QUINN'S WAY

BY

STEVE GRAY

AuthorHouse™
1663 Liberty Drive
Bloomington, IN 47403
www.authorhouse.com
Phone: 1-800-839-8640

© *2011 Steve Gray. All rights reserved.*

No part of this book may be reproduced, stored in a retrieval system, or transmitted by any means without the written permission of the author.

First published by AuthorHouse 1/10/2011

ISBN: 978-1-4567-7175-1 (sc)

Printed in the United States of America

Any people depicted in stock imagery provided by Thinkstock are models, and such images are being used for illustrative purposes only. Certain stock imagery © Thinkstock.

This book is printed on acid-free paper.

Because of the dynamic nature of the Internet, any Web addresses or links contained in this book may have changed since publication and may no longer be valid. The views expressed in this work are solely those of the author and do not necessarily reflect the views of the publisher, and the publisher hereby disclaims any responsibility for them.

For H, who asks for so little and yet gives so much.

CHAPTER 1

Monday November 18th. 7-45p.m.

Give or take a few seconds Lucy Thomas had only three minutes to live. She was just thirty-six years old, married and the mother of an increasingly precocious eight-year-old daughter, Annie. It was Annie who had just interrupted her thoughts as she finished washing the dishes from the early evening meal.

'Mummy, can I stay up a bit longer?' A pause as she waited for Lucy to respond, and then an almost desperate plea,

'Please?'

Lucy smiled. Straightening herself at the kitchen sink she shook the remains of the washing up water from her hands and reached for a hand towel. As she did so she caught her own reflection in the window.

'Still looking good,' she thought, and indeed she did. She was not tall, only just a couple of inches or so over five feet. A natural ten she could at a push, and depending on brand, squeeze into a size eight. Even during her pregnancy she did not carry any excess weight. Her hips and waist were still slim and her buttocks nicely rounded. Her face was slim with high cheekbones, a straight elfin nose and a small, if somewhat pouty mouth. She had hazel eyes and shoulder length dyed blond hair parted down the centre. An attractive lady who could still turn heads but whose features and demeanour had a hint of steel about them. Turning, she looked down at Annie and ran her fingers through the girl's blond and curling locks.

'Fifteen minutes and then bed,' she answered with mock severity. Lucy glanced at the clock. She was due at the gym in fifteen minutes anyway so David, her husband, would have the problem of Annie's bedtime.

She bent down and placed her arms around Annie giving her a brief but hard hug and as she broke the embrace she gave her a loving, if perfunctory, kiss on the top of the head.

'Be a good girl for daddy.'

Annie headed for the stairs. 'I will be good, I'm always good,' she answered in that sing song voice so beloved of small children. Lucy smiled again. She would have to watch Annie she knew. The child was growing fast and already developing an attitude. Still, at least it was a positive attitude. Like herself she was no shrinking violet. Lucy however projected herself as a way to compensate for what had once been a lack of confidence and self esteem. Annie lacked neither. Lucy followed her almost to the top of the stairs. She glanced momentarily at the Monet print at the end of the landing and, as always, the memory of what she had done on the floor beneath it flashed across her mind. Involuntarily she fingered the Saint Christopher medallion hanging from the delicate chain around her neck, but the patron saint of travellers would not protect her this night.

She watched Annie safely enter the bedroom where David was already surfing the net and shouted,

'Bye! Be back about half nine,' before retreating back down the stairs. There was no response and Lucy had no desire to repeat herself or kiss her husband goodbye. She prayed silently that he was not gambling again. She believed they had put his addiction behind them but she knew the plumber was still to be paid for the recent bathroom renovation. Although David said the payment was in hand she was dreading the night time knock on the door, the doorstep argument or worse, the bailiff.

'Bye Annie!' she shouted, a little louder this time. Still no answer from Annie but she heard a distracted 'OK' from David as she headed for the door.

David had never truly been the centre of her life although Lucy loved him in her own way. He was after all the father of her beautiful daughter. When first they met she had disliked him immediately, and he her, but mutual animosity made each of them a challenge to the other. They dated tentatively before being swept along on the tide of expectation, rather than emotion, which had led to the ultimate social battleground of marriage. To this day Lucy did not know why she and David had married. It was just what all their friends and family appeared to have expected of them. They still had a physical relationship but any real passion had long since died.

David was unfaithful to her even before they were married and again just after the birth of Annie. Lucy found out about David's affair with a young and very busty hairdresser. They separated for some months but he came back begging forgiveness and vowing to change. It was New Years Eve and in a moment of weakness, loneliness got the better of her and she allowed him back. She told her friends that it was for Annie's sake, as she did not want her to suffer the same dysfunctional childhood that she herself had endured. Her own mother neglected her as a child often leaving her for hours on end to fend for herself. Lucy could never forget being farmed out to relatives to care for her. Nor sitting in the large oak-panelled courtroom as her parents, lawyers and social workers debated, argued and negotiated her future. In the end she lived with her father who coped as best he could with the spirited and rebellious teenager that she became.

Lucy sometimes wondered if this was why on several occasions she found herself attracted to an older man. Was it something to do with the relationship she had with her father? Or was it just the mercenary streak in her that made her believe that an older man would be wealthy enough to take care of her and that when he died, she would still be young enough to enjoy those riches?

Although Lucy would always deny it she liked being the centre of attention. She had developed an inner hardness, which helped her to cope with an abortion when just fifteen years old. Indeed, she had the operation and then within hours went out on her paper round. The money had been that important. She didn't sleep around however; she had just been unlucky. Now, approaching middle age, she compromised her own happiness to save Annie from any emotional trauma.

Lucy flirted constantly, both at work and socially, and enjoyed it. She kept herself well under control however and only once had her coquettish behaviour got seriously out of hand. She fell in love with the wrong man at the wrong time and found herself in a situation way over her head. For a time she contemplated leaving David, but found herself trapped by circumstances which for once she could not control and the relationship ended acrimoniously. She also suffered a miscarriage but that had been a blessing. Lucy had not wanted to face the fact that she was unsure whether the father was her husband or lover. All that was left now of the relationship were the memories and the St. Christopher hanging from her slender neck. Despite everything though, she considered herself to be a good mother. When Annie was grown she would have her fun. This was a promise made to herself and would be, she believed, her time in the sun.

The final minute began. She donned her wrap over her designer tracksuit, picked up the car keys, mobile phone and handbag and stepped out into the darkness. The night was cold and clear, the temperature just above freezing. As she closed the door she gave an involuntary shudder. It was unusually dry for the time of year and the local weather forecast warned of snow before morning. Despite the secluded nature of the terraced cottage there was sufficient light pollution from the nearby town and the rising moon to be able to see clearly. The building had originally been home to six families who worked on the nearby canals, but had long since been converted into four unique homes. She could never make up her mind which to call the front and which to call the back and she never would.

It was thirty metres from the door of the cottage to the garage. She took in the broad expanse of westerly facing lawn, which had so attracted her to the house, and where she and Annie loved to play. In her hand she held the keys to her husbands' company car which was parked directly behind hers. Both cars were outside as the garage was full of Annie's playthings. Lucy often used his car for her twice-weekly visits to the gym.

Despite buying all the appropriate clothing she had never properly worked out a training programme. She didn't realise that probably the best time for her to train was in the morning. Gym sessions produce endorphins in the body, which in some do not make for a good night's sleep. Still, even she would admit that she rarely broke sweat. Not through being naturally fit but through lack of effort. Like thousands of other members of gymnasiums across the country she viewed her Rednall Fitness Centre membership card as a fashion accessory. She often joked that the gym was no more than a coffee bar with keep fit equipment but she would never deny that the attentions of the young and fit instructors were good for her ego.

As she stepped forward her thoughts returned again to David. When they first began dating she knew that he liked the odd flutter. Along with friends, the two of them enjoyed several days out at the local racecourse and she herself loved the atmosphere, the excitement and the glamour. Just like many other race goers she placed small bets with the course bookmakers but had never been remotely interested in betting away from the event. She entered the sweepstake at work for the Grand National and did the lottery every week but that was all. David however discovered internet gambling sites and had run up a serious amount of debt. Only the intervention of his parents prevented them from losing the house. For almost a year now he had been, or appeared to have been, 'clean' but of late there had been phone calls at odd times of the day. Gambling or an affair? A confrontation would surely come soon and if there was indeed a problem she hoped he was having an affair. Losing David to another woman she could cope with but losing all the equity in the house, losing her home, Annie's home, was unthinkable.

Lucy passed the end of the garage on her left with only seconds remaining and was momentarily distracted by a car passing further to her left beyond her neighbour's garden. As she walked between the two parked cars the sensor for the outside light picked up her heat signature and illuminated the drive. She sensed, rather than saw a presence and felt the hairs stiffen on the back of her neck. She caught a brief glimpse of shadow. Time split into fractions of a second. A half turn was not enough to save her life. An arm clamped across her mouth stifling her attempted scream. Her momentum carried her forward pulling her head back and exposing her throat. Her arms flailed helplessly as she lost her balance.

She felt only a moment's pain and then intense panic gripped her as the knife penetrated her neck.

'No!' her mind screamed.

Lucy always boasted that if anyone attacked her she would fight back but she had no time to react. Her knees buckled and she felt the warmth of blood spilling from her on to her breasts and then a further momentary horror as her bowels gave way.

'No! God No!' Screaming in her mind constantly, desperately, but no amount of exhortation to God could save her now.

She felt herself being lowered to the ground and saw her attacker's eyes. Although from her position she was looking at her assailant upside down she knew who it was and felt confusion mixed with hurt, anger and sheer terror. She tried to scream but the only sound was a gurgling, choking noise and she knew that she was dying. She heard muffled words, but she was beyond comprehension or pain.

'No, No, No………'

She had a last fleeting memory of Annie and then mercifully the darkness engulfed her. Her body would not be discovered for another two and half-hours.

It was 7-48 p.m.

Chapter 2

Tuesday November 19th.

Today should not have ended like this. Here I am, alone, sat with the remnants of a last glass of red wine, an empty bottle and the dying embers of the fire. It's just after eleven o'clock in the evening, it's my birthday and I'm here on my own and feeling decidedly sorry for myself. I'm certainly not playing the part of the merry widower tonight. Even my two kids haven't managed to ring. Sam, my not so little girl is the eldest and Charlie, eighteen months her junior is definitely no longer my little boy. They both have an excuse I suppose, serving overseas in the armed forces but still, it's just not right!

When I woke up this morning the day had promised so much.

The radio alarm startled me from my dozing state at six.

'Hi! You're listening to the Harry Benstead show waking the county. Morning to you!' He always raises his voice an octave or two when he announces the start of the day, as though someone has just given his testicles a quick squeeze. How do these early morning presenters always manage to sound so alive and cheerful? Wouldn't you just love it if one of them actually sounded a little grumpy, just like the rest of us for once? In fairness to Harry, his is one of the better shows and having met him a few times at the golf club, he's a decent bloke who does more than his fair share for good causes. I felt as though I had just gone to sleep.

I had not had a good night. My face, shoulder and ankle all hurt from the stupid fall I took the night before. Every time I rolled over during the night the pain in my shoulder jolted me awake. I tried sleeping on my back and then front but you know what it's like, you drop off to sleep and then involuntarily begin to move about. The graze on my cheekbone was still stinging from the antiseptic I had, bravely, applied to it. The ankle throbbed, but not too badly, certainly not as badly as I feared it would. The shoulder worried me though as I had injured it before. The joint stiffened during the night but I was reasonably certain nothing was broken or fractured. Despite feeling knackered I threw back the duvet, swung gingerly out of my massive bed and tested the ankle. It hurt enough to cause me to limp but the bleeding had stopped. I went into the bathroom and put on a fresh plaster and then stepped back into the bedroom and threw back the curtains. Although still dark I could see that the predicted snowfall had not materialised. It would make my planned journey easier, although my Range Rover Sport copes well enough with most conditions.

I hate this time of year. Even my birthday doesn't help. It's just one more lap ticked off in the race to the grim reaper. I hate the cold, the damp and gloomy days, early darkness and the long, seemingly endless nights. If global warming brings longer summers and a warmer climate then I'm all for it. After all, I'm not going to be around to see or suffer the consequences. The thought of spring being so far away only deepens the gloom. My doctor reckons it's a clear case of winter blues. SAD she calls it. Seasonal Affective Disorder. She reckons it affects over half a million people every winter with symptoms including depression, sleep problems, lethargy and loss of libido. I think she looks too deep. I just feel a bit pissed off. But then, November was also the month when my wife Lynn died.

The house however was lovely and warm. During the winter months the central heating is on continuously and controlled by several thermostats. I never shiver when I get out of bed. I pulled on a T-shirt with some difficulty. I had, as always, slept in a pair of shorts. I took my horrendously expensive wristwatch, a Chopard Mille Miglia, from the nightstand and snapped it on to my wrist. Then I picked up my mobile, and headed carefully downstairs. I limped into the kitchen and took my trainers from the rack. The ankle had minimal swelling but the bone was clearly bruised. I put on my tracksuit top and then grabbed a bottle of water from the fridge. I took a quick pull and then unlocked the back door, took out the keys, turned on the outside light, stepped out and headed for the garage. Any residual sleepiness was quickly swept away by the bitter cold. I was tempted to turn round and go back to the warmth of the bed but I am nothing if not disciplined nowadays.

As I walked the twenty yards to the garage the pain in the ankle subsided a little, probably from a combination of the cold and movement. I noticed the side door to the garage ajar and felt a moments panic as I realised I had not locked or shut it properly the night before. A silly thing to do but as I'm well off the beaten track its highly unlikely anyone would venture down the lane. But you never know? I opened the door and snapped on the light. When I drive in the light comes on with a sensor. Everything appeared just as I had left it. The back half of the garage I have converted into a small gym and it is separated from the front by a heavy drape. I pulled it tentatively aside and then smiled to myself. No one else was in the garage and nothing had been disturbed. Nevertheless the tension got the adrenaline going and I was not noticing the cold as much. I turned on some music and went through my repertoire of stretches and then did thirty minutes on the cross trainer. There is minimal shock to the ankle on this machine so I was able to manage. I warmed down with a few more stretches and then went back to the kitchen for a light breakfast. The shoulder still ached a little but was otherwise fine and the ankle still throbbed gently but at least I no longer felt the need to limp. I caught the seven thirty news from the local radio station. The world was relatively quiet. Locally, a body, understood to be that of a woman, had been discovered in Rednall, a town some thirty miles away. The police were making no further statement but they had cordoned off an area of the town.

'There will be more on this story throughout the morning as and when we receive further information' roughly translating as 'the police are telling us nothing and we need to get someone over there pronto!'

'Thank you Izzy and now it's over to the weather report.'

The weatherman, another unnaturally cheerful soul, had now decided that despite the bitter cold the day would warm up a little and that there was more chance of rain than snow. I finished breakfast, put the few pots in the dishwasher and then went upstairs for a shave and shower. As I stepped out the shower I heard a car in the lane and looked out. It was only my next door neighbours, Rachael and Andrew, leaving for work. I watched Rachael pull her car from the garage and noticed that she was giving her friend Sarah a lift. Andrew was just climbing into his own car, which had been parked in front of my garage. I was quite surprised as I thought he would have left earlier. I watched them drive away and then dressed casually in a polo shirt, faded designer jeans, black leather bomber jacket and black hand made soft leather driving shoes, before leaving the house just before eight thirty for the nigh on four hour drive north to see 'me dear old mam.'

As I put the Range Rover's gear selector into R to reverse out of the garage my mobile sounded the anvil clank indicating a message. It was a text from one of my staff, Jake, and it read simply,

'IT IS DONE'

I smiled and decided to turn off the phone. The company could do without me for a few hours. I eased the car out of the garage, clicked the button to roll down the electric entrance door and tuned in the radio for the local station. The news came on and the main story was yet more on the body discovered in Rednall. The police were not confirming that it was a case of murder merely that the death was suspicious. They had closed an area in the Mereside district of the town and were holding a man in custody for questioning. There was no doubt in my mind that this would definitely turn out to be a murder enquiry.

The drive north was an easy one. Apart from five miles either end, the entire journey is either motorway or good dual carriageway. The Range Rover eats up the miles in both comfort and style. When I reached the motorway I set the cruise control at a shade over seventy, confident that breaking the speed limit by a fraction wouldn't cause the law any great sweat, switched over to the CD and relaxed. The local traffic news indicated no hold ups and the radio's inbuilt warning system would automatically cut in and tell me if there were any problems. The wonders of modern technology.

I have a great lifestyle and I know people envy me but life hasn't always been this good. I've been comfortable but ironically I only began to experience real wealth after Lynn died. Girlfriends? Certainly the lifestyle, wealth and flash motor do wonders for the pulling power but I've never been one for airheads and one night stands. They usually get two chances to impress! I have no live in lover. Well, not quite. My current lover, Rachael, resides under the same roof but with her husband Andrew next door!

Rachael is in her early forties and she is a stunner. She's ten years younger than me and, despite a trace of laughter lines around the eyes, could easily pass for being in her twenties. She is an exception to the saying that 'men mature and women grow old.' She's five foot four, a natural blue eyed blonde, slim, got great legs, pert breasts, flat stomach, a wonderful arse and narrow hips despite the rigours of giving birth to two kids. Don't ask what reaction I get when she's out bending over weeding the garden in her tight jeans! She's also intelligent, gentle and self-effacing. Despite her association with me, she's what I term a quality person. If she were a vintage wine I would drink her by the case full.

Watching Andrew drive away this morning made me really excited at the prospect of receiving a special birthday present this evening from Rachael. The anticipation was however tinged with some surprise and a little disappointment. As it is very rare for me to be away early on Tuesdays, I have an informal parking arrangement with Andrew. He is almost always away before six on Tuesdays, having worked at home from mid afternoon on Mondays, and doesn't get back until Wednesday evening. I'm almost always home on Mondays before either of them and as Monday night is football night on satellite TV I rarely go out. Andrew leaves his car in front of my garage so that Rachael can put hers away when she gets home. It's a minor inconvenience considering the rewards! I had hoped for a few minutes with her but it didn't happen because for some reason he left late.

In any event the horrible Sarah had been in attendance. Rachael sometimes gives her a lift to work. Why do pretty women always have an obnoxious friend? I could understand it when I was a pimply teenager. The girls always hunted in pairs. The pretty ones hung around preening and keeping their undies padlocked while the ugly partner stood by, reflecting in the glory, with a knowing and expectant, smile. Any self respecting Saturday night warrior always chats up the uglier one in the pair because as a general rule they don't take much drink and it's easier to get inside their undies. OK, you do get the odd pig in knickers and I've woken up next to some where it might have been preferable to chew my arm off rather than disturb them, but do we really care at the time? The old beer glass's have a wondrous effect on most of us blokes! I've never bothered to find out if women feel the same. Aren't they just grateful? We change as we get older and get a bit more choosy. Or at least most of us do. The values I held as a teenager are somewhat different today. I wouldn't touch Sarah with a broom handle. She's certainly not a true friend to Rachael either. I once overheard Sarah in the supermarket queue talking about Rachael in less than flattering terms. I didn't tell Rachael. Why upset her?

On reaching my home town I made a detour to the local hospital hoping to see my old mate who is a Doctor. Fortunately she was on duty and gave me a quick once over, redressed my wounds and then took great delight in sticking the needle in my bum to administer the tetanus injection. Then she told me to take it easy for the next week or so. She was hoping I was going to be in town for a few days. Unfortunately for her, she was old news. Been there, done that, moved on. But she was still a useful contact. Professionally of course.

I enjoyed a great lunch with me mam. A good couple of hours having a simple meal in the local pub and enjoying the Geordie banter followed by another hour in her neat little bungalow catching up on all the family gossip. I lost me dad in a mining accident when I was an infant and mam never re-married. She'd bought me a very nice jumper for my birthday which no doubt I will donate to a local charity shop within weeks. Mothers never learn. I also got the customary lecture. Having hinted about Rachael on a previous visit, more to stop the 'when are you going to find another woman?' discussion, this time she became a bit more direct. Much to her frustration, I kept deflecting her.

'You think you can talk your way out of most things Joseph Quinn but God will be your judge,' she grumbled.

It made no difference. In any case, hopefully God will have to wait a long time. I gave her a big hug and got the expected tears before I took my leave and headed back down the motorway. Such was my mood that I was halfway home before I realised that my mobile hadn't rung all day. I fished in my pocket, not very sensible at seventy miles an hour, glanced down and realised that I hadn't turned the bloody thing back on! The next service area was only a mile away so I waited until I had pulled over before turning on the power. The strength of these tiny handsets never ceases to amaze me. It clanked loudly almost immediately indicating several missed calls and half a dozen text messages. Before I could sort them out however it rang. It was Rachael.

'Where the hell have you been?' she demanded angrily. I was

surprised by her tone as it's not like her to be angry or possessive and in any case she knew where I was going.

'I left the phone off because I was driving.' Well, I wasn't going to admit that I had left it off by accident was I. 'What's up, are you missing me?' I said cheekily.

'No.' She was still angry but her tone was definitely softening.

'Come on, what's up, you knew where I was going?'

'Andrews home tonight.' Talk about instant deflation, but before I could respond she rushed on, 'and have you heard about the murder in Rednall?'

'I caught it on the news this morning. Why?'

'The police have given out the woman's name and where she worked. She worked for the Hatton Group Joe. Her name was Lucy, Lucy Thomas.'

Bad memories surfaced again. Lucy Thomas was a name from the past and a previous long term lover.

CHAPTER 3

Rachael was by turns frustrated, angry and worried and the more she worried the more angry and frustrated she became. She had hoped to catch Joe that morning but Andrew did not leave for the office at his usual Tuesday time and she had been unable to snatch a moment alone with her phone. Worse, when they woke that morning, Andrew told her that he would be home that night as there was a head office meeting on Wednesday that required his presence. Andrew being at home that evening completely ruined her plan to have dinner with Joe. She even thought about sending a text to the local radio station wishing Joe a happy birthday on air but Andrew was listening to the news regarding the discovery of a body in Rednall. Then, Sarah arrived unannounced begging for a lift to work, denying her any chance of leaving a little later and going round to see Joe. Sarah was her usual chatty and catty self on the drive to work preventing her from finding any opportunity at all to ring Joe. At odd times throughout the day she tried to phone him but his mobile provider continually announced that his phone was turned off. She knew he was visiting his mother but she didn't have a contact number. She desperately needed to warn him about Andrew, wish him happy birthday and just, well, talk to him.

It had been many years since she had felt this emotional. She felt like a teenager again with a crush but despite telling herself that was all it was she didn't want the feeling to stop. She was on a real roller coaster of emotion. At times so elated that she couldn't stop smiling and yet at others more than a little frightened. Then as she drove home at five-o clock she heard the announcement that the woman found dead in Rednall the previous evening had been murdered. The police were naming the deceased as Lucy Thomas, married and the mother of a young daughter. She was employed at the Hatton Group as an account assistant and the directors had issued a statement expressing their shock and horror. Rachael guessed correctly that this was the same Lucy Thomas who had once been involved with Joe. Rachael was not the jealous type but when Joe told her the story of their affair she felt that he was still a little in love with Lucy. She was unfinished business. Or had been she thought ruefully. She surprised herself by feeling just a little pleased with the news and felt a little ashamed that she was jealous of a dead woman. Joe would need someone to talk to and somehow she would make sure, despite Andrew being at home, that it would be her.

Rachael could not have told anyone when it was that she became bored with her life. It was almost as though it had crept up on her and finally settled like a dead weight around her shoulders. She was only just turned forty-one. She would, and did, describe herself as middle class and although she and Andrew did not have money to burn, they were comfortably off. At eighteen, she had breezed through her 'A' levels and gained a place at university. She was to read law and hoped eventually to do criminal law and be called to the bar. It was at university that she met Andrew. He was one of her tutors, twenty-two years her senior and married with three children not yet in their teens. She had been young, overawed, headstrong and fell hopelessly in love with him. She soon found herself pregnant but alone as Andrew made a belated attempt to save his marriage. Andrew's wife Gill was not to be persuaded and the divorce descended into a bitter and acrimonious battle with Gill determined to have her pound of flesh.

Despite her parents objections Rachael married Andrew just one month before their eldest son Mark was born. The ceremony had been a very quiet and sparsely attended occasion. The scandal wrecked Andrew's career and called what she hoped would be a temporary halt to her studies. Andrew soon found a job in the fledgling computer industry. Even now, as he headed towards retirement, he still worked long hours. She suspected that he had conducted several affairs over the years but she was never able to obtain conclusive proof. She still loved him but was not in love with him. Their marriage yielded another son John, who was born only eighteen months after his elder brother. Any thoughts of Rachael resuming her university studies ended as she became a full time mother and housewife and Andrew fought with the economics of effectively running two households. Both boys were now at university and both looked likely to graduate with master's degrees. They were good boys who adored their mother and, despite the difficulties of having to share their father, they loved and respected Andrew in spite of his sometimes cold and aloof manner. Both had been adult enough to accept the difficulties that their father had faced.

Rachael now worked full time at a local primary school as a teacher's aide, a job she enjoyed but which didn't particularly challenge or fulfil her. The money though helped her to have a little independence. Their marriage had been a long financial struggle, which had only begun to diminish over the last few years. Gill had, despite eventually moving on with her life, quite rightly continued to see that Andrew made proper provision for their three children. For their part, the children for some time played father off against mother and it seemed to Rachael that Andrew sometimes put their needs ahead of Mark and John. Despite his faults however Andrew had done right by all his children, and indeed, as they got older both sets of children tolerated each other remarkably well.

Rachael made the best of things. She had always been good with her hands and made many of her own clothes. She was quite a trendy, if conservative dresser. She was proud of her 34-24-34ish figure although she had once wished that her breasts had been a little bigger. She kept in trim with a sensible diet and plenty of exercise visiting the gym twice a week, where she always trained hard and ignored the suggestive comments of the instructors. Indeed, she gained their respect by not rising to the bait. She knew she looked good and not just for her age. She was comfortable in her own skin. The thought of having an affair however never entered her head until she and Andrew moved into Canalside.

She was proud of her home and had fallen in love with the converted warehouse as soon as she saw it. Situated at the end of a quiet lane through a wood and with the canal flowing at the end of the back garden it was both remote and idyllic.

Despite it being a semi detached they paid the full asking price immediately. They knew that the developer and vendor, Joe Quinn, was also their neighbour but it made no difference. When they moved in Joe was away and it was some two weeks before they met. Andrew took an instant dislike to Joe. He didn't say as much but she knew. She could also tell that Joe was not particularly enamoured with Andrew either. They were courteous enough to each other but from the first time they met she felt that a major disagreement between the two would occur one day. That, she now knew, was a racing certainty.

Despite Andrew's protests she invited Joe for dinner shortly after they moved in and Andrew found that he and Joe possessed little in common. Andrew worked long hours while Joe appeared to do very little and made a lot of money doing it! In his free time Andrew fished. Joe raced cars and got paid for the pleasure. Andrew felt that Joe was a working class playboy and seemed to object that he had risen above his working class roots, whilst Joe kept his thoughts on Andrew to himself. He did however have a withering contempt for fishing which Rachael found highly amusing.

'I've never seen the point of fishing for fun,' Joe said. 'All that sitting around on a river bank for hours on end just waiting for a piece of plastic on the end of a piece of string to move and then when it does you pull the poor fish in by it's top lip, drag it from it's natural environment, wrench the hook from it's mouth and then throw it back again, just so that you can repeat the process a couple of hours later! I'm surprised that the fish don't develop hair lips from the amount of times they get hooks through them.'

'You DO miss the point,' Andrew answered pompously. 'The sport is a great trial of wits between man and fish and it takes great patience and skill to outwit your prey. You're not just sat doing nothing. You have to concentrate and make constant adjustments to your equipment.'

'So what you're saying is you sit on the riverbank playing with your tackle and having a battle of wits with a species that has a reputed memory span of five seconds?' Joe asked with barely concealed contempt. Rachael laughed out loud and although Andrew claimed not to be offended she knew this was not true. She noted the flushed cheeks and the pursing of his lips as he fought to keep his anger in check. Joe immediately smiled his gentle smile and moved the conversation on.

Her first reaction to Joe had been one of surprise. He was not tall at around five foot six. She had been expecting him to be much taller and overweight. She didn't know why, other than it being a stereotypical view of how builders were supposed to look. He had a compact, muscular and powerful body and was clearly very fit. He was lightly tanned and seemed to shine with vitality. He was certainly not an ugly man but nor could she describe him as being film star handsome. He always had a faint, pleasant musky odour to him which she could never quite make out. Was it just the expensive cologne or his own natural aroma? Despite his age he had a youthful outlook on life and possessed the cheekiest smile she had ever witnessed and a very irreverent sense of humour.

The more she spoke with him the more she liked him. He talked with a soft, slight Geordie lilt which became more pronounced when he became excited and never failed to make her smile. Although proud of his roots, Joe admitted that he had made a real effort to soften his accent and whilst he had practically succeeded his grammar would often betray him. More often than not he would use the word me instead of my, and his mother was always referred to as 'me mam'. Still, she found him funny and intelligent, capable of debating with her on a vast array of subjects. He was a good listener, often just allowing her to air her problems and fears without passing any sort of judgement. She also sensed a vulnerability about him, a loneliness, which she ascribed to the death of his wife, Lynn.

The first few months after they moved in, Joe was away quite often and she did the neighbourly thing and offered to keep an eye on the house. They swapped mobile numbers and the first time he had been away racing she had, on impulse, sent him a good luck text. Now, sending a message before he raced had become a tradition. She did not want to admit to herself that she was falling, or had fallen, in love with him but she found it increasingly difficult to banish him from her thoughts. Then, one Tuesday evening she overstepped the boundary between dutiful wife and adulterer.

Andrew was away, as he was most Tuesdays, and she thought Joe was away visiting his family in the north. She had bathed and then dressed in her short silk nightgown and matching negligee, retired to the lounge. She loved her lounge with its high ceiling and double bay windows. The room was furnished simply but tastefully with a deep red carpet and cream suite with elephant print scatter cushions. The fire had a heavy wooden surround with a mirror over and she had placed scented candles liberally around the room. One of her friends remarked that the room appeared to have an African theme but that had not been her intention. What happened that night however bordered on savage. She had lit the candles and settled down with a bottle of very chilled white wine, her favourite Sinatra CD and a magazine. Feeling a bit lonely but mellow she found herself thinking of Joe. The drink and the fire warmed her and she allowed her negligee fall open. Her nightgown had ridden up slightly and she began to tease herself gently between the thighs, something which she had not done for years, searching for the spot and feeling herself becoming moist. At that moment her phone beeped, startling her and she pulled her hand away guiltily. It was a text message. Seeing the name and number she opened it immediately.

'HOW R U?'

It was Joe. She felt a rush of excitement. Her thumb moved quickly on the tiny keypad.

'FINE. WHERE R U?'

'HERE!'

They had played this game before. Sometimes it irritated her but in the right mood she found it funny. Tonight she was in the right mood but she wanted more than a text.

'RM' Ring me, she sent.

Almost immediately the phone rang.

'Hi,' she answered in her most whispering and teasingly seductive voice.

Joe laughed on the other end of the phone and said,

'Andrew's not there then?'

'No. You should be here,' she said huskily, 'we could have shared this bottle of wine.' She was safe flirting over the phone because had he truly been there she doubted that she would have held herself back.

'You're teasing again. If I were there you'd run a mile,' he said chiding her gently.

'Not tonight, the mood is right,' she teased softly. She was in the mood but the distance would keep her safe.

'Yeah, you're right. It's time I licked you into shape,' he answered just as she heard a gentle but persistent knock at the door.

'Damm,' she said, her voice changing tone. 'There's someone at the door. Just hang on the line whilst I see who it is.'

'Be careful Rache, you never know what weirdo's are about,' said Joe.

'I'll be fine. The chains on and besides I'm sure I can rely on you to be my knight in shining armour and come chasing down the motorway to rescue me. It's probably Sarah so if it is I'll call you back later' she whispered into the phone as she moved through the kitchen.

She placed her eye to the security peep-hole in the solid wood door and recognising the person doing the knocking she smiled, ended the call and removed the security chain knowing that when she opened the door, as she knew she would, her life would never be the same again.

CHAPTER 4

Waiting was always the hardest part. The cold damp doorways of winter or a warm park bench in summer both required the same level of patience and intense concentration and over the years Jake Smith had developed an abundance of both. He was also a meticulous planner and earlier that Monday afternoon Jake had made the final preparations for the evening's work. It was always a source of amusement to him when Joe Quinn, his current employer, preached the mantra 'piss poor planning leads to piss poor performance' because Jake was anything but a piss poor performer. He had learnt all about the value of careful planning long before the night he met Joe Quinn and in a much harsher environment.

Jake was satisfied that everything he needed was in place. For him, tonight's enterprise was a relatively simple task. Things could and sometimes did go wrong but he was a good improviser, supremely confident in his own abilities to overcome the unexpected. He planned to be back in his penthouse apartment home no later than midnight and whilst his anxiety level would be a little heightened, he felt no real fear. He had performed far more onerous and much more dangerous tasks in the past. Still, he would never allow himself to become complacent.

As far as he was aware no one, apart from Joe, had the slightest suspicion regarding the truth of his previous life. In the days following their first meeting Joe attempted to gently question him but when he realised that Jake was not going to be more forthcoming he abandoned his efforts, happy in the knowledge that Jake would do his bidding. Joe was probably the nearest human being since childhood he had ever allowed close. Past was past, but the skills he had learnt could not be forgotten. In any event Jake loved his work and felt he was as skilled as any surgeon. Always calm, never flustered and always in control. He wasn't a big man, just five feet eight inches tall, but he was slightly heavy set. The bulk however wasn't fat, it was all muscle. He was forty two years old and kept himself in peak condition by working out at the gym in the highly fashionable apartment complex where he now lived. He was light on his feet and could move with the stealth of a cat. He was not a handsome man but nor was he ugly. He had long since shaved his head and facial hair and despite his slightly dusky complexion even an expert would have been hard pushed to accurately define his birthplace as being anywhere other than England. His accent bore just a trace of Kent and his passport proclaimed him to have been born in Dover. He possessed the great skill of not drawing attention to himself or standing out in a crowd. Most who met him would describe him as courteous, kind hearted, good humoured, well liked and respected by his colleagues.

Jake Smith was content with his life. It was a far cry from his days as an operative for the Mukhabarat, the Iraqi intelligence service. Born Ali Hussein al –Tikriti his father had been a cousin and devout follower of Saddam Hussein. The young Ali had enjoyed the patronage of the Iraqi leader. He had been well trained in the art of espionage and knew many ways to end a person's life and countless ways of inflicting serious non life threatening injury and pain. He was not a sadist like Saddam's sons. He was never cruel for the sake of cruelty and he didn't kill for the sake of killing either but he did acknowledge that the moment he extinguished a life gave him an almost sexual high. Jake was also homosexual and although he knew that nothing would ever come of it, in love with Joe Quinn.

CHAPTER 5

'Drink Bob?'

'Bob? Who are you calling Bob?' Detective Superintendent Robert Buxton wanted to reply. No one, apart from senior colleagues, both in rank and age, called him Bob. He was Robert to his wife, Boss to his subordinates and several other less complimentary names to the villains he put away.

'No thanks,' he answered and turned his back. 'And I wouldn't accept a drink from you if I was dying of thirst in the desert you crook' he thought. 'That's the trouble with the Rednall Golf and Country club nowadays,' he had opined earlier, 'declining standards. A few years ago people like him wouldn't have got in the car park, let alone the bar and as for getting tickets to the annual ball.' He had let the sentence hang in the air.

Still, the evening on the whole had been a success. Buxton, a twelve handicapper, enjoyed both the golf and the social events the club organised. In one years time he could look forward to plenty of golf on his retirement. Buxton was of medium height, a blunt no nonsense Lancastrian who, despite not living in his home county for several decades, had never lost the accent. He had receding grey hair, an expanding gut and a liking for red wine, which he drank every night. No one however, ever saw him drunk and unlike some officers he never kept a bottle of spirits in his desk drawer. He had a world-weariness and cynicism about him that suggested too long in the job. But to those who knew him and those who worked with him he was a good hearted, fundamentally honest man and a hard working, respected if somewhat stubborn police officer. An attitude which, along with his scant regard to paperwork, often caused unnecessary friction and frustration to some of his more enterprising colleagues. Especially when he refused to change his opinion or contemplate an alternative viewpoint. Thinking outside the box was not a phrase that could ever be readily applied to DS Robert Buxton.

'I'm just doing it by the book' was his mantra but only when it suited. Still, no one could deny his ability to catch villains however slovenly his methods.

A few minutes after eleven, Buxton, along with his long suffering wife Rose and their two guests, had just retired to the bar when he felt the vibration from the cell phone in his inside pocket. He excused himself claiming a call of nature. Rose, seeing his hand travel to his inside pocket, guessed that work had just interrupted their evening. By the time he vacated the bar the phone had stopped vibrating, but he knew that for someone to ring him this evening then the call was likely to be serious.

Finding a quiet corner he hit the recall button and connected almost immediately with Detective Sergeant Andrew Davies, his junior officer and young man who Buxton saw as a new generation of high flyer. He liked him however and while he saw nothing of himself in him other than a desire to catch criminals, he was enjoying mentoring him. They had worked together for nine months and there was no jealousy or animosity in the relationship. Davies quickly told him of the discovery of a body in the Mereside district of town. Buxton made a mental note of the address and returned to the bar to make his excuses. Rose was not happy but she knew that Buxton would put duty first. He apologised to their guests who agreed to see Rose home and left the gathering.

Rather than wait for the car that Davies had offered, Buxton decided to take one of the taxis lined up outside the club. He gave the address to the driver and settled down in the back seat for the short journey across Rednall. The town was relatively quiet and within ten minutes the taxi approached the Mereside roundabout. Turning right off the arterial road into Mill Road they were immediately stopped by a marked patrol car. Buxton decided to walk the remaining few hundred metres and paid off the taxi driver. The two uniformed traffic officers in the patrol car were in for a boring night. The only people usually heading into Mill Road at that time of night would be courting couples heading for the car park beside the mere and the cold evening wasn't particularly conducive to couples copulating in cars. As Buxton walked on he could see further vehicles and the large white caravan used as a mobile incident room being manoeuvred into position at the junction of Mill Road and Mere Lane. Uniformed officers had already cordoned off the entrance to the lane. As he turned to the left a young constable lifted the tape for him to duck under. He acknowledged the officer with a curt nod and as he stood up he could see to his right the top of a large awning, just visible over a high hedge, being erected over the crime scene. Floodlights were already in place and their glow together with the flashing blue lights from the marked police vehicles were creating quite a light show. The scenes of crime officers, referred to throughout the force as SOCO, were on their knees examining the ground. Dressed in their disposable white coveralls they appeared almost ghost like beneath the powerful lights. As Buxton approached he could see the police doctor examining a heap on the ground which he knew would be the body. Davies spotted Buxton as he approached and walked across to meet him.

'Nar then Andrew,' Buxton said, his northern roots showing even more, as they always did when he had consumed several drinks.

'Evening boss, sorry to spoil the evening.'

Buxton shrugged and smiled, but he was feeling the chill having left his coat at the club.

'Forget it, what's the story?'

'Call came in about ten twenty. The occupant of the cottage, a Mr. David Thomas, discovered a woman's body. He says it's his wife, Lucy, who had been out for the evening. She's clearly been murdered, her head is almost severed and there's a great deal of blood.'

'I imagine there would be,' Buxton responded with a thin, taut smile. He could see that Davies was a little uncomfortable and knowing that it was his first murder case realised that sarcasm was not what was needed at this time.

'Husband?'

'He's in the house. DI Kirk and a WPC are with him. He's badly shocked.'

'I'm sure.' Buxton glanced around the scene. The well-oiled machine that is a murder investigation was moving along. The doctor was still examining the body and would, in due course, have it moved to the lab.

'It, no longer a person,' Buxton thought. He sighed, they were all in for a long night and turning to Davies he said,

'Get the strobes turned off Andy. I know we are out of the way here but let's not advertise our presence too much.'

Davies nodded acknowledgement.

'There's also a kid in the cottage boss, a little girl. I gather the husband called his parents after us and they are on their way.'

Buxton merely grunted at the added complication and said,

'Let's go talk to the husband. Is there another way in? I don't want to disturb anything.'

'We can get in round the back. We need to walk down Mill Road. This lane runs down to the mere and the angling club. The road that runs down the side from the roundabout goes to the Old Mill at the rear. The river is just beyond that. There's a small conference centre and a couple of craft shops, all owned by the council. There are four cottages here. The ones at either side of this one have their gardens and vehicle access to the sides but this one has its access off Mere lane. Anyone could come and go from here without disturbing the others. They all back onto the Old Mill and have small courtyards. I think all the buildings round here probably belonged to the old Rednall Brick Company.'

'Alright,' said Buxton. 'Tell uniform to watch out for the parents and for Gods sake keep them well away from the body. Make sure they escort them to the rear of the house.'

Davies quickly relayed Buxton's instructions whilst Buxton glanced around the scene admiring the professionalism of the officers. No one was just stood chatting. They all had a sense of purpose. Davies returned and the two of them walked down the road towards the corner. A uniformed officer touched his helmet in acknowledgement as they passed and turned to the rear of the building. Buxton noted the conference centre and shops and thought that there would be some unhappy occupants in the morning if the lane remained closed. It was hard enough earning a living in Rednall at the moment. Two more uniformed officers stood outside the French doors which appeared to be the only other form of access to the cottage. Buxton gave a brief thought to the budget. Overtime would wreak havoc and no doubt the chief would be having a word in the morning. Still, he couldn't help when people died violently and this was certainly a very violent death.

'Evening Robert,' PC Pete Brown, the older of the two officers, greeted Buxton.

'Evening Pete. Chilly night.'

'It is, but we get used to it' he replied with just the right amount of sarcasm to let Buxton know that those in uniform had the less glamorous role. Buxton didn't rise to the bait.

'Go straight through the kitchen. DI Kirk and Jenny Holmes are in the lounge on the left with Thomas, the husband. He's pretty shaken,' Brown added.

Buxton nodded and entered the house with Davies. Kirk and the young WPC were seated in easy chairs on either side of Thomas who was sitting on a large sofa and staring vacantly ahead towards the fireplace. The two officers stood as Buxton entered the room and Kirk swiftly made the introductions. Thomas, who was shaking from head to foot and having difficulty lighting a cigarette, didn't react. Buxton noted from the ashtray and the heavy atmosphere in the room that it was not his first smoke of the night. However, despite his demeanour, at this moment in time Thomas was the prime suspect.

'Mr. Thomas, I know this is a very difficult time but I have to ask you a few questions.'

Thomas just continued to stare ahead his eyes seemingly focused on the fire. Buxton wanted to react, to shout at the man. Buxton knew his temper was short probably due to the lateness of the hour and the alcohol he had consumed at the golf club. With an effort he continued.

'Please, just tell us what happened this evening.'

Thomas turned and looked at him. For an instant Buxton thought Thomas was going to cry but then he pulled himself erect and began to speak, slowly at first and then more quickly as the nightmare events that had become his evening began to unravel.

'Lucy left about quarter to eight. She always goes to the gym on Mondays. She said I'll see you about half nine, but when she didn't come home I thought she may have gone for a drink.'

'Did she do that often?'

'No, no, not really, just sometimes with the girls,' he answered haltingly.

'Go on Mr. Thomas, take your time.'

'I put Annie to bed, read her a story and then went back on the computer. I was looking for holidays. I suppose I forgot about time and then when I looked at the clock it was after ten. I went outside for a cigarette and thought I'd ring her. I walked down the path and then I could hear her phone ringing. I went round her car and the outside light came on. She was there, laid on the floor.' He stopped, his breath having caught in his throat, clearly distressed.

'There was so much blood.' His voice tailed away and he fell silent, his head bowed, clearly reliving the moment life had turned to hell. Buxton had been through this before. Questioning relatives in the immediate aftermath of shocking death never got any easier and he knew that if it did, or if he ever became immune to the grief, then he would be somehow dehumanised. He softened his approach.

'Mr. Thomas. David, you don't mind if I call you David do you?'

David shook his head.

'Did you touch her?'

'No, I knelt forward but I could see the blood and she was just staring at the sky. There was an awful smell and I just wanted to get away. I was sick on the lawn. I ran back and phoned you from the kitchen. Then I rang my parents, I thought they would have been here by now.'

'Is there anything you've not told us David?'

David paused, collecting his thoughts and then blurted out, 'My car! My car is missing!' Then he gave them the make, colour and registration number.

'It's my company car. I sell BMW'S for the Hines Motor Company in Birmingham,' he said, his voice softening to a whisper as he lowered his head.

Kirk left the room and organised the circulation of the vehicle details. The WPC was dispatched to the kitchen to make tea, the great cure all. Buxton resumed his gentle probing.

'Is there anything else you can tell us about your wife which would help us further tonight?'

At that point however they were interrupted as Constable Brown entered the room followed by a middle aged couple who Buxton guessed were the parents. The female didn't wait for any introductions.

Before anyone could intervene she immediately rushed to her son and embraced him. Buxton led Davies from the room leaving the family with the WPC who had returned from the kitchen. She may have felt uncomfortable but sometimes sitting unobtrusively can bear fruit. This would prove to be one of those times.

'C'mon then Andy, what do you think?' Buxton said hunching his shoulders against the chill night air.

'Robbery maybe? Although it's a bit out of the way for an opportunist thief. Could have been a petty thief on his way to rob the couples in the park by the mere and it got out of hand?' Davies answered.

Buxton smiled.

'I doubt that. Besides you're assuming she went to the gym. She may have been murdered earlier. The doc can tell us that. You don't think it was the husband then?'

'No. I know it's my first murder but his reaction seems genuine.'

'I agree but we can't eliminate him yet. We are going to have to take him in I'm afraid. The parents will presumably take the girl and I want a warrant to search the house. I'll ask his permission but I don't want any comebacks. I want someone on his computer. SOCO won't be finished for hours outside. Has anyone been to the neighbours?'

'Kirk had uniform do it as soon as we got here. One couple are away and the others neither saw nor heard anything.'

'I'm not surprised. This place isn't overlooked from what I can see. Makes house to house easier anyway,' he smiled ruefully.

'Do you want to see the body in situe boss?'

'No, I've seen all I need to see and it's only more boots tramping over the scene. Leave it to the doctor and SOCO. They know what they are doing. We won't get the interim report till morning and I doubt we can get anything more from Thomas tonight. We need to find the car of course. Any CCTV in this area?'

'I'll check it out with traffic. I'm pretty sure there will be a camera at the roundabout and there's definitely a camera pointing down the lane from the complex at the rear.' Davies answered.

Buxton nodded, 'Excellent. Get the tape or whatever it is we use nowadays and don't be frightened of ringing the council even at this time of night. Unless the killer came up from the mere, or it's the husband, it could be more than helpful. In any event one of the recordings will hopefully show the car being driven away which will help to confirm the time of death.'

Both men returned inside and Buxton explained what they intended. Thomas didn't object to a house search and even volunteered the passwords to his computer. From their body language it was clear his parents seemed non-too sure at his acquiescence but they made no comment. He didn't mention a solicitor either. Buxton agreed to let Thomas wake the girl although they were all in no doubt that at her age she would be too tired to notice anything amiss and probably wouldn't remember a thing about the events the next morning. Buxton was thankful that he would not be the one to tell her that her mummy was not coming back. Buxton and Davies stepped outside and Davies spoke to one of the constables, who then radioed for a car. When the vehicle arrived a few minutes later, Davies elected to accompany Thomas to the Rednall Central Police station. The parents followed their son out with the little girl wrapped in a blanket. She had remained asleep in her bedroom, on the opposite side of the house to all the activity. It wasn't until after they left that the young WPC attracted Buxton's attention.

'Excuse me sir.'

'Yes Jenny.'

'When you were out, the mother said she always knew that the tart would cause bother, but not like this.'

Buxton immediately knew what his first question would be the following morning and although he didn't know it at the time, the following day would prove to be long but ultimately very rewarding.

CHAPTER 6

It's now almost midnight. The predicted snow has begun to fall and I'm having a last brandy before retiring to bed, still alone. I can't help thinking that just a few feet away on the other side of the wall is the beautiful woman who I should have been making love to tonight. Instead she's lying next door with her husband!

When it comes to attractive women I've always had a serious weakness. And a massive blind spot. Most blokes will admire and not touch. Not me. Never let it be said that I allow common sense to get in the way of my ego. It's not that I go out of my way to chase skirt. I don't, honestly, but if I get a flicker of interest them I'm off and I don't know when to stop. Why Lynn put up with it for so long God only knows? I did, or do, have some rules though, one of which is never to chase another man's wife. I stuck to it too. Well nearly! There was the Car Hire Manager's wife from Mildenhalls in Madley. Very blond and very pretty she was a really nice, but desperately lonely lady. Her husband was so possessive he stifled her. At company functions she was almost too frightened to talk to anyone. She was just sixteen when he married her. They had six kids, the youngest having just started at nursery when I came on the scene! Obviously he had decided that keeping her pregnant was the best way to stop her running off! He was right. No matter how wonderful she was between the sheets she came with far too much baggage! Besides which, he was a very big bloke! I can take care of myself, but there's no point in tempting fate to often so after half a dozen passionate daytime encounters in the local Travelodge we ended it before anybody got hurt. For sure I took advantage of her unhappiness. The affair was a kind of revenge for her husbands back stabbing ways. Another particularly venomous individual in the motor trade who would say one thing to your face and another behind your back. I like to think she learnt something about herself those days that would perhaps sustain her throughout her sad life. That's my excuse anyway!

And then there was Lucy. No excuses, I should have walked away but she made the first moves and at that time in my life I thought I could walk on water. My career with the Hatton Motor Group was really taking off. I was being groomed for a senior directorship. Quite a coup for a Sales Manager who had not risen through their ranks, or more pertinently was not a member of the family, and had joined from another company. Like I said, although she worked at a different branch, Lucy made the early moves and I couldn't resist. Trouble was I was breaking another golden rule, 'don't poke the payroll.' Despite several warnings from friends and colleagues who suspected what was going on, I wouldn't give her up. Then one grey November morning my castle in the air came down faster than the setting sun on the equator. One phone call from a trusted colleague and suddenly the planned promotion was no more.

Lucy had been acting strange for a few days and now she wouldn't return my calls or texts. Her assistant insisted that she was out of the office and I couldn't find an excuse to drive the twenty odd miles to head office to see her. I had been dumped. No word of explanation. No call, nothing. Just the humiliation and that horribly impotent feeling of knowing that there was absolutely nothing I could do about it apart from admitting defeat and walking away from both her and the Hatton Group.

One-week later Lynn died. I will forever be haunted by the question, why? Did she really just lose concentration and genuinely not see the tanker heading her way. She was at times absent-minded or did she do it on purpose after a long summer of neglect by me. I'll never know. She died instantly. All the side impact beams and airbags in the world won't save anyone when they are hit by forty tons of tanker travelling at forty miles per hour. The tanker was within the speed limit and the driver escaped with just a few bruises and severe shock. He came to see me but what could we say to each other? Lynn's Aunt Mavis and Uncle Alan had been staying with us and they were in the car with her. Again,

I wondered if Mavis, with her constant yapping from the rear seat had distracted Lynn. Miraculously, sadly, both she and Alan escaped with just bruising and minor cuts from the flying glass although Mavis tried to make the most of the situation, as she always did.

Lynn's mother died giving birth to her. Her dad, stricken with grief and faced with the enormous responsibility of bringing up Lynn alone committed suicide when she was only three months old. Mavis and Alan, parents of an eight year old son John, were more than happy to step into the breach and adopted her. Mavis had always wanted a daughter and of course, the financial legacy had nothing to do with their philanthropy. Lynn, never knowing any different, took everything in life in her stride, although even she realised that Mavis and Alan were not like her friends parents. With her sensible and calm nature Lynn always felt a strong responsibility to her guardians and Mavis constantly played on it. She never let Lynn forget what she had supposedly sacrificed to bring Lynn up.

Cousin John adored his new 'sister' and to Lynn, he was never anything other than a much loved elder brother who never displayed a hint of jealousy towards her. His relationship with his parents however, was always extremely difficult. He was a rebel and eventually tired of Mavis and her hectoring ways. He married young and he and his pregnant wife Judy fled to Australia. Judy hated the life down under and was back within months having given birth to a daughter Amanda.

After Lynn's death, I endured the two blackest months of my life. The funeral was like a bad dream where you pray you'll wake up and it will be over. I was so proud of my kids, Sam and Charlie. They were so strong. Mavis made it to the ceremony of course, on crutches. Her doctor, an old friend of ours, somewhat unprofessionally but understandably fed up of her wasting time and resources, confided in the kids that she didn't really need any assistance to walk or stand. He kindly put her theatrics down to shock, but it was clear what he really felt. Mavis spent most of the service sobbing loudly but with surprisingly few tears to show for all the supposed emotion. Despite what Mavis told everyone, she and Lynn had never been really close. This was the woman after all who threw Lynn out of the house when we had first discovered she was pregnant before we were married. Then, when Lynn went back to get some clothes, Mavis attempted to push her down the stairs! The Social

Worker who was present wanted to involve the police but Lynn, being the type of person she was, wouldn't allow her. Several years later, when Lynn was seriously ill and off work for just over a year, Mavis didn't even contact her to see how she was or if she could help in any way. Unless she was the centre of attention and getting her own way she was never interested in anyone else. John has only ever returned from Australia once although he keeps in touch. He didn't make the funeral either and I could understand why. I have visited him a couple of times since in Oz and he's a good bloke, happily re- married with a lovely wife Elaine and two girls.

Judy also re-married, several times! She turned out to be a real tart and the inevitable occurred. She turned Amanda loose and the poor girl finished up with Mavis and Alan. Mavis repeated history by putting her on the streets after some meaningless spat. Lynn and I took her in and then got accused by Mavis of doing it for the money! Apparently we could have claimed some state benefit but we never did. We never gave a thought to any form of financial payment. We just did what we felt was right despite all the disruption to our lives the situation caused. Amanda stayed for a few months and then returned to her mother.

Throughout our married life Mavis constantly tried to interfere. There are no words which adequately describe the utter contempt I felt for her. Selfish, lazy, self-centred, bitter, twisted, two faced malingerer are probably the closest. From a very early age the kids couldn't stand her. She really was the 'mother in law' from hell, a real witch, a real harridan.

Alan was heartbroken when Lynn died but he was never allowed to show his emotion. I only found out just how much he felt about Lynn when John found the old man's diary. At the funeral Alan remained silent and dignified but not once did he attempt to offer any assistance or condolence. I tried to speak to him but he just mumbled something unintelligible and shuffled away. He was so far under his wife's thumb that he was almost invisible. Neither I nor the kids ever saw either of them again after the funeral. Mavis sent them Christmas and birthday cards but apparently they went in the bin. Harsh? Maybe, but indicative of the strength of feeling towards her.

About a year after Lynn died and just as I was beginning to make some real money I received a phone call from Mavis claiming that

Lynn had borrowed £10000 from her and that the loan had never been repaid. I knew it wasn't true and that she was just trying to cash in on my growing success. I took great pleasure in telling her where to go and hanging up the phone as she screamed obscenities at me. She then followed the call up with a particular obnoxious letter, which I ignored of course, and despite hearing from a mutual acquaintance that she was telling all and sundry that I would never have amounted to anything if it wasn't for her, I never heard directly from the bitch again.

Eighteen months ago Mavis was found dead at the bottom of the stairs in her immaculate house and Alan was found equally bereft of life in his bedroom. Alan had died from suffocation and was found in his bed with a pillow over his head. The gossip mongers decided that she killed him and then fell down the stairs accidentally. Poetic justice or what? Tellingly, the coroner recorded a verdict of accidental death for Mavis and a verdict of unlawful killing on Alan. The police were not carrying out any further investigations which confirmed what everyone thought they knew. There were two separate funerals and me and the kids went to Alan's because Lynn would have wanted us to. John came over and he was genuinely upset over the death of his father and was further moved when he found that Alan had left all his worldly goods to him. I went to the other funeral and was one of only ten souls in attendance. And that included the priest and pall bearers. Clearly others were of the same low opinion of her as I was. I only went to make sure the coffin lid was screwed down securely and the ovens well stoked!

The kids were, and are, great. There were no recriminations after Lynn died, at least not to my face. In any case I doubt I would have noticed as I was too wrapped up in my own self-pity. I began drinking rather more than I should. Not drunk but just enough to dull the pain. Or so I kept telling myself. I was grieving for Lynn, grieving for Lucy and grieving for my job. But most off all I was grieving for me.

Christmas and New Year were a nightmare. Everyone was trying to help but no one, or so I felt, could really understand. I was almost an embarrassment. Then, early in the New Year, there was a knock on the door and it was two very nice men from an insurance company. It seemed my insurance broker had done his job and contacted them. I filled out all the forms and gave them a copy of the death certificate and a week later they came back with a cheque. It was for far more than I expected. It was colossal! Lynn was always good with money and had been investing for our old age.

Suddenly life seemed an awful lot better. A thorough search of the house revealed more savings books and share certificates. Money doesn't buy happiness but there are more people poor and miserable than there are rich and miserable. Shallow? Yes, I've stepped in puddles deeper than me, but at least now I had some focus and the wherewithal to have some purpose. And fun.

I am now the majority shareholder in a property development company. I found myself involved in this almost by accident. I needed to invest some of the money from the insurance so what better place than bricks and mortar? Sure, property drops from time to time, but long term the value always goes up. Besides, the company can weather any storm. Our borrowings are carefully managed and we have plenty of spare capital in our rainy day account. The company name, Moreton Jeffries, was chosen by that great scientific method of sticking a pin in a map and then checking that no one was already using the name. I have one co-director, Nigel, who I can trust totally to run the business in my absence. I met Nigel when we worked together at Mildenhalls. A very good number cruncher, I doubt he has a dishonest bone in his body. He has a small shareholding, as does the bank, but their combined holdings nowhere near equal mine so I can never be outvoted. Our secretary, Lizzie, is a seventy-year-old widow who is supremely efficient and a real mother hen. We also have Jake.

Every company should have a Jake. I would trust him with my life. We have offered him a directorship but so far he has refused. I'm sure he has his reasons. Nigel and I handle all the big projects but Jake has the responsibility for the 'subbies.' We decided not to abandon the small jobs like the one off garages, conservatories, kitchens, bathroom extensions and general maintenance but sub contract the work to other small independent tradesmen. We get them the work, but they handle everything else including final pricing. The materials they buy on our account to help their cash flow and we take a cut from the final price after deducting the costs. The final invoice to the customer has to match the original price unless the client alters the specification. Not only that, we don't allow work to commence until a simple contract has been signed by all parties. We like to think our tradesmen are the most professional in the country. Projects are priced fairly and accurately. Our builders don't just chuck a price at a job in the hope that it will be somewhere close and then disappear to the pub. By and large the system works but occasionally we get an 'anomaly' which is handled with quiet efficiency by Jake.

We had one general builder, Frank Holmes, who attempted a bit of free enterprise with a gullible client. Having finished the job and been paid, Holmes then went back and said he had underestimated the cost of materials and that he was still owed another grand. The client foolishly paid up, but through a friend of a friend Jake got to know. Jake then checked back and found that it wasn't the first time this had happened. The client's were reimbursed. Holmes didn't work for us for awhile again. Come to think of it he didn't work for anyone at all for six months after a visit from Jake! Still, he got the opportunity to mend his ways. Everyone always gets a second chance on the basis that only idiots make the same mistake twice.

Jake also handles debt collection if clients don't pay. We don't have a problem with the big stuff but occasionally the 'subbies' get someone who won't cough up. After a visit from Jake the problem always goes away. No one argues with Jake. I particularly liked the way he handled one miscreant by arriving one night in a JCB. The client paid up on the spot. Well, you would wouldn't you if someone had an excavator bucket poised over your new conservatory!

I have invested well in other properties, which bring in a good rental income, and I own half shares in two used car dealerships, which keeps me in touch with my working roots. I try to spend a couple of days each fortnight visiting a few local main dealers and buying their unwanted stock. I even deal with the Hatton Group nowadays. I also have the occasional punt on the stock market and have quite a diverse portfolio of shares. One recent speculation in a small oil exploration company proved to be a spectacular success. Priced at just ten pence I bought twenty grand's worth. Three months later they discovered oil in some remote part of Kazakwotsit, or some such ex Russian state, and the shares leapt. At just short of two pounds a share I sold out. The profit will buy a few cheaper properties for renovation and rental.

Funny old world isn't it? When I needed the cash I had nothing but my wits and now, when the wits are supposedly on the wane, I have more money than I ever dreamed possible. Still, it does allow me to indulge myself without worrying. I started motor racing in my early twenties but a lack of cash prevented me from progressing. I kept my hand in over the years with a few one off drives, but nothing of any great note. When Lynn died and the insurance money arrived I suddenly rediscovered the passion. I entered a few kart events in the Club 100 championship, by far and away the country's premier 'arrive and drive' kart series. Pay a fee, turn up, race and then go home. No greasy fingers, no worrying about breaking the machine and no transportation concerns. A cost effective way to start on the motor sport ladder in a brilliant, professionally run championship. The competition was fierce but the camaraderie is something I still miss to this day. I didn't perform badly but felt that cars, not karts were where my future lay so, through the business of course, I bought my own sports car to race. I turned out to be pretty quick, even at my age, and I now drive for an old friend of mine who has his own team. I even get paid! I'll never be Formula 1 World Champion but I can more than hold my own in sports cars. It's a good hobby and allows me to travel extensively, usually at someone else's expense.

Buying the disused warehouse on the side of the canal also proved to be an inspired decision in more ways than one. It is situated at the end of a lane through a wood alongside the canal, which once served the numerous gravel pits and quarries in the area and now serves the narrow boat lovers. The canal is actually a spur from the main waterway, which runs into the river, so very few boats use it save for the odd overnight mooring. As the building stands back from the water by about fifty metres with the towpath on the opposite bank it is remote, quiet and private. My first intention had been to convert the building into an upmarket waterside hotel. However, when the architect had a look he felt it wasn't quite big enough. Conversely, when I thought it would make one large house the architect felt it would be just a bit too big to be practical! So we compromised by dividing it to make two homes. This still gave me more room than I would ever need and selling the other half meant the whole project was not only self financing but turned a handsome profit. My only concern of course was what the neighbours would be like, but at least I could veto any sale. The estate agent described the buyers as a middle aged professional couple. Hmm. Close enough I suppose.

I didn't meet Rachael and Andrew until after they had moved in. The estate agents handled it all. What a bunch of parasites they are! At least they were reasonably efficient though. Then again, they should be. Despite my hard negotiations with them and the fact that they handle the company business, their fee was still disproportionate to the amount of work they did even though I gave them a very hard time. None of this showing potential buyers round for me, that was their job. I was even away when Rachael and Andrew moved in and they had been there for two weeks before we met.

The first time I met Rachael it gave me quite a jolt. Apart from hair colour she and Lucy could almost have been sisters. Roughly the same height, same build, give or take a few pounds and almost the same bone structure, but where Lucy had a slightly hard face Rachael's looks are softer. It's just a subtle difference but they could easily have been cast from the same mould. In temperament though my first impressions were that they were worlds apart. Where Lucy was flirtatious, mouthy and enjoyed making an entrance, Rachael was restrained. She certainly wasn't shy just quietly reserved. Until I got to know her better of course. She is witty, intelligent and surprisingly passionate.

Andrew however is a real prize prat. Fortunately I suppose, otherwise I might have felt guilty. I was surprised that he was quite a bit older than Rachael and he looked it. We also didn't appear to have much in common, apart from Rachael. It wasn't until much later that I found out that he also had a weakness for the opposite sex. His only passions appeared to be work and fishing. He can't fish the canal though. Much to his annoyance I hold the rights to the spur and nothing will persuade me to let him or anyone else fish there. He's humourless and self possessed. The years have not been kind. He might have been six feet tall once but he's beginning to stoop and put on weight. Rachael showed me a photograph taken just after their first son was born. You would not believe it was the same man. In fairness to him Rachael tells me that he has always worked hard but then he's had to. His first wife apparently bled him dry and putting five kids through university can't have been easy. According to Rachael she is sure he has had a number of affairs since they were married, although she only can only be reasonably certain of one and that was not long after they were married. Looking at him should serve as a warning to me and I should calm down. He looks old and tired.

I never forget the first time with any woman. Some I may want to but I can always recall them. Even I though wasn't prepared for the intensity of my first night with Rachael. She wasn't expecting me to be home. I knew Andrew was away on some training course so I made certain I returned home early from playing the dutiful son up north. I freewheeled the car into the drive and swapped text messages with her while I waited for her to ask me to ring. When she did I left the car and walked quietly to her door. I wasn't certain how she would react when she saw me there but what the hell. She opened the door and her face was a picture. I paused only briefly before putting my arms about her and placing my lips firmly over hers. There was just the tiniest fraction of resistance before she kissed back and then my hands were loosing her shoulder straps and as her slip fell to the floor she was pulling me back towards the lounge. I have never removed my kit so fast in all my life, although I had a willing helper, and we were quickly joined together and into our stride screwing each other like there was no tomorrow. It was fast, furious and almost violent and when she came she actually screamed! It was not a scream of fear or pain but it was, well, primeval, if that's the right word, in its intensity. Pure lust. I climaxed seconds after and then we lay locked together. The second time we made love tenderly and explored each other's bodies. I love her small, pert breasts and my ability to make her nipples come alive. I stayed until the new day began to dawn and then I left her. Later that day I sent her two dozen carnations and we have been lovers ever since.

CHAPTER 7

The morning after the murder Buxton arrived at the police station just before eight, having slept soundly and enjoyed a hearty breakfast. Davies, he knew, had stayed all night at the station using the put-me-up in the corner of the office to snatch a few hours sleep. He was not surprised to see his younger colleague looking less than his usual debonair self. He could remember when he had been that enthusiastic. Just. Nevertheless, despite his demeanour, Davies had already been busy. The interim report from the police doctor confirmed that Lucy Thomas had died from haemorrhage and shock due to a single, deep and violent stab wound to the right hand side of the neck. The knife had then been torn from the wound by a pushing and twisting action that almost severed the head but missed the cervical vertebrae. It made determining the height of the killer more difficult but the best estimate appeared to give the assailants height at between five feet four and five feet eight. There was no evidence of any further bruising or impact damage to the skull indicating that she had been lowered, rather than dropped, to the ground. The position of the wound clearly indicated that she had been attacked from behind and that the killer was likely to be right handed. The core temperature of the body indicated that the time of death was between seven thirty and eight so she had been murdered before going to the gym. The SOCO team had been at the murder scene all night and the operation was now being scaled down. A surprising amount of detritus had been collected, bagged, and would now be painstakingly analysed along with the contents of the victims handbag, which had revealed a second mobile phone.

Examination of the personal computer belonging to David Thomas revealed that he was heavily into internet gambling and looked to have something of a debt problem. It gave Buxton his second line of questioning.

Of the missing car there were no reports. The CCTV tape was now ready for viewing and Buxton decided to look at this before talking further to Thomas. As they went down the corridor Buxton bumped into Sergeant Bill Russell. Not far from retirement Russell was one of the few people allowed to call Buxton, Bob. He was just leaving having done a double shift thanks to the night's events.

'Can't stand the pace Bill?' Buxton enquired humorously.

'It would have been a quiet night but for this murder and if I'd not stopped to chat I'd have been 'ome tucked up in my pit,' answered Russell smiling ruefully.

'Serves you right for being such a gossip. You're worse than an old woman. Not much doing then?'

'No, quiet all afternoon and evening apart from you lot. Liveliest thing was someone trying to nick a narrow boat from Woodgate basin.'

'Some drunk on his way from the pub?'

'If it was he was pissed early. It happened about half eight. The bugger rode off on a bike!'

Buxton laughed and moved on. Over the last few years, since the canals re-opened, boat crime was on the increase and causing some anxiety among the residents and boat owners. Almost always, it turned out to be the high spirited antics of drunks on the way home from the many pubs along the canals, but just occasionally a boat did get moved or burgled. It was becoming not just a nuisance but a serious concern for the force. It was bad enough trying to police the streets without having to patrol the canals as well.

The footage from the cameras mounted on Mereside roundabout showed several cars but only one pedestrian approaching from the direction of the town. The pedestrian, a jogger, passed beneath the camera at 7-29p.m. Despite the recording being monochromatic and somewhat grainy the runner appeared to be dressed in black, wearing what seemed to be some form of tight running suit and was clearly carrying a rucksack type bag on his, or possibly her, back. As the runner went down Mill Road he, or she, crossed over and ran beneath a road sign on to the pavement before disappearing from view down Mere Lane. Crucially though, the runner was also wearing some form of headgear which masked their features. Both Buxton and Davies instinctively knew that they were looking at the likely killer. Several cars were also shown, but they were only interested in the search for one and at 7-49 p.m. a BMW five series passed the camera heading towards the town having entered Mill Road from Mere Lane. This, they recognised from the registration number, was David Thomas's company car. It also showed very clearly that the driver was wearing a dark balaclava with twin eye-holes. Buxton had by this time pretty much made up his mind as to what had happened. He sat back and stroked his chin reflectively.

'Well Andy lad, I reckon the runner is our man. He either waited outside until she came out or he was just an opportunist thief who wanted a ride home. What do you reckon?'

Davies wasn't entirely certain whether his boss was joking but he picked up the train of thought,

'If, IF the runner is the murderer then I don't buy the theory that this was an opportunist attack, or a robbery. The handbag was left behind. I know we have some weird people on our streets these days but I don't buy into this guy, or woman, going for a run and then deciding on the spur of the moment to kill this woman and then pinch the car. Why come all the way from the town centre? Why not just go into the nearest car park? I know it's remote down Mill Road and there's less chance of a witness, but if you went out with intent, how are you going to know that you are going to meet someone down there anyway? If this is some mad psychopath then surely they would just act.'

'Not necessarily. Could have been after someone at the mere?' Buxton mused.

'No. If that were the case you would have gone later, after the pubs shut.'

Buxton smiled. 'So many questions aren't there Andy. Gut feeling is that's our man and I'm convinced it's a man. I reckon he knew her, and he waited knowing that she would be there at that time, which lets the husband off the hook. I'm certain this was personal. It was no random attack.' Buxton stood abruptly.

'C'mon, let's put Mr. Thomas out of his misery. We do need to ask him some searching questions so I'll lead, but unless he surprises us and makes a confession he's not our man. We'll try not to waste too much time with him. He needs to spend today with his family.'

Davies rang the front desk and arranged for Thomas to be escorted to the designated interview room. Buxton made a couple of internal calls and then led Davies down the hall. As they entered the interview room Buxton was not surprised to find that Thomas was now accompanied by a solicitor. He guessed rightly that the parents had organised this, fearing for the welfare of their son. Thomas stood politely but Buxton waved him to sit. Despite a largely sleepless night, Thomas seemed alert although he was pale and clearly still very shaken. He had been kept in a holding cell overnight and had been offered breakfast which he declined. Buxton felt more than a little sorry for the man.

'Morning David,' he said. 'I'm sorry to have kept you waiting but I'm sure you appreciate that I have to ask you some further questions.'

Thomas nodded. The solicitor, John Todd interrupted before Buxton could continue.

'Is my client under arrest?'

Buxton's previous dealings with Todd had shown the solicitor to be a competent if pompous brief. He didn't like him and suspected that the feeling was mutual. Todd was short, obese, and balding with pinched features which always reminded Buxton of a cartoon rat. Buxton addressed his answer to Thomas totally ignoring his solicitor.

'It is your right to have a solicitor present but you are not being charged at this stage and I'm sure, and I hope, that we can quickly eliminate you from the enquiry and you can get home to your little girl. She will need you today.'

Thomas nodded. He was dreading seeing Annie. Todd, suitably chastened, settled back in his chair, notebook in hand.

Buxton leant forward and said, 'your mother called your wife a tart David, why was that?'

Thomas looked as though he had been slapped in the face but gave Buxton his full attention. Some of the colour also returned to his cheeks.

'She had an affair a few years ago and my mother never forgave her.'

'Did you?'

For the first time that morning Thomas smiled if somewhat mirthlessly. 'I didn't kill her.'

'That wasn't the question.'

'I know.' Thomas took a large breath before continuing. 'Yes, I forgave her but I guess I never forgot. Look, Lucy was a free spirit. She was a good mum but we didn't have the greatest of marriages. I'm sure you'll find out even if I don't tell you that we separated not long after Annie was born and we spent several months apart before we got back together.'

'Whose fault?'

'Mine, I left her because I was having an affair.'

'And since that time?'

'I've had the odd one nighter but nothing serious,' Thomas answered almost defiantly.

'I'm not here to judge you David, I just want to catch whoever killed your wife,' Buxton said gently. 'Did your wife have any further affairs that you knew of?'

'She might have been seeing someone, yes, but we haven't discussed it.'

'So you were jealous then?'

'No, but if she was having an affair then I think it might have resulted in our going separate ways.'

'How long were you married David?'

'Long enough' he answered but then realised how crass his response sounded and gave Buxton the exact date and a brief résumé of the marriage. Buxton sat nodding his head and drumming his finger lightly on the table between them.

'What made you think she might have been seeing someone?'

'I don't really know. It was just little things. Her phone would go sometimes and she would say it was a wrong number. She always kept her phone with her.'

It was something that had annoyed David because he could never get a look at her phone.

'She kept two phones. We found a second in her handbag.'

'So she had been up to something,' thought David. He knew that the look on his face had given away his thoughts. Buxton looked at Davies. The unspoken question was on both officers' minds. Was this a motive? Was it sufficient reason to follow your wife down the path, then practically sever her head and return indoors to wait a couple of hours before ringing the police? Could he have driven the car away and left the child alone? Perhaps he had a lover and they had planned the attack together? Was David Thomas a liar?

Buxton changed tack.

'Do you gamble much David?'

Thomas smiled. He knew they would ask him about his habit and was not at all fazed.

'I gamble too much but it's not a crime is it?'

'No, it's not, but big debts could be a motive for murder especially if the victim turns out to be insured.' Thomas paled.

'Lucy is insured and yes I have some debts, but I didn't kill her,' he said with just a hint of panic.

'How much debt Mr. Thomas?' Davies asked.

Todd shifted uncomfortably in his seat, but did not try to intervene. The atmosphere had changed as Davies asked the question. It was the classic good cop, bad cop routine but Thomas had known since the early hours that this line of questioning would be inevitable and he wasn't going to attempt to hide the truth.

'I owe getting on for a hundred thousand pounds,' he answered trying desperately to keep his voice calm. Even Todd raised his eyebrows.

'That's a great deal of money David,' Buxton said before Davies could ask him any further questions. If Buxton was shocked he didn't show it. He changed the course of the interview again, trying to catch Thomas off guard.

'Who was her previous lover David?'

Thomas winced inwardly. Even though it had been several years earlier and despite his own infidelities his pride still hurt.

'Joe Quinn, his name was Joe Quinn,' he answered quietly.

'Are you sure it was over?'

'Yes I'm sure. As far as I'm aware they haven't seen each other for years. They both worked at the Hatton Group. He left. The relationship ended when I found out.'

'How do you know?'

'Lucy came home in tears. There was some row between them that I never did get to the bottom of although I didn't try very hard to find out what it was. To be honest I didn't care why the affair ended, I was just pleased it had. Everyone knew about them but me. She made lots of excuses and denials. I wanted to believe her, so I did.'

'No recriminations then?'

'No.'

'Ever seen Quinn since?'

'No. In fact I've never met him.'

'You weren't tempted to go round and confront him then?'

'No. I'm not the confrontational type.'

Buxton nodded before continuing,

'Are you seeing anyone at the moment David?'

'No. No I'm not,' Thomas answered shaking his head.

Buxton stopped and surprised everyone by suspending the interview, suggesting that they have a break. He left the room with Davies and walked down the corridor to his office. As they walked Davies asked,

'You went a bit easy in there Boss I thought. Was there a reason?'

Buxton stopped in his tracks.

'He didn't do it Andy that's why.'

'How can you be so sure? We have two possible motives.'

'Maybe, but it's not enough to charge him and I still don't see it. Despite the debt, I think it would be way too much of a gamble to kill her for the insurance money. He could have paid someone of course but that scenario just doesn't work for me. I know there's no template for this sort of thing but I just can't see him as the murderer. A gambler and a foolish man perhaps, but not a killer. I can't see him leaving the child alone either. If he wanted rid he would have just walked away, got divorced, sold the house and paid off his debts without fear of being caught out.'

'I see,' Davies answered quietly, clearly unconvinced.

Buxton was quite clearly oblivious to his concerns and as they walked on he turned to Davies and asked,

'Where do I know Joe Quinn from?'

'If it's the same Joe Quinn that I know of' Davis answered, 'and I'm sure it is, because my parent's bought a car from the Hatton Group a few years ago and he dealt with their complaints. He's made a fortune from property development and he's quite a successful racing driver. You will have heard him on the sport news and you must know the story about how he started his company. Wife died in a car crash and the insurance payout set him up in business.'

'Aah yes, you're right, I know who you mean, just didn't know he had a connection with the Hatton Group. Come to think of it I met him briefly at the golf club sporting dinner last year. Well liked as I understand it. His company is doing the big development around the old Harpley docks.'

'Interview him?'

'Perhaps. If we don't get any further with Thomas we will if only to eliminate him. I take it we took swabs and prints from Mr. Thomas last night?'

'Yes, he was fully co-operative even though he was badly shocked. I think he's more worried about the little girl.'

Davies went on to explain that he had organised a briefing of what would be the murder squad for ten o'clock. Buxton told Davies to get everyone together and that he had decided to release Thomas. Buxton himself returned to the interview room, walked in and without preamble said,

'Mr. Thomas, thank you for your time and patience and please accept my condolences at this difficult time. I'm going to arrange a car to take you to your parents and I know this will be difficult, but please try not to discuss the case with anyone outside of your immediate family. We already have the media sniffing round so it is inevitable that they will find you and try to get some detail. To that end I'm going to instruct uniform to place a discreet watch over your parents' home and in due course we may ask you to appear at a news conference. The local news hounds are pretty respectful, but news is news. I'm not going to give you the old cliché about not leaving town and we will keep you in touch with any developments. There is a family liaison officer assigned to you and she will answer any questions you need to ask. You will have to formally identify the body of course, and we will be keeping your wife's personal effects for the time being. There is nothing else I can say to you at this moment. Is there anything you want to ask me?'

Thomas shook his head, relieved that at least a part of his ordeal appeared to be over.

'Go home and care for your daughter David' Buxton said with genuine sympathy. Thomas began to shake and Buxton could see that he was on the edge of tears. He did not envy him the next couple of hours.

Buxton shook him by the hand and nodded to the solicitor as they left the room escorted by a uniformed officer. Buxton followed and headed to his office, pausing to get a coffee from the machine. He sat at his desk deep in thought, wondering if they would get a break. The break came with the ringing of the phone.

'Boss, we've found the car at Webbers Wood and it's intact.'

CHAPTER 8

David Thomas did not want the journey from the police station in Rednall to his parent's home in Dunley to end. Fifteen miles, twenty minutes give or take. Twenty four hours earlier the last thing he thought he would be experiencing was finding Lucy murdered and having to spend the night in a police cell. The first pangs of hunger were beginning to gnaw at his stomach. Unsurprisingly he had hardly slept. The police questioning had been relentless but they were only doing their jobs. When they ended the session Buxton appeared genuinely sympathetic. As he left the station the younger officer, Davies bumped into him as he went down the corridor and handed him his card, telling him to ring if there was anything he needed to find out. The gesture surprised David as he felt Davies considered him to be the prime subject. If the last twelve hours had been bad however he knew that this was going to be the worst day of his life.

No one spoke in the car, not even to ask him directions. He assumed that the vehicle was equipped with satellite navigation. The silence just made everything worse. The realisation of Lucy's death and what he now had to do was beginning to hit home and hit hard. He couldn't get the image of her lying there from his mind but worse, was the horrible smell which still seemed to cling to him and the thought that in a few hours time he was going to have to see her again and make the formal and positive identification. He knew he hadn't loved her as he should but she had been the mother of his child. How strange it was to think of her in the past tense. He couldn't make any sense of it. He really had no idea who would have wanted to have killed her. Was she seeing someone else? He had his suspicions but there was nothing he could prove and indeed he had never tackled her about it. The discovery of a second mobile phone was a real revelation. He had never considered that possibility. If she was having an affair then who was it or rather who could it have been? Someone at the gym? Someone at work? He didn't know. But then, he hadn't realised that she had been having an affair with Joe Quinn until one of his best friends told him about their relationship and even then, he hadn't accepted the truth. Were there any comparisons between then and now? He didn't think so. Quinn was never a topic of conversation between them again after the affair ended, despite Quinn's success and the attendant publicity. A veil had been drawn across the whole sorry mess.

This time, he knew his suspicions were different and that it had been more an inbuilt defence that made him constantly, if silently, question her actions and movements. He realised now that things had never really been right between them since her affair with Quinn.

As the car entered the outskirts of Dunley his thoughts turned again to Annie. She adored her mother. They had been so close and despite her faults Lucy had been a good mother. He knew that Lucy had only taken him back because of Annie and that Lucy would have done anything for her. Annie had always been her priority. Annie was the glue in their relationship. He began to feel his stomach churn as the car turned into his parents' road and then into the horseshoe shaped driveway of their mock Tudor home. He saw the front door opening before the car pulled to a halt. As he stepped from the car his mother, Nancy, came towards him with her arms outstretched. She had always been protective of him despite the fact that he was almost a foot taller than she and had been since his early teens. His father, Eric, stood in the doorway. It was clear he did not know what to say or how to react. He was a big man, used to dealing with the hard men of the construction and plant hire industry. It made him think of Joe Quinn again and he wondered why they had never met and why his father, who was after all in the same line of work, had also never met him as far as he knew. Eric had been fond of Lucy despite her infidelity. He saw it as her revenge for David's own unfaithfulness and told David so in no uncertain terms. David gently broke the embrace and they went inside, crossed the hall and entered the lounge. None of them heard Annie coming down the stairs and were not aware of her presence until from the lounge door she said,

'Daddy,' and they turned as she continued in a low voice, 'where's my mummy?'

CHAPTER 9

Buxton replaced the phone. He was surprised to learn that the abandoned car was not a burnt out shell. This troubled him but did at least mean that there was a likelihood of clues. SOCO were already on their way to the car, which was in the car park at Webbers Wood, a small picnic area on the outskirts of Rednall. Buxton knew from his uniform days that there were a number of paths radiating from the car park. Webbers Wood was a popular place for dog walkers and, after dark, lovers. It had also been the site of some environmental protests when the new bypass had been built. The council overcame all the asinine objections, invested money tidying the wood and paved the previously pot holed parking area. The picnic area was only just off the access road to the by-pass and the Birmingham to Rednall canal bordered the site. Buxton remembered how scruffy the canal had once been. In recent years it too had received a makeover and was now well used by the growing band of narrow boat enthusiasts. Rednall itself was moving away from its industrial roots and was re-inventing itself as a tourist centre but not without some economic pain as factories closed or re-located.

Davies entered the office without knocking and before sitting, Buxton informed him of the latest development. He then told Davies that he should visit the site as he intended to take the scheduled briefing along with Kirk. It took Davies only ten minutes to get to Webbers Wood and as he pulled his unmarked car to a halt a short distance from the entrance, a uniformed officer was quick to approach. He recognised Davies and escorted him to the car park. As is common practice nowadays the entrance had a large metal height restrictor over it to prevent any unauthorised over night camping or worse, an infestation of travellers and the disruption they would inevitably bring. The site was already taped off and Davies could see a white suited SOCO operative moving carefully round the metallic green BMW. It was the only vehicle parked within the confines of the park. Davies was surprised to see the head of SOCO, Lee Park, in attendance but not dressed in his white oversuit. The last time he had seen Park he had been on his hands and knees at the murder scene in Mere Lane. Park looked, and was, very tired.

Park saw Davies and came across and explained that when the call came in he had just been about to go home having worked throughout the night. It was because he was tired that he was not examining the car in case he missed something. He was however going to stick around. It transpired that the car was locked. It had also rained on this side of town during the night. So, although they were going to do a fingertip search of the immediate area around the car, the concentration of effort would, naturally, be on the car itself which they were intending to move to the station garage on the back of a low loader.

'We can't shift it yet because of the restricted access. With the car being a company demonstrator the supplying dealer is also the registered keeper. We made contact with them and they have despatched a driver with a spare set of keys. He contacted me a few minutes ago and reckons it will be an hour before he gets here,' said Park.

'Anyone looked through the window?' asked Davies.

'The officer who found the car. There's a mobile phone in the rear footwell behind the driver's seat and what appears to be a bloodstain on the passenger seat but nothing else. A lot of these car dealers insist on personal belongings being kept to a minimum inside their demonstrators.'

Davies nodded. Yet another mobile. Davies guessed that it was this that was keeping Park's attention. He would want a breakthrough as much as anyone. Certainly David Thomas never mentioned that he owned a second phone and Davies felt certain he would have, which meant that the killer had almost certainly left it. But why? And if it had fallen from his or her pocket why not go back for it? Davies didn't see any point in staying with the car. As always in a murder enquiry much of the work done requires a great degree of patience as the various specialists get on with their jobs. With this in mind Davies decided to return to the station where he could catch the remainder of the briefing. As he pulled away he made a call to David Thomas and ascertained that he did not own a second mobile. He also noted that there were no CCTV cameras in the vicinity of the wood.

By the time Davies returned to the station the briefing had still not commenced, Buxton having been delayed by a call from the Chief Constable, mainly concerning the need to be mindful of overtime and its effect on the budget. It was not a call that Buxton had enjoyed or appreciated. Davies quickly explained why he had returned and then Buxton surprised him by telling him to take the briefing. At first Davies thought that Buxton was having a joke at his expense. When he realised he wasn't Davies brought the crowded room to order. He then picked out a point on the wall at the rear of the room so that he could avoid eye contact with his colleagues, some of whom he knew would attempt to distract him. Despite it being a very violent incident there would still be plenty of 'mickey' taking. The jokes and sarcasm helped relieve the stress. As he began to run-through the elements of the case, beginning with the discovery of the body, the likely identity, Mrs. Lucy Thomas, married, a mother of one, a senior accounts administrator at the Hatton Group and the questioning of her husband David Thomas, the nerves began to leave him and although he knew his delivery may be a little disjointed he would get by.

Two teams of two would again interview the neighbours and the other handful of homes in and around Mere Lane. SOCO were still on site, although they had completed the examination of the drive and were just finishing in the house. They were also searching the undergrowth between the roundabout and an area fifty yards beyond the house heading down to the mere. Buxton interjected at this point as he felt that this would be a waste of time as it was more likely that the killer had driven straight from the house. Davies resumed by explaining that the car had been found and was now undergoing examination. Buxton interrupted again and said that he would be giving a short briefing to the press with the usual appeal for public help. No decision had yet been made to involve David Thomas in the press briefing and the victims name was also being withheld until after the formal identification. As yet there was no clear motive and no weapon.

The assembled officers were all making notes and no one interrupted until Davies mentioned that Mrs. Thomas was known to have had a previous love affair. Then he informed his audience of the name of her former lover, Joe Quinn. There was no missing the buzz of comment to which Buxton responded.

'Somebody want to speak?'

'Is this the property developer from Harpley?'

'We believe so and if it is, apart from a speeding ticket five years ago, he has no form. It seems this affair is from a few years ago when Quinn worked for the Hatton Group and there is nothing to suggest that he was still seeing her, but it may be that we question him later today.'

Davies raised an eyebrow not having been told of this.

'Any CCTV?' From the floor.

Davies responded.

'There are cameras on the Mereside roundabout. We have examined the recordings and it shows a runner heading towards the lane some fifteen minutes before the time we believe the incident took place. It also shows a number of vehicles on the main road before a green BMW, which is Mr. Thomas's company car, passes the camera around ten to eight. There's also a camera on the Old Mill complex but it appears it was turned off.'

'What about the industrial units. Are there any with surveillance?'

Both Davies and Buxton mentally cursed. Neither had thought about this. Apart from the complex to the rear of the cottage there were some much larger industrial units on the town side of the roundabout. Buxton responded by telling the officer who had asked the question that he had just volunteered himself to check.

'What about the husband?'

'Bet he did it!' someone shouted from the back.

Buxton sensed that Davies was beginning to lose the room so he stood and raising his voice said,

'Pipe down, lets stay focused on what we have for now. I've spoken to him and whilst he's not been totally ruled out, we need to get down to the Hatton Group and start interviewing those who worked with the victim. She was not due at work today and so far we've restricted news to the discovery of a body but this is a small town and news will travel fast. It won't be long before someone tries to get hold of either Mrs.

Thomas or Mr. Thomas and then starts putting two and two together. Inspector Kirk will be in touch with the MD at the Hatton Group, as he knows him personally. I don't want us going down mob handed either so Kirky will pick who will be involved. I'm sure the company will be co-operative. Lets get to it people.'

With that, Buxton left the room with Davies in tow. He needed a cup of tea and wondered how many more cups he would have this day? How much caffeine? Rose would give him hell but he could take it. This might be his last murder case and he was determined to solve it and solve it quick.

CHAPTER 10

By midday Lee Park was beginning to generate some results despite being almost out on his feet. Strong black coffee and adrenaline were keeping him going. The BMW had been moved from Webbers Wood to a sanitised and secure area within the police garage. The driver with the spare keys arrived at Webbers Wood just prior to the low loader, negating the need to break in. Broken glass, or a damaged door lock, was the last thing the forensic team needed. The car's interior was now undergoing microscopic examination. The position of the driver's seat indicated that the last person to drive the car was between five four and five feet eight. Park however concentrated his personal efforts on the three mobile phones, all of which revealed fingerprints. He checked the numbers of all three phones, recorded them on his note pad and wrote LT against the first number, bag against the second and BMW alongside the third.

The first phone, found by the body, was a top of the range model and clearly the most used, the casing being scratched and generally worn. The phone was also covered with fingerprints matching those of Lucy Thomas. The contacts folder within the phone was full and the history of phone calls was also extensive. The numbers of the other two phones were not listed. Park put the phone to one side, rationalising that this phone was the one Lucy Thomas used on an everyday basis.

The second and third phones, one found in the victims handbag and the other discovered in the abandoned BMW, were both identical, inexpensive devices and on 'pay-as-you-go' contracts. Park called up the service provider on both phones and received an automated response giving the credit balance for each device. There was only a little credit left on either phone.

The phone from the handbag provided one clear print and it was obvious from its casing that it had not been subjected to heavy use. Dried blood was also present indicating that it had possibly been handled by the killer. The blood type matched that of the victim. There was only one phone number held in this phone's memory and the call records showed that only one number had been contacted either by speech or text. Checking his pad he put a tick beside the number of the third phone, found in the foot well of the BMW at Webbers Wood.

It came as no surprise to Park when the third phone also contained only one number in its contacts folder. It too, had only ever been used to connect with one other number. Checking his pad again he smiled and placed a tick beside the second number. Although the records on each phone only stretched back a couple of weeks he felt sure that records provided by the phone company would prove this had always been the case. The last phone, found in the BMW, also offered up a partial print and a few bloodstained smudges. The partial print would however, Park knew, be enough to identify the handler. DNA traces would take a little longer to verify, but he was pretty certain he knew which way the evidence was pointing. The last text sent at seven thirty the previous evening from the third phone stated,

'PLSE DONT END THIS'

This message was staring at Park from the screen of the second phone.

Even as he sat back a junior colleague gave him the news he had been waiting for. The service provider had revealed the names to whom the phones were registered and would, in due course, supply a detailed list of calls and texts from the two phones. The phone found in the handbag was registered to Lucy Thomas. Both phones had been purchased on the same day and at the same time from one of the many mobile phone shops in Rednall shopping centre. Although it would take a little longer, data taken from the positioning of the transmission masts would allow the company to give the locations of the phones on the days they had been in use. Park now possessed hard evidence to give to Buxton and he himself could get some well earned rest. He was confident that the rest of the team could confirm the test results from the bags of detritus collected from both the murder scene and the car and that these would confirm his suspicions. As far as he was concerned they were looking for a right handed male, probably no more than five feet eight tall who picked his nose and bit his fingernails. With luck, they had their man. For Stuart Green of 35, Suzanne Road, Rednall, the registered owner of the third mobile, today looked as though it would turn into a very bad day. Park reached for the desk phone.

CHAPTER 11

Buxton took the call from Park as he and Davies drove to the Hatton Group's head office in Rednall. The advance investigation teams had left some two hours earlier under the supervision of DI Kirk, and they entered the premises of the motor dealers as discreetly as possible given the circumstances. The accounts and administration departments of the company were located about one mile away from the main showroom in a drab building, which would not have looked out of place in a sixties cold war movie. The teams would attempt to cause minimum disruption to the running of the business, but would fail miserably as the gossips and rumour mongers got to work.

As Buxton answered his cell phone he indicated to Davies to pull over. Park quickly but methodically related all the evidence he had collated. Buxton didn't ask any further questions. He simply thanked him and then told him to go home and get some well earned rest. Buxton trusted the system. The name Park had given him, Stuart Green, meant nothing to Buxton, but with a policeman's intuition he called the Hatton Group. The female switchboard operator answered the call on the second ring and he asked for Stuart Green. She immediately told him everything he needed to know. Green did not work at the Rednall branch but was the manager of the Hatton Group's Harvington branch. Harvington was a medium sized light industrial town some fifteen miles to the north east of Rednall. The operator didn't give Buxton the number. Instead she offered to transfer him internally which Buxton gratefully accepted. She placed him on hold and Buxton endured a few sentences of the company's latest special offers before another female operator answered. When Buxton asked for Green he was told that he wasn't in that day as he was away on a course and would be back, as far as she knew, the following day. Buxton wasn't about to wait until the following day and turned to Davies.

'Forget Hatton's Andy. Suzanne Road, number 35, it's near the canal.'

Davies nodded. He knew the area and turned the car around as Buxton got back on his mobile and requested a single unit to meet them at the address.

It took less than ten minutes to drive to what in the warmer months would be the leafy suburb containing Suzanne Road. As Davies turned into the road he instinctively took in the nature of the estate. No litter or decaying autumn leaves in the gutters, the district of which Suzanne Road was a part was one of the more prestigious areas in Rednall. The development had only been completed four years earlier and already any property coming on to the market, usually sold very quickly and at a premium. Most of the houses appeared to have security gates although as he drove past number 35 he noted that the gates were open and that there were no vehicles parked on the drive. Davies reflected that it was clear that management remuneration in the motor industry appeared to be way in excess of pay in the police force. Almost at the far end of the road a marked patrol car was already in position. Davies came to a halt opposite the car and the two uniformed officers got out. Buxton was pleased to see that one of the officers was Sergeant Noel Render, known affectionately throughout the local community as 'Nobby'. Buxton asked him if he knew the area well and then realised what a stupid question it was to ask. Render was an experienced officer who had never worked anywhere other than Rednall. He told Buxton that they were very rarely given cause to venture on to the estate. There was a lane at the back of the houses, on the same side as number 35, which separated the development from the main Birmingham to Rednall canal. Some of the owner's kept boats on the mooring pontoons and occasionally some holidaymakers would moor up for the night, before moving on to Woodgate basin where several canals converged. It did occasionally cause some friction with the residents.

Buxton directed the two officers to the lane at the rear of number 35 in case anyone exited from the back of the property. As he and Davies were about to move their car however, a bright red Ford Focus turned into the entrance to number 35 and a woman, who Davies judged to be in her mid thirties, emerged. Davies reversed and parked, blocking the driveway. The woman paused in the act of unlocking the front door but showed no great alarm as Davies called,

'Mrs Green?'

When, without hesitation, she confirmed she was, both he and Buxton strode forward and introduced themselves by word and with a flourish of their respective warrant cards. Mrs. Green gave them only a cursory glance.

She was a small woman, around five feet tall. Although a little on the chunky side she was not unattractive and clearly dressed well. Her dark hair was cut back from her round well made up face, although no amount of make up, however skilfully applied, could hide the remains of what had once been a very black eye. She invited them in, showed them into the expensively furnished lounge and when asked, confirmed that her husband was not in but would be back around seven as he was in London for the launch of a new car. Looking at her eye Davies asked the inevitable question and received the inevitable answer,

'Clumsy of me, I walked into a door.' But she looked away.

Both Davies and Buxton smiled sardonically. It was not the first time and it would not be the last that a beaten wife had given that answer. Her answer may have been true but both men were already building a mental picture of Stuart Green.

'Mrs. Green, can you tell us yours and your husband's whereabouts last night?'

She looked confused but answered,

'We were both at home.' But again she averted her eyes and before either officer could ask another question she offered them tea, needing a moment to herself to collect her thoughts. Both officers accepted the offer, not pressing her yet, and she went through to the kitchen. As she reached for the kettle there was a knock on the back door. Opening it she was confronted by Sergeant Render who asked to speak to Buxton. She invited him in and Buxton, having heard the exchange met him in the hall.

'Sir, can I have a word?'

Buxton excused himself and left Davies with Mrs. Green. He

followed the sergeant out of the kitchen and as they walked down the garden path Render said,

'I think you need to see this Bob.'

Just inside the gate was a wheelie bin screened from the rest of the garden by a panel fence. Somewhat sheepishly Render said,

'I'd just finished a chocolate bar and was putting the wrapper in the bin.'

He lifted the lid and Buxton looked in immediately wrinkling his nose at the smell from the accumulated rubbish. At first glance he didn't notice the source of Render's concern but then his eye was drawn to a piece of cloth mainly obscured by a cereal box. He took a pen from his inside pocket and carefully moved the box aside revealing the cloth which was red stained and rolled up. Poking through was the unmistakable tip of a large knife. Buxton felt a surge of adrenaline. If this was the murder weapon, and he was in no doubt that it was, then this case was going to be solved very quickly indeed.

'Good spot Nobby. Let's not rush this. Call it in and get the nearest available car to block the opposite end of this lane. I don't want a fuss so tell them no blue lights or sirens. Don't let anyone near the bin and make sure SOCO are informed.'

Then he realised that he was patronising his experienced colleague and said, 'Sorry, you know the drill.' Render nodded, turned away, and began speaking into his lapel radio.

Buxton returned to the house and made his way to the lounge where Mrs. Green sat nervously with Davies. Now was the time to put her under some pressure. As he sat he asked firmly,

'Mrs Green, do you know a Lucy Thomas?'

'Yes,' she answered uncertainly, 'and her husband. They are friends of ours. Lucy and I worked together at the Hatton Group. It's where I met Stuart and she met David. Lucy still works there. I left when I had the kids. Stuart is still with the company but at a different branch and David left some time ago. Please, tell me what's going on,' concern now evident in her voice.

Davies looked at Buxton wondering how far he would go. Buxton carried on,

'Mrs Green, we are investigating a very serious incident and we believe that your husband may be able to help us.'

Mrs. Green, already pale, looked as though she was about to vomit.

'This course that your husband is attending in London, did he travel alone to the city?'

'No, he and some of the other managers were meeting at the service area at junction 12 and travelling in one car.'

'Do you have your husband's registration number?'

'No. It's a company car and they change them quite regularly. I never take any notice and I doubt that Stuart even knows. It's a blue Mondeo if that helps.'

Buxton nodded and replied,

'Mrs Green, I'm sorry, I don't know your first name.'

'It's Wendy.'

'May I call you Wendy?' Buxton asked gently.

She nodded uncertainly and Buxton continued. 'I'm going to get a WPC to stay with you. I must ask you not to try to contact your husband. We do need to speak to him urgently and I would prefer to intercept him before he gets home, if only to prevent the neighbours from having a free show. I know you must be worrying but hopefully we can resolve this quickly and everything will be back to normal. There will be some other officers about and I would like your permission to search the premises.'

'Why?' she asked, clearly bewildered and despite Buxton's assurance very worried.

'It's routine and it would help.'

'Too right it will,' thought Davies, rolling his eyes, not in the least surprised that Buxton was steaming forward without thought of obtaining a search warrant. Warrants were another area where Buxton could be extraordinarily cavalier. Davies believed that one day Buxton's luck would run out and he had long since decided that he would take a more rigid approach. He did not want to lose a cast iron case on a technicality but Wendy Green clearly had more on her mind than formal procedures.

'What's he done?' her emotions were getting the better of her and she was beginning to get angry. 'He's having an affair with Lucy isn't he?'

Both Buxton and Davies wondered what made her jump to that

conclusion, but they both remained silent and just looked at her. She immediately knew it was what they thought. Stuart always fancied his chances with Lucy and she knew that given any encouragement, being a mate of David's wouldn't stop him. When Lucy's affair with another manager became common knowledge, his jealousy had been very evident. He had been even more aggressive with her just recently and she wondered why? Now she knew, or thought she knew. Always quick tempered the previous week he had hit her. She came home early on his day off and found him slumped, drunk and asleep, in front of the television with his trousers and underwear round his ankles. A box of tissues lay by his side and one of his disgusting films was playing to itself. She berated him at some length. What if she had come home with her mother or the kids? And then he lashed out, knocking her to the ground.

But she was confused. The police didn't investigate affairs she thought, so just what was this all about? Then a sickening dread tightened her stomach. She remembered the news bulletin regarding a body on the morning news but she could not remember if they had broadcast a location. Could it be Lucy? God, what had he done? Suddenly she knew what she must do. If Stuart was up to no good then he could pay the price. 'Go ahead,' she said, 'do whatever you have to.'

Buxton was relieved. He hated it when a woman broke down. He rose to leave but before he could speak she spoke, her voice quivering very slightly,

'Inspector. I'm sorry, I lied earlier. I went out last night with a few friends. You can check. Stuart babysat.'

'What time was that?'

'I left about seven and returned about eleven. Stuart was in bed when I got home.'

Buxton thanked her and instructed Davies to wait with her until a WPC and search team arrived. He himself would get the registration number for Green's car from the Hatton Group and organise the intercept. It was not yet mid afternoon and they had made startling progress.

CHAPTER 12

Jake snapped the mobile phone shut and smiled. The text he had just transmitted should have been sent the night before, but he knew that Joe would not have a problem about the delay. In fact he knew that had he not sent the message at all, Joe would not have questioned him. Joe, he knew, had complete faith in him as Jake, equally, had total trust in Joe. Trust was a strange emotion for him. His life had been lived in a world of constant mistrust but his relationship with Joe was different. Jake loved Joe. Love was also a new experience. He had loved his parents but this was not the same. He didn't lust after Joe. He knew it would get him nowhere if he did. Nor was he jealous of Joe's women. He didn't like them, at least those that he met, as they all seemed very shallow. For Joe, they were nothing more than a release for his sexual tension. He always entertained them in one of the show flats. They were little better than whores. Rachael he sensed was different. They had yet to meet but Joe confided in him about her and he was unaffected, despite, or perhaps because of, Joe's clear depth of feeling towards her. He was actually pleased for Joe.

He pushed back the glass sliding door on the penthouse flat and stepped out onto the balcony. He shivered as the cold morning air hit him. It reminded him momentarily of the cold mornings in the training camps, before the sun began pulverising the desert wastes. There was no sun to warm him and no promise of it either, the sky being a solid grey overcast. He stood for a few moments surveying the boat basin below him. The moorings were quiet at this time of year with only a few hardy souls in their canal boats. Over the far side of the basin the building crews were already hard at their labours on the final phase of the dockside development. He could hear the shouted instructions, someone singing loudly and tunelessly and a joiner hammering away. A canal boat below him edged its way gently from its berth. Another three months, if the weather stayed kind, and the final phase of the Harpley dock development would be completed and Moreton Jeffries could look forward to yet more profit. He smiled, pushed himself back from the rail and turned to go back inside. A sudden flash in his eye corner made him throw himself down. He waited for the explosion, the bull whip crack of a bullet, the searing pain ripping through his body.

Nothing happened. He lifted his chin and saw the welder working high on the superstructure, knowing that if the flash had been a bullet he would have already been dead. Dodging bullets was all very well on television, or in the movies. The reality was that had the flash preceded a real and accurate bullet, then no matter how good his reactions were he would now be lying in a rapidly expanding pool of blood. He laughed at himself and did ten push ups in case anyone had seen his odd behaviour and then stepped back inside. Old habits die hard. A penthouse in Harpley was a long way from his native Iraq, but he knew that despite all his tradecraft and all his precautions, he could never be completely safe.

Jake did not believe in God. Despite his upbringing he felt from a very young age that the existence of any sort of Supreme Being was totally illogical. His beliefs did not prevent him from praying or following the religious doctrines of his country. Life was safer that way. He had been recruited early by the Mukhabarat and went into the desert camps to learn his trade. The harsh regimes hardened him still further. The monomaniacal instructors honed him into a man capable of killing without remorse. He was born with a gift for languages and his looks, more western than Arabic, made him an ideal candidate for recruitment to Directorate 9 of the Mukhabarat, which specialised in operations of sabotage and assassination outside Iraq. He killed with knife, gun, bomb and bare hands and returned to his home country rarely. As a practising homosexual this suited him well, although he chose his partners with great care. On his sporadic returns home his sexuality caused him no great problems but Saddam made the practice illegal in 2001 and he would return to his homeland even less. In any event he knew that the international noose was ever tightening around the Iraqi dictator and that a wind of change would eventually blow through his country. He was determined that when the regime fell he would be long gone. Sadly for him, his plans didn't work out as he intended.

Iraqi operations abroad were severely curtailed after the 1991 Gulf War but Jake continued to do his masters bidding. He knew that sometime in the future America and its allies would wage a war against his country again and when the planes hit the twin towers of the World Trade Centre he was appalled. The loss of life mattered not at all, but he knew that this would give the enemies of his country the excuse they needed. Personally, he had no quarrel with the Americans or westerners in general. In fact, he enjoyed his lifestyle away from his own country. He even thought in English now and adopted western ways. He was certain that there was no link between Iraq and Osama Bin Laden but it would make no difference. He felt Bin Laden was a fool and a barbarian. Indiscriminate killing of citizens was all very well for creating a spectacle and causing public outrage but it didn't strike at the heart. Better a surgical strike at the politicians to instil real terror. All the planes should have been directed at one target, the seat of government. After all, were western politicians not just the same as the leaders in his native country? Did they really care about the populous or were their interests just as self serving? When President Bush announced his war on terror Jake was not surprised. Throughout the following year the sense of foreboding heightened as the Bush regime became ever more aggressive in its rhetoric.

That following summer Jake received word that his father was ill. He returned home to find a country in fear. It was clear that the administration of his country was falling apart and the behaviour of Saddam, his family and followers was becoming ever more despotic. Jake's father passed away and he left the country again heading for Paris under yet another false identity, intending to keep his head down. As Christmas approached he knew that representatives of the head of Iraqi intelligence, General Tahir Jalil Habbash al Takriti, were in touch with Vincent Cannistarvo, the head of counter terrorism at the CIA, but he felt that the talks would prove fruitless. The west, or certainly the Americans with British support, wanted war. In their attempts to justify conflict the Americans had even forged a letter from the General to Saddam, stating that the ringleader of the 9/11 plotters, Mohammed Atta, had been trained in Iraq.

In March the following year Jake received another message to return home. This time it was his mother who was ill. Returning to Baghdad had not been on his agenda. He knew that invasion was imminent but he knew he had no choice. By the time he arrived his mother was in hospital and plainly dying. The doctors were doing what they could to ease her suffering. However, there was by now a drastic shortage of medicines. Jake stayed in the family home at Dora Farms, a farming community on the outskirts of Baghdad and only two hundred metres from the entrance to one of the Royal compounds used by Saddam and his family. In the early hours of March 19th, Jake's mother passed away. It angered him that her last hours were spent in so much pain but he was also thankful that it was now over. Returning home he was aware of an eerie silence which had descended on the city, broken only by the distant roar of a far off jet engine. Was it just his sense of personal loss or a portent of things to come? The distant whine of the jet engine penetrated his thoughts. Was the noise getting louder? He was only one hundred metres from home when he realised it was. A split second too late, he hit the brakes. There was a mighty roar and then all hell broke loose as the missiles rained down. Jake saw his family home disintegrate before him as a stray cruise missile landed. The Royal compound was clearly the target. His car was blown over by the shockwaves. The earth shook and the air pounded around him filling his mouth and nose with dust. Jake struggled from the wrecked car. He could not believe that his home was now destroyed. There was no one inside but crucially his passport and money were still in his bedroom and now lost under the mound of smouldering rubble. He knew it would be pointless to search. In any event he wanted to be as far from Dora Farms as possible. He had no intention of being caught in the city if this was the start of the invasion, so he joined the exodus of refugees and headed for Jordan. It would take him eight months to reach England during which time he stole, begged and murdered to survive, but survive he did eventually reaching London in mid November.

CHAPTER 13

Bob Dance was thoroughly fed up. It was bad enough that he had lost the 'spoof' and been forced to drive his three colleagues to the new car launch meeting in London, but to have had to suffer Stuart Green's drunken, boorish behaviour, particularly in view of the news they received regarding the death of Lucy Thomas, pushed him close to doing something which he would have enjoyed, but that would almost certainly have caused him long term professional regret. On a personal level he didn't know Lucy well but she was a long time colleague and he was stunned by the news and manner of her death. Green however merely continued drinking copious amounts of free red wine and making insensitive comments throughout the afternoon. Were it not for him finally falling asleep, Dance might well have stopped the car. As he drove up the motorway he was thankful that Green remained comatose.

His other two colleagues, Jeff Jones and Mick Atkin, had also been deeply shocked at the news regarding Lucy and after Green nodded off they speculated amongst themselves as to who could have murdered her, or why? None of them thought for one moment that they were actually travelling with the prime suspect. Dance was totally oblivious to the unmarked police vehicle which had taken position behind him, three junctions earlier.

Buxton glanced at his watch. It was 6-45p.m. and the waiting was testing his patience. His fidgeting was beginning to annoy Davies. The unmarked patrol car had radioed in some fifteen minutes earlier and was holding station a couple of hundred metres behind the Mondeo transporting the four sales managers back from London. Buxton, with the discreet help of the Hatton Group's managing director, had been able to obtain the registration numbers of the cars used by the managers known to have travelled to London. He and Davies made the short trip to the service area and found three of the four cars parked alongside each other leaving the fourth as the car being used for the journey. This was the Mondeo being driven by Bob Dance which was now approaching the service area.

Dance exited the motorway at junction 12 and spotted the marked patrol car parked on the overpass. As he drove round the roundabout and headed into the service area, he warned his two wide awake colleagues to be careful when they drove out. Dance had remained sober throughout the day but Jones and Atkin had drunk a little too much of the complimentary wine. Compared to Green however they were relatively sober. They were all prepared to risk their driving licences and careers on the basis that it couldn't possibly happen to them. Atkins and Jones were to be lucky. Stuart Green would be the odd one out.

Buxton had been re-joined by Davies in the late afternoon. Mrs. Green co-operated completely with all their questioning. The knife had been removed from the bin. Mrs. Green herself put the rubbish out earlier in the day and she had not noticed anything untoward. She hadn't looked in the bin, merely lifted the lid and dropped the rubbish in. She consented to a swab being taken. There were no prints on the knife but the blood type had already been matched to that of Lucy Thomas. There was no doubt whatsoever now that this was the weapon used to end her short life.

Buxton also had a busy few hours. By the time he returned from Suzanne Road, David Thomas had formally confirmed the identity of the body as being that of his wife. The information was given to the local press and radio. The press was not happy because the news came too late for the final edition, but the local radio station was now carrying the murder as their lead story. Buxton decided against a full press conference, as he wanted to see how the day developed. How much more satisfactory to be able to announce that a suspect was in custody? Forensics had given him a further report. They had found two cigarette butts at the murder scene and one in the BMW. DNA taken from them indicated the same smoker as did several bitten fingernails and nasal hairs, which Buxton noted with distaste, were encased in nose droppings.

Buxton parked only a few bays from the three Mondeos, all company cars owned by the Hatton Group. Two were the same mid range specification but one, allocated to Stuart Green, was of a higher grade. Buxton's original plan had been to detain Green at the service area as soon as he arrived but the arrival of several football coaches altered his thinking. Davies rightly pointed out that the extra crowds gave Green the possibility of flight and football fans were not always well disposed towards the police. Buxton agreed and felt that Green would take a direct route home, south, down the dual carriageway that connected Rednall with the motorway. Three quarters of a mile down this road was a lay-by frequently used by traffic police and Department of Transport officials for routine vehicle checks. A marked patrol car would follow Green and indicate to him to pull over just before the lay-by.

Davies spotted the silver Mondeo as it drove towards them. Dance pulled past, still oblivious to the fact that he was being followed and was being watched. He stopped behind the three cars but didn't attempt to park in a bay. Three doors opened and the other occupants stepped out. All the passengers wore suits and were somewhat dishevelled from the journey. They were also a little subdued and one of them appeared a little unsteady on his feet. Buxton surmised that they had been told of the death of Lucy Thomas. It was highly unlikely that once her name had been released, no one from the company would have been in touch. Indeed Buxton thought it likely that from the first moment the police arrived at the Hatton Group that the phone lines would have been very busy across the various branches. The managers bade each other farewell, but there was none of the boisterous energy of a lad's day out. Davies identified Green from the photograph given to him by Mrs. Green. Tall, tanned, fair haired, a fine example of the genus 'spiv.' Both he and Buxton were pleased to see that he had not swapped cars with either of his two colleagues. Buxton instructed the other unmarked vehicles to hold back and follow him.

Dance drove away first followed moments later by the other two managers. Green stood by his car, his head to one side with his mobile pinched between his skull and shoulder. If he was trying to ring his home he would not get through. Mrs. Green had been asked and duly complied with a request to turn off both her mobile and the landline. Very frightened, worried and more than a little angry, she decided to spend the night with her parents and had been taken there earlier along with her two children. Green took his phone from his ear and looked at it clearly annoyed that he was getting no response. Turning, he got into his car and as he drove away he placed a cigarette between his lips. It would be his last nicotine shot for some time.

The driver of the marked patrol car, positioned on the outside of the roundabout above the motorway, had kept his engine running. His presence would not arouse suspicion as police vehicles often parked at the spot giving them a good overview of the motorway. In any event Green would not see the car until he committed to the roundabout and if he did try to flee he could not outrun the high performance vehicle or the police helicopter, which had been circling on standby a mile to the east and was now moving towards the dual carriageway. As Green pulled away Buxton alerted the rest of the cars. One minute later Green drove by the patrol car on the roundabout. If he was concerned it didn't show in his driving. The lights were at green and he indicated to turn down the exit to Rednall, at which point the driver of the patrol car accelerated away, took the same exit, and put on his blue lights. He caught Green within four hundred metres and for a moment thought he was going to flee, but a quick burst on the sirens brought an instant response. The Mondeo indicated left and sensibly reduced speed before pulling into the lay-by. Green knew he was in serious trouble.

The patrol car pulled by him and parked across his front at an angle. Green was so preoccupied watching it he did not see the three unmarked cars pull in behind him. Constable Tim Harris, six months in the job, climbed out of the passenger seat and walked back towards the Mondeo. As the window came down on the car a haze of smoke, combined with the unmistakable aroma of alcohol assailed his senses. Stuart Green was facing at least one charge this night.

CHAPTER 14

'Gotcha,' thought Buxton as he put down the phone.

'Forensics has matched the fingernails, nasal hair, saliva on the cigarette butts and the partial finger print to Green. The blood on the seat is the same type as the victim,' he said to Davies. It was just after midnight. Both Buxton and Davies were tired, hungry but more than slightly elated. Buxton looked like a man who had just won the lottery. Davies looked and felt crap, tiredness eating into his bones. It had probably been the longest day of his life. Or did he class it as two days? He had not seen his own bed since the previous day. Buxton showed little sign of the stress of the day and Davies had to admire the older man's fortitude. Despite all the stress and the long hours however the day had brought immense satisfaction.

Stuart Green did not put up any resistance whatsoever when arrested for drink driving. No matter what his future held or how good his legal representation turned out to be, this was one charge he would definitely answer and would lead to a minimum twelve-month ban and a large fine. A lengthy suspension of his driving licence however was looking like the least of his worries. When the line of enquiry turned to the subject of Lucy Thomas, Green appeared to rapidly sober up. He was clearly shaken and more than a little confused. Questioning him further however had been suspended on the intervention of the police doctor who advised Buxton that Green was still technically under the influence of alcohol. Buxton reluctantly agreed, not wanting to give Green any loopholes for his legal team to exploit. Although frustrating, Green was going nowhere and if a good night's sleep made him more alert then the same held true for the two officers. The break gave Buxton and Davies the opportunity to examine the many statements and the forensic evidence that had been collated throughout the day.

The statements taken from the staff at the Hatton Group's administration building had not revealed much. Lucy's colleague, Mandy Frost, who worked across the desk from her, confirmed that Lucy was a 'happy go lucky' sort of person. She liked a laugh and a joke, was an incorrigible flirt, but by and large was popular with the staff, if not some of the more senior managers as she delighted in making sarcastic remarks and putting them down. Mandy knew that Lucy had an affair a few years earlier but did not believe that Lucy was involved with anyone now. They had worked together for several years but were not particularly close. Lucy's life seemed to revolve around her daughter, whom she idolised. None of the statements indicated that she was in any sort of clandestine relationship. The chief accountant, who sometimes had to endure publicly her sarcastic, if somewhat witty rejoinders, praised her as being a conscientious and reliable employee.

Stuart Green however was a different matter. It was clear that he was not a popular member of staff. His office at the Hatton Group's Harvington dealership had yet to be searched, but the desk in his study at home had been very illuminating. Several pornographic magazines were discovered. Eighteen bankbooks from different banks and building societies discovered beneath the base of a drawer showed substantial investments over a lengthy period of time. The amounts recorded did not tally with the amount Green earned at the Hatton Group. He was clearly a man with expensive tastes, including a high specification motor cruiser moored on the canal immediately behind his home. His personal computer revealed hundreds of pornographic images, some of them involving children. In his attic the search team found several boxes of magazines, films and photographs. Buxton knew that several of his officers would be taking a keen interest in 'researching' these items. Buxton had many questions for Green to answer and was looking forward to the following day.

'Well Andy, I think we can sleep safe tonight knowing that we have got our man. Your first murder investigation, what do you reckon?'

'It looks that way,' Davies answered. 'It all seems a bit of an anticlimax though. I thought the investigation would take much longer.'

Buxton stretched and stifled a yawn.

'Sometimes you need a bit of luck to go with the plod, as we got today. Most murders are domestics and not professional hits. Most are committed by people who know the victim. All the evidence regarding the phones points to Lucy Thomas and Green being in a relationship. Three years they have had those phones. Three years,' he repeated with some feeling before continuing, 'it's a long time to keep a secret like that. She probably learnt from her mistakes the last time and was more careful. It would not surprise me if they used the boat. Tests on the seats and bedding will hopefully give us something. I'm sure he was on the take from somewhere. The motor trade is notorious for backhanders although the amounts look quite large to have just come from a local used car trader. His salary would not sustain the lifestyle. It's a very expensive house and it's well furnished. I have no idea what the boat cost but I'll bet it wasn't cheap. Looks to me as though Mrs. Thomas wanted to end the relationship for reasons we may never know. Maybe she found out about the kiddy porn or maybe she just grew tired of him. It happens. I really don't care too much why? Now that forensics can place him both at the scene of the murder and in the car he's going away for a long holiday courtesy of Her Majesty's prison service.'

'But Mrs. Green says that he never left the house last night.'

Buxton smiled.

'She said he babysat. That doesn't mean he didn't leave the house. It's not the first time, nor will it be the last, that a wife has covered unwittingly for a husband. She'll change her mind when she's had a night's sleep and the shock wears off AND she finds out exactly what he has been up to. You saw the initial reaction when she thought he was having an affair. Mark my words she'll want her pound of flesh and it will be her turn to put the knife in.'

Davies smiled at the unintentional pun and Buxton continued more seriously,

'As I said, Stuart Green is going away for a very long time. What's more, we've done it all without having to call in the criminologist with all her physco babble. You should be pleased Andy, twenty-four hours of hard graft and we've solved your first murder. C'mon, you can give me a lift home. Tomorrow you can savour the adulation showered down from on high for saving the chief constable's money. Sorry, I meant the taxpayer's money,' he said smiling cynically.

As they left the office Davies snapped off the light. Despite Buxton's confidence he still had the uneasy feeling that the investigation was progressing a little too easily.

CHAPTER 15

On Wednesday morning, just as the digital readout on the big electric clock in the corridor flicked over to 9, Buxton and Davies entered interview room 2 at Rednall Central Police Station. A now sober Stuart Green and his solicitor, Guy Pepper, were already present and seated. Green was dressed in a disposable white forensic suit, his clothes having been taken for examination. This was more a case of Buxton applying a little psychological pressure, as he doubted that Green's clothes would yield anything of significance. Green was gnawing at the nail of his little finger and, having bitten a piece off, he discarded it on the floor.

An hour earlier Buxton and Davies had met with DI Kirk to review the evidence thus far. One of the team had worked into the early hours reviewing the CCTV tapes from the roundabout and from the industrial units on the opposite side of the road. They got lucky, as one of these cameras was mounted down the side of a building at right angles to the main road and pointing over the front yard with Mill Road in the background. Although the camera was not strong enough to see all the way down Mill Road, it did give sufficient imagery to record both the runner and traffic in Mill Road. Of the runner returning there had been no sign. They did not rule out the possibility that the runner was not the murderer as he or she could just have carried on down to the Mere and exited the park by a different route. The camera on the roundabout on the main road had recorded several cars, ten of which had not gone on towards the town but turned down Mill Road. Of these, nine were recorded going down the road between 7-10p.m. and 7-20.p.m. Eight made the return journey between the same times indicating that they had been dropping a person, or persons, off at the centre. One had gone the road down but not returned until 9-30 p.m. The final car was recorded by the camera at 7-25 p.m. and did not reappear until 7-45p.m. It was this car that was causing Kirk the most interest.

The vehicle was registered to the Hatton Group. Unfortunately, until the branch opened at nine, he wouldn't be able to identify the allocated driver. Buxton asked why so many cars had gone down Mill Road at that time of night and Kirk told him that the small conference centre in the Old Mill was used several nights of the week by a local drama group. Between 9-15p.m. and 9-30 all ten cars were recorded in Mill Road heading away from the conference centre. Apart from the car registered to the Hatton Group the remaining cars were all privately owned and Kirk had obtained the names and addresses of all the registered keepers. Kirk deduced that the first car to arrive and last to leave probably belonged to the tutor. Certainly when they had been called out to Mere Lane the Old Mill and craft shops had been empty. Buxton was pleased with their work but didn't anticipate it would be of high importance apart from finding out if anyone had seen or heard anything. He was convinced that the killer was in custody.

DI Kirk was given the responsibility by Buxton of taking a team to the Hatton Group's dealership in Harvington where Green was General Manager to interview the staff. The interviews would help to build a profile of Green. Buxton was hoping that the staff would play, 'lets stab the boss in the back.' He also wanted a report on the car registered to the Hatton Group.

Buxton turned on the recording machine and commenced the interview with the formal introductions. He then proceeded to take Green through the overwhelming forensic evidence against him. Cigarette ends found at both the murder scene and in the car had been smoked by him. Several chewed fingernails found at the two scenes were from his fingers. Green involuntarily moved his left thumb and forefinger to his nose and Buxton told him that they had found nasal hair and nose droppings at both sites. Green's hand dropped guiltily to his lap. The phone found in the car was not only registered to him but had an impression on it which matched his thumb print. Davies showed him the phone encased in a plastic bag.

'It's not my phone,' he responded.

Buxton smiled but without humour and continued. Text messages had been sent from the victim's phone to the phone registered to him. Messages, still in his phone's memory, had been sent to the victim's phone. The final message from his phone appeared to indicate that Lucy Thomas was trying to end something that he didn't want ending. Again Davies indicated the phone in the bag. Green shook his head. Buxton moved on. The murder weapon had been found in the refuse bin at his home. Green remained impassive but inside he was beginning to panic. The blood on the knife was the victim's blood. Both Buxton and Davies saw the change in Green's expression, but he quickly regained his composure and continued to fix his gaze on Buxton, his mouth slightly open. Buxton was convinced that he had his man and that Green was like a punch drunk boxer flailing in desperation. He would soon admit defeat and confess his guilt. Davies though, whilst accepting that Green was frightened, thought that his expression was one of incredulity. Buxton ended by leaning towards Green and asking in his most low and threatening voice,

'Why?'

Green seemed almost relieved to get the chance to speak and replied, his voice rising several octaves,

'I didn't kill Lucy Thomas.'

'Oh, I believe you did,' retorted Buxton. He spread five black and white photographs across the desk showing the mutilated body of Lucy Thomas. 'You hid behind the garage and then did this,' he said with disgust. 'Then, when you realised what you'd done you lowered her gently to the ground. Your temper got the better of you. What was it, a lover's tiff gone wrong? Had she found someone else, we know she had other affairs?' Buxton brought the palm of his hand down hard on the desk making the other three start with surprise,

'Tell me!'

'I didn't do it!' the rising panic now even more evident in his voice.

Davies interjected. 'Come on Stuart, what do you expect us to believe? You've heard everything we have so far. Think of your family and David Thomas and his little girl. Better to get it off your chest and save them any further distress.'

'I didn't do it!' he responded angrily. His solicitor reached across and touched his arm to calm him. Davies smiled at him.

'How often do you hit your wife?'

Green paled. He knew just how wrong he had been, but he was still in denial and chose to lie.

'I don't hit my wife. I have never hit my wife, she fell,' he responded desperately.

On and on the questioning went. First Buxton and then Davies with the relentless interrogation but Green would admit nothing. He didn't hit his wife. He had no knowledge of the phone. He did not know how his DNA was at the scene. It must be a mistake. He had been at home all night. His wife would confirm it. He had never seen the knife. He didn't kill her. Of course he knew her and had done for years. Her husband was one of his best friends. Although they worked at different branches he spoke to her most days on the landline. She did the accounts for his branch.

'I didn't do it.' He broke. The tears began to flow freely and his head dropped forward on the desk.

'I didn't do it, I didn't do it. It's a setup,' he sobbed.

'Really?' Buxton responded dryly but Green just sat, his body wracked by sobs. Pepper, his solicitor, intervened requesting a break and reluctantly Buxton suspended the interview at 10-20.a.m. The two detectives left the room leaving Green to consult with Pepper. Outside Buxton ran his hand across his bald pate.

'Still think it's easy?' he asked.

'No boss. It's bloody frustrating. I thought if he was guilty he would just crumble.'

'He will. He's trying hard, I'll give him that, but he will, he will. The tears are just the start of it. One more nudge and he's over the edge. His fear, or perhaps his temper, will get the better of him.'

Buxton decided he needed a drink and they headed for the vending machine. As they turned the corner their thoughts were interrupted by the sound of laughter. It was Sergeant Russell and two younger colleagues.

'Good joke Bill?' asked Buxton.

Russell turned and without the slightest hint of embarrassment replied,

'Mornin' Robert. Just had a call from Harpley. It seems they had a report of two bodies in the river. They scrambled the rescue dinghy and it capsized. The boys got a dunkin' and the bodies turned out to be two of them models what they dress up in shop windows. Unfortunately the TV station had a crew down there doing a piece on the swans and they recorded the whole scene. Lookin' forward to the telly tonight,' he chuckled.

Buxton smiled. There would be some sarcasm over the phone lines today, and even more tomorrow, all over the division and it would be sometime before the boys from Harpley would be allowed to forget the incident. It would have been different had anyone been hurt. He slapped Russell on the back good-naturedly and accepted the drink proffered him from the machine. Davies got his own drink and they headed for Buxton's office. They had just sat down when the phone rang. The caller was DI Kirk with information on the car belonging to the Hatton Group and recorded in Mill Road. It was being used by Nigel Preece, the Used Car Director at the Hatton Group.

'He's not at work today. He's away on this new car launch that Green was on yesterday, along with three other directors. I've spoken to him on his mobile though and he confirms that he was there. His wife belongs to the drama group and she was a little off colour and had been undecided about going. That's why they were a little late. Apparently he waited outside in case she decided not to stay and I've spoken to the tutor who swears that Preece never got out of his car.'

Kirk then gave Buxton a progress report on the interviews at Harvington. Every employee questioned was painting a picture of Green as a man who was vain, aggressive and a bully. He was not felt by his staff to be a good manager although the Harvington branch was one of the leading performers in the Hatton Group. Apparently the sales team believed the good results were all down to them and that they had been doing well before Green's arrival and would continue to do so. Their success was in spite of him not because of him! None of the staff could confirm that he was having an affair and all of them interviewed so far had put two and two together and expressed great surprise that Lucy Thomas could have been in any way attracted to Green. There was no surprise that Green should be attracted to her and he had admitted at various times that he would love to, as they put it, 'give her one.' Three female members of staff had reported that Green had made improper suggestions to them but had been rebuffed. None of them made a formal complaint, as they thought it would fall on deaf ears as Green was considered to be a Directors pet. Some of them referred to him as 'Teflon' Green as it always appeared that no blame ever stuck to him. A search on his company computer revealed several soft porn images and some of the sales staff reported that these were used in sales meetings as part of what Green termed 'a team bonding exercise.' He used other exercises such as 'farting competitions' and thinking up different terms for women's breasts. Although these games caused some embarrassment, no great offence appeared to have been taken. Green was tolerated for his position but not respected. His first love appeared to be his boat and his children. There were pictures of both the boat and the children on his desk but nothing of his wife.

Buxton replaced the phone and drummed his fingers thoughtfully on the desk. He related the conversation to Davies, which didn't serve to alleviate the doubts that Davies felt. Buxton didn't attach any great significance to what Kirk had told him, but would still probably get someone to take a formal statement from Preece. He decided that when they went back to the interview room he would try a different approach. They finished their drinks and went back down the corridor. Russell was still informing everyone he could of the mishap in the river at Harpley.

Buxton and Davies entered the room, sat down, and Buxton again switched on the recording machine and recommenced the interview. Green had regained much of his composure, fortified by the break and some quiet words of encouragement from his solicitor. Buxton focused on the discovery of the pornographic magazines in Green's home and the images found on his computer hard drive. Green had worried overnight about his collection of photographs, knowing that if the police searched his house, as they inevitably would, eventually they would be found. Green forced himself to stare straight back at Buxton.

'No comment,' was his surly response.

Buxton wasn't looking at Green however, his gaze had shifted to Pepper who had paled slightly at the mention of pornography and shifted uncomfortably in his seat. Buxton knew something of his background. Buxton moved on to the bankbooks.

'Tell me about the bankbooks. Why were they hidden away under your desk drawer?'

'No comment,' Green answered again. His mind was reeling though. If they had found the bankbooks and some of his collection of porn then they were leaving no stone unturned. He could feel the panic beginning to well inside him again. If they had found his collection of child pornography what then?

'What can you tell us about Nigel Preece?' Buxton asked unexpectedly. 'It seems he was in the vicinity of Mill Road and Mere Lane at the time of the murder.'

'That's it! It had to be Nigel, the bastard' thought Green. It seemed that he had been thrown a lifeline and he wasn't about to waste the opportunity. Both Buxton and Davies noted the shift in his body language. He asked for a five minute break to consult with Pepper which Buxton, much to Davies's surprise, agreed to. When they returned Green appeared as though a great burden had been lifted from his shoulders and he calmly proceeded to tell the two officers exactly where all the money had come from, despite the fact that it implicated both he and Preece in massive fraud.

'Better fraud than murder and they will turn something up on Mr. Preece. This is a murder investigation and they will be very thorough,' Pepper advised after Green told him his story. Not only were he and Preece guilty of taking massive bribes, but they had defrauded the revenue as well. Green clearly took the view that if he was going down then Preece was going with him. Whenever Buxton turned the conversation back to Lucy Thomas however he wouldn't give an inch.

'I didn't kill her.'

By lunchtime Buxton began to feel frustrated and needed a break. He decided not to charge Green yet and had him returned to his cell, despite the expected protest from Green's solicitor. For Stuart Green this was the loneliest and most frightening time of his life. Buxton and Davies returned to Buxton's office.

'He's got some bottle this one Andy.'

'Boss, what if he's telling the truth?'

'If not him then who?' Buxton answered clearly exasperated with his young colleague.

'Preece maybe?' replied Davies. 'We can place him near the crime scene by his own admittance and at the right time. Suppose he was getting greedy and he wanted Green out.'

'Two big flaw's though Andy. Who stole David Thomas's car and the tutor swears that Preece never left his car? He couldn't be in two places at once even though they are close together.'

'Maybe Joe Quinn's still involved.'

Buxton shook his head, beginning to lose patience.

'That's quite a leap you've made there lad. There is nothing to link Quinn with any of this other than his past relationship with the deceased and as far as we know it ended, what, four or five years ago? Preece will be interviewed by the fraud boys and we will also be having a chat but I'm still convinced that we have our man. The physical evidence is just too strong. As for Quinn.' Buxton sighed and was about to say 'forget him.' Then he saw the crestfallen look in his young colleagues face.

'What the hell,' he thought. He needed a break. Green was going nowhere and a period of solitude might just soften him up a little. Preece was in London and wouldn't be back until late evening. A trip through the countryside might just give him some time to think and help clear his mind.

'Alright, you buy me lunch and I'll humour you. Where do we find him?'

'Give me five minutes to find out.'

Buxton sat back in his chair and closed his eyes. No sooner had he done so than Davies walked back in. Buxton realised almost guiltily that he had dozed off.

'I've rung Quinn's company and he's not expected in the office this afternoon. His secretary reckons he should be home mid afternoon. I told her I was from the waterways board.'

'Do you have an address?'

'It's Canalside, Harpley. It's not in the town. It's about a mile outside and as the name suggests it's by the canal.'

Buxton couldn't help thinking that there seemed to be an awful lot of canals in this investigation.

CHAPTER 16

By the time Buxton and Davies left the station it was half past two and they had missed lunch. Buxton, after some pressure from on high, had attended to some routine matters including yet another call from the Chief Constable regarding overtime whilst Davies spent his time reading over some of the witness statements collected at the Hatton Group. Nothing new had come to light. He had just picked up a forensic report and was in the process of reading about the fingernails, cigarette butts and the amount of dried colloidal mucus found at the murder scene when Buxton put his head round the door and told him to get the car. He put down the folder immediately without fully comprehending the contents.

Buxton instructed Davies to save time by using the motorway for the journey south to Harpley, more miles but in theory quicker. Unfortunately an incident on the northbound carriageway, though not serious, caused traffic to back up as 'rubber neckers' on the southbound lanes slowed to look at the devastation, delaying the traffic flow. Buxton took the opportunity to ring his counterpart in Harpley, Detective Superintendent Darren Moore, who he had first met at the police college in Hendon many years earlier.

'DS Moore,' he answered on the first ring.

'Dazla! How's it going?' Buxton asked amiably.

'If you've rung to take the piss about the river incident I'm not in the mood,' Moore answered, frustration evident in his voice. It had been a bad morning.

Buxton laughed.

'No my friend. Crap happens; it'll be old news by tomorrow. Or the day after. Do you know anything about a Joe Quinn?'

'Joe Quinn as in property developer and racing driver?'

'That's the one.'

'I know Joe socially.'

'Same lodge as you lot is it?'

'I've told you before, there are no freemasons at this station, they've all been promoted.'

It was a long standing joke between them. Moore was a Freemason and proud of his membership. Buxton had politely declined any overtures to join the society. He didn't like the aura of supposed secrecy. Moore went on,

'Joe's a good bloke. Very approachable, runs a good business and does a fair bit for charity. As far as I know he's never been in any bother. Always good for a laugh at the golf club. Why are you interested?' Moore asked.

'His name came up in the course of this murder investigation but it's probably nothing. I'll let you know. Thanks for the heads up, I'll catch you later if I need anything. And by the way, I know a good swimming instructor!' Chuckling, Buxton snapped his mobile shut as the traffic began to move and before Moore could think of a suitable retort.

Exiting the motorway at the first Harpley junction the two officers were then held up on the northern ring road by the sheer volume of traffic trying to negotiate the two-lane highway. Harpley was noted for its traffic problems having only two crossings over the river, which effectively cut the city in two. It was just after four by the time they eventually found the lane leading to Canalside. The irritating female voice on the sat nav had twice directed them incorrectly and Buxton's mood had grown darker, just like the late afternoon. Having located the lane the address was easy to find as it was the only house and was situated right at the very end of the road. The surrounding woods only served to heighten the remoteness although both officers knew they were only a mile from the outskirts of Harpley.

As they pulled to a halt in front of a double garage they were dazzled by a security light over the doors. Climbing from the car both men were surprised to see that the house was a large semi-detached. It had clearly been some form of industrial or agricultural building and someone had spent a great deal of money on the conversion. The right hand half of the building was in darkness and Buxton made a mental bet that this would be the one belonging to Joe Quinn. Buxton spotted the number 1 on the wicket-gate and thought they had got lucky. This house was illuminated. Davies told him thy needed number 2, which elicited a grimace from Buxton. They could not see an entrance to the darkened house. Realising that they needed to go back into the lane and round the back of the garage did nothing to improve Buxton's mood, particularly when Davies could not produce a torch. Davies reversed the car out into the lane and shone the headlights to illuminate the pathway. Rounding the garage plunged them back into darkness but there was now just enough reflected glow to locate the gate. As they went through the security light from the garage extinguished itself. Fortunately there were no obstructions on the path leading to the door. Several attempts on the bell push and hard raps on the door produced no response. Joe Quinn was clearly not at home.

Fearing an even more irascible Buxton on the return journey to Rednall, Davies suggested that they at least talk to the neighbours. To his relief Buxton agreed and they reversed their steps from number 2 back to the car. Davies extinguished the lights leaving the car where it was parked. As they passed in front of the garage the security light came back on. Davies thought it was badly adjusted as its pool of light did nothing to illuminate the lane and access to number 2 was made somewhat awkward. He surmised that there was a more direct route from the garage but wondered why there was no security light system between the garage and door to the house.

They went through the picket gate and down the path to the door of number 1. From the garage light there was more than enough illumination to see. Davies knocked on the heavy wooden door surprised that there appeared to be no doorbell. There was only a moment's pause before they heard footfalls from within. They heard the steps halt at the door and guessed that they were being viewed through the security spy hole. The door opened but was held by a strong security chain. Davies immediately took in the very pretty female face framed by blond hair and felt his groin tighten. He initially thought she was in her late twenties. There was some concern in her intensely blue eyes and he guessed that they did not get many unexpected callers in this location.

'Can I help?' she asked, the concern clear in her voice. Davies thought she most definitely could help him with something but put the thought from his mind as he produced his warrant card,

'I'm sorry to trouble you, Miss?' he asked hopefully.

She inspected the warrant card without holding it but noted the rank and station and answered.

'Mason, Mrs. Rachael Mason.' Davies struggled to hide his disappointment.

Buxton produced his identification and she undid the chain, opened the door and invited them in.

'Please don't be alarmed Mrs. Mason, we just need to ask you a few questions regarding your next door neighbour,' said Buxton. Davies noticed a change of expression, from concern to apprehension, and thought she was about to say something but she appeared to check herself and as she turned she asked them to follow her. They had entered through the kitchen door and she led them across the large stone flagged room and into a wide, sparsely furnished but tastefully carpeted hallway. Buxton admired the décor and Davies the rear of Mrs. Mason. 'This is one very attractive lady,' he thought, although he now realised that she was older than she first appeared. They were shown into a large lounge where a much older man sat in a leather wing chair by an open fire reading from a folder. He made no attempt to get up but peered at them from over the top of his spectacles.

'This is my husband Andrew,' Mrs. Mason said. Both men hid their surprise and before she could speak further Buxton interrupted, determined to exert his authority and clearly annoyed by Mason's lack of manners. He introduced both himself and Davies and both men flourished their warrant cards. Without waiting to be asked and without any attempt to shake hands, Buxton sat on the sofa and Davies followed suit, with Mrs. Mason seating herself opposite. Davies could not help but admire her legs and wondered how such an attractive lady could end up with someone as obnoxious as Andrew Mason appeared to be. 'Perhaps it was money' but he dismissed the thought. Although seated, Davies guessed that Mason was around six feet, overweight and the wrong side of sixty. His grey hair was lengthy and somewhat unkempt. Buxton continued, now in definite control of the situation.

'Mr. Mason, as I just said to your wife we're sorry to trouble you but I wonder if we might ask you a few questions regarding your neighbour? We believe his name is Joe Quinn?'

'That's correct,' answered Mason in a tone that was almost questioning. Davies continued to look towards Mrs. Mason who shifted uncomfortably in her chair, but she stayed silent as Buxton continued,

'Please don't be concerned. There is nothing to worry about; we just believe he may be able to help us with an ongoing investigation.'

'What investigation?' Mrs. Mason asked just a touch too quickly. Before Buxton could respond Mr. Mason spoke, glancing briefly at his wife,

'We're not concerned; we don't see him that much.' He clearly did not want to be involved and both officers noted the trace of animosity in his voice. Buxton answered Mrs. Mason, ignoring her husband.

'I'd rather not say.'

But Mrs. Mason answered back sharply and in a voice, which Davies felt was betraying just a hint of panic.

'It's about the murder in Harpley isn't it?'

Buxton settled back.

'What makes you think that Mrs. Mason?'

Davies stared at her but she quickly regained her composure.

'Well you're from Harpley, there has just been a murder there, the dead woman worked at the Hatton Group and I know that Joe worked there in the past.'

Buxton smiled and nodded noting to himself that she used Quinn's first name. Her line of thought, the connection, concerned Davies.

'When did you last see him?'

Before Mrs. Mason could speak Mr. Mason answered. He had been staring at his wife throughout the exchange Davies noted.

'The night before last. I came home mid-afternoon and parked in front of his garage. He was at home then. He was in the back garden. We said 'hello' but didn't have a conversation. He has a gym at the back of his garage and he was heading towards it. He was in his shorts.'

'Why did you park in front of his garage?'

'I always do on Mondays. It's so Rachael can get her car in the garage. We only have a single unit and I'm usually home before her on Mondays but away early on Tuesdays. It saves having to swop the cars around early in the morning. He's happy with the arrangement, in fact he suggested it. When he's home on Mondays he rarely goes out and in the evening he likes to watch the football on TV. I don't get back until late on Wednesday.'

Mason glanced at his wife and Davies couldn't help notice the slightest flush in her neck. He wondered about this as Mason continued,

'Later on I stepped out for a cigarette. My wife doesn't allow me to smoke in the house.'

'What time was that?'

'Around 7-45. I'm not a great football fan, I prefer Rugby, but I do watch West Bromwich when they are on. I was born near the ground and one of my uncles played for them. Once a Baggie, always a Baggie,' he smiled. Davies thought he had better taste in women than he did his choice of football team. He resisted making any comment as Mason continued,

'I went down the garden and I could see him through the upstairs window. He uses that room as an office and I could see him sitting at his desk. I saw the light go out and then the lounge light came on. I came back in, watched the first half and then went out again at half time. He was back upstairs. I didn't linger as it was cold. He was still there when I came back in. I watched the rest of the game and when I went out again for a last cigarette he was in the lounge, I saw him moving about. I've not seen him since. The lights were on last night and he's not asked us to watch the place, so I assume he's been at home.'

Buxton nodded. 'What about you Mrs. Mason, when did you last see him?'

Davies was watching Mason for a reaction but he was staring at his wife impassively.

'I don't really remember. He comes and goes. As my husband said, at this time of year with the dark nights, we don't see much of him. He tells us when he will be away for any length of time. He's away quite a bit in summer. He drives racing cars you know and it takes him abroad quite a lot. We keep an eye on the house.'

'I bet you do,' thought Davies who glanced towards his boss. Buxton responded by getting to his feet and thanking them both for their time.

Mr. Mason remained in his chair and uttered an almost inaudible goodbye. Davies stepped forward and proffered Mason his card.

'If you do think of anything further please don't hesitate to contact me' he said firmly. Mason blinked at him and reluctantly accepted the card. Mrs. Mason rose and showed them out, this time through the front door which was at the side of the house. Davies thought he would love to be a fly on the wall, convinced that Rachael Mason and Joe Quinn were more than just neighbours.

Outside Buxton said, 'I still think we are wasting our time here. I'm going to break the habit of a lifetime and let you buy me a pint. I'm sure we passed a pub on the main road. We'll give it half an hour and then come back. If Quinn's not here we let it drop. The Masons have given him an alibi, not that I thought he needed one, and I sensed the animosity from the husband, so I don't think he would cover for him. Quinn couldn't be in two places at once. We'll drop a card through the door asking him to ring.'

He changed the subject by saying, 'Attractive woman that, I saw you giving her the eye. Reckon she's got a thing for Quinn?'

Davies smiled and nodded and was about to speak but Buxton continued sternly as they got in the car, 'Maybe, maybe not. It's none of our business. We are only sticking around because it's a long way back and traffic at this time of night will be hell. Half an hour, back, and then home with or without seeing Quinn.'

Davies reluctantly agreed, turned the car around and headed back towards the main road.

CHAPTER 17

As Rachael closed the front door behind the two officers she leant her back against it, and breathed a huge sigh of relief. Her legs felt as though they would buckle at any moment. Their arrival had been totally unexpected and she offered up a silent prayer of thanks that she had been able to keep her composure. She was worried however. Was it guilt that was making her feel as though her every movement these days was being scrutinised? She had watched the younger officer observing her and guessed at least some of his thoughts. She knew what effect she had on men and she usually found it quite amusing. She had never used her sexuality to influence any situation, at least not since she and Andrew were married. Had the officer though suspected her? Did he sense that all was not well with her marriage? Andrew had also become even more withdrawn of late. Did he suspect her feelings? It had ruined her week when he had not gone away on Tuesday, but it happened occasionally. Usually he gave her plenty of warning but this time he surprised her when he came home early. It was out of character.

'Tea,' she thought, 'I never offered them tea. What must they have thought?'

She felt a little foolish. Why on earth should she bother about tea? She moved away from the door, went to the kitchen and despite herself, put the kettle on. She thought about Joe, but then these days she thought of little else. Not since she was a teenager had she felt or acted like this. Joe had an almost hypnotic power over her and yet he never chose to use it. Maybe he just didn't realise how he affected her. Was he that blind and self-centred? No, she was convinced it wasn't that. The sex they shared was something else. She had never experienced sexual joy like she experienced with Joe. She realised now that she had never before experienced a true orgasm until Joe. Although their lovemaking was sometimes a little over enthusiastic, she was a willing enough participant. Mostly he was kind, gentle, courteous and made her laugh. Even when she first fell in love with Andrew, with all his sophistication and maturity, she had never felt like she felt with Joe. Joe made her come alive. She had never thought of herself as particularly repressed, and she wasn't but this was just so different. Andrew had been her first experienced lover and she had enjoyed his seduction, but with the passing of the years, their encounters had become mechanical, spasmodic and yet routine. There was no spontaneity any longer and hadn't been she knew for many years. Her life, she had begun to realise more and more, was fast approaching a crossroads and it was both exciting and frightening.

She knew Joe could not be involved in the murder of Lucy Thomas. After all he had been at home, not in Rednall. Even Andrew, who delighted in putting Joe down, confirmed that he had seen him at home. She wondered what Lucy had been like. Joe would not tell her the full story despite her probing. He always brushed aside her questions, gently but firmly. He had not seen Lucy since he left the Hatton Group, or so he said. Rachael suspected that the police would still want to speak to him. She was desperate to warn him, but how?

She made a pot of tea, placed it on a tray with two cups and a few biscuits and returned to the lounge. Andrew had resumed his reading. As she walked in he put the documents down by his side and steepled his hands. She was instantly on her guard.

'Bit of excitement.' Was he asking her, or telling her she wondered?

She nodded, and then with some effort to keep her voice steady replied,

'Yes, I know Joe worked at the Hatton Group but that was some time ago. I suppose they are just looking into the dead woman's background.'

'Or maybe he is a crook and he hired a hit man to take her out as they say,' Andrew replied with just a hint of malice. He was however smiling and Rachael was unsure whether he had just made an attempt at a joke. He carried on,

'You know I don't like him Rachael, but I don't think he's a murderer and he was at home.' She sensed that he wanted to speak further, but to her relief he picked up the folder and resumed his reading. Rachael poured the tea and then feigning a call of nature she went upstairs. Locking herself in the bathroom she tried Joe's mobile. It was turned off. She felt a pang of jealousy and wondered where he was. She held no rights over him but it didn't stop the longing inside. She needed and wanted him desperately.

'Get a grip girl,' she thought. 'You're a respectable forty one year old with two grown children, not a silly schoolgirl.' Nevertheless the ache would not go away and she sat on the loo, close to tears.

CHAPTER 18

As I drove down the lane towards home the headlights picked out the last remnants of the light snowfall. I was glad it had not been heavy. Snow might look pretty on Christmas cards, but it plays havoc with building schedules. My mobile suddenly clanked twice demanding attention. As I was only two hundred metres from home I didn't stop. I went round the little kink in the lane and noticed that the security light over the garage was on, but the trees and bushes were obscuring whoever had triggered the sensor. Slowing, I pulled into the entrance to find a car I didn't recognise parked in front of my garage door. As I stopped the two occupants, one an older man, medium height and the other younger and taller, got out.

Both men immediately turned towards me and away from the bright light. I got out of the Range Rover but left the motor running. I was only slightly uneasy; I can take care of myself.

'Sorry gentleman, do you mind moving so that I can put my car away?'

Both men ignored the request and the older one asked,

'Mr. Quinn? Mr. Joseph Quinn?'

Only me mam calls me Joseph these days, and then only when she's trying to be firm. No prizes then for guessing who they were.

'I am, but whatever you're selling I'm not interested. I don't accept cold callers.'

The older man set himself as though he were about to give vent, but instead of getting aggressive he introduced himself and his colleague with exaggerated politeness.

'I'm Detective Superintendent Buxton and this is Detective Sergeant

Davies from Rednall Central. I'm sorry to bother you, but we would appreciate a few minutes of your time.'

As he spoke he waived his ID card at me, as did the younger guy thus confirming my suspicions. They just had that look about them, an air of supposed authority. In any case I was half expecting them.

I didn't tell them that since news of the murder broke and a phalanx of police invaded the Hatton Group, the phone lines had been doing overtime. The motor trade is a hot bed of gossip at the best of times and this news had certainly travelled fast. Rumour and counter rumour was doing the rounds with everyone having their own theory. I must have taken thirty calls throughout the day from managers, salesmen and other motor traders on the pretence of selling me some stock. What they were really after was my thoughts on the murder and if I possessed any salacious gossip. Some of them knew of my past relationship with Lucy Thomas. The word was that the police were holding Stuart Green, General Manager at the Hatton Group's Harvington branch in custody. In the end I turned my phone off for a couple of hours.

'Look,' I said reasonably, 'let me put the car away and then we'll go inside.' No sense in antagonising them for no good reason. Still, it wouldn't hurt to give them a little test.

Buxton nodded to the younger guy, Davies, who got back into the car and drove out of my way. I got back in the Range Rover and pressed the remote to open the garage door. It rolled up, the automatic light came on and I drove in pressing the button to close the door as I came to a halt. Buxton however stepped into the entrance and the auto stop sensed the obstruction, halting the door and allowing Davies to join him.

'Round one to the Feds,' I thought ruefully. As they moved inside the door rolled down. I could see from the look on Buxton's face that he knew he had won some kind of small victory. I opened the car door and swung my legs out. I couldn't hide the grimace as my foot hit the floor. I saw Davies look but he said nothing and Buxton appeared not to notice my discomfort.

'Nice car,' Buxton said.

With a shrug of the shoulders I said, 'Yeah, it does the job.'

I was not going to be distracted by talking cars. I wanted them gone. I pulled back the curtain that divides the garage and held it back for them as they stepped by. I could see them both taking mental notes of the surroundings. It was clear that Buxton had not seen a gym for sometime. Davies looked a bit more athletic and seemed suitably impressed by the exercise machine, weights and punch bag. His eyes seemed to be darting everywhere. Buxton seemed more interested in the assortment of garden and DIY tools and the golf clubs in the corner.

'Do you play much?' Buxton asked indicating the clubs.

'Not often, I struggle for time,' I answered. They both looked at one another with a kind of disbelief. Had he been making enquiries? 'Best not be flippant,' I thought. I played occasionally with one or two officers from the force in Harpley. I unlocked the side door and flicked the switch to illuminate the back yard. We stepped out and I locked the door. The internal sensor would take care of the garage light. We went down the path, I unlocked the back door, turned on the light, turned off the alarm and they followed me in. I had already decided that the kitchen was as far as they were going and I offered them seats and tea or coffee. Much to my relief, Buxton, with an impassive wave of his arm, declined for both of them but in doing so, managed to knock over an ashtray containing some loose change and one of my many lucky charms. Superstitious lot we racing drivers.

'I'm so sorry,' he said as he collected the shrapnel and put it back in the ashtray. I merely nodded.

'One each,' I thought.

Neither of them attempted to remove their coats even though it was quite warm in the room. Davies wrinkled his nose as he sat and he noticed that I noticed, otherwise he may have remained silent.

'I'm sorry,' he said, 'there's a peculiar smell.'

I almost retorted that I had not noticed it until they walked in but thought better of it, my own warning repeating itself in my head.

'It's probably a contaminated log. I've had a few lately and you get used to it.'

Buxton ignored the exchange.

'I'll get straight to the point Mr. Quinn,' said Buxton. 'We want to talk to you about your period of employment with the Hatton Group and in particular your relationship with a Mrs. Lucy Thomas.'

I nodded in acknowledgment. Surprise, surprise.

'I'm sure that you are aware that Mrs. Thomas was found dead on Monday evening.'

I nodded again. 'I heard it on the local news.'

'Your name came up when we were interviewing some of the staff and we were told that you had an affair with the lady.'

Straight to the point he certainly was. Not an alleged affair then. He had obviously made up his mind that what he had heard was the truth. It was.

'That's right. Lucy and I are ancient history though. I haven't seen or heard from her since I left. We move in different circles.'

'Why did you leave?'

'It was time to move on,' I answered smiling.

Buxton didn't press the issue, he just nodded and then changed tack.

'Do you mind telling us where you were the night before last?'

'This guys not big on small talk,' I thought. I had a vague recollection that I'd met him before, but I couldn't place where or when.

'I was at home. I usually am on Mondays at this time of year. I keep my diary fairly clear so I can catch up on some paperwork at home. Household bills and the like. In the evening I like to relax with a drink and watch the Monday night football.'

'Were you at home all day?'

'No. I attended a site meeting in Harpley about two. There are some flats I'm renovating, or rather the company is, just back from the dock development and the architect wanted to show me some proposals. I was home mid afternoon. I spent some time in my gym, had a meal, did some more work and then watched the match. It was a poor game. I was in bed just after ten. It was an early night because I wanted to be up early on Tuesday as I was going up north to see me mother. As it happened I overslept.'

'Did anyone see you after you got home?'

'Yes, I saw Andrew from next door when he got home. We said 'hello' but that was all.'

'Were you alone?'

'Yes, completely,' and I put on my 'I don't think that's any of your business face.'

'Just asking,' he smiled having clearly noted the body language. He went on, 'Your neighbour confirms that he saw you in the garden and again later on that night. He was out having a cigarette.'

I smiled. 'Gives me an alibi then?'

'Why, do you need one?' Davies asked abruptly. Until that moment he had just sat on the stool, looking inscrutable. Before I could answer Buxton interrupted, ignoring his junior colleague.

'I take it you know Stuart Green?'

'Of course. I worked with him at the Hatton Group. I still do business with him from time to time.'

'We understand that the two of you didn't get on,' Davies interjected determined not to be left out. So who gave him that nugget of information I wondered?

'You shouldn't believe all you hear Detective. We had our differences at work, but it happens. The motor trade can be a competitive business and both of us aspired to greater things.'

Davies went back into his shell and Buxton asked,

'When did you last see him?'

'Err, last Monday morning. I called in to see if he had anything to sell. I have a share in a garage business, as I'm sure you know, and we needed some stock. I probably call in on him every other week.'

'Did you know he was having an affair with Lucy Thomas?'

'No, but it wouldn't surprise me.'

'Really, you're the first person who has indicated that.'

'I knew he always fancied his chances and if she could go out with me then she could go out with anyone,' I answered self effacingly. 'He did drop the odd hint but I never enquired.'

'What sort of hint?'

'I'm sorry, I don't really remember. I just remember getting the impression that he was seeing someone on the side, as it were. I wasn't really that interested.'

'I see,' Buxton said. He then asked me a few more questions about my time at the Hatton Group. Nothing complicated or deep, just general stuff about what I had done there and since. He duly noted my success and confirmed that we had in fact met at a golf club evening. I remembered him then. Davies just sat quietly but as they got up to leave he suddenly said,

'That's a nasty graze on your face, how did you get it?'

'I slipped on the path.'

'When?'

'Monday, Monday night.'

'So you went out then?'

'Only to make sure the garage was locked. I hurt my ankle at the same time,' answering the unasked question and making sure that my tone reflected that I found the question irrelevant.

'I see. You keep yourself pretty fit I notice.' I thought he was going to say 'for an old one' but he carried on, 'I take it that's because of the racing?'

Now I can talk about my racing career till the cows come home. 'Are you a fan?' I asked.

'I'm a Formula One nut. I read all the magazines and I've seen your name a few times. You've had some good results I've noticed and some good rides.'

For a moment I thought he was being facetious but then I saw from his face that he was actually being serious.

'Yes, I've been very lucky. I have some good contacts.'

For the first time Davies smiled. 'I always wanted to be a racing driver but never found the time and I suspect I don't have the talent. My mother bought me a racing driver suit and a pedal car one Christmas. I had the helmet, black balaclava, underwear, the whole works. The balaclava was useful. I could be a racing driver one minute and a bandit the next.'

I relaxed and laughed. 'I always wear white,' I answered. Perhaps I had misjudged him. He held out his hand and I gave him mine. He shook hands so enthusiastically that I felt a twinge again in my shoulder and grimaced. He noticed.

'I'm sorry,' he said, 'are you alright?'

'Yes, yes I'm fine. It's an old injury and it plays me up from time to time. The cold and damp at this time of year doesn't help,' I answered. He smiled in response and didn't look unsympathetic.

I shook Buxton's hand gingerly and he handed me his card with the usual 'if you think of anything which may help us with our enquiries please don't hesitate to contact me.' I showed them out making sure I turned on the lights so they could walk round the garage safely. I remembered my mobile and checked the two messages. The first was from Lizzie telling me that someone from the water ways board was trying to contact me. I guessed it was probably the police trying discreetly to track me down. The second was from Rachael warning me that the police had been to see her and Andrew. Well, now they had seen me as well. Lucy Thomas was dead and now she really was history. Stuart Green was in custody and would get what he fully deserved. How much more fall out would there be at the Hatton Group from all this I wondered? I settled down on the stool thankful that I could now draw a line under a very unhappy period in my life. The memories will fade in time but as I sat I couldn't help but think back to those times a few years earlier. How different all our lives had become in the space of those few short years since I left the Hatton Group.

CHAPTER 19

Nigel Preece, Group Used Car Sales Manager at the Hatton Group, was not a happy man. The weekend sales results from around the group spread out across his desk in front of him were the source of his mounting irritation. All the figures were relatively good, but one particular set of numbers was outstanding. His contract with the company dictated that he earned a percentage from the profit of each dealership, so whilst the figures were good for his wallet, this one dealership, or more particularly its sales manager, was causing him concern. From his point of view this sales manager was just too good.

Six months earlier John Hatton, the Sales Director, had appointed Joe Quinn to run the sales department at the Hatton Group's failing Harpley dealership. It was the first time John Hatton had appointed a senior sales manager without consulting him and, despite the fact that he knew Quinn was a highly experienced sales manager and would probably bring success to the dealership, Preece was highly irritated. Now it was becoming increasingly annoying, as the name on everyone's lips at the moment seemed to be that of Joe Quinn. It seemed he could do no wrong. The Harpley dealership was on the up and beginning to challenge the Rednall operation, for so long the company's number one branch.

Preece enjoyed his position within the company. He had worked for the Hatton Group for thirty years and risen from being a salesman to his senior position. He was paid a good salary, but modest compared to what others in a similar position in other large groups received. He enjoyed a good standard of living and had built a substantial nest egg. However, a large percentage of his income was made by being dishonest.

The money though wasn't all he desired. He was still ambitious and like all greedy men he wanted much more. He craved the heady, intoxicating elixir of power.

Preece knew he couldn't leave the group and seek a senior position elsewhere. Other groups were too well run and he was aware of his limitations. The Hatton Group suited him. Fred Fox, Group Managing Director, was only a year senior to him but was planning to retire early, and not before time. It was becoming increasingly obvious that Fox had a drink problem, but everyone from the chairman down appeared to be turning a blind eye. Preece wanted his job, or at the very least a seat on the board.

Although he knew the brothers' would never relinquish their seats on the board, as Managing Director he would be a major part of the decision making process. He would have his power. He would be a mover and shaker. He could control the whole company just as Fred Fox did, even though he had no great interest in the service, spare parts and body repair departments. The sales operation was where the big money was won and lost. Normally, the much younger John Hatton was easy to influence. His office was next door to his own and John dropped by on a daily basis for a chat. If Preece could elevate himself to a position on the board then his protégé, Stuart Green, could take over his post. Whilst he himself would no longer be dealing with the corrupt, or as he preferred to call them, 'friendly' elements of the motor trade, he could retain his revenue stream through Green.

When Preece joined the Hatton Group it was not his intention to become corrupt. He thought of himself as an honest man. He still did. The company, or at least the sales department he joined, was however riddled with dishonesty. The sales team had a scam going with road fund licence discs. They were removing discs from the windscreens of vehicles taken in part exchange and surrendering them to the relevant tax authority in their own names. The appraisal form, completed by the sales person to record all the vehicle particulars, make, model, condition and mileage for these part exchanges, almost always showed that the road fund licence was about to expire. An analysis undertaken by one of the accountants showed that imminent expiry of road fund licence appeared to be the prime reason for customers wanting to change their cars. How little the bean counters knew. The sales team made sure that just enough discs were surrendered in the company's name so as not to arouse suspicion. The Sales Manager never checked because he had his own money making scheme. In his first month at the branch Preece took a car in part exchange which he felt he could retail at a good price and earn himself a good commission. To his surprise and disappointment, when he went into the manager's office, he saw on the stock board that the information card for the car had been placed in the sold column. He was even more surprised a few days later when he saw the car parked on the drive of his Sales Manager's home, and then advertised in the classified adverts of the local paper. Preece checked the sales invoice and found that the name on it was not that of the Sales Manager. He didn't complain however, he just decided that if that was how the system worked then he would play it to his advantage, and play it well.

Joining the firm had been an act of desperation for Preece as his planned career went catastrophically off the rails. He had been the assistant manager of a large department store and destined for greater things. Unfortunately he couldn't keep his hands off the younger female members of staff. His lascivious nature would prove to be his downfall. He didn't see anything wrong in the odd pat on the rump or ribald comment but the more he got away with, the braver he became. Some of the girls complained to their supervisors. Their claims were always explained away as acts of spite, or girlish stupidity, until one day he crossed the line once too often. He made a particularly lewd suggestion to a newly appointed trainee. What he didn't know was that the trainee was the favoured niece of a senior director. His leaving was swift.

With a young family and a mortgage to service he needed to find another job quickly. He saw the advertisement in the paper for a car salesman at the Hatton Group's dealership in Rednall and rather than write a letter of application he walked round to the garage. The General Manager was impressed by his initiative and his employment commenced the following day. At first, unlike his colleagues, he kept his nose clean and earned a steady living but he watched, learned and planned. The world of car sales is very competitive and he found himself becoming more and more devious in his efforts to become and remain the number one salesman. Nobody could deny however that he was anything less than committed. He worked long hours and would often forfeit his day off in order to make another sale. He aimed to be the number one salesman across the group and he didn't care how he achieved this. He had no conscience when it came to sabotaging the efforts of others.

Preece viewed selling as a numbers game and the more customers he saw the greater he felt his chances were of making a sale, so he made sure that he saw more potential buyers on the sales pitch than anyone else. It was not an uncommon occurrence for a sold car to have developed a fault when the time came for delivery to the customer. Faults never occurred on any of his cars though. It was always one sold by one of his colleagues. A flat battery for instance, caused because Preece, the last man to leave the dealership, turned on the ignition in the car and left it on over night. Arriving first the next morning he would turn the ignition off and the salesman would be none the wiser. The dead battery meant that the car would not start and whoever the salesman was he would be forced to spend time sorting the problem thus missing the opportunity to speak to new customers. Or it might be that keys went missing only to turn up in the workshops on a bench or on odd occasions, disappear altogether. Preece would always try to assist but always break off when a customer came on to the site. Never once did it happen to a car sold by Preece. He was just too careful and when the General Manager chastised the staff for failure to organise themselves properly he would always hold Preece up as a shining example of how things should be done. In any event salesmen rarely stayed longer than eighteen months as they couldn't compete with Preece. A few came close but when they did Preece would actively encourage them to seek senior positions outside the group. He was everyone's friend, confidant and helper.

It came as no surprise to anyone when he was invited to fulfil the role of Sales Manager, the previous incumbent having moved to another group. He took the promotion and was rewarded with a higher basic salary and better car but quickly realised that he was actually being paid less money than he had previously been as he no longer received commissions. Indeed many salespeople within the group who lacked anything like his enterprise were now earning more than him. Within weeks of his appointment a solution presented itself.

Preece thought that he was unlikely to rise very high in the family run business so when he was offered a 'sweetener' by one of the traders he thought, "why not?" A part of his managerial responsibilities was the disposal of trade vehicles at the branch. These were vehicles which the company did not consider fit to be retailed from their premises. They could be older vehicles, vehicles with high mileage, unpopular vehicles that didn't fit the company's profile, niche cars or cars that required so much refurbishment as to not be economically viable. These trade vehicles were disposed of through a network of small independent retailers or traders, generally one or two man operations. Managed properly, the system worked efficiently from most main dealer's point of view. A car comes in and a trader removes it thus saving space and time, and with time being money, improves cash flow. Unfortunately, the system can be open to massive abuse.

Roger King was one such trader. He took Preece out to lunch and passed him an envelope. It was, he said, a thank you for selling him a particular car. The envelope contained £100 in cash, a substantial amount of money at that time. From that moment on every car that Roger King purchased from the Hatton Group was bought for at least £50 less than its true market value. Half of the £50 found its way to Preece and as he controlled the orders and invoicing, no one ever checked. Preece had no fear of auditors as they didn't check the actual value of goods they were more concerned in the mathematics of transactions. In any event, anyone minded to check would have found it impossible to verify the value of a vehicle which had been passed on. Preece could argue that it was damaged or suffering from mechanical trouble. Provided he didn't massage the figures by huge amounts he would never get caught. The extra cash more than made up for any salary shortfall. It paid off his mortgage and allowed him to indulge in his passion for flying and exotic holidays.

His success as Sales Manager at Rednall did not of course go unnoticed and he developed close relationships with the directors who were based on the second floor at the dealership. He was not afraid to make tough decisions and any staff who failed to reach targets consistently were quickly removed. He also kept control of his predatory nature and by and large he was not an unpopular member of staff. He liked to consider himself as everyone's friend. When the opportunity arose to become Group Used Car Manager he seized the moment. He would no longer be responsible for the day to day disposal of used cars but Stuart Green, then a young and ambitious salesman would step into his old role. Albeit diluted, Preece would still get a cut in trade sales transacted at Rednall. He would now get a bigger salary and better yet, he could now influence the trade sales across the whole group. His new position gave him enormous scope.

He knew of course that it was unlikely that he was the only corrupt used car manager across the group, so he immediately instigated a group policy for the disposal of trade vehicles. Instead of each individual branch having responsibility for the disposal of stock, everything would now be invoiced via head office, or more specifically the Group Used Car Department, at a value set by himself. Traders were initially banned from all the dealerships. They were given no choice but to see him and negotiate with him alone. The system worked, but he quickly became overloaded and he was forced to allow the managers to deal with any vehicle with a value of less than £500. He policed the system with a rod of iron and any manager who kicked up too much of a fuss was soon brought to heel, or simply forced out of the company. The smaller independent traders relied on the bigger groups for their survival. Preece could afford to be hard and careful. Some traders' he dealt with correctly but others were only too happy to grease his palm. He made sure that he didn't get too greedy and gave an occasional profit back to the dealerships. The directors were happy. His department was profitable, even if it was at the expense of the dealerships. All he was doing was moving profit around on the balance sheet. The managers lost commission on their bottom lines. Commission went to Preece and although substantial it was less than the company would have paid to the individual managers cumulatively. The bottom line was that the Hatton Group made more money. The directors were convinced that they had a good system which prevented any manager from stealing, little realising that good old Nigel was making a tax free fortune.

His other main responsibility was to make sure that all the branches were fully stocked. He therefore had to buy cars in bulk. The main manufacturers all have their own used car schemes for selling their own company vehicles such as management vehicles and press demonstrators. It is common practice for dealer groups to buy centrally from the manufacturers at one price and then 'sell' the vehicles to their own branches at a higher figure. By adding just a nominal amount to the internal invoice, head office retains profit whilst ensuring that any errors made by salespeople such as under selling or over estimating part exchange values are paid for by the branches. This accounting procedure also lessens the liability to commission payments to salespeople and managers.

Better manufacturing processes have ensured that more and more cars have been built. There is a massive oversupply of new cars and to get these cars registered and maintain market share, manufactures often sell these cars at huge discounts to car hire companies. The hire companies frequently find it advantageous to sell these cars after a few months with minimal depreciation and then buy new again. The dealers buy these used vehicles and then sell them on to retail customers at a huge saving on the price of a brand new car. Although profitable it can also be self defeating as customers who would normally buy new could be persuaded to buy used, thus leading to pressure on new car targets.

Preece however wasn't bothered about new cars. He quickly found that those in charge of disposing of these nearly new and relatively low mileage used cars were under pressure. He realised that if he was willing to pay just slightly over the odds for these cars then the sellers were more than willing to pay him introductory commission. He couldn't lose. He was now getting paybacks from both buyers' and sellers within the trade. As long as the group remained in profit it was unlikely that anyone would ever question what he was doing. To all intents and purposes he was a long serving and loyal member of the company. No one questioned his lifestyle. Apart from his plane, which everyone thought was owned by a syndicate, and his foreign holidays he was never too overt with his spending. He lived in a large house but not too grand that it could cause suspicion.

Now though, this new Sales Manager, Quinn, was causing him more than a little aggravation. Not only were his figures good but he was inventive too. Only the previous week Quinn had suggested to John Hatton that the group's disposal policy was inefficient. He felt that the group should adopt an auction only policy whereby every single vehicle for trade disposal no matter what age, mileage or condition, should be sent to auction. His argument was that it would save time and money. By not having to deal with any traders at all, it would free up time during the working day and allow managers to concentrate their efforts on retail sales. Sales teams would gain a greater knowledge of the true worth of cars by cutting out the middlemen. Preece knew that this was how the big groups worked. He also knew that their reasons were not totally altruistic, their main concern being to prevent corruption among the managers.

Preece was forced to admit that the sales figures were impressive. In the two years since the Hatton Group took over the Harpley branch from another group, no one had managed any sort of success until Quinn joined the company. He set about his new position with relish. He introduced a proper sales process and weaned out underperforming staff, replacing them with people he had worked with before. His organisational and motivational skills were of the highest order.

Year on year unit sales were only marginally better but unit profit, apart from finance and insurance, was now the best in the group. Overall performance was up by a phenomenal seventy five per cent and it was only the better finance penetration, customers buying on finance plans, at Rednall that was keeping that dealership ahead. It was fortunate that the Business Manager at Rednall was acknowledged to be one of the best in the country.

During Quinn's first few months with the group, finance performance at Harpley showed a significant improvement. Quinn had clearly forged an instant bond with the incumbent Business Manager, Billy Hogg. A quiet word from Preece in Fred Fox's ear regarding Hogg's private life had been sufficient to wind Fox up and Quinn came under pressure to get rid of him. Preece had it on good authority that Hogg was a user of recreational drugs. Fox was easily convinced that if Hogg's habit ever came to light it could cause a problem to the Group. Quinn was unhappy but Fox would not be deflected and Hogg had been removed. Even Preece admired Quinn for the way he carried out Fox's wishes. Knowing Hogg was himself ambitious, Quinn left his office door open whilst on the phone discussing an opening with a rival company. Hogg overheard the conversation and acted accordingly. Within days he was gone. Quinn struggled to replace him but now a new man was on board and the signs were looking positive. Good for the branch, good for the company, but not for Preece.

John Hatton entered his office without knocking and immediately noted the spreadsheet across Preece's desk. He had been perusing the same report in his own office.

'More good figures from Quinn,' Hatton said as he sat himself happily in the chair opposite Preece.

'Yes,' Preece responded forcing a smile, 'he's doing OK but new car sales could be better.' Preece was determined to bring a negative to the discussion.

'I agree, but no one has had good new car penetration on that site for years. The parking situation is horrendous. Joe doesn't seem to think it will be a problem when we move to the new site,' Hatton answered. Preece mentally noted the use of Quinn's first name.

'Any news on the new site?' Preece asked, hoping to change the subject.

'Yes, the plans are done but we won't have the funds until next year.'

'Pity,' Preece answered without conviction.

'Yes, still if Joe can keep this up, with the profit he's making it will bring the project forward. His performance so far is outstanding. I think he's going to be a good choice for the General Managers post. He's very direct, aggressive almost, but the staff are responding well to him. He strikes a good balance. Gives his people positive reinforcement and always makes a point of thanking them when they sell a car. Who knows, if he keeps this up he could even become a candidate for Freddie's job,' Hatton said as he rose from his seat and stepped out of the office still smiling happily.

Preece was inwardly horrified by that statement, but his face remained impassive. The conversation gave him an idea. He reached across the spreadsheet, picked up the phone and dialled an internal number. It was answered on the second ring and he said,

'Stuart, get your arse up here, we need to talk, NOW!'

CHAPTER 20

Flattered. Enormously so. If anyone had asked me how I felt when John Hatton from the Hatton Group first contacted me about joining the company, that was how it was. The Hatton Group was a medium sized, well established, family owned local motor group with several different franchises, operating from twelve dealerships spread across the region.

I first came across their name some twenty years previously mainly as a result of their motor sport involvement. At that time in my life I was a mere spectator with ambitions of motor sport glory but no money. I had no professional contact with them as I was based in the insular North East with Mildenhalls and the Hatton Group was based in the South Midlands. It wasn't until I was promoted and moved south that I came into what I thought would be direct opposition to them. Mildenhalls were at that time one of the largest multi franchise motor groups in the country and operated nationwide. The Hatton Group was probably one sixth the size of Mildenhalls, preferring to remain local and independent rather than compete nationally with the bigger groups. Although in theory Mildenhalls and the Hatton Group were rivals in the same part of the country, I was based in the small city of Madley, which turned out to be far enough from the Hatton Group's dealerships for there to be very little cross over of customers. I met some of their managers at manufacturer meetings and developed a good working relationship with them. We would occasionally help each other out with new car stock when either of us needed a specific vehicle.

When I was approached regarding the possibility of joining the Hatton Group the timing could not have been better. Mildenhalls wanted me to move to London, a prospect which did not appeal. Apart from the horrendous house prices the thought of living in the capital filled both Lynn and I with dread. I knew I would be on rocky ground when I turned down the promotion. No one ever refused senior promotion at Mildenhalls. Instantly my working life became hell with constant, unremitting pressure. Previously agreed targets and budgets were suddenly revised. Meetings would be hastily arranged at head office only to be cancelled at the last minute. The Group's internal audit department, whose powers were way in excess of their use to the company, descended twice in six months and on both occasions managed to find some minor misdemeanour which resulted in a financial penalty to the department, wholly disproportionate to the actual infraction.

'You failed to sign off this cleaning docket.'

'And?'

'You failed to sign it off. You're not being thorough enough.'

'It's one ticket in two hundred.'

'Doesn't matter, it'll have to go in the report.'

What always made it worse was that the rebuke was usually delivered by some snot nosed young graduate with a non-descript degree from some non-descript university and no experience of selling, industry or life in general. I heard one of them once in a pub near head office, boasting about how they had got a sales manager the sack. The attitude just sickened me. I had built a good sales team at the Madley branch but it made no difference. Twenty years loyal service to the company meant nothing.

A senior manager at the Hatton Group heard of my plight and made some recommendations to the Sales Director John Hatton, who was also the grandson of the company's founder. I attended a couple of informal interviews with him and the Managing Director, Fred Fox, and felt that John was a man with whom I could do business. Fox was a different matter. At our first meeting I found him to be cold and aloof and subsequently came to realise that he was devoid of any motivational skills whatsoever. The man was a bully who liked to rule by fear. Worse, his decisions were inconsistent. What was right one day was wrong the next. Given that John introduced him as the driving force behind the company, I found Fox surprisingly resistant, apathetic even, to change. I was offered the General Sales Managers job at the Harpley branch. It was an ideal position as Lynn and I had bought a house midway between Madley and Harpley. The money was less than I was commanding at Mildenhalls but the move seemed to have potential. Or so I first thought.

Like many other motor groups the Hatton Group grew from humble beginnings. Arthur Hatton founded the company in the mid thirties. A big but very dextrous man, Arthur began his working life as a blacksmith's striker wielding a large sledge hammer. Using a pair of tongs the blacksmith would hold the hot iron in one hand whilst using a small hammer held in his other hand to tap the metal and indicate where it needed to be struck. It was hard unrelenting labour. Arthur got on well with his employer, Fred Empson, but he knew that the era of the village blacksmith was in decline. Occasionally Arthur would get the opportunity to repair a tractor. Fred had no interest in what he termed 'them new fangled blots on the landscape' and preferred to continue with his core business of making farm implements and shoeing horses. It was during one such operation that Arthur suffered an accident, which was to prove a curse at the time, but which would ultimately prove to be a blessing. A particularly feisty mare caught him with a hefty kick to the side of the knee. It was an injury severe enough to cause him restricted movement in the joint for the rest of his life.

Fred always blamed himself for the accident and when the time came for him to retire, blessed with no children of his own, he handed the premises over to Arthur. Although the forge was in the tiny hamlet of Marton, a few miles north of Rednall, it was situated on a main road. Arthur quickly built a reputation for first class workmanship and reliability at a competitive price. Being located on a main road, Arthur often found himself being asked to repair broken down motor vehicles and soon found that he was devoting more and more time to this side of the business. Arthur soon realised that he needed larger premises and he found a suitable workshop which also had the benefit of a small bungalow adjacent to it, a few smaller sheds and a couple of petrol pumps. It was also at this time that his elder cousin Dennis Hatton re-entered his life.

Dennis was ten years older than Arthur. On leaving school, and determined to better himself after a lifetime of being told he would never amount to anything, he left his home in the somnolent countryside to seek his fortune in the big city, in this case Birmingham. A big, hard and good looking delinquent he quickly established a reputation with the criminal underclass. Over the years he built up quite an empire with interests in several clubs and other small business's forged from the proceeds of numerous armed robberies throughout the land. Arthur knew nothing of this, and although he suspected that Dennis wasn't an entirely legitimate businessman, as far as he was concerned Dennis was just a man who had taken his chances and made good. When Dennis offered to fund Arthur's business expansion he readily agreed. The rate of interest Dennis wanted on the loan was very reasonable so Arthur felt he couldn't lose. All Dennis expected was that the repayments were made on time, work done on some of his vehicles and the use of some of the empty outer sheds Arthur owned, for storage of some of his stock. He also arranged for large safe to be installed in the concrete floor of the pantry in Arthur's home.

Arthur also found time to marry his childhood sweetheart Amy, a kind and gentle soul who doted on Arthur and who had always known that she would marry him. Within a year of marriage their first son Peter was born. A few months later Hitler invaded Poland and the Second World War broke out. Arthur was quick to offer his services, but his knee injury prevented him from joining up. Although he was frustrated by this, and eventually helped to form the local Home Guard, his indisposition didn't cause Amy any great distress.

Britain's pre-war production of motor vehicles peeked at almost half a million units in 1937. Some three hundred and seventy nine thousand of these were cars. Between 1940 and 1945 less than twenty thousand units were built. These pre- war cars were not the most reliable and with a lack of supply to the private sector Arthur's repair business, particularly as he possessed a great ability to improvise, thrived. At the outbreak of war an army transport depot and an airfield were built close to the garage. It gave Arthur even more opportunities. Petrol rationing had been introduced within three weeks of the outbreak of war and in 1942, it was banned from civilian use. Nevertheless civilians continued to obtain supplies via the black market. Servicemen of all branches of the forces were happy to supply and Dennis was happy to provide the funds with which to buy the precious fluid. Arthur was able to extract the dye from the forces fuel using charcoal filters and he also fitted auxiliary tanks to any vehicle Dennis needed for a job. The sheds rapidly filled with commodities such as cigarettes and clothing, all stolen by Dennis. Arthur did not consider himself dishonest; he was just a businessman fulfilling the laws of supply and demand. Besides, he now had another mouth to feed with the arrival of a second son Reginald in the first year of the war. The deprivations of war hardly touched Arthur's young family, but he was careful not to allow any signs of what Amy termed 'flash.' Throughout his life he never invested in a large sovereign ring or huge watch but over the years, as his wealth increased, he did keep the obligatory 'wedge at the hip,' his wallet in his back pocket never containing less than five hundred pounds in cash.

Although food rationing was in force the family maintained a good diet. Arthur was often called out to the local farms to repair machinery. If parts were needed, and couldn't be obtained, then he would make them. An indebted farming community often paid in kind and food was never a problem. He also bought and sold cars. The RAF was a particularly good source of used cars. He was often able to buy from the estates of dead aircrew and Arthur made good profits from the officers and gentlemen of both Army and Air Force.

Dennis also continued to thrive until April 23rd. 1943 when his luck finally ran out. The worst of the bombing raids on Birmingham were long over but on this night, Dennis was entertaining some of his associates in one of his gambling clubs. They never heard the stick of bombs which hit the club and surrounding buildings. Of Dennis, or his associates, nothing was ever found. It left Arthur with a large cache of cigarettes and, once he had cut his way into the safe, a substantial amount of cash and no debt.

At the cessation of hostilities he needed larger premises and he put his deceased cousin's cash to good use. With the employment of three mechanics he donned a suit and began to expand his sales operation. It would be another five years before petrol rationing ended but the Army and Air bases remained open.

By the early fifties Arthur had made sufficient profits to enable him to purchase two more outlets in Crowle and Abberton, both small affluent market towns to the south of Rednall. He changed the company name to Hatton's Garages Limited to reflect his growing success. His growing reputation, combined with the funds to back him up, began to attract the attention of several manufacturers all keen to grant him a franchise. He invested in even larger premises in Rednall, which became the new head office, and son Peter joined the firm. Peter was born to be a salesman and with more people able to afford motor cars the business continued to prosper. Reginald, or Reg as everyone knew him, joined the firm on leaving school but there would be no internecine rivalry. Reg was no salesman, having inherited his mother's softer nature and his father's dexterity with machinery. Arthur and Amy moved from the small bungalow into a much larger house commensurate with Arthur's ever increasing standing in the local business community.

During the sixties both Peter and Reg married. Their respective weddings were opulent affairs paid for in cash siphoned off from the business. It was proving a simple matter to sell a vehicle for £500 but invoice it for £450. Invariably customers never asked for invoices and revenue checks were rare. Again, neither Arthur nor his two sons felt they were doing anything dishonest. They were merely maximising their earnings and besides, everybody else in business was doing it so why not they? Peter was also enjoying a burgeoning reputation as a racing driver, again assisted by money from the company which was never recorded on the accounts.

The seventies saw the sons with families of their own. Peter's wife June, presented him with two sons, Trevor and Michael, and a daughter Jane. Reg's wife Hazel also gave birth to two sons, Melvyn and John. Expansion of the company stalled through the decade as political unrest, heavy inflation and growing competition from the Far East began to have an effect. The Inland Revenue and Customs and Excise also developed a bite to go with the bark.

Tragedy struck the family in 1980 when Arthur, just a few months short of his planned retirement, and by now a very wealthy man, collapsed and died whilst hosting a dinner party. His devoted wife Amy died the following year having never recovered from the loss of Arthur.

Peter and Reg now held the reins of the company and whilst discussions were often heated with regard to the direction the company should take, they usually resulted in agreement. Both brothers felt however that two men at the helm was not an ideal scenario in the decision making process. They needed a third person to bounce ideas with and to allow them a little more freedom. Their respective sons were far too young and inexperienced and so in 1984 they appointed the saturnine Fred Fox as Managing Director. He was a somewhat surprising appointment but he turned out to be the perfect foil for the two brothers. At the time Fox was employed by the finance arm of a leading car manufacturer and was very aware of the politics involved in running a large organisation. He was instrumental in the company diversifying into car hire, truck rental, leasing and contract hire. It was Peter though who was the driving force behind sales and who was responsible for the majority of the company's money making schemes which, if not entirely illegal, were very often unethical. He was also the instigator of the change in name to the Hatton Group.

During the 50's and 60's the company sold more than it's fair share of 'clocked' cars and cars which were the subject of sub standard, cosmetic repairs. The 'clocked' cars were those where the odometers were wound back to show the car having done far less mileage than it had actually covered. This allowed them to buy high mileage cars cheap, 'clock' them, and then sell them as low mileage cars at an inflated price. Cosmetic repairs were often carried out using baked bean tins, chicken wire and body filler to cover up rust holes in bodywork. The company drew the line however at selling stolen or 'ringed' cars. Joining the front of one stolen car to the back of another was just too dangerous to contemplate. As the company became larger and its profile increased, trading standards officials became more vigilant and the company ceased these activities. However they still needed to make money and Peter became ever more inventive.

The general public probably perceive all car salesmen as being economic with the truth. Indeed, probably all salesmen, or women, whatever the product are perceived this way. It's not true of course but the motor trade does have its share of bad apples. The salespeople are the ones who may lie about a cars performance, or the number of owners, to make a sale but to a certain extent these are minor infractions compared to the schemes dreamt up by the likes of the Peter Hatton's of the industry.

One of his more cunning strategies involved the fitting of tailgate wash and wipes. In the late 70's and early 80's more and more manufacturers began producing small saloons with lift up tailgates as opposed to the conventional saloon with a boot. These hatchbacks, as they were christened, filled the gap between saloon and estate models. Peter would order these cars as base models from the manufacturer but specify that they must have a tailgate wiper and wash system fitted. Then, when the cars arrived at the dealerships the rear wipers were removed, the panel on the inside of the tailgate door unclipped and the wiper motor and wash pipe made secure behind it but out of sight from outside the car. Two rubber grommets were then used to cover the holes and the internal rear panel clipped back into place. From the outside the cars looked like base models without wash and wipe systems. The sales teams were then incentivised by way of additional commission to sell these cars with the wash wipe systems fitted as an extra and charged out at a dealer fitted rate. When fitted as the car went down the production line in the factory these systems could be fitted and retailed for less than £100 still giving the dealer a profit. If fitted at the dealers the cost would be almost triple that figure, as the dealer would have to buy in the parts and then have a mechanic fit the system in the workshop. By ordering the system as a factory option Peter maintained the best of both worlds. Factory fitted cost price but dealer fitted retail price. The worst case scenario for the company was that the sales teams would supply the odd system free of charge. Even that small loss in profit still produced an upside as the customer perceived they were receiving something for nothing which made for a very satisfied buyer. As customers demanded more and more specification on cars as standard items the practice died out, but the scam was good while it lasted. The same fraud could also be used with radio systems, driving and fog lamps.

Reg, in his role as Service Director, developed his own schemes for maximising revenue. A customer would bring in a car for a routine service. Having left the car he would then be rung just after lunch and told that his pride and joy required extra work, brake discs and pads being the favourite. Usually a safety related item, particularly if it had been noted that the car had a child's safety seat fitted. When a child's safety is at risk what customer would refuse? Some service items, particularly oil filters, would be charged for but not fitted and if the garage were to be caught out an apology usually sufficed. Customers though rarely checked. Oil, bought in bulk, was sold at inflated rates. Even water became a chargeable item.

The manufacturers became concerned at some of these practices within the general motor trade, and in an effort to improve the public's perception of the industry, insisted that any item taken from a car was the property of the customer and should be returned to them. Most customers refused to take away the rubbish but then the dealers received some good luck when society began to develop a green conscience and environmental control became an issue. The dealers were given the responsibility for waste disposal. It was a heaven sent opportunity to pass on a further cost to the customer under the heading Environmental Charge, which in the new green age the customer was morally obliged to pay. As garage premises became more customer friendly with lounge areas and coffee machines, so the labour costs charged went up, often up to ten times that which was paid to the mechanic who completed the job. And heaven help you if you were a woman bringing your car in for a service!

With Fox's arrival the Hatton Group began a period of steady, if unspectacular, expansion. Peter continued as a national racing driver of some note which all helped with the company profile. The four sons joined the company although ironically Peter's sons Trevor and Michael both found their niche in aftersales. Their cousin Melvyn, always a quiet and studious individual, became an accountant. Cousin John proved to be totally hopeless at anything either academic or manual and moved into sales. He was not like his uncle Peter however and would even admit that he couldn't sell a car to save his life. He was happy to tell people that if it were not for his birthright he would not have the position he held. Whilst being refreshingly honest, his frankness did nothing to endear him to his subordinates who struggled at times to afford him any respect.

Jane joined the company some time later having spent her teenage years being indulged by her father and her twenty's travelling the world. She eventually found herself working in the company's personnel department as it was apparent that she could not work within a large department. She was prone to remind everyone that she was a member of the family and therefore everyone should defer to her. She was not a popular woman.

As production techniques became more sophisticated the manufacturers began to build more and more cars and expected greater results from their dealers. Consumer choice became greater and competition fiercer. Then Peter, for so long the real driving force behind the company, was killed whilst testing his racing saloon.

The loss of Peter left Reg as the sole chairman. Fox continued as Managing Director and the sons now joined the board. Trevor and Michael became joint aftersales directors and Melvyn was given the title of Accounts Director. John was appointed Sales Director, but the sales and marketing decisions were made by Fox with John acting as a mouthpiece. The company continued to expand and increase its dealership coverage across the region. Increasingly however, growth was being funded by manufacturer loans and mortgages on the Group's previously freehold properties. A solid reputation, built over the years with the banks, held them in good stead. The Hatton Group was asset rich having bought, or built, its early dealerships. Sadly, it was no longer a cash rich company as its borrowings and debt continued to grow.

When John Hatton first made overtures to me I understood he represented a go ahead organisation with proper systems, policies and procedures. I would be joining a well run, professional, honest and ambitious company so I accepted his offer to become the General Sales Manager at their Harpley dealership. I should have taken the time to have a good look at the dealership but I was so keen to get away from Mildenhalls I didn't bother. Harpley turned out to be a dump and I quickly found that none of the dealerships in the Group were as plush as the head office at Rednall. Many presented a good façade but were seriously dated inside. There was no formal sales process in place, no integrated computer systems, no staff training programmes and very little investment other than in vehicle stock. Beauty truly was skin deep. The group desperately needed an infusion of new and enthusiastic blood and I, having had the benefit of big group training and experience, was just the man to supply it. Besides which, the challenge of changing the sow's ear which was Harpley into a silk purse was professionally too good an opportunity to miss.

CHAPTER 21

Stuart Green loved pornography. He knew he was addicted to it but she didn't care. To him there was nothing perverse or immoral in pornography and it didn't matter what the material depicted. Images and films were capable of making him laugh or turning him on. His home computer contained hundreds of images and video clips. He owned hundreds of videos and DVD's the majority of which he kept in his loft. Some were in his spare briefcase in the boot of his car. He even kept some at work and had a selection of video clips and images on his office computer which he sometimes used to provide a laugh in morning sales meetings. It never occurred to him that he might be causing offence.

His dream was to make his own film. He had even tried to persuade his wife to participate but she was not interested. He hadn't attempted to force the issue and she continued to turn a blind eye to his predilection. He had become adept with his digital camera, scanner and computer software, at producing his own images. On the pretext of taking promotional pictures of the used car stock he would take photographs of female members of staff. It was easy to appear to be taking a picture of a car when he was in fact taking shots of the staff as they walked by. In the privacy of his own home he would superimpose their heads on pictures of female models in various stages of undress or being used by their male counterparts in his collection of magazines. These images were definitely not for public consumption.

Nigel Preece knew about his hobby but Green knew that there would never be any disciplinary action taken against him. Preece turned a blind eye because he was a frequent borrower from his extensive collection of films. Even Fred Fox would occasionally stop by his office on his way home and depart with a film safely tucked away in his briefcase.

Green was thirty three years old and had been with the company since leaving school. He had grown with the company and found a mentor and patron in Preece. He began his career as a storeman but his cocky demeanour soon brought him to the attention of Preece, who suggested moving him to car sales. He proved to be very good and in time his success saw him promoted to Sales Manager at Rednall. He felt that in the eyes of the company he could do no wrong. His department sold the most cars and made the most profit within the group. It didn't make him popular with the rest of the Sales Managers in the group who viewed him as an arrogant, conceited bully. His unpopularity however was not known to him and even had he known he wouldn't have particularly cared.

When his office phone rang he was in the process of downloading a clip of cartoon sex from the internet. It was his intention to use this in the morning sales meeting the following day. He wasn't surprised when Preece rang him. He was expecting the call. Preece had taken to ringing him every Monday morning when the figures were in from the other branches. There would be some trade deals where they could make some cash. Green went upstairs and didn't knock before entering Preece's office. Nor did he wait to be asked to sit.

'How have we done?' he asked.

'Not bad, Harpley has done well.' A pause, 'again,' Preece replied.

'We were top though,' Green said indignantly.

'You sold one more unit,' Preece responded dryly as he relaxed back in his chair, 'and this spreadsheet doesn't show a profit breakdown. If it wasn't for your Business Manager having the best finance figures in the Midlands you would be behind. Quinn is catching you. What do you think of him?'

'Personally or professionally?'

'Either.'

'I don't know him that well but I don't like him. He thinks he knows the job inside out and I get the feeling he's always trying to take the piss when he's talking to me. He takes the occasional car from us and we from him. He always cooperates. He's clearly doing a decent job at Harpley even though I think he's a wanker. I know some of the staff don't like him either.'

'That's always the case when we get a new man.'

'I know and I'm sure there are some people who don't like me, but I don't know who?'

Preece raised his eyebrows not certain Green was being serious. He asked,

'Do you see him as a problem to your future career prospects? Your ambition is to be the General Manager at Harpley when they build the new dealership is it not?'

'Well yes, but I've already been told that that's the company plan as well. You know that. Have you heard different?' he asked, the concern evident in his tone.

'No but things change. Quinn is doing well and what's more he has Johnny boys' ear. John seems to think he's the best thing since beer was invented at the moment. He thinks Quinn's so sharp he could cut himself without a razor. Remember he appointed him. Apparently Quinn has a saying about the job being all about 'attitude, effort and commitment' that John keeps repeating. I can't deny he's doing a good job and more people than John are beginning to take notice. The other Managers seem to like him as well.'

'Why should that affect me?'

'John let slip on Friday that when they build the new showroom at Harpley the board are considering relocating head office and all the admin departments.'

'What, leave Rednall?' Green asked in disbelief.

Preece gave a clipped 'Yep' and paused before continuing,

'If you think about it, it makes some sense. It's a much bigger site. It has good links to the motorway. It's more central with the rest of our operational area. By moving the accounts, vehicle administration and fleet departments from Flushing Road it frees up land which can be sold for redevelopment and that will help the company at the bank.'

'I can't believe we would shut Rednall though.'

'We won't but it will be a much smaller operation. This place was state of the art when it was opened and it has been updated but it's getting long in the tooth. Times and styles change. We could even sell this site and move somewhere smaller. If Quinn carries on doing a good job you may not get a look in at Harpley. He might get the job as GM.'

'But it's been promised to me,' Green whined.

'Well, promise or no promise your biggest threat is Quinn. If he continues to do well it will make it difficult to move him. I can keep being less than enthusiastic when Foxy is around but I can't deny his success forever. It'll just make me look stupid. At the moment we have the better site here and you have the better staff, particularly your business manager. I'll make sure you have the better stock but we need to keep an eye on him. I would suggest that when he has a customer for one of your vehicles you tell him it's sold or out on loan. Avoid his calls if you can. I'm sure you can manage to be uncooperative without being obvious. We need to formulate something to torpedo him. Give it some thought and see if you can think of something. Anyway, what's that new film you were on about? Wife's out tonight and I could do with a distraction,' he said lecherously.

CHAPTER 22

It was just after six on a warm, late summer evening in September when I took the call that was to change my life irrevocably. The consumer rush that had been the registration plate change on the first of the month had begun to die down and I was having a bit of a tidy up in the office and clearing some paperwork. Apart from the duty salesman and the showroom cleaners all the staff had left for the day. It was just over a year since I joined Hatton's and I knew that I had done, and was doing, a very good job. By and large I had the staff working for me who I wanted and trusted. Customer complaints had all but ceased to be an issue. No sales person was ever guilty any longer of not returning a customer's call and we were all pulling in the same direction. I had a good working relationship with my General Manager, Michael Hatton who was also of course a Director, and with John Hatton the Sales Director. Even the Group Used Car Manager, Nigel Preece, had become something of an ally. When I first joined the company I sensed hostility from his direction, but over time I appeared to have convinced him that my methods were good and I had no hidden agenda. He even took on board my suggestion to put all the trade vehicles through an auction rather than through individual traders. I had nothing against traders but time was saved by not having constant interruptions during the working day. These traders had supposedly been banned some years earlier but they still called in at the dealerships to view the stock before speaking to Preece. The fact that trade cars were going through a small independent auction in Rednall made little difference to me. Based in Rednall made it easier for Preece to get to the auction and guide them through the process. He could easily be on hand to sort any problems.

He and I seemed to work well together and he had even taken to ringing me on a regular basis to canvass my opinions, although I did upset him a little when I spoke directly to the auction manager about some of their administration charges. It was not a long conversation as the man, Jack Swift, referred me back to Nigel. I was only trying to help. The other Sales Managers within the group were always cooperative, apart from Stuart Green at Rednall, who never went out of his way to help but was never overtly obstructive.

I answered the phone which had been switched to manual, the receptionist having left at six.

'Hatton Group Harpley. Good evening, how may I help?' I asked in my most professional voice.

'Joe?'

'Yes.' I replied guardedly, knowing but not quite placing, the voice.

'It's Reg, Reg Hatton.' The chairman! I had never spoken to him at length before apart from a brief introduction when I joined the company. Nevertheless there was no mistaking the Rednall burr.

'Glad I caught you, are you free to speak?'

'Just a moment,' I answered and got up to close the door. I trusted my staff but there would inevitably be gossip if anyone knew who I was speaking to. Salesman have notoriously big ears when it suits and even bigger mouths. I sat back down wondering what was coming next.

'Go ahead Mr. Chairman,' I said.

'Please, call me Reg. I just wanted to congratulate you for your efforts over the first eight months of the year. You're well ahead of your budget. We'll alter that next year of course,' he chuckled. No surprise there. Achieve your targets and up they go. 'I want to give you something to think about,' he continued. 'You must understand though, that this conversation has to remain between you and me for now. It is not open for discussion with anyone, and I do mean anyone. Is that clear?' he said firmly.

'Perfectly Mr. er, Reg, you can rely on it.'

'Good. Over the next couple of years we need to continue to push the business forward. These are exciting times. Foxy will be retiring and I won't be around for ever. One of the boys will no doubt take over as chairman. Perhaps all of them may have a joint role. However,

I am toying with the idea of restructuring the whole business and I'm considering forming an informal committee to discuss ways and means to achieve this. A sort of think tank. Bear in mind that these chosen few are likely to be offered very senior positions within the restructured company. Would you be interested in this?'

'Of course,' I replied. Well, who wouldn't be?

'Good, I'm going to be speaking to a few others over the coming weeks. As I said, this is not for discussion with anyone including your wife. If I hear that you have discussed this with anyone or that any of the others have discussed it then I won't take the idea any further other than to say that career prospects with this company will be seriously jeopardised, if not ended. Is that understood?' he said with just enough of a hint of underlying malice to make me feel slightly uncomfortable.

'Perfectly,' I answered.

'Excellent. Keep up the good work and I'll be back in touch soon.' And with that the phone went dead. I replaced the receiver and sat for a moment slightly bemused. Then elation got the better of me and I stood up and punched the air as though I had scored the winner in the Cup Final. Wealth and power beckoned.

CHAPTER 23

Jack Swift, the owner and chief auctioneer at Rednall Motor Auctions replaced the phone in its cradle on the desk, sat back and exhaled. He looked across the desk at his cousin Nigel Preece, who asked,

'Think it worked?'

'He didn't question me and I didn't detect anything in his manner. He's only spoken to me once remember and I think you've made certain he won't ring me again' Swift replied, smirking.

'I think you can count on it. That was a bloody good imitation of Reg. I reckon you would have fooled me. Unless we are very unlucky he won't speak to the chairman and if he did mention this, I think he would just make himself look foolish. It's unlikely that Reg will ring him and I can't remember the last time he went to Harpley. He's content nowadays to sit in his office with the racing page and let Foxy get on with it. Quinn's ego will keep him quiet,' Preece said.

'What happens now?' Swift asked.

'To be honest I'm not absolutely certain. We'll give him a couple of weeks to think about things and then we'll drip feed him a little bit more when I've thought things through a little more carefully. There's no rush, we have plenty of time. Harpley being built is a while off. We have the land and premises for the new dealership but planning permission for the conversion has yet to be granted. Besides, the company is a bit short of cash at the moment.'

'Perhaps you should lend them some Nigel,' Swift suggested playfully.

Preece grinned. 'You and I both need Stuart Green at Harpley and then one day stepping into this job. Putting trade vehicles through you won't last forever unless we get rid of Mr. Quinn. One day that clever little shit will cotton on to the costs and suggest to John that we use one of the bigger auctions. The big boys are only too willing to do a deal.'

'And you'll lose your cut,' said Swift.

'Quite, and you'll lose a large slice of business. We all have too much at stake. As I have said Quinn is doing a good job, but I'm not going to allow him to leap frog me or Stuart in the pecking order. I've not worked out how yet, but I'll think of something that will really discredit him.'

'Well, I'm happy to help,' Swift responded. 'Your cars coming through have given us a huge boost. If it continues I'm going to have to increase staff.'

'When you do, I'll have to have a bigger cut,' Preece responded as he got up from his chair, smiling,

'C'mon Jack, you can buy me and Stuart a pint, the lads not had a very good day.'

'How so?'

'We were interviewing a prospective new trainee salesman this morning and the boy was a bit cocky. At the end of the interview Stuart tried to catch him out, but it didn't quite work.'

'In what way?'

'Stuart tried to use one of Quinn's interview techniques. For all I can't stand Quinn he does have some good ideas, one of which is that at the end of an interview he always asks the candidate to tell a joke.'

'Why? No pun intended, but are you having a laugh?'

'No, not at all. Actually the theory is quite good. The candidate has just finished the interview and they start to relax so you hit them with a totally unexpected question. Usually you get one of three responses. One, they tell a joke straight off. Two, they sit ringing their hands and squirming with embarrassment or three, they collect their wits and tell a joke or apologise that they don't know any jokes.'

'That's four.'

'Whatever. The point is that if they hit straight back then they are going to be good at thinking on their feet and are quite confident. The squirmers are likely to react that way with a customer and will probably finish up lying. The ones who slightly defer the question are the ones who are likely to respond to a customer in the manner of, I don't know but I'll find out.'

'Interesting.'

'Yes it is. It's not definitive of course but I can see the benefits. If nothing else it widens the repertoire of jokes.'

'So what happened to Stuart?'

'It didn't work quite as it should. You know how the back wall of his office is covered in mirror tiles? Well, the lad asks if the joke can be visual so Stuart looks at him a little bemused and says OK. The lad asks him to turn round so Stuart does and of course he's looking at himself in the mirror, whereupon the lad says there's your joke and gets' up and walks out!'

Both men began to laugh as they pushed open the showroom door and headed towards Green's office. Green was just shutting down his computer as they walked in.

'Fancy a drink Stuart? Jack's in the chair. Just one thing though, you'll have to tell us a joke!'

Green turned crimson. He was not a happy man.

CHAPTER 24

For six weeks I heard nothing more. Nevertheless the conversation with the chairman had given me a massive boost and I went about the business with an added spring in the step and was, even by my standards, a little more cocky than usual. The department continued to thrive. Then, early one Thursday evening late in October, as Lynn and I were preparing for a long weekend away, the phone rang at home. Lynn took the call and passed the phone over to me. It was the chairman.

'Good evening Joe. Sorry to bother you at home. I just wanted to touch base with you before you went away. I hope I've not rung at an inconvenient time?'

'No, not at all, I'm just clearing up one or two bits and then Lynn and I are going to our son's for a few days. He's home on leave.'

'Excellent. It's always good to see the family. We shall be moving things forward on the other front and I just wanted to sound out a couple of ideas with you.'

'Fine,' I answered. I was deeply honoured and consequently full of myself.

'What do you think to the idea of Harpley becoming the new head office and moving accounts, car administration and fleet departments over there?'

I couldn't see any problem and said so. After all, it could only increase the prestige of the new dealership. And me of course.

'Good. I thought you might approve. Second thing, this sales process you use that John keeps banging on about. I think we need to adopt this across the whole group when we move. What do you think?'

Now when it comes to a proper sales process I'm completely in favour and said so. I couldn't believe it when I joined the Hatton Group and found that they had no written sales process. A new salesperson just appeared to be told to get on with it.

'Here's an appraisal pad and price guide. The brochures are over there. Now go sell me a car,' appeared to be how they worked. Well, not in my dealership. Properly trained sales people and a controlled and managed process are the keys to lasting success.

My standard format was for the salesman to meet and greet the customer within, at worst, two minutes. Not turn the other way and pretend to be busy. And if eye contact is made always respond immediately. There's no need to make a big fuss or dash forward and grab them by the hand, which tends to frighten most new customers anyway. A smile, always, and a simple greeting are usually enough and always in a positive manner. Not some indistinct mumble which some sales people seem to cultivate. Just the use of plain and sincere good manners goes an awful long way. Then it's on to fact finding and qualifying. The salesperson has to be sure that the car they want to sell is suitable for the customer's needs. The customer might want a certain car but will they be happy in the long term with what they buy. Imagine an eighty year old who wants a two-seater sports car. It might be the least line of resistance to supply the car the customer wants but it almost certainly would not be exercising good judgment. Try walking into a showroom and when the salesperson asks if they can help say 'No.' How many of them give up at the first attempt? Where's the grit and determination to succeed? Or tell them you want to buy a new car but you don't know what type or model. If the salesperson is any good they will sit you down, make you relax and then fact find and qualify you so that what they want to sell you will match your needs. It's about taking control. Yet most salespeople give in and allow the customer to control the sale. Then we move on to presenting the product in a pleasant and professional manner, including an accompanied test drive. Not just fasten a set of trade plates on the car and let the customer drive off on their own. What good is that? The salesperson should drive first and properly demonstrate the features and benefits. Then change places with the customer at a safe spot and let them enjoy their first experience of what will be their new car. If the customer is allowed to drive unaccompanied, apart from the obvious danger of the car being stolen, how can any objections the customer may raise, be easily overcome? When the customer is sold on the car, then we get down to the numbers and always with the involvement of the Business Manager. I prefer to present the deal as a monthly payment as most people are on a monthly budget anyway. The Hatton Group's preferred system appeared to revolve around finding out how much the customer wanted for their part exchange or how cheap they could sell them a new car. That's not selling, it's order taking. It's the lazy salesman's way of earning a living and doesn't maximise every customer coming through the door. It's reliant on having a lot of customers through the door so it doesn't matter if a few get wasted. But what happens when you use this method and customers are in short supply? It's also the lazy Sales Manager's way of running a department. Lack of involvement means a lack of control and a lack of accountability. Failure is always someone else's fault, usually the salesperson. I can't understand sales people who are given fantastic opportunities through proper training and scripted formats and yet fail to grasp the nettle because they think following a script sounds silly. They are just being idle. If only they would realise that retail is detail and the more you practice the better you get, and the better you get, the more money you earn. There is no doubt that if sales people apply a structured sales path and follow it consistently then it will result in them being able to supply a volume of vehicles professionally and profitably, with good customer care resulting in repeat and referral business in the future. How many careers are there where you get a nice car and the chance to earn big money without any formal qualifications whatsoever? And a good Sales Manager will always thank a salesperson, and say 'Well done' when they have done a deal because the deal should be the one the Sales Manager has structured. Again, it's a question of control and let's face it; the job title is really a clue to the job spec! It appeared that the chairman was on my side.

'When you return I'm going to send you a letter of intent which will outline the aims of the committee. It will of course contain a confidentiality clause. Don't copy it, just sign it and return it through the internal post. Mark it for the attention of Jenny in the fleet department and I know this will sound strange but I want you to mark the envelope with a smiley face in the top left hand corner. Is that clear?'

'Perfectly,' I answered and before I could say anything further he wished me a good holiday and ended the call.

I was bemused. My first thought was that this was a bit cloak and dagger even for the motor industry. Still, he was the chairman so who was I to argue?

CHAPTER 25

In Nigel Preece's office in Rednall, Jack Swift put the phone down and burst out laughing.

'He'll never fall for all this,' he said shaking his head in disbelief.

'Sounds to me as though he already has,' Preece answered chuckling, 'but even I thought the smiley face was pushing it a bit far. He thinks he's Billy Big Time but I intend to turn him into Billy No Mates. Sales process indeed. He'll have us taking car keys off customers and throwing them on the roof so they can't get away without buying a car at this rate. We are going to make him so cocky he'll think he can walk on water. Then I'll make sure he drowns. I have a few more ideas to destabilise him and run his operation off the rails, then our good friend Mr. Green here can step in and rescue the situation.'

Stuart Green, who was sat quietly in the corner, smiled and said,

'Are you really going to send him a letter?'

'Of course.'

'What if he makes a copy?'

'What if he does? What can he do with it? If he revealed it, it would just make him look stupid. Let's face it, if you got caught out with something like this would you want to broadcast it. Besides, who can he accuse? I reckon he will follow our instructions to the letter provided they are not too outrageous. The trick will be to keep things just believable. Over the next few months I'm going to blow his ego up like a balloon and then when it suits I'll stick a pin right through it.' Preece imitated pricking an imaginary balloon. 'Pop!'

All three men laughed. Green then decided to share a conversation he had had earlier that afternoon.

'I rang Harpley today to speak to Quinn. He was on a half day so I spoke to the Business Manager. Turns out they worked together at Mildenhalls. He was quite chatty. He tells me that Quinn is something of a ladies' man.'

'Really?' Preece answered with genuine surprise. 'Now that is interesting. I bet that's not on his CV.'

'It seems he was poking a sales girl he worked with a few years ago. Apparently it caused one hell of a rumpus. Gives a whole new slant to fucking the staff,' Green replied with a sly smile.

'Did she have a white stick and a Labrador?' Preece asked grinning. They all laughed again. 'Well, it's not a crime but it might help us,' Preece said thoughtfully. 'Perhaps we could put temptation in his way.'

Swift and Green remained silent as Preece continued, 'Lets all give it some thought. Look, this financial year is drawing to a close. Quinn's had a successful year and we've sown a few seeds in his mind. I'm going to get him to run his stock down as we head into the quiet time of the year and then when he's crying out for stock in January he might just find that I'm having difficulty with supply. I think Mr. Quinn is in for a very bad year next year. Let's keep our heads down and see what develops.'

With that, all three men left for the evening. Preece couldn't remember feeling so excited about a new trading year ahead and the prospect of furthering his career at the expense of a man he now loathed.

CHAPTER 26

With just three weeks left of the calendar year and the company's financial year it was time for a break. The motor trade always goes quiet in December. Not unnaturally buying a replacement car is not uppermost in people's minds. Santa holds sway. My department had produced a very profitable year and I was well pleased. As was John Hatton, so when I suggested at very short notice that I could do with a holiday he was happy to grant my request. I had heard nothing further from the chairman. He passed through the dealership one day, but apart from a cursory nod in my direction he said nothing. It seemed a little odd but I was not too concerned. Word on the grapevine was that the new development had been delayed but that the company was stretching itself a little further with the banks to buy some more land surrounding the site. The future was looking very bright.

My friend, the Group Used Car Sales Manager Nigel Preece, had asked me to reduce the used stock to a third of its normal level. I achieved this with comparative ease. A couple of sale weekends in November helped and most vehicles still left in stock had been bought at the right price. Preece oversaw some of these being sold at auction and most of them returned a small profit. It was job well done. Other branches were not so fortunate and their manager's were given a bit of a kicking. Everything in my garden seemed rosy and I felt that Lynn and I deserved a couple of weeks in the sun as a reward for all the hard work and long hours throughout the year. It was agreed that my Business Manager, Paul Jones, would be left in charge and Lynn and I jetted off to St. Lucia for two weeks in the sun.

I find it quite difficult to turn off on holiday. At Lynn's request, or rather at her insistence, I left my mobile phone in the car at the airport but I made the mistake of leaving the details of where we were staying with Paul. Now Paul is a good lad. He's not the greatest finance and insurance salesman I've ever worked with but he tries hard, is basically honest, thorough with his paperwork, very committed and does as he's asked. I have a very simple philosophy. All I ask is that my staff do what they say they are going to do and then everything works. By and large Paul does just that. He is prone at times to 'big up' his contribution to the department and he does have a habit of putting his foot in it and volunteering information without being asked. As one former colleague so aptly put it, he has a job holding his own water.

I should not have been surprised therefore when I received a message in the hotel to ring him. Lynn was livid. Breakfast time in St Lucia, tea time in England and a dampener about to be put on the holiday. I rang Paul and after he apologised he told me that there was a memorandum, circulated by e-mail within the company, which was less than complimentary about my department. The memo emanated from Stuart Green and had been copied to all the Directors, General Managers and Sales Managers within the group. I obtained an e-mail address for the hotel and Paul forwarded Green's missive to me. Sure enough Green was being critical of the standard of preparation of used vehicles at Harpley. Cleaning was sub standard. Cars were not serviced prior to sale and we were using his prime stock to top up our own inventory.

I was stunned. And very, very angry. Apart from his statement being largely untrue, I thought he had acted in a gutless manner by sending it out when he knew I was on holiday. Other Sales Managers within the Group warned me about Stuart Green when I started working for the Hatton Group but he had not previously given me any problems. It was clear he was not well liked although no one could question his success. The negative comments regarding him I attributed to a touch of professional jealousy. I could concede his point that we took stock from his dealership. In truth, I encouraged my sales team to take stock from every dealership within the group if it meant making another sale. We made every effort to sell a customer a car, not just let them walk off to another dealership probably outside of the Group. As far as I was concerned the stock belonged to the company not the individual branches. I couldn't for the life of me understand why he had stuck the boot in. I knew I could refute the allegations. Lynn begged me to leave it till after the holiday and I didn't want to cause a ruck whilst we were away. Male pride wouldn't allow me to just let the subject drop however. So I sent a response to Green which simply stated my annoyance and a promise that we would discuss the situation when I returned. The whole thing put a real downer on the holiday. Despite sending him an e-mail I couldn't get Green's treacherous behaviour out of my head. Had we been in England I am sure I would have driven to Rednall and given him a good slap. Then again, had we been in England he certainly wouldn't have had the courage to have attacked me.

The first thing I did when I returned to work was to contact Green. He immediately apologised. He claimed he was feeling pressured, a couple of deals had turned sour. He had arranged for a car to come from my branch and it was dirty. He realised he had been hasty and hadn't known at the time that the car he borrowed had only come into stock the same day. He had forgotten I was on holiday. He whined on. He was lying of course and I told him I would be e-mailing a formal response to his comments later in the day and circulating it in the same manner as he. I cut the connection midway through his response. I had heard enough. I make it a rule never to argue with an idiot because they are apt to drag you down to their level and then beat you with experience. If he wanted a war then he was going to get one.

My deliberations were interrupted by a call from Nigel. He started with the expected pleasantries regarding holiday and health and then moved on to the problem of Mr. Green. His suggestion was that the wisest course of action was to e-mail Green and copy it to him and not the other Managers and Directors.

'Everyone knows what Stuart is like and if you respond in kind you will just be lowering yourself to his level. You've had a good year. John is singing your praises from the rooftops. 'Outstanding' is how he's describing you. I came across and checked your stock and gave it a clean bill of health. It's no worse than others. I reported the facts to Foxy. Let it go, enjoy the Christmas break and come back refreshed for the new challenge.'

In deference to him I did just that. He was right. My department had produced a very good year and I could feel justifiably proud of my efforts. Little did I know that a year from hell was just about to begin.

CHAPTER 27

At first, when Nigel Preece received the copied e-mail from Stuart Green regarding Joe Quinn and the Harpley dealership, he was absolutely livid. Fortunately for Green, Preece was unable to locate him and having given himself time to think, he began to see some possibilities. He was not however about to let Green off the hook. Green got the message from reception and went upstairs to find Preece sitting behind his desk and looking like he was about to explode. Green suspected what it was about and any lingering doubts were dispelled when Preece greeted him. Green was already beginning to regret his actions.

'Close the door.'

He did so and sat.

'What the fuck did you do it for?' Price asked his voice surprisingly level and calm.

Green turned crimson, thought seriously for a split second about braving it out, then sensibly realised that it wouldn't be any use. Even he thought his answer was a bit weak.

'I thought it would help,' he said lamely.

Preece then proceeded very quietly and calmly to remind Green of his responsibilities both to the company and their own long term plans. Green realised that certainly as far as the other managers would be concerned, he had shot himself through the foot. No one would trust him now. He was not a happy man when he returned, very chastened, to his own office in the showroom.

For Preece though, every cloud had a silver lining and he knew that he would have to embark on some damage limitation which could, he felt, be turned to their advantage. Quinn was, after all, on holiday, and the furore would have died down before he returned. Most would have their thoughts on Christmas by then.

Closing his door he sat down, rang Fred Fox and told him that in the light of the e-mail he really should visit Harpley to check the situation. Fox readily agreed. On arriving at Harpley he proceeded to give the stand in manager Paul Jones an uncomfortable time. Jones had been more than helpful and was keen to deflect any criticism from himself. Consequently he gave Preece more useful information regarding Quinn. Preece was more than thorough when he inspected the stock. In truth it was, without any shadow of doubt, the best prepared and presented in the group. Quinn clearly had good systems in place. Still, when you look hard enough you can always find fault. Jones also confirmed that Quinn had a weakness for the opposite sex and could be a bit to aggressive at times towards the staff. By all accounts he once had a salesman by the throat in their previous employment. Luckily for him, after an apology, he escaped without further sanction. The story amused Preece and as he drove back to Rednall he was beginning to formulate a plan. He immediately reported back to Fox who, somewhat fortuitously, was chatting with the chairman. Preece lost no time in putting the boot in.

'We need to tighten up some of the stock preparation across the whole group. Harpley is bad and some of the others are very poor.' he said. Call them all poor but call Harpley bad. No one could accuse him of bias. Much. The next group Sales Managers meeting would have a few indignant employees. He had dumped on them all but he knew that he would get away with it. A few drinks and comforting arms round the shoulders would still any dissent.

'According to Jones it's him that does most of the admin, Quinn is just a figurehead, strutting around, pricing a few cars and taking all the plaudits.' Preece knew this was untrue. He was also aware that no one would challenge his assessment. Yet another seed of doubt sowed on a fertile field.

'Still, you can't deny he has had a good year. Profit is up and the Customer Satisfaction Programme results show a remarkable increase,' said Fox.

'That's true I know. Trouble is, I think you might find there is more to the CSP results than meet the eye,' Preece replied, 'I had an interesting conversation with a customer who brought in his CSP questionnaire.'

Fox raised an eyebrow and gave him a knowing look, guessing what was going on at Harpley.

'So our star may not be as bright as he seems?' he asked rhetorically.

'It would appear not,' Preece answered anyway.

'Do we need to know more about it at this stage?'

'I don't think so.'

'Right. Well, I'll trust your judgement so we'll leave it to you and John to sort out. The Sales Manager of the Year award can go elsewhere. He'll still get his pay rise to bring him in line with the other managers and we'll see how he performs under a bit of pressure. We might have to consider bringing forward the time table to move some of the Managers. I know we have talked in the past about Stuart going to Harpley. John was against the move because he's a Quinn fan. I think I need to have another conversation with John and we'll see what transpires. Thank you Nigel.'

As Preece left the office he was smiling contentedly. The customer bringing in the CSP questionnaire had been a real bonus, particularly as Trevor Hatton had been with him at the time. Trevor had been puzzled as to why a customer should bring in the form and be expecting a tank of petrol for his trouble. Preece told him that he was sure there would be a logical explanation and it had been left at that. Preece knew exactly what the explanation was, as it was he that had suggested to Quinn what he needed to do to get the CSP score to an acceptable level.

CSP, or CSI as it is sometimes known, is the abbreviation for manufacturers Customer Satisfaction Programme or Customer Satisfaction Index and is the manufacturer's way of measuring how well or how badly, they and the dealers are performing in the service they offer to the customer. All the manufacturers introduced these programmes in the late 80's not just to measure performance but to also show that they were taking positive steps to give the industry a better image. The dealers received rewards depending on the scores. The trouble was, motor dealers being motor dealers, some of them decided that the easiest way to increase the scores, and probably the way that came most naturally, was to cheat.

The simplest way was to coerce the customer. The salesperson would tell the customer that about one month after delivery they would receive a questionnaire from the manufacturer. The salesperson would then play on the customers emotions by saying that if the form gave him, or her, a bad score then it would directly affect their commission payment,

'And of course Mr. Customer, as we have got on so well and you've had such a great deal you wouldn't want that to happen would you?' whilst gently stroking a picture of their family strategically placed on the desk.

The other way was the simple bribe.

'Bring the form in Mr. Customer and then we can fill it in together because they can be quite complicated. We will of course give you a full tank of fuel for your trouble.'

Initially it was probably only a few dealers who cheated the system. Then the manufacturers had the bright idea of cutting the dealers discount margin from 17% to 7%. Not unnaturally the dealer body complained about this sudden cut in profits. To appease the dealers the manufacturers gave some of the profit margin back by giving parts credits and incentive payments some of which were linked to new car registrations and to good customer satisfaction ratings. Suddenly the dealers had even more incentive to cheat. Salespeople, who had seen their own commissions cut, were given bonuses for good individual customer satisfaction scores. The programmes descended into farce with zone managers from the manufacturers turning a blind eye to the cheating, mindful of their own targets. The system of questionnaires being sent out has been largely superseded by many manufacturers who now rely on their own call centres to carry out the surveys by phone. Only by doing the job properly can the dealer get a good score, which is as it should be.

Quinn had been having a lengthy conversation with Preece one day regarding CSP ratings and Preece told him,

'You do what you have to do.'

'So the company is happy to give away free fuel?'

'You know the drill Joe,' he said, 'no one is going to give you a written memo but there's too much money at stake to rely on customers giving good scores. Even if we do the job one hundred per cent right, we will still get customers who will only give us nine out of ten. It's the way we are in this country. I do it in hotels and I bet you do too. We always allow room for improvement.'

Quinn took the advice on board and immediately implemented it; not giving a moments thought that Preece now had something he could hold against him.

CHAPTER 28

New Year and a new financial year. It doesn't matter how well you did the previous year, come January everyone sets out on a level playing field. Almost. Some playing fields are always a bit more level than others. I believed I had every reason though to be optimistic about the coming year. I'd just been granted a big pay rise. The deadwood in my department had been removed and replaced with the staff I wanted. The new recruits received proper training from me and were showing the right attitude and commitment. I knew they would put in the effort. We were a team and they knew that I would back them to the hilt. The new dealership was on the horizon and with it the promise of promotion for me and increased sales, and commission, for the team. The budget for the next twelve months had been increased as I expected and I wasn't concerned. I felt sorry for one or two branches that failed to reach their targets the previous year and still had their budgets increased. I have never been able to understand that particular anomaly within the motor trade. Some directors, usually those who are not from a sales background and more often than not accountants by profession, seem to think that just because it is a new year then everything changes. Now don't get me wrong, I'm not saying all accountants are useless. I've worked with some very commercially aware number crunchers who do appreciate that without sales people doing the business then they wouldn't have a job. Sadly however, all too often accountants believe that the sales teams exist for the benefit of the accounts departments and that the accountants are the prima donna's of the business. They totally forget that the retail motor industry is a people business. They don't look at why a dealership has failed to achieve its objectives and seek to put it right, they just come up with a new set of numbers and tell you to get on with it. There are many good managers who have been sacked from failing dealerships because of a knee jerk reaction from a senior manager wanting to send out the 'fail and you're out' message, instead of recognising the true reason for failure and giving proper support. And if the guy stays in his job and succeeds it's never a 'well done' scenario, they just get questioned as to why they didn't do it the previous year! Then, the numbers go up again and when they fail they get fired. A replacement then comes in and the budget occasionally gets adjusted down to give the new incumbent a chance. The treadmill starts again. It isn't as though senior managers or accountants care. Failure, even by a small fraction, is just another reason to belittle a Sales Manager and his, or very occasionally her, team. It's never the senior managers or accountant's faults; the blame is always deflected elsewhere.

Conversely there are many bad managers who have been lucky enough to be placed in a good dealership and risen higher than their talents deserve, before eventually being found wanting. It's either promotion or the sack. Fortunately for me I was looking at promotion. The storm clouds however were gathering.

The first week in January John Hatton organised a sales meeting at Rednall to outline the strategies for the New Year. All the Sales Managers from the various branches were in attendance. John cried off with illness so Jim Ashton, the Group Marketing Manager, chaired the meeting along with Jane Hatton, who spent most of the meeting staring in my direction, presumably trying to make a feeble attempt at making me feel uncomfortable. Or perhaps she was just fantasising!

I liked Jim, even though I felt his role in the company was a little superfluous. He collated information from the various branches and produced the weekly sales figures for the board and the branches. He did a bit of marketing and attended meetings but I thought his contribution was overblown. Still, there were a lot of senior employees within the Hatton Group who seemed to do very little for their pay. Yet another company top heavy with sycophantic non-productives. When Jim announced that internal service charges were to be increased every Sales Manager realised the real reason for John Hatton's absence. By increasing the internal charges, the company effectively made it more difficult for the sales departments to make a profit, thus cutting commission payments to sales staff, including sales managers. The profit was being redistributed to the service department so the company as a whole didn't suffer at all. I silently swore that if anyone told me to consider the big picture, I would punch them!

A main dealership can be a really dishonest business. Not only do we fleece the customers but we even try to shaft each other. Each of the main departments in a dealership, Sales, Service, Bodyshop and Spare parts are run as separate businesses within the branch. They all have separate budgets but it is only in the sales department where the staff rely on commission from sales to make up the bulk of their salary. Consequently, if the company can find a way to retain profit and pay less commission then they will implement it. For instance, the sales department buys in a used car for eight thousand pounds to sell at ten thousand. If it sells for ten the government takes approximately £298 in VAT. The car needs paintwork so the bodyshop makes a charge. It may not charge the normal retail rate so for arguments sake we'll say it costs £300. Two thirds of this will be internal profit. Then the car requires servicing. The service department, in its role as the expert, advises sales how much needs to be spent. Invariably it will be more than anticipated. A couple of tyres which have suddenly got cuts in the sidewalls. Brake discs and pads are needed or new shock absorbers. It's easy to make a good shock absorber appear to be leaking. A smear of dirty oil usually does the trick and then when new parts are authorised just clean off the oil. Before long another £500 has come out of the profit or been redistributed to the service department. Incredibly, or perhaps sadly, there are a great many sales managers who are too lazy to actually check that what they are being told by the experts is the truth.

Then the car gets invoiced to the customer. The company, as part of the commission scheme, has decreed that all sales will be the subject of a £250 house charge to cover administration and warranty costs irrespective of whether the salesman has sold a warranty. The parts department has made its money on the materials supplied to the service department. The sales department is then left with the net profit of which, as a generalisation, the salesperson gets 10%. The company has of course made a much bigger profit. Is there any wonder that there is a high turnover of sales staff, or that some sales people resort to dishonesty in their desperation to make a sale when they are so reliant on commission to live?

As for Jane, she really gets on my nerves. She is a really unfortunate young woman having been a long way down the queue when they handed out good looks. She makes a Pug dog look handsome. When I first joined the company I had a few dealings with her over the phone and to be fair to her she was really helpful. She had a pleasant telephone manner and I was quite looking forward to meeting her. When she called in at the showroom one afternoon I got the shock of my life. Certainly not a woman you could ever describe as raw boned. Six feet tall and big, very big. Her ankles and calves are surprisingly finely proportioned. Sadly, from the knees upwards everything had gone wrong. Big thighs, big hips and a pot belly, big shoulders, huge pendulous breasts and features that to describe as ugly would be an understatement. It would be wrong to describe her as fat in any conventional sense, although shedding a few pounds wouldn't have hurt her. She was just big! Her dress sense was non-existent which didn't help her at all. Occasionally she would wear short, tight skirts which made her look even more repulsive to me as her stomach would fold over her belt. When she gets pressured she hops from foot to foot like a demented stork. She really is very odd, a true BUF!

I've also found out as time has gone by that she is as thick as two short planks. A gnat has a bigger IQ. She has no formal qualifications to run a human resources department. It was clear from some of the advice she gave me when I had to discipline a member of staff that she did not know what she was talking about. Left to her, anyone who fell under suspicion was guilty and should be sacked without recourse to a proper disciplinary procedure. Another one in the company who only has a job because she was born to the right family. The day she made a pass at me I was appalled. She suggested we meet for lunch at a quiet hotel and it was obvious what was in her mind. Hopping into the sack with her would have been like a mouse trying to hump an elephant! She has never got over my refusal and from time to time has caused aggravation. She is nasty, vindictive and a bare faced liar. Hell hath no fury like a woman scorned.

Stuart Green was his usual voluble self. He talked a lot without actually contributing anything useful. It didn't particularly bother me other than the fact that he was just wasting time. Any good ideas suggested by the other managers were met with negative criticism. His own ideas were of course brilliant. At least to him. Still, as far as I was concerned he was yesterday's news. By the end of the meeting I was so bored I had almost lost the will to live and I couldn't wait to get away. I also did not want another confrontation with Ms Hatton. Unfortunately, as I crossed the car park Green came after me and delivered a metaphoric kick in the gut.

'Can I have a word?' he asked.

'Sure, what's the problem?' I replied wondering what minor infraction he was going to make a mountain out of. I thought maybe he was going to wish me a Happy New Year. No, lets not be silly.

'I'm sure you must have heard the rumours, so I just want you to tell you your position won't be affected one bit.'

I looked at him like he'd just grown two heads.

'What are you talking about? What rumours?' I asked with a mounting sense of dread.

'Sorry, I shouldn't have said anything. I just thought you would have heard.' He was obviously, and surprisingly, a little uncomfortable and clearly struggling to recover his composure as he couldn't stand still or look me in the eye. Then he obviously realised he had me at a disadvantage.

'Still, better to get it from the horse's mouth. I'd prefer it if you didn't discuss it with anyone as it's not yet official.'

'What's not official?' I asked angrily.

'When the new branch at Harpley opens I'm going to be the General Manager,' he said smiling smugly.

Now it's not often that I'm speechless but this was one of those few moments. Livid? I was apoplectic! He repeated that he didn't want me to discuss it with anyone and that he had probably said too much. He had. I needed to think before I did something stupid. Like belt him. I got in to the car and drove back to Harpley. Fast. By the time I got back to the branch I had not calmed down. If someone had placed a kettle near me it would have boiled instantly. I headed straight for Michael Hatton's office, knocked and without a hint of a pause barged straight in. Now Michael is an alright bloke. He might be a Director but I always found him down to earth and sensible. I trusted him but I felt not the slightest bit of guilt at the direct approach. Nor with what I said to him.

'What the fuck is going on? I've just been told by Stuart Green that he is going to be the next GM here.' I didn't shout but I did raise my voice. Michael looked aghast as he settled back in his chair but he recovered his composure quickly.

'Calm down,' he responded with a smile which kind of took the wind out of my sails, 'that's not happening. I won't deny that it's been a discussion point in the past but I can assure you it's not happening.'

As I sat down I could feel some of the tension leaving me but I was still angry because I had allowed Green to get to me.

'Mr. Green has obviously got the wrong end of the stick and I will be speaking to him about it. You have nothing to worry about,' he said firmly.

We had a few more minutes' discussion. He did a very good job of placating me. I've always found it difficult to stay angry with someone who is smiling at me pleasantly. I left him after apologising for bursting in. He was his usual genial self and like I said, I liked him. I asked Paul if he had heard the rumours and he had which irritated me no end. I guessed he was hedging his bets. After all, if the rumours had been true he wouldn't want to upset Green for fear of retribution. I called a sales meeting to inform the staff that if they heard anything further they should just ignore it. I didn't want them unsettled and losing focus. The rumours persisted though and I was to call several more meetings along the same lines over the next few months.

CHAPTER 29

For the second time in a month Nigel Preece was having difficulty in controlling his temper. The source of his anger was yet again Stuart Green who sat across the desk from him, with a look on his face that could only be described as defiant.

'What the bloody hell did you do that for? Why can't you just learn to keep your mouth shut? What are you trying to do? I'm taking Quinn on a journey to professional destruction which is to both mine and your advantage and you,' he paused and jabbed his finger angrily at Green, 'you are trying to sabotage me. Foxy has a few minutes conversation with you and you think promotion is a done deal. Well it's not. You're not as good as you think you are. It may come as a surprise to you that not everyone within this Group thinks that you,' he paused again to emphasise the point, 'you, are the world's greatest Sales Manager. This is the last discussion you and I will have on this subject. You do things my way or I'll make sure you rise no further in this company or any other for that matter. My way or not at all. Do you understand?' Preece ended his tirade with enough menace to deflate Green who made a valiant, if somewhat futile, attempt at conciliation.

'It'll unsettle him though won't it,' he said weakly.

'I don't care,' Preece responded angrily, 'he'll be unsettled enough by the time I finish with him. I just don't want him as a loose cannon. I'm about to give him something that will keep him out of our hair for a good while and now I don't feel I can share my plans with you. You can't keep your mouth shut can you?' he ended nastily.

Green sulked. Grudgingly he was forced to accept that Preece was right. The trouble was, when out drinking after work with some of his team, the alcohol and the ambience had loosened his tongue and he boasted about his expected promotion. He thought his staff were loyal to him and wouldn't say anything, but he was wrong. It never occurred to him that his team laughed at his jokes and put up with his behaviour purely to humour him. He was determined to find the source of his betrayal and someone would pay. He also knew that he needed to find a way to placate Preece. And then he had a 'eureka' moment.

Quickly he outlined his thoughts to Preece and he could tell by the look on his face that he had caught his attention. Preece said, 'you know Stuart, for once in your life you might just have saved your day. I'd actually seriously considered paying someone to cosy up to him. Much as I hate to admit it, your suggestion might just work. Let me give it some thought. I'll handle the detail though, not you. You just keep your head down and do your job. And keep your mouth shut.' Stuart Green was a very relieved man as he left the office.

Preece sat for a good hour thinking about Green's idea and came to the conclusion that it would fit in very well with his own scheme. He now knew exactly which direction the plot against Quinn was going to take. He picked up the phone and dialled an internal number.

'Used accounts,' answered a female voice.

'Mrs. Thomas, you and I need a little chat about some important changes which are being proposed. Can you call at my office when you leave?'

'Sure, no problem, I have some tax discs to bring round anyway.'

'Good, see you later then.'

He put down the phone and then picked it back up and dialled another internal number. It was answered on the second ring.

'Stuart Green.'

'SG, meet me back here at quarter past five.'

'OK. What'

But Preece broke the connection before Green could finish his question. Preece knew Green would be there. He always was. Green was his boy. As for Quinn, he was going to fail in the biggest and most embarrassing way possible. If everything worked as Preece intended nobody in the motor trade would touch Quinn with the proverbial barge pole.

CHAPTER 30

January turned out to be a very bad month for the department. Nigel Preece was apparently having difficulty replacing the stock I had traded during late November and December. I had helped the company's cash flow, but it wasn't helping my bottom line. No profit equated to no commission. We were having to rely on borrowing stock from other branches for clients to view, and with stock in short supply, the managers were not too keen to help. They had their own profits to worry about so I couldn't blame them. Borrowing stock is not a very a good option. Running the company on a shoestring meant that there were never enough part time drivers, so it meant taking bodies off the showroom floor. Mildenhalls always kept a few retired people on the books who they could call on at short notice to transport vehicles from branch to branch. The Hatton Group paid so poorly that even the elderly looking for something to fill their time weren't interested, and understandably salespeople are reluctant to leave the showrooms and sales pitches to ferry cars around because of the potential for lost sales opportunities.

On a personal note though things were not so bad. Only a few days after the Manager's meeting at Rednall I was in my office waiting for John Hatton to arrive to discuss the new service charges when the phone rang. I answered it in my usual professional manner. It was the chairman.

'I want you to go to the fax machine and ring me when you are in position. I'm in Nigel's office.' And then the phone went dead! Abrupt or what?

I was surprised that he was in Preece's office but as Nigel had rung me only a few minutes earlier from his car on his way to the auction, I supposed he was in there purely because the room was empty. I did as he requested and within seconds the machine printed out the message and I headed to the bog for some privacy. I read the contents, which basically stated that I was not to concern myself over any rumours of job opportunities in connection with other staff members. I needed to concentrate on my own position which would be far senior to anything that was offered to any other Sales Manager. The chairman was also asking me to consider who I should have as my assistant and he was suggesting a senior accounts administrator, Lucy Thomas, who I already knew. I signed the bottom of the message, placed it in an envelope, which I addressed in the usual manner to Jenny in the Fleet Department and marked in the corner with a smiley face. Then I put it into the basket containing the rest of the internal post. Only a few minutes earlier the driver who collected the post from all the branches had arrived and was on his drinks break. The envelope would be with the chairman within the hour. I didn't make a copy and made sure that no one else saw the contents. It never occurred to me to question why he sent me a fax rather than just say what he needed to say over the phone. Nor why I had to sign and return it.

Lucy Thomas turned out to be one of the few bright spots in a crap month. The other points of illumination turned out to be two cars which we borrowed from Rednall. The first, a Renault Megane, arrived and was so damp in the boot that there were fungi growing. Obviously Mr. Green's staff were not opening tailgates on a regular basis to keep fresh air circulating. At Harpley, or any dealership I run, the first thing that is done every day, apart from in seriously inclement weather, is to open all the tailgates. Not only does it keep vehicles aired but it shows that we are open for business. Needless to say I was quick to point out to Michael Hatton the poor standard of preparation at Rednall. I'm no grass but it was case of doing unto others as they would do unto me. The second car, a Vauxhall Astra estate, highlighted even more the incompetence of Stuart Green.

We sent the car across to Rednall on the last day of the month. We couldn't sell it and I wanted it out of the way before doing the monthly stock check the next morning. The vehicle could only just have arrived in Rednall when my phone rang. It was Green.

'This car you've sent me is shabby,' he said with an air of superiority. 'It's filthy inside. The ashtray has stale ash in it. The CD radio is the wrong spec and there's no spare wheel. It's typical of the standard of car we get from you. I want it removed or I'll have to report the matter to John Hatton.'

Remarkably he didn't wind me up. Indeed I was happy for him to continue berating me until he paused for breath, giving me the opportunity to reply,

'It only came to us on Friday and we haven't had time to clean it up I'm afraid,' was all I said, almost apologetically.

'Well why have you sent it to me? None of my team has an enquiry for a car like this,' he answered. I could almost feel the sense of superiority he was feeling. He was gloating at my supposed discomfort.

I paused. This was a moment to savour and I was wishing I could have been there to see his face.

'I agree the car is in a poor state. Our customer wouldn't buy it and we were in fact reluctant to let them see it.' I then lowered my voice and carried on in a more menacing tone.

'We borrowed it from your branch on Friday afternoon when you were off. It's been on your forecourt for over two hundred days. You really do need to exercise better control of your stock Stuart.' I'm sure I heard the phone hit the cradle and a frustrated scream from thirty miles away. What a sweet moment, I almost wet myself laughing. As did all the other managers when I repeated the tale!

As for Lucy Thomas, I first met her within days of joining the company. I was given a conducted tour of all the facilities by John Hatton and met Lucy in her office in the central administration building at Rednall. Lucy was responsible for all the used car accounts across the company. She didn't exactly crunch the numbers but made sure the numbers were there for the senior accountants to feed on. Some groups have administrators in every branch. Others, like Hatton's, have centralised the system in order to cut costs. Ours had been a brief introduction but my first impression was that she was an attractive lady, slim with long dark hair and a no nonsense attitude. I only saw her once a month when I went to Flushing Road for an accounts meeting, although I did speak to her at least once a week regarding our invoicing. Our conversations were always polite and businesslike with the odd flirtatious comment from me, to which she barely responded. There was rarely any personal content to our chats regarding families or relationships. Indeed, any attempt at talking about anything personal was usually rebuffed. She wasn't rude; she was just the lady on the other end of the phone who did the provisional accounts. She was just doing her job. Even at the annual company get together she practically ignored me and my sales team, preferring to spend her time with the rest of the accounts staff. She made no attempt to circulate although it was noticeable that some of the other sales teams, particularly Green's, did gravitate towards her and her colleagues some of whom were very fit young ladies indeed. Like moths to the flame.

I suppose I really should have noticed the shift in our relationship. It probably happened around mid January although the change was quite subtle. As I said, I rarely saw her, but in between coming back from holiday and Christmas, I made a point of going across to Rednall and taking her a bottle of Jack Daniels as a thank you for her help and efforts throughout the year. I told her it was from all the team. Good account administrators are hard to find. Generally they lack any commitment. I've worked with some where their work has to be constantly checked and as a rule they are chronically underpaid, which probably explains why, as in most things in life, you get what you pay for. Lucy Thomas however, was as good as they come.

Other people noticed the change in our relationship before I did. Our phone conversations increased from one or two a week to every day. It was always about business but little bits of personal information began to creep in. Calls that normally took a few minutes began to stretch to ten minutes or more. Then she began ringing me at lunchtimes and I found myself closing the door so that no one else could hear. I began to look forward to going to work for the wrong reasons. I was looking forward to hearing from her and I knew that I had begun to take my eye off the ball. Not that I would admit it to anyone though.

Commercially the month was bleak. I had a budget to sell sixty used cars but I started the month with a stock of only thirty. Nigel was not coming through with fresh stock and at his behest, apart from not only borrowing stock, I was now being requested to take other branches overage units. The stocking rule at Hatton's was ninety days and then if a vehicle was still in stock it was supposed to be sent to auction. It was not a rule that ever seemed to be implemented. At Mildenhalls I had known the stocking rule to be as low as forty five days with financial penalties for the branch if it was not adhered to. The Astra came back from Rednall to Stuart Green's undoubted joy. Nigel also asked me to do him a favour and move some Mondeo estates. Great cars normally, these were high mileage units for their age and Nigel had paid far too much money for them.

'Don't worry about the price as long as you can return what we forked out,' were his words.

We sold them all and broke even. The profit per unit line on the accounts was decimated. The department lost money against its budget for the first time since I joined the company. Other branches had suffered as well from stock issues but we were bottom of the pile. Still, what did I care? I was falling in love.

CHAPTER 31

Nigel Preece was elated and allowed himself the luxury of leaning back in his chair and placing his feet on the desk. The January flash reports from around the group showing the predicted month end profits from actual units sold were on the desk in front of him. It had been a hard month and most branches had struggled. Harpley, to his great delight, had bombed. Given that the branch started the month with only thirty units in stock to sell forty had been a creditable achievement but it was way short of the budgeted sixty and in any case, thanks to the Mondeo estates, the profit per unit was way down. He knew he shouldn't have bought them but the commission paid directly to him from the hire company made the transaction worth the risk. Rednall, on the back of finance sales, had returned a decent month. No one it seemed realised just how much Rednall relied on the finance sales. If every branch employed a Business Manager like Philip Bentley at Rednall there would never be any pressure from the banks. Bentley was exceptional, even if his methods were a little dubious. Only the previous week Preece had been forced to deal with an irate customer who found that the money taken from his bank by the finance company wasn't quite what he understood it should have been.

Bentley had been guilty of 'double docking.' In this case the customer had been quoted hire purchase terms to buy his new car, which were acceptable. Bentley, at the point of sale, attempted to sell him a Protected Payment Plan. Known in the industry as PPP these plans covered the customer against accident, sickness, redundancy or death. In this instance the customer decided that the premium was too high and that as he was paid when he was off sick he did not need the plan. When the customer collected his new car it was late and he was tired. Bentley tried one last time to sell him PPP. This time he used the assumptive method. He 'assumed' the customer wanted the protection and produced three sets of finance documents. One set showed only the balance financed with no insurance. The second set showed the balance financed plus a further section showing the PPP payment. The third set showed the balance financed and a section for death benefit. Bentley's first action was to place the documents showing the PPP payment in front of the client and then asking him to sign where he indicated. The customer signed without reading, partly because he was tired and wanted to be away in his new car and partly because he was thoroughly fed up with listening to Bentley making inane small talk. He was given a copy of his document and went on his way. The other two sets of unused documents Bentley filed in the waste bin in the corner of his office. One month later, when the first instalment came out the bank, the customer realised a mistake had occurred. In fact he felt conned. Preece however showed him a copy of the signed document and claimed that neither Bentley nor the company was at fault.

'It's all here in black and white sir,' Preece argued.

'I've seen the damn copy thank you but I told him I didn't want any protection.'

'Then why did you sign for it sir?'

It was only when the customer threatened violence that Preece backed down. It took some time to sort out the mess with the finance company. Nine times out of ten Business Managers throughout the industry would get away with assumptive selling. The method was also condoned by some of the manufacturer's own area managers who turned a blind eye to the practice, mindful of their own targets.

Preece also knew that Bentley occasionally lied about the interest rate being charged and would make sure that when the customer signed the finance documents his finger was placed strategically over the box showing the rate. Bentley was adept at telling customers that they were being charged one rate and then upping the rate by a few tenths of a percent. A rate of six point one per cent at point of sale became six point nine per cent at delivery. Payments were also 'penced.' A payment of ninety pounds and ten pence became ninety pounds and ninety nine pence. All of this made extra commission for the company and it was very rare that a customer ever noticed.

Preece picked up the phone and dialled the number for Fred Fox. Fox answered within three rings with a curt, "Yes?"

'Have you seen the flash reports?' Preece asked.

'No, tell me the worst.'

'Rednall's done alright but the others have struggled. Harpley has done particularly badly and it's well bottom of the league. The lack of part exchanges from new cars has caused the problem,' Preece told him deliberately neglecting to mention that he had failed to supply the branch with any fresh stock.

'New cars will always be a problem. I'm not going to get excited over one bad month but we'll need to keep an eye on Quinn. I know you have reservations so let's see what develops,' Fox said.

'You're right,' Preece replied, 'I do have reservations. However, for the sake of the company, I will continue to give him my full support.'

He heard a grunt down the line as Fox terminated the conversation.

'He'll have my support alright' Preece thought, 'all the way out of the company's front door.'

He reached down for his briefcase and took out a folder marked Quinn. A copy of the flash report went into the folder which already contained the fax message signed by Quinn regarding his proposed position and that of Lucy Thomas. Stuart Green's big mouth almost caused a major problem and Preece had needed to move quickly to placate Quinn.

His opportunity came when John Hatton told him he was going to Harpley for a meeting with Quinn. The two service directors were away from the building briefing the service managers across the Group. Foxy was away on personal business leaving Preece as the senior manager at a virtually deserted head office. He rang Jack Swift and explained what he needed him to do and then rang Quinn from his car in the car park telling him that he was on his way to the auction. When Swift, in his role as the chairman rang Quinn and told him what he required Quinn had readily complied. It then proved to be a simple task for Preece to intercept the internal post delivery and extract the envelope with the smiley face sent by Quinn. He then cut the top off the message to remove the Rednall fax number, copied the remainder, and destroyed the original. The remaining copy would eventually form part of the evidence to prove that Quinn was a manipulative abuser of a vulnerable member of staff.

CHAPTER 32

Ali knew that it was pointless going to any of the safe houses. The old regime was long finished and it was likely that all his old 'official' haunts were compromised if not discovered and closed down. Someone, somewhere, quite probably possessed a file with his name on it but he had planned for this eventuality.

Many years earlier Ali rented a small flat with direct access to a lock up garage below in an anonymous block in south east London. All the transactions he completed in his assumed name. The real Jake Smith was once his lover. Meeting the real Jake Smith had been a stroke of massive good fortune. Ali was between operations. They met in a bar in Brighton, notorious locally for its reputation of catering primarily for members of the 'gay' community, one warm spring evening. For the real Jake Smith it was love at first sight. For Ali it was no more than lust and a pleasant diversion from the stress of his nomadic and often violent lifestyle. When he realised that Jake was his age and build, a plan quickly formed in his mind. The opportunity was too good to miss. Over the next few months Ali and Jake became inseparable. Jake was a self employed builder based in Ramsgate with no living relatives or close friends. He was quite a shy man who kept himself to himself and it was easy for Ali to persuade Jake to move in with him and re-locate his business to Brighton. It gave Ali the opportunity to literally steal Jake's identity. Bank account, National Insurance number, drivers licence, passport, everything was placed in the address of the flat which they shared just back from the beachfront in Brighton. For the real Jake, for the first time in his life he knew true happiness. Despite the so called liberated society his sexuality and shy nature had condemned him to the life of a loner. Then one autumn night the two of them went out on a fishing trip into the channel on the small motor launch which Ali had persuaded Jake to buy. Only one of them came back. Ali killed Jake with his bare hands, strangling him as he was sodomising him. He wrapped Jake's body in an old anchor chain and dropped him into the cold, deep, grey waters of the channel. The next day Ali gave notice on the flat, paid the outstanding rent, sold the boat, loaded up the van and moved to London where under his new identity he spent a few nights in a cheap, nondescript hotel while completing the formalities on his new flat. From that day onwards Jake Smith continued to pay his taxes and file his accounts through a small accounting firm in east London. He returned to the flat periodically to clear the accumulation of junk mail. The neighbours bothered him not at all. He had chosen the area well. Unlike some districts this was an area of many mixed races who tended to keep themselves very much to themselves.

On reaching London after his arduous journey his first port of call was to the flat. It was dark and before attempting to gain entry he stood discreetly opposite the building watching for any signs of life. He saw nothing to concern him and being cold and tired he took the chance. The key to the flat was long since lost but the lock would be easy enough to pick. There was enough light for him to see and he noted with concern that there appeared to have been some work done on the door. It took him only seconds to gain entry and his worst fears were realised. Someone had been in the flat. He stepped silently over the pile of unopened mail on the floor. He tensed, were they still in there, waiting silently in the dark? Was this to be the end? He closed the door silently behind him and stood, his eyes squinting to adjust to the darkness and his ears straining for any sound. He waited for a full minute, holding his breath. Nothing happened and he exhaled, allowing some of the tension to release from his body. He overrode the electric curtains, pulled them across the window shutting out the night, and snapped on the light. The glow would not arouse any suspicion as all the lights were set on a timer so they would have been turned on and off at various times of day. The curtains had been similarly programmed. He looked carefully round the room. The furniture had been moved. Surfaces had been dusted to, he presumed, hide any finger prints, and he surmised that it was only recently as there was no great re-accumulation of dust. He went through to the bedroom and checked the wardrobe. His clothes had been rearranged. He was convinced however that it was not a professional job. There were too many mistakes. A professional would have taken more care and made sure everything had been put back exactly as it had been found. It was clearly no thief either as the room had not been ransacked.

He went through to the bathroom and carefully removed the bath panel. There were no signs of scratches on the five screws and the slots on the heads were still in the same sequence, twelve o'clock, one o'clock, two o'clock, three o'clock, four o'clock and five o'clock. Reaching up behind the bath his fingers sought, and found, a plastic bag containing a drivers licence, passport, both in Jake's name, spare door key and a key to the padlocks on the inside of the main garage door.

He left the flat via the kitchen and descended the internal flight of stairs to the garage below. The entrance door was closed but clearly showed signs of being forced and with very little care. He opened it carefully feeling for the light. He was less tense now, but still wary. The garage would be a good place to apprehend him. There were no windows and he had carefully sealed round the outer door to avoid any spillage of light. The plain red scruffy Transit van was still in place but the building tools had been disturbed. But far worse, his inner sanctum had been breached. Jake had built an internal wall across the back of the garage. The door had been crudely prised open. Whilst the added room stretched the full width of the garage it was really only a large cupboard but it had contained a box, similar to the type held in safety deposit vaults, containing a wad of cash, bank books and spare identities. Several tins contained two hand guns, ammunition of various types and a small quantity of plastic explosive, in this case the ubiquitous C4, plus other sundry items related to the business of terror. An AK47 assault rifle was propped in the corner. It had been a calculated risk leaving the gun there but Jake had not found time to conceal it or get rid of it the last time he had stayed at the flat. The tins were still there but the box had gone and right now this was far more important to Jake.

Jake now faced some hard decisions. He sat on a forty five gallon drum, with his feet propped against a wheelbarrow, deep in thought. He had been compromised but by whom? British intelligence? No, too sloppy and besides they would have had a watcher and he would surely have been taken by now. The Americans then? No, same reasons. His own countrymen? No! The country was still in disarray and besides they had no reason to suspect he was still alive after the invasion. He was known to have been in Baghdad and staying at his parents home when the bombs began to fall. The likelihood was that he had been presumed dead. Many of his countrymen would have changed sides and whilst his activities would certainly have come to the attention of security services around the world in the past, he had never been apprehended. The landlord? No reason. The rent was paid on time; he knew he worked away a lot. Jake had told him that he was working on a large building project in Germany. The accountant? No, surely not. But the longer he sat and thought about it the more he became convinced it must be. For some reason he must have grown suspicious. Jake knew he had to see the accountant and quickly. He also realised that the flat had served its purpose and that his identity may also be compromised. If the accountant had the box he just might possibly know too much about his activities now.

Jake reached up to a shelf and pulled down an oil can. Unscrewing the top he took out a plastic bag containing the ignition key for the van. The battery would be long flat. Disconnecting it after using it previously, knowing that he was likely to be away for sometime, he hoped had saved it from permanent damage. He quickly connected the battery and booster pack and turned the key. The engine turned but didn't fire. The fuel gauge was only just registering a tiny amount of diesel in the tank. He tried again and was rewarded as the engine burst into life. He shut it down immediately not wanting to choke on the fumes or draw attention to the noise. The cold and pangs of hunger were beginning to gnaw at him. He went back upstairs and slipped out of the flat after first removing the pile of junk mail and placing it on the table with the other unopened letters. He would never know that this simple act would result in several needless deaths. He left the door unlocked after finding that the spare key was useless. The lock had been changed he now realised giving further credence to his theory about the accountant. He used the time honoured method of placing a hair across the crack in the door to warn him of anyone entering the flat in his short absence. There was a shop only a few hundred yards away which he knew would still be open, even though the hour was late. From there he bought a loaf of bread and some cheese. It would have to do. Water he could get from the tap in the flat. He returned to the flat, the hair was still in place and he remained in the dark and ate. It wasn't long before sheer exhaustion overcame him and he slept but already a plan had begun to form in his mind.

CHAPTER 33

Why do the young believe it is only they who are allowed to fall in love? It is not their prerogative. The middle aged and the old are just as susceptible to the emotional and physical attraction of another human being. We may not be looking for it to happen but happen it does and probably the most incredible part of the whole process is that we never know when it's going to occur. That and the fact that and no one has ever come up with a rational explanation for the chemistry between two people which we define as love. Throughout the ages many have tried.

Perhaps the two most popular explanations for the phenomena are opposites attract or, they appear to hate each other so they must be in love. An explanation which is usually accompanied by a nod and a knowing smile. What is surely true is that there are different levels or types of love. The love for a parent or the love for a child. The love of a friend or the love of a pet. The love of a place or the love of an object. Or perhaps the love of a God. So how then do we differentiate between love and lust? Is it lust or love that causes us to experience that nagging, constant ache somewhere deep inside? Which of these two emotions is it that causes us to eat like we are constantly starving or conversely to be unable to eat? What causes us to have the object of our desires on our mind twenty four hours a day, seven days a week? To make us do things we don't want to do and then when we look back we wonder what kind of insanity made us do it. Then we swear we'll never get caught again. No one will make us look or feel foolish again. Who are we kidding? It's true that there are some more strong willed than others and who are able to bury their feelings. Are they the lucky ones? Some never cross that line that separates, supposedly, the right and wrong paths. Me, I suppose I'm amoral.

After the department's terrible performance in January, February was no better. I should have been concentrating on the job but I was well and truly distracted by Lucy. I didn't see it but some of the staff did. The telephone calls were becoming more and more intimate and lengthy. If a member of staff came to the door when I was on the phone to her they couldn't get in. The door was firmly closed. Then one day she asked me out to lunch. Who was I to refuse?

I actually took the day off work. I made a big effort that Thursday morning. I must have cleaned my teeth and flossed half a dozen times and by the time I picked her up I was practically shaking with excitement. I felt like I couldn't put one foot in front of the other. It never occurred to me that she would be just as nervous. I didn't show it of course. Not me, not Joe Quinn. I met her at her office. How stupid was that? We made no attempt at discretion. She looked stunning and had clearly made an effort. She stood a mere five foot five in her heels. Her shoulder length auburn hair, parted down the centre, shone in the sunlight and accentuated her narrow face and high cheekbones. Her black dress emphasised her slender frame. The hem hung just above her knees and rode nicely up as she sat. She wore black, sheer tights, or perhaps they were stockings? Lucy looked all woman to me. I was most definitely in lust!

Driving away from Flushing Road I could see some of her colleagues looking out of the office window. I was in no doubt that we would be a major topic of conversation and I didn't care. She directed me to a local pub and I was surprised that she chose a route which took us past the main dealership and that the pub was quite close. If anyone from head office chose to have a pub lunch it was odds on that this would be where they would go. Unless of course they were doing what we were. She didn't appear at all bothered that anyone would see us. I naturally bought the drinks. She ordered Coke and despite desperately wanting some alcohol to steady the nerves I stuck to mineral water. I didn't want to blur my senses and become over confident. Neither of us wanted food. We made some inane small talk, as people do on a first date. Both of us were experienced enough to know that we were dancing around each other. Suddenly, as if tired of the pretence, she seized the initiative and moved our relationship up a gear.

'How unlucky can I be?' she asked. 'I'm married to a man who has already cheated on me and now I've fallen for a guy who is old enough to be my dad and has a worse reputation for being a womanizer than probably anyone I've ever met.'

I laughed. So she had fallen too!

'It's not funny,' she retorted attempting to look severe.

'I know, but my reputation is over hyped. You've been talking to Paul. I've been married for a long time remember so I can't be all bad. I have a mate who is on his fifth marriage.'

'Another motor trader no doubt,' she said. 'What is it about you lot that makes you think you can snap your fingers and we girls come running?'

I thought she was being a little unfair, and told her so with just a hint of indignation. Then she grew serious and covered my hand with hers.

'Look Joe, I don't know where this is leading.' I hoped I knew! 'But there's something we need to get clear. My daughter, Annie, is the single most important thing in my life. No matter what happens she always comes first. I took David back after his affair because of Annie. Admittedly it was a moment of weakness. It was the New Year and I was lonely and Annie was missing her Dad. I was wrong, but I made a promise to myself that I would make the marriage work and that it wouldn't be me who wrecked the happy home. Annie adores her dad and we both adore her. I have no doubt he will cheat on me again, if he hasn't already despite what he said and says. One day we will go our separate ways. Only the other night he was talking about buying some expensive hand made wardrobes. I told him there was little point in buying something that would last forever, because our marriage won't. He was shocked and I laughed it off but it's true. Breaking up yet though is not on the agenda but, as I said, nothing lasts forever.'

She took a sip of her drink as I pondered.

'Are you really that cynical?' I asked.

'Yep. One day he will have another affair or perhaps when Annie's grown, I will.'

'What of us?' I asked.

'There is no us. Not in the sense you think or want.'

'Then what are we doing here?'

'Two good mates having lunch.' She smiled, took my other hand in hers and stared straight into my eyes. 'You need to understand how it is. I know we've grown close and I do like you. A lot. I enjoy our chats but it will go no further than that. I can't risk hurting Annie.'

I felt like I had been slapped but I was determined not to let it show.

'OK, I understand,' I replied, 'I'll just go with the flow. We'll just be good friends.' I tried to sound sincere. 'For now,' was what I thought.

She smiled, released my hands and made no comment. The talk turned back to work. I was half expecting her to mention the Chairman's committee, but the subject never came up. Either the Chairman had yet to discuss it with her or she was being ultra discreet. We finished our drinks and left the pub. I drove her back to the office and dropped her off. As I drove away I realised that we hadn't even kissed and that I had never attempted to. Not even a peck on the cheek. Despite what she said however I didn't feel that our relationship had ended before it had begun. On the contrary, this was a beginning and in any case I liked a challenge and this was one I was going to relish.

CHAPTER 34

As Lucy strode back into the office she was met with a wall of silence. All her colleagues had their heads down and appeared to be working. They were doing no more than shuffle paper. She sensed that her date had been the lunch time topic of conversation and wondered who would be the first one brave enough to speak. She smiled and was tempted to say something as she hung her coat behind the door. Waiting though would keep them all on edge just a little longer. Without so much as an acknowledgement she went through to the small kitchen and cloakroom.

Lucy was a mixture of confused emotions. Happy that she had been to lunch with Joe and yet there was a growing sadness within her. She first realised that she was attracted to Joe some months earlier but she did nothing to indicate her feelings towards him. She didn't even really know what attracted her to him. At first she treated him with indifference. She never discussed anything personal with him, just business and his first attempts at polite conversation she had not taken up. She was notionally in charge of the Used Car Accounts Administration Department at the Hatton Group, so she oversaw all the invoicing of used car sales throughout the group and reported only to the head of the whole admin department but her role, while important, gave her no real influence. She was a 'doer.' The job was relatively straightforward with none of the complexities of dealing with new cars and worse, the new car manufacturers and their increasingly complicated marketing programmes.

As a result of her ease of working, Lucy was able to negotiate a very advantageous contract with the company which almost made her a part time employee and allowed her to care for Annie. Her work and experience was highly valued. She only worked two full days every week. Tuesdays and Thursdays she left at three and didn't usually break off for lunch. On Wednesdays she had the whole of the afternoon off. The efficiency of her department didn't suffer and she was flexible with her time. On the rare days when she did have a lunch break she would leave at four. If month end, with all the attendant pressures of making sure everything was invoiced at all the branches, fell on one of her half days then she would re-arrange her schedule to suit. The timetable worked well. The company saved on wages and still got the job done. She was well able to balance the demands of work and her responsibility to her family. It also allowed her to have some time to herself.

Lucy liaised on a regular basis with all the Sales Managers within the group. She spoke to Joe every week on the phone. He was always polite and had a somewhat irreverent sense of humour. He made her laugh but she never let on how good it made her feel. Even if she rang him with a problem, which was rare, nothing was ever a crisis. He dealt with everything quickly and calmly. There were never any histrionics like she got with some of the other managers. Even at month end when the pressure was on, he never got ruffled. The deal envelopes containing the history of the transaction from the sales person's first customer appraisal to the final invoice came over to her from Harpley ready sorted, in a logical order and on time. Joe made life easy for her and she appreciated it.

What she was not prepared for were her own feelings towards him. Over time she began to look forward to their chats and she found herself looking for reasons to ring him. She was overjoyed one month when she had to go to Harpley for a routine audit. She came back slightly deflated because if he had any special interest in her he gave no hint. She had flirted with him but whilst he was friendly towards her he seemed to treat her no differently to any other of the female members of staff. He flirted with every female, no matter what their age might be. She found it mildly irritating. Normally she could wrap a man she was attracted to round her little finger. She hated the feeling of not being in control. She couldn't understand what was happening. When she thought about him, which seemed to be most of the time, she couldn't make sense of why she felt as she did. He was not tall and he was quite slim but he carried himself well and she imagined that he had a powerful body. There was no sign of any middle aged spread like others his age. His hair was cut fashionably short and simple without being severe. When she got close he smelled of expensive cologne. He looked fit despite the fact that he was old enough to be her dad. He wasn't the best looking guy she had ever known but he was no ogre either. He had a confidence about him but it was not fuelled by arrogance. She was excited by him in way that she had not experienced for a very long time. She could feel the stirring of desire deep inside whenever he was near and in her own bed at night she frequently fantasised about him, even when engaging in sex with her husband David. Lucy no longer believed that she made love to David. The act was a chore, a duty.

Then, shortly after Christmas and just over a year after Joe joined the company, their relationship noticeably changed. The telephone conversations suddenly grew longer. She took to ringing him just to say goodnight. Then one day she had taken a gamble and not rung him. Just as she was about to leave he rang her. The stakes had been raised and she spoke to him again from her car. Lunch was the outcome.

Yet even in the excitement of this first lunch date and the promise of more to come she knew it was all an illusion. Nigel Preece had rung her and if he knew about her lunch date with Joe he didn't let on. Those few minutes with him though would have a profound effect on her whole life she knew. She and Joe might share a summer of passion, of love even, but it was a relationship that was doomed. She knew he was hooked now and so was she. She though was not just hooked by Joe, she was hooked by her past. Hooked by a stupid mistake she had made several years previously and a selection of photographs which could, and would, destroy her if they ever came to light. They would cause untold damage and pain particularly to Annie. The realisation hit her very hard and she sat on the toilet and felt the growing pangs of despair. Then she got angry. Angry at Joe. Angry at Nigel Preece, at Stuart Green, at David but most of all at herself. And then she began to weep silent tears.

CHAPTER 35

The week after my lunch date with Lucy the chairman rang again. This time he wanted me to attend a meeting at The Crown Inn in Barrow, a small village only a few miles from his home and about forty from mine. Still, what was a bit of inconvenience with so much at stake? This was, he said, to be the first meeting of the new committee. The meeting was scheduled for 7-00 p.m. on the Friday evening. Lynn was not pleased as we had arranged to go for a meal with some of her friends but she played the dutiful wife and cancelled. We had begun bickering more and more and I certainly was not paying her enough attention. I left home giving myself plenty of time and then half way to the destination my mobile rang. I glanced at the tiny screen and pulled over. It was the chairman. The meeting was cancelled. He apologised, told me he would contact me on Monday and rang off before I could get a word in. I returned home feeling very pissed off and walked in to face the inevitable row with Lynn. Also that day, Lucy told me that she would be going on holiday the first week in May, just six weeks away. David's parents owned an apartment on the Costa del Sol. I was already feeling apprehensive about her going. It was only for ten days even though it would seem like a long time. I realised my work was suffering as a result of our growing relationship and I just didn't care. The staff were becoming restless but I thought I had them under control. The rumours regarding Stuart Green replacing me were still doing the rounds. I continued to pour scorn on the idea. The lack of quality stock was killing us as a department but I was just accepting everything Nigel told me. There was no point in complaining, life was easier that way and like I said, I had other things on my mind.

Lucy was pulling the strings, something that was a new experience for me. The following Saturday she came to the branch with her daughter Annie. A real cute kid. It threw me a bit. Lucy was her usual chirpy and flirtatious self. She left her car with us whilst she went into Harpley, shopping. There were some very knowing looks from some of the staff but nobody, after she left, took the piss. That in itself should have served as a warning.

The following Monday the chairman rang again. He had decided that Lucy would definitely be the perfect person to head up the new Used Car Accounts Administration Department. Although her job specification would remain virtually unchanged with the planned expansion the size of her department would be increased with additional staff recruited to assist her. It would be a very major promotion with a much bigger salary to reflect her increased responsibilities. She would be a senior manager and would be expected to report to the board. More importantly she would be directly under me, a statement which I thought was most appropriate! She was the final piece of the jigsaw. I was over the moon. This would bring a new dimension to our relationship and make it easier to see one another. I couldn't wait to tell her but when I did she seemed less than enthused, despite the promise of a much increased salary package. I thought maybe it was just the time of the month. Well, you would wouldn't you?

A strange thing happened a couple of days later. Michael Hatton announced that all the managers were required to go the new site. There was much excitement at this. We all knew where the site was and indeed I had been up a few times to have a look. Unfortunately I was never able to gain access to the interior. It was a big warehouse with some land and I could see the massive potential. When we arrived we were all directed to drive into the warehouse. Inside the building seemed huge, the lack of any dividing walls accentuating the overall size. I was surprised to see the chairman and Freddie Fox already there along with John Hatton. My colleagues were all greeted with a warm smile and a handshake. Not me though. When it came to my turn the chairmen barely acknowledged me let alone find a moment to hold a conversation. Freddie Fox grunted at me and even John Hatton had the grace to look slightly embarrassed at his lack of manners. It was all very bizarre.

Fox outlined the plans for the new dealership and even produced some working drawings for us to peruse. Everyone was very enthusiastic as well they might be. This would probably be the biggest dealership in the Midlands and whoever was running it would have a very high profile within the industry. I reckoned I could safely handle the pressures of being both the General Manager at Harpley and the Used Car Sales Director for the Hatton Group. Despite the chairman's indifference my chest was puffed out like a pigeon when I left the meeting.

The next day there was more good news, or so I initially thought. Stuart Green handed in his notice. No one could quite believe it. This was a man who had been with the company since leaving school and although most of the staff viewed him as a wanker he appeared highly rated by those that mattered. Even I had to admit that despite the animosity between us, he appeared on the face of it to have done a decent job at Rednall. It was true that his Business Manager saved him on occasions but still, most sales managers would have swapped dealerships and results and been delighted. My main thought was that given the resources he had at his disposal I could have done better. The normal procedure in the motor trade is that when you hand in your notice you are usually gone within days. Surprisingly it turned out he had given three months notice and hadn't got another job to go to. I immediately decided that his resignation was some sort of protest which turned out to be right on the money.

Lucy and I continued to have long telephone conversations and the odd lunch. We never seemed to manage to have a real date. It was an odd sort of romance but patience is a virtue. And then the time came for her to go on holiday. I gave her an old St. Christopher, which was a family heirloom, to protect her. She was surprisingly touched. She was obviously not happy about going away and sent me several text messages from the airport which softened the blow of our separation.

The sales results in both March and April turned out to be very poor. A couple of salesmen handed in their rifles and went off to work for the opposition. I was angry, even though I could see their point of view. The lack of stock was leaving them with a poor choice to offer and low sales meant low wages. One of them though particularly upset me. This was a guy who I went out on a limb for after he had wrecked his company car a few months earlier. He went out one night and had been with one of our customers at her home. She was a divorcee who came onto him and despite being in a long relationship he succumbed to her advances. Coming back from her home he lost control of his demonstrator on a treacherously wet road and crashed through a fence. He then panicked and despite the car having its radiator holed, he drove off leaving bits of wreckage behind. By the time he reached home all the water had been pumped out of the engine. Not only did the car need extensive body repairs, the engine was terminally damaged as a result of severe overheating. These were costs which the department would have to stand as the company insurance policy had a huge excess. He rang me the next day and I picked up the pieces, literally, including placating the homeowner who agreed not to pursue the matter after the lad agreed to pay for all the damage to the fence and garden, backed up with a guarantee from me. I gave him a real bollocking, not so much for the damage to the car, but because it was caused through playing away from home. I conveniently forgot that I was in the process of doing exactly the same thing. One rule for me and one for the rest. He of course expressed his eternal gratitude for saving his job, his driving licence and most probably his relationship. A few weeks later we had a disagreement over his sales targets and I sent him home for the weekend to cool off. When I returned to work after the weekend his company car keys and letter of resignation were on my desk. Of him there was no sign and I never did see him again. The prat. So much for eternal gratitude and a typical example of the insincerity within the industry.

Still, what did I care, Lucy was back the following Wednesday, a far more important event!

CHAPTER 36

Nigel Preece was having a very good day. He picked up his office phone and dialled a mobile number. It rang once before Jack Swift answered,

'Yes Nigel.'

'Now Jack. Can you find space at the auction for ten cars? I've got no room here and there's a good chance that you'll get the chance to dispose of them.'

'I can always find room. What's the story? Have you had a sudden busy period?'

'They all belong to our preferred finance company. Our friend Mr. Quinn has exploited the rules and it's entirely legal. For once I take my hat off to him. I wish I'd thought of it. Fortunately this time his knowledge will favour us and I reckon it's going to cause quite a stir.'

'What's he done?'

'Only exposed the motor trade's best kept secret.'

'What's that?'

'Suppose you buy a car on a hire purchase agreement. On the finance form there is a section regarding halves and thirds. I've never yet come across a salesman or Business Manager who has explained this section to the customer and I doubt whether any customers read all the small print either. If they ever do they probably don't fully understand it. Once you've paid a third of the total amount payable on the agreement if you default on the payment the finance company has to go to court to get the car back.'

'I know that.'

'But I bet you don't know that once you've paid half the total amount payable then if you no longer need the car you can tell the finance company to take it away and you owe them nothing.'

Swift answered with genuine surprise, 'I didn't know but why would you want to?'

'Let's say you took out a long term agreement to keep the payments down. You know how easy it has been to get credit in the past. Some customers have been able to borrow more than the car was worth and we've helped of course by adjusting invoices to show a deposit if need be. There might have been finance outstanding on the part exchange or the customer might have had no cash but a good credit record. Trouble is two or three years down the line, when the customer wants to change the car again they owe far more than it's worth. Quinn has started convincing clients to exploit the rules and just hand the car back. The finance company gets heavy with the customer of course and threatens that they will be on a blacklist but it's all just hot air. There's nothing they can do about it because it's the law and Quinn is convincing more and more customers to exploit the clause. I'm not convinced he doesn't ring the finance company himself on the customer's behalf. We have a meeting tomorrow with the finance rep. No doubt they'll threaten us with changing the system in favour of personal loans which means a cut in our commission and VB.'

'What's VB?'

'Volume bonus. It's the commission we get in relation to how much money we've sold, or rather that the customer has borrowed. We get a cut from the interest on each agreement plus a scale of commission on the volume of business the company does.'

'Sounds like a good deal.'

'It is. When our Business Manager Bentley gets to hear about Quinn's methods, because we sell more cars here, there will be more and more profit opportunities for us. As you know Bentley is the best. I reckon more and more Business Managers across the group will adopt the strategy even if it is only short term, so I want to keep our finance company sweet for as long as possible. I'm sure you can do something on your rate without affecting my cut of course.'

Swift sighed. 'You are a greedy bastard at times Nigel. Get the cars down here. I'm sure we can sort something out.'

Preece laughed and cut the connection just as John Hatton walked into his office holding a letter which he handed to Preece.

'Did you know about this?' he asked belligerently. 'It's a letter of resignation from Stuart Green.'

Preece knew. In fact he had told him to do write it.

'You know the reason he has handed in his notice' Preece answered forcefully, emphasising each point. 'You know Foxy told him months ago that Stuart was going to be the GM at Harpley,' he continued letting his impatience show. 'I know it's not been talked about since and he's pissed off. I accept that Foxy was slightly inebriated at the time but Stuart's ready for a new challenge and I think he's earned it. Harpley will be the jewel in the company crown and he wants it. It's clear the new dealership is some way off but if we move him now he can steady the ship and the transition will be that much smoother. It makes sense John. Your man is hardly setting the world on fire. In fact he's taking the place backwards,' Preece ended forcefully.

'New car sales are showing an increase,' Hatton retorted.

'Only on the back of this new scheme of his which is something else we need to discuss. I'm concerned the whole thing will backfire.'

Hatton knew that he was probably right. The sales results from Harpley, despite a slight increase in new car sales, did not make good reading. The situation would have to be addressed and he was not looking forward to it. He hated confrontation. He couldn't understand why Harpley had gone pear shaped. Quinn had done so well the previous year, but his mind was clearly not on the job despite his brainwave regarding finance customers. Perhaps the rumours of an affair with Lucy Thomas were true. He had dismissed them when they were first mentioned and reports of lengthy phone calls also reached his ears. However the phone bills didn't record internal calls and he never experienced any difficulty getting through to either of them. Still, he was going to have to find a way of broaching the subject with Quinn without causing offence.

'Face it John,' Preece went on, 'Quinn's not up to it.'

'He did it last year. He just needs better stock and more of it and he is taking in more part exchanges against new cars' Hatton answered with some irritation.

'But they are not our cars John they belong to the finance company'

Preece smiled wearily not in the least bit surprised that John had failed to grasp what Quinn was up to. 'There is no way that I am sending him good stock when he doesn't perform. Foxy would have my balls if I supply Harpley at the moment. Joe Quinn is more interested in shagging the staff than doing a proper job running his department.'

'But that's just rumour and gossip.'

'Rumour and gossip my arse. There's no smoke without fire John. If it were up to me he would be out the door. However, I know you like him so why not compromise. Send Stuart to Harpley and stop him from leaving. Move Harry Morgan from Harvington to Rednall. He deserves a chance with a bigger dealership and move Quinn to Harvington. He can hardly make a mess there. The place is well organised and full of long term staff. You know it makes sense,' Preece ended pleased that he had not gone over the top and said 'even you could run it' which was what he was thinking.

Hatton knew he was being manoeuvred but he had to admit the logic was sound. Perhaps moving Quinn was the answer. Maybe a shock would get him back on track and performing to his capabilities.

'Let me talk to Freddie and Dad about it,' he said rising from the chair, knowing that he was beaten.

Preece allowed himself a smile. His plans were all going rather well.

CHAPTER 37

It had been a long ten days but the following day Lucy was due to return to work. Unwittingly I threw myself back into work and we produced a decent week and a half's performance to report to the board. The reason for the improvement didn't register with me at all. I was just putting the finishing touches to a deal when the phone rang. It was Lucy.

'Hi,' was all she said, all she needed to say. My mood instantly lightened.

'Hi yourself,' I answered. 'Didn't think I would hear from you until tomorrow.'

'I made an excuse as soon as we got back. We only landed two hours ago. I've missed you and I needed to talk to you.'

'I've missed you too,' I said. I was surprised by her show of emotion. It wasn't like her, she was never normally a needy person. We chatted for ten minutes and then she made her excuses and rang off. I spent the rest of the afternoon feeling as though a weight had been lifted from my shoulders. I didn't even snap at one of my more irritating salesman when he came in for a price. We had christened him 'village' and he thought it was because he lived in one. He was most surprised when someone enlightened him by adding 'idiot' on to the nickname. Still, it could have been worse. I worked with a guy once who we christened 'Thrush,' and he never did work out why? A cruel world to be involved in at times is the retail motor industry.

The following day I had plans to make. It was the annual Hatton Group staff get together that evening. All the car sales teams, accounts and admin staff go to an old country mansion so that the Directors can tell everyone how great they are and hand out a few awards. The Sales Managers award for the previous year was not going to be presented to me which I found somewhat surprising as we had performed so well. Still, at least Green hadn't won it either.

Monkhampton Grange is a fine old Elizabethan house set in large grounds with a small lake. It has been converted into a small and very select hotel. The owners erect two marquees for the company. A small one to use as a bar and a much larger one to use for the speeches or to eat in should the weather become inclement. Someone once described the event as the annual Hatton chip insertion. Others as the annual brainwashing. Still, the drinks and food are free and most of the staff just use the evening as an excuse to get ratted at the Directors expense. The downside is that everyone has to endure a speech from Foxy and a bit of glad handing. Fox's speech usually involves telling the assembled throng what a great job everyone at Rednall is doing and then handing down varying degrees of criticism to the other branches. I had agreed to give a couple of the lads a lift so they could have a drink but now I knew Lucy was going to be there I told them they would have to make their own arrangements. The looks of annoyance barely registered. Something far more important had come up. Or at least I hoped it would! There had been enough long chats and the odd lunch and it was time to get serious. If there was the slightest chance of taking Lucy home I was making sure that I was in a position to do so without any other encumbrance.

When Lucy arrived that evening she made quite an entrance. She looked stunning. Despite it being early May, the evening was very warm. She was wearing a very colourful gypsy skirt and a white, lace edged, centre buttoned sleeveless blouse. It accentuated her recently acquired tan and I'm sure I wasn't the only one there wondering how far the tan extended. I was the only one likely to find out however. Her earrings were huge gold rings which on anyone else would have looked pretentious. On her, they merely enhanced the Romany look. She wore dark glasses and I knew that this was to disguise which way she was looking. She carried a white shawl and a small leather shoulder bag. I could see several of the blokes giving her the eye. It made me quite jealous. I watched Stuart Green leering at her as she conversed with him and Nigel. From the body language it was clearly not a conversation she was enjoying and she quickly moved away. I just wanted to hit Green. Not surprisingly he had withdrawn his notice although no one was giving a reason for his change of heart and I wasn't concerned. I acknowledged Lucy when she arrived with a barely discernible nod. Earlier in the day we had agreed to keep a low profile and not draw attention to ourselves together. Part of the reason for that was that I didn't want to look like the lost sheep following her around. We thought we were being so discreet. In reality of course our relationship had become the talk of the company.

After several rounds of welcome drinks everyone was herded into the larger marquee to hear the gospel according to Freddie. It went pretty much as I expected. Rednall was a fine example of a well run dealership with an outstanding sales department. What a yawn. He neglected the fact that without a colossal amount of finance income, over which Green had no control, then the performance would have been quite mediocre. Or that Rednall had more stock, by far the biggest catchment area and was the biggest dealership in the area with decent parking facilities. Still, it would be a different matter when the new Harpley branch was completed. We would see who was king of the hill then. We did manage some praise for the previous year and then took some stick for our year to date performance. Even our CSP rating only got a passing mention and we had made the greatest improvement by far of any dealership in the Group, even if it had cost us a few tank full's of fuel and free mud flaps or mats. I could see some of the lads were taking it personally. The chairman stayed in the background. I did give him a cheery 'Hello' when I first arrived. All I got in return was a frosty look. It was a far cry from the warmth of his telephone conversations.

By the time Foxy ended his speech and made several awards the evening sunshine had given way to darkness. The company had organised some further entertainment so there was a short break and I took the opportunity to take some fresh air. I sensed Lucy was close by as I could smell her distinctive perfume on the balmy night air. Turning, I could see her standing alone by the lake. I walked across, took her hand and guided her behind the rhododendrons lining the lake. We were out of site of the marquee. We kissed, hungrily. The sense of longing hung in the air. Without speaking we followed the path by the lake and found ourselves at the rear of the marquee.

'Wait a second,' she said giggling, 'I'm desperate for the loo.'

I released her hand thinking a moment of promised passion had escaped but she was back within two minutes.

'Let's get out of here,' she whispered. With no one in sight we carried on to the makeshift car park and like two naughty school kids playing truant we made good our escape. I drove away steadily not wanting to draw attention to our departure. Lucy gave me some directions and I quickly realised that we were heading towards Rednall.

'Am I taking you home?' I asked.

'Eventually,' she answered softly. Her hand strayed to my inner thigh. She just rested it there and I could feel myself becoming aroused. From the slight smile on her face I knew that she was also feeling my discomfort and enjoying the power she was exerting over me at that moment. I knew that there was only one way I was going to get comfortable! We reached the outskirts of Rednall and she directed me on to the ring road. I had never taken this route before having always entered Rednall from the opposite side of town.

'Take the first exit,' she said 'and then the third exit off the roundabout.' It was just like taking a driving lesson. I did as I was instructed and realised we were in Hornsby Lane. I knew, or thought I knew, exactly where we were heading.

'Do I turn right at the next roundabout?' I asked.

'Of course,' she answered with just a trace of humour.

I was beginning to feel slightly disappointed. Turning right and then left would take me into the lane that led to her house. Turning right and going straight on would take me to the complex behind her home. I didn't argue. I turned right and then she said,

'And now left.'

As I turned left her house was on the right. I almost indicated right but she said quickly and with more than a trace of amusement,

'And go straight on,' she chuckled. 'You didn't really think I was going home just yet did you?' I hoped this would be the only tease of the evening. I smiled and drove quickly past her home and down the narrow winding lane until we reached the mere. The council had done a wonderful job with the mere which was actually a man made lake formed from excavations by the old and long defunct brick company. The lane led only to the angling club. There was however a car park of sorts, which had been roughly constructed by the side of the mere. It was a popular spot for courting couples. At this time in the evening it was deserted as we were a little early for the quickie brigade who would be here when the pubs kicked out. In any event she directed me right to the end and I found that with a little careful manoeuvring we were out of sight of the car park entrance and with a view over the moonlit mere. It was a beautiful setting with just a very light mist beginning to appear on the surface of the undisturbed water. Not that we gave each other much time to appreciate it! I turned off the engine and said a silent prayer to the erection God to quell my nerves.

Almost without pause Lucy reached across and pulled me towards her. As our lips came together my hand reached down for the seat recline lever. I pulled it and she fell back sharply pulling me with her. Her hands were at my belt and mine at her blouse. Her skirt had ridden up and I realised that she was naked beneath its folds. My trousers were heading towards my ankles and as I unclasped her front loading bra my mouth searched hungrily for her tiny nipple. As she slipped my jockeys down I raised my head and we paused and looked into each others eyes. Then I felt her hands pull my buttocks towards her as she raised her hips to greet me. She gave a small gasp as I entered her. The erection God had heeded my prayer and the following day I was forced to clean the inside of the car windscreen myself to erase the outline of her footprints.

CHAPTER 38

As the speeches ended most of the employees headed towards the bar to escape the oppressive heat inside the marquee. Two of the managers had begun to roll up the sides to give everyone a degree of comfort before the light entertainment began. Preece spotted Lucy leaving the marquee but resisted the temptation to follow her despite wanting to apologise for Green's crass behaviour when she arrived. He greeted her cordially enough that evening as she arrived at the Grange. The conversation had been brief. He wanted to remind her quietly of her responsibilities. Then Green mentioned holiday snaps. Lucy flushed and told both Green and himself to leave her alone. He expected these minor setbacks from time to time. He was in no doubt however that in the long run, she would keep her side of the bargain. With so much to lose she was left with no real choice. He smiled as he saw Quinn leave the marquee and he rose from his seat, went to the front of the marquee and joined John Hatton and Freddie Fox who were sitting together, deep in conversation. Fox's ruddy complexion suggested that he had already enjoyed quite a few drinks. A good time to put the boot into Quinn.

'Noticed anyone missing John?' he asked as he pulled up a chair.

'No, should I?' Hatton asked in return slightly annoyed that Preece had joined them without invitation.

'Well, I can see all the managers with their respective teams but the Harpley manager seems to be missing,' Preece said as though he was imparting a great knowledge.

'Maybe he's gone to the loo.'

Preece grinned. John Hatton was clearly embarrassed and he wasn't about to let him off the hook with Foxy in attendance.

He didn't dislike John, no one did, but he was a real limp wrist as far as he was concerned. A distinct lack of backbone. The thought that there was any chance of him one day becoming chairman filled him, and others, with dread. Everyone, from the yard sweeper to the senior managers, agreed it would be the beginning of the end for the company should the day ever come to pass that John Hatton became the head of the Hatton Group.

'I can't see our used car accounts lady either. Maybe she's gone to the loo as well,' he said with just a hint of sarcasm.

He could see Foxy was getting annoyed with the exchange, so he continued.

'You're really going to have to do something about this situation you know. Their relationship is interfering with work. I have a job getting through to either of them on the phone and some of the other managers have complained as well. Both their lines seem to be engaged all the time. And it's not just their work that is suffering. Other people are spending time gossiping and speculating. These things can be bad for morale and God knows what will happen if her husband gets to hear anything or his wife finds out?'

'But there is no proof that anything is happening between them,' Hatton answered, his anger and frustration mounting. He didn't need this conversation in front of Foxy and really wanted to tell Nigel to mind his own business, but he knew it would be futile.

'No John?' Foxy interjected, 'if they've both left its proof enough for me. Speak to him John and make it soon. At our next board meeting I shall be insisting that we implement the management changes we have discussed. I think we are being more than fair in giving Quinn a second chance. It's only your loyalty to him that's saving him from sanction. I agree with Nigel. He's lost the plot. As for Mrs. Thomas, she's always been a flighty bitch ever since we employed her. I thought marriage and motherhood might mature her but she still likes the sound of her own voice far too much for my liking.'

As Preece took a sip of his drink he noted with satisfaction that John had become more than a little flushed and, unlike Foxy, it was not through drink. He had to admit to himself however that he was jealous of Quinn.

Preece was no different from many other of his male colleagues in lusting after Lucy, and although he had half heartedly suggested a date, he had always been rebuffed. He had seen the photographs of her and Green teased him with the knowledge of his one night with her. The thought that Quinn was probably getting something he felt he should have had years ago gnawed at him. Far from consuming him with jealousy however the situation only served to strengthen his resolve. Lucy actually falling for Quinn had not been part of the plan. Still, if it led to Quinn getting the boot and Lucy being another casualty then so be it. He could live with that.

CHAPTER 39

For Lucy the evening proved to be the best of times and the worst of times. She arrived at the Grange with her colleagues determined that she would spend time with Joe despite their both agreeing to keep a low profile. She didn't give a damn any longer what people thought and she was fed up of just talking to him down a phone line and having the odd lunch. Nigel Preece, Stuart Green, the photographs and the stupid plotting could go to hell as could David. Annie would have to understand. She would make her. Yet even as she arrived, her resolve, so positive when soaking in the bath earlier, began to weaken. Bravado is a great conviction in relaxed solitude, quite another when in public and faced with reality.

The first two people she met as she stepped into the marquee were Preece and Green. Preece merely asked if she had enjoyed a good holiday. Green asked leeringly if he could see the holiday snaps. She knew what he was really referring to and that she was in their grip. She despised them both and herself and was tempted to turn around and walk out and then, as she wheeled away, she spotted Joe and knew she must see him. Perhaps she could find the courage to tell him about the photographs but even as she thought came into her head, she knew she couldn't take the risk. Besides, it wasn't just the photographs now.

The photographs had been taken only a few weeks after she and David were married. He had gone away on a stag weekend and on the Saturday night she decided on impulse to go to a friend's party. The only reason she went was to get her own back at David for going away. The first person she met when she walked into the party was Stuart Green. She had known him for several years having joined the company around the same time. Although they knew each other well enough they were not close friends. He asked her out several times but she always refused. He wasn't a bad looking guy, he just wasn't her type. To his credit he never took offence at her refusals. She could never accuse him of acting like a spoilt child even though he persisted in his pursuit of her right up until the day of her marriage, despite David supposedly being a close friend of his.

The party was in full swing with music pounding to a heavy beat when she arrived. There was plenty of drink flowing and she knew that some of the partygoers were doing drugs. Pills or joints were not her scene however, and never would be. She circulated. There were plenty of people she knew and Stuart always seemed to be on hand whenever her glass became empty. She enjoyed herself but just before midnight she began to feel a little unsteady and went upstairs in search of somewhere to lie down. Two of the bedrooms were in use, with couples copulating furiously. A third room, which turned out to be the master bedroom, was locked. As she tried the door Stuart conveniently appeared at her elbow and produced a key. She felt a moments concern but was to dizzy to object to his presence. He unlocked the door and pushed it open. Inside, the bed had clearly seen some action but she was too tired and disorientated to care. She was only just aware of Stuart following her into the room as she crossed the floor and collapsed on to the bed. It was her last memory before she woke up naked the next morning with an equally naked Stuart Green beside her. Her head was pounding and she rushed to the adjacent bathroom and was violently sick. Returning to the bedroom she was confronted by a now wide awake Stuart Green grinning at her from the bed and looking like the cat that had got the cream. He reached out to her but she grabbed her clothes and locked herself in the bathroom. Dressing quickly she opened the door to find Green standing naked in front of her. Her eyes were drawn to his erect penis and she wanted to vomit again. Taking a deep breath, she evaded his grasp, pushed past him without answering his entreaties to stop and fled the house. She got into her car without looking back and as she drove away she began to cry. She could not believe she had been so foolish. Was it a blessing or a curse that she could not remember?

That Sunday had been awful. She was badly hung-over and feeling deeply ashamed. She could not get the image of herself and Green out of her head. She found herself wanting to bathe all the time in an effort to feel clean. But no matter how much she scrubbed it made no difference. She couldn't even cry rape because she could remember nothing at all from entering the bedroom until waking in the morning. She was dreading David coming home and frightened of her reaction if he wanted to make love to her. Fortunately, when he arrived home, he was also suffering from the effects of too much alcohol and not enough sleep. He had gone almost straight to bed. That night she struggled to sleep and when she did finally drop off her dreams were haunted by the events of the previous evening. She awoke several times fearing that it was Green laid beside her and not David.

Over the next two days at work she managed to avoid any calls from Green but she knew it could not go on. Then, on the Wednesday after the party he appeared at her office. He said he had a present for her and tossed a large envelope on to her desk before turning away and leaving without further comment. Her first reaction was to throw the envelope in the bin but she knew she had to open it. The contents shocked her so badly that she almost fainted.

The envelope contained photographs of her taken from several different angles. She was apparently having sex with a man who she assumed was Green. She couldn't be sure as his head had been obscured. Some images depicted her kneeling before him with her face against his groin. Others showed her on all fours with him behind her. Some were taken from above with her on her back and there were more with her knelt astride him with her eyes closed facing the camera. All were dated and she knew that the copies she held in her hand were not the originals. She dashed to the toilet and retched so violently that she could taste blood in her mouth. She could not believe that she was capable of doing some of the acts she appeared to have committed nor believe that she had been photographed committing them. She remained seated on the toilet seat for almost half an hour and then decided that the only course of action was to confront Green. She found an empty office and rang him. She hoped the call wouldn't go to his voicemail. It didn't.

'What do you want?' she asked, hating him with all her being and dreading the answer.

'Nothing, nothing at all. It's our little secret. Just remember I have the originals as a souvenir of our night of passion. You really were quite a tiger. We must do it again sometime,' he laughed.

'You fucking evil, sick bastard!' she hissed with growing hysteria as she slammed down the phone and once again fled to the cloakroom. She tore the photographs into tiny pieces and flushed them down the loo. With a supreme effort she managed to compose herself before returning to her desk.

The following day Green rang her regarding work and acted as though nothing had ever happened. Despite her hatred and disgust of him she acted professionally, dealt with his query and had continued to do so. Surprisingly for several years Green never mentioned the photographs again and her relationship with him took on a modicum of civility particularly after he began dating one of the admin girls from Flushing Road, Wendy Burrows, who Lucy knew quite well. She was tempted to warn Wendy off Green but thought better of it for fear of any backlash from her actions.

Lucy was determined to make her marriage work. Green eventually married Wendy and Lucy and David attended the ceremony, although she persuaded David not to perform the duties of best man. But any illusions she harboured that the images had been totally forgotten were to be cruelly swept away. Nigel Preece had rung her requesting a meeting in his office. She complied with his summons, not the least bit concerned. Even Green's presence in the office did not surprise her. Then she saw the brown envelope on the desk and tensed as the memories came flooding back. She wasn't surprised that Green had shown the photographs to Preece. She knew, despite her angry protestations, that she would have little choice other than to comply with what they explained they wanted her to do. David didn't particularly matter any longer but now there was Annie to consider. And nothing would be allowed to cause Annie any pain. It was ironic that she had only just admitted to herself that she had strong feelings for Joe Quinn, and now this.

The charade had been running for some months now and she begun to fool herself into believing that there might be some way that it would not all end in tears. Indeed, she found it remarkably easy to follow the occasional instructions she received from Preece.

The holiday had been a complete disaster. No matter how she tried she could not stop thinking about Joe. She, David and Annie had gone with two friends to his parent's holiday home in Malaga. She actually looked forward to the break even though she knew she would miss Joe, but she and David bickered constantly. The situation was made even more tense with Annie being taken ill with a tummy bug. It was one evening, whilst taking a walk by herself on the beach, that Lucy had decided to sleep with Joe and to hell with the consequences. The first thing she did on returning home was to make an excuse to go to the supermarket ostensibly for some medication for Annie. She rang Joe from the car park. She knew she had fallen in love and made herself believe that it would all work out. Resolve is a wonderful thing. Until the moment of truth we can all do anything we wish.

After their first night of passion Joe dropped her off just around the corner from her home and as she approached the house she could see that it was in darkness. She was relieved that David had gone to bed and she hoped he would be asleep. She unlocked the door quietly. There was no sound anywhere and by the light of the moon she went to the kitchen and made herself a coffee. She retired to the lounge, turned on a table lamp and curled up in the corner of the sofa. When she and Joe had parted earlier she felt so happy and content. There was none of the post coital depression that she felt immediately after having sex with David. And, by making love to Joe, she had exacted a kind of revenge on Preece, Green and to some extent David. She and he were now both equals. They were both adulterers.

She imagined she could still feel Joe inside her and then the realisation of her predicament began to hit home. For a few hours she had escaped from reality but she knew that she was still trapped.

'Oh Joe,' she whispered into her coffee mug. And then, not for the first time, she began to weep. There would be many more tears over the coming months.

Chapter 40

The straw that broke the camel's back came for me on the last Monday in May just a few weeks after Lucy and I truly became lovers. May was shaping up to be yet another bad month. New car performance was poor and the used car department was still in dire need of an infusion of fresh stock. We were way behind budget and without the proper stock level there was no chance to make up the shortfall. The chairman though was still in a buoyant mood. There had been no more meetings arranged although he had taken to ringing me every ten days or so with a message of support. It was much appreciated but it didn't alter the fact that we were doing badly. And performance had to be bad for it to be concerning me.

Lucy was hit and miss. Some days she couldn't live without me and would surprise me with a text message or an unexpected call. Other days she would be cool, miserable and distracted. Lynn was just cool and distracted and our relationship was getting rapidly worse.

I've never enjoyed Mondays, either personally or professionally. For us managers in the motor trade it's a time of intense activity. Mondays mean endless reports and forecasts. Doesn't seem to matter which company it is the directors always want chapter and verse as to what has happened over the weekend. Monday to Friday results never get the same scrutiny. Saturday and Sunday you have to do well. You can break all the sales records going during the week but it will never receive the same acknowledgment that comes with a good weekend. There are an awful lot of sales managers who hold back deals in the week just so that they can report a good weekend. I know, I've done it myself.

This particular Monday I was reporting a bad weekend performance on the back of an equally bad week. More often than not I fax the results to head office to save Jim Ashton, who coordinates the results for the directors, from having to ring. It saves him time. Unfortunately I got caught up dealing with a customer complaint so I had no chance to transmit our results. Now, as non productives go, Jim is not a bad bloke but this day when he rang, he hit a nerve. I gave him the figures with as much enthusiasm as I could muster and then he said,

'That's not very good is it? Rednall produced a cracking weekend and Harvington wasn't far behind. You're lagging badly.'

As I have said Jim isn't a bad bloke and maybe he was just trying to have a joke, but I wasn't in the mood. I snapped.

'Who the fuck do you think you are to criticise me?' There was a voice in my head telling me to calm down and put my brain into gear but it was way too late.

'Had a good weekend did you?' I continued. 'Sat by the fire watching the tele whilst I'm at work flogging my guts out to keep people like you in a job? I've got no fucking stock and consequently no profit and all I get is shit. If I don't start getting some support here this company can go fly!' and I slammed the phone back in its cradle before he could respond.

I knew I shouldn't have reacted like that and it was unfair on Jim but it was too late now. I thought I would give it an hour and then ring and apologise. I was way too late of course, the damage had been done. I was not surprised when thirty minutes later the phone rang and it was Fox's secretary requesting my presence in his office at 11-30a.m. I could have done without a bollocking as I felt bad enough as it was. Then I realised it would be a good chance to get things off my chest. I knew he wouldn't sack me. After all I was still the chairman's blue eyed boy. Looking on the bright side Lucy was off work in the afternoon, having swopped her usual day off, and being in Rednall would give me the excuse to pop round. Maybe some afternoon delight was in the offing?

All the way to Rednall I was running through my head what I was going to say. Home truths there would be plenty of. After all good old Freddie wasn't on the committee so he had no future. I was kept waiting outside his office for ten minutes and then his door opened and John

Hatton appeared. I was surprised to see him. I hadn't given any thought to him being present. Regardless, it didn't really matter.

John apologised for the delay and ushered me in. Fox instructed me to be seated at the conference table with an imperious wave of his hand and John seated himself opposite.

'I won't beat about the bush,' Fox said in his usual brusque tone.

I thought, 'this will be a first,' but kept quiet.

'It's time for change,' he droned on, 'so we are moving Stuart Green to Harpley and Harry Morgan to Rednall. You will go to Harvington. We like,' but I let him go no further. As I listened to his pronouncement my blood pressure went through the roof. I felt my fists clench and through gritted teeth I snarled,

'So finally we get the truth. Nearly six months I've had to put up with denials, and having believed the crap you've spouted and told my staff this change would never happen, it does. What kind of people are you? Run a company, you couldn't run a fucking bath!' It felt only a little better. Fox turned red with anger but managed to control himself while Hatton just sat in embarrassed silence.

'Do I have a choice?' I hissed.

'No.' Fox paused doing very well to keep himself under control. 'Well yes, I suppose you do have a choice,' he answered smiling at his own little piece of wit. Was he hoping?

'I suppose the other two know do they?'

'Yes, they have been informed.'

Should I quit? I was tempted but I had a future to think of. Just what was going on? I had the chairman singing my praises but Fox was moving me to a smaller dealership. It didn't make sense.

'When does this take effect?' I asked, fighting to keep calm.

'The other two are telling their teams now so you need to inform yours and then we want you at Harvington tomorrow. Nigel Preece has agreed to be the on site General Manager at Harvington as well as his role of Group Used Car Manager so you will report directly to him. He will remain here though for the time being until we decide when his appointment will take effect. I, we, expect you to liaise with him when the need arises.'

So Nigel was to be my boss. He had always been notionally the General Manager at Harvington. It had always been just a paper appointment to appease the manufacturer who as part of the franchise agreement insisted on a General Manager at each branch. There were so many things I wanted to say. Hatton sat silent and obviously discomforted. I wanted to belt him. I was in turmoil. I got up, said 'Thanks' as sarcastically as I could manage and left the room. I thought about slamming the door but didn't. Instead I just left it hanging open hoping it would express my contempt for the whole situation.

I was shaking with anger and shock by the time I got back to the car. It was so unfair and then I realised that if I repeated that out loud I would sound like a real loser. I sent Lucy a text message and she rang me back but when I asked if I could pop round she told me that Annie was off school and that she'd rather I didn't. I didn't press the point and told her what had happened. She was surprisingly indifferent. She didn't mention the future either professionally or personally. She just said she would talk to me the next day and cut the connection.

I sat there feeling more than a little hurt. This was turning into a really bad day. I was just about to drive away when the phone rang. It was the chairman.

'I know you think you've just been given some bad news but don't worry about it. Nothing has changed for the future. Look on it as good experience. Stuart Green won't do any good at Harpley. He doesn't have your flair, experience or intelligence.'

'So why make the changes?' I asked.

'You have to understand that there are a lot of politics involved in running a family business and Freddie is the Managing Director. It's important for you to remember that he isn't part of the committee. There was no real point in his membership as he will be retiring. He just wants to flex his power a bit before he goes. Just do what he asks for now. The building work has now commenced inside the new premises so I reckon it will only be a matter of months before you're back at Harpley and in a much more senior role.'

I was buoyed by this and said so. He replied,

'Just get on with it Joe. You will inherit some good staff at Harvington and it might give you some ideas. Harry Morgan has done a good job there. If you have any problems with Mrs. Thomas you can tell her that I will have a letter of intent for her shortly and when she has signed it we can work out her contract. I think as we get into the latter part of the year then things will progress quite quickly.'

With that he rang off. My mood had altered totally. I wasn't looking forward to telling the staff but it had to be done. Harvington would not be so bad. It would be a change. It was closer to Rednall and closer to Lucy. I was completely overlooking the fact that I was leaving a dealership that was in deep crap, in no little part through my efforts, or lack of them, and going to a dealership that was doing very well. I was still heading for the top and no one could stand in my way.

CHAPTER 41

Jake woke with a start. He threw back the blankets instantly alert and then realised that the noise was only the sound of the bin men in the courtyard below. Rising from the bed he went through to the kitchen and broke off some more bread and a little cheese. He was hungry but he was used to hunger and the simple meal would sustain him. Splashing cold water on his face revived him. He did not allow himself the luxury of a shower. Better for now to remain as a tramp with his lank, unkempt hair and straggling beard. He needed to contact the accountant. He needed answers and more, he needed the missing box and could only hope that the accountant had not done something precipitous. The temptation to use the phone in the flat was almost overwhelming. It was still connected and he was certain, having dismantled it to check, that it wasn't bugged, but the line could be tapped. He was now even more convinced that the break in had been the work of an amateur. The tidying up had just been too sloppy and he was certain that had it been the security services he would either have been in custody or dead by now.

Jake left the flat and walked purposefully down the road towards a phone box on the corner. He rang the familiar number and the call was answered on the third ring.

'Anderson Building,' a female voice announced. 'How may I direct your call?'

'Nelson accounts please,' Jake responded.

'One moment sir.' There was only a few seconds pause before she came back on the line. 'I'm afraid that business is no longer listed in this building sir.'

Jake felt the tension within him increase as he asked,
'Do you know where it has located to?'

Despite his training and years of experience he was sweating now. He wanted to reach down the line and grab her by the throat. She seemed to take an age but in reality it was only seconds before she came back on the line.

'The business has transferred to Harpley sir,' and she gave him an address and telephone number.

'Thank you. One last thing, how long ago was this?'

There was another pause. Was she reporting his interest or just getting irritated by his persistence?

'Two weeks ago.'

He cut the connection. It fitted with his suspicions. He tried the number the receptionist had given him. It was unobtainable. Odd, but he did have an address. Where in the name of Allah was Harpley? He had an atlas in the flat but first he needed to be sure that the reaction from the receptionist had been innocent. For the next hour he wandered up and down the street mingling with the crowds and pausing to look in shop windows but never losing sight of the phone box. Nothing happened to arouse his suspicions and he returned to the flat. He found Harpley on the map and realised that there was not enough fuel in the van to get him there. In any event Harpley would have to wait. He needed to sanitize the flat, the garage and all its contents.

Working calmly through the afternoon Jake constructed a bomb. All the supplementary equipment he needed had been concealed in various innocent looking cans around the garage. He had fuses, spent cartridges, smokeless gunpowder, mercury fulminate powder, sulphur, potassium chlorate powder, several cans of petrol and an electric ignition, bought from a hobby store, which would normally be used to power a tiny rocket motor in a model boat. Connecting the device to an ordinary kitchen electric timer would give him ample time to be well away before the detonation. By late afternoon he was set. He left the flat and walked two miles to the nearest major bus station. It didn't take him long to ascertain that there was a National Express service running North, which passed through Harpley although it was a circuitous journey leaving late in the morning. He had enough cash left for the fare but buying further food would be a problem.

Returning to the flat Jake rested through the early part of the evening, until the sound of car doors slamming in the courtyard below woke him around nine. He looked cautiously round the curtain and saw the landlord, Sadiq Khan and his family, returning to their flat. Feeling hungry again he ate a little more of his meagre rations before placing the remainder in his rucksack. As he sat back on the sofa he felt a coin roll from his pocket and in the act of retrieving it he put his hand down the back of the cushions and was elated to find further coinage. A search of the other chairs revealed further errant coins. His find didn't amount to much but at least it would provide further sustenance before he met the accountant.

Just before midnight he went down to the garage. He had long since removed the chassis identification plate from the Transit and ground away the numbers from the engine block. He placed one of the cans of fuel in the van before opening the garage doors and then climbing into the driver's seat. The vehicle started on the first turn of the key, the battery having been on charge for most of the day. Depressing the clutch he attempted to engage first gear. The gear stick would not move. It had happened before and Jake turned the motor off, put the gearbox into second and turned the ignition key. The van lurched forward and the clutch freed itself. The brakes stuck momentarily and then also freed. He drove out of the garage, stopped, got out, closed the doors, got back in and drove away. If anyone saw him he knew not, but the risk was worth it and after tonight he hoped it would no longer matter.

He only drove a short distance before turning into a disused factory and parking at the rear. There were a number of burnt out vehicles close by. Working quickly he removed the number plates and placed them on the drivers seat. Then, he doused the interior of the van with petrol, tossed in a burning rag and walked away. By the time he had gone a hundred yards the tinder dry ply lined interior of the van ensured that the vehicle was well alight. By morning it would be a burnt out shell already beginning to rust and just another statistic. He doubted that the police would even bother filing a report let alone investigate it.

He walked back to the flat and by three in the morning he was ready to leave for good. Loading the wheelbarrow with the remaining bomb making materials, guns and ammunition took him only seconds. The building block sized lump of C4 he placed on top of the load.

Cautiously he went outside and walked to the garage next door but one to his which was below the flat occupied by Sadiq Khan, the owner of the row of flats. The lock yielded easily to him and he opened the door slowly and noiselessly. He returned for the wheelbarrow, having noted that the landlord had left his car parked well to one side in the garage. He pushed the wheelbarrow to the rear of the garage before setting the timer for twenty minutes. He closed the door and returned quickly to his flat. Entering he turned off the electric at the mains so that there would be no premature spark, turned on the gas cooker and left the flat quickly making sure that the door locked behind him.

Jake was almost a mile away when the bomb detonated. He could have sworn that he felt the shockwave. The explosion blew out windows up to half a mile from the blast centre. Sadiq Khan, his wife and three children were atomised in the initial explosion along with all his accounts and records of his various businesses. The secondary gas explosion, which occurred almost simultaneously, and the resulting fireball removed any remaining trace of Jake or his activities. In all ten people were known to have died in the blast which totally levelled the row of flats leaving a crater ten feet deep and twenty feet wide. The police admitted that the death toll could be higher as they had no way of telling how many of the flats were occupied. Jake's driving licence and passport were still on record at the Brighton address and apart from the accountant the only persons who could connect the flat to Jake were now dead.

Although no group claimed responsibility, suspicion fell on the landlord who was known to visit a mosque also frequented Islamic militants. It was never proved beyond doubt but after forensic teams had spent many days on the site and found micro traces of explosive, the investigation concluded that the garage at the centre of the explosion had been used as a bomb making factory and security across the land was heightened still further.

CHAPTER 42

Nigel Preece stood in the window of his office overlooking the car park and watched as Quinn walked briskly to his car. He could tell from his body language that Quinn was not a happy man. Preece had been informed that morning that the proposed managerial changes would be announced during the day. Preece was not unhappy about the changes and indeed, he had encouraged them, although there was a possible danger that they could compromise his own schemes. Much depended on Quinn's reaction.

When he originally devised the plan to get rid of Quinn he did not envisage moving him to Harvington. He was prepared to improvise however and it would be to good effect. If Quinn had been dismissed today he would undoubtedly have started asking questions, which would have provoked other questions regarding his supposed promotion, and which could have caused embarrassment despite Quinn's demise. Preece was confident however that he had covered his tracks, with the exception of Quinn's increasingly close relationship with Lucy. She was the one weak link but they were all too far down the line to turn back now. She may have wobbled on a few occasions but came quickly back onside when reminded of the consequences of any precipitate action. He was in no doubt that he would need to speak with her again. Even Quinn resigning at this point would not have suited Preece. There would be loose ends, in particular the problem of an unfinished relationship. In any event however, he had been reasonably sure that Quinn wouldn't fall on his sword. Quinn still believed he was destined for greater things. Quinn also continued to have the support of John Hatton despite the perceived abject performance at Harpley over the previous months. Given the level and quality of stock which Quinn had at his disposal he had actually done a far better job than anyone realised. The problem for Quinn was that the Directors didn't look at the minutiae of the accounts. The bottom line and performance against budget was all they were interested in. Stock detail was not high on their agenda. John Hatton had all the answers, but no one would explain it all to him. Preece knew that one of the Group accountants was more commercially aware than most of the other bean counters and he hinted to Preece that the situation was unfair. Preece told him to stick to what he was good at and not interfere. None of the other accountants were inclined to worry about the stock problem at just one branch.

Quinn was sinking slowly and that suited Preece just fine. He didn't just want Quinn out of the company; he wanted him out of the industry. If Quinn left before Preece was ready for him to go he might, at some time in the future, make a comeback. Preece wanted him destroyed. Destroyed, humiliated and with his reputation torn to shreds so that no one in the industry would want to be associated with him. Quinn would be lucky to get a job selling pedal cars or push chairs by the time Preece was finished.

He watched Quinn get into his car and pull out his mobile. He guessed that he would be ringing Lucy. Preece pulled his own mobile from the inside pocket of his expensive suit and hit the speed dial for Jack Swift.

Swift answered immediately knowing it was Preece as the number showed in the tiny screen. Preece had forewarned him anyway.

'I'm watching him now. He's not moving so hit the button when I tell you,' Preece growled,

Swift had already retrieved a second mobile from his own pocket and was moving towards the private office at the end of the corridor. This phone was just a cheap pay as you go mobile with only one number programmed into its memory. It was the only phone Swift used in his guise of the chairman to contact Quinn. Quinn had been told to use only this number and to never attempt to contact him on a landline. So far the ruse had worked. Quinn had no need to contact the real chairman in the day to day running of the business. Swift reached his office and closed the door. He would not be disturbed.

Back at Hatton's, Preece saw Quinn take the phone from his ear and prepare to drive off.

'Now,' he said to Swift and cut the connection.

He saw the exhaust fumes as Quinn started the car and it moved forward slightly before stopping abruptly. The fumes ceased as Quinn turned off the engine and answered the call.

Preece smiled with satisfaction and moved away from the window. He sat at his desk and pulled out his diary. With Stuart Green now on his way to Harpley, Preece was going to have to rectify the stocking problem and he knew he could expect a hefty bonus from the suppliers. This would be easy money. He also needed Quinn to carry on failing at Harvington. Preece had only been the notional General Manager at Harvington and now the board wished to make the appointment a bit more permanent. He resisted their wishes citing too heavy a workload at Rednall. He compromised by saying that he would keep a close eye on Quinn. He didn't want any of the failure coming Quinn's way to reflect on him. If anyone tried to implicate him he would merely shrug his shoulders and point out that he had been warning of Quinn's deficiencies for some time. He would decide when he was going to Harvington, if at all.

Preece had however a soft spot for Harvington and Harry Morgan in particular. It was he who had recommended Morgan's elevation from salesman to Sales Manager. Morgan was one of his 'boys' who did exactly as Preece told him to do without question. If everything went to plan he would make sure that Morgan was well rewarded. Preece didn't draw him into his plans however as he was aware that Morgan liked a drink and after a few pints he was apt to become loud and indiscreet. Stuart Green caused him enough problems without any further complications. Still, he did look after him. Preece frequently manipulated stocking records so that vehicles appeared to have been in stock for far less time than was true. He successfully hid an overage stock problem. Over the next few days he would begin to alter the records to more accurately reflect the truth. It would be gradual process however. Preece was confident that Quinn would not notice. Lucy would keep Quinn's mind off the job. He instructed Stuart Green to uncover as many errors, both procedural and administrative, as he could find at Harpley. There would be inevitably some things that Quinn had overlooked. There always were. And in the event of not finding any then he would have to manufacture something.

Preece also intended to destabilise the Harvington sales team.

Morgan was popular with his team and it would not be difficult for him to persuade a couple of them to follow him to Rednall. Two of them actually lived in the town. There would be openings there as Green intended to take a couple of his team to Harpley to fill the vacancies that Quinn had, as yet, been unable to fill. Quinn would also attempt to entice some of his team. A few false promises, such as possible promotions, would prevent any of them from joining him without causing any fuss. Quinn would have to look outside the company for replacements and Preece intended to make this difficult. He had already discussed with Freddie Fox the need for better quality staff and been given the green light to organise a recruitment night at a local hotel. Preece would make sure that this event would not take place for another couple of months. In the meantime he would veto any Quinn appointment, citing the Directors wish for the recruitment night. He would sympathise with Quinn but he would tell him that his hands were tied. Quinn would be short of staff, short of stock and under pressure. He would be marginalised and well and truly stuffed.

CHAPTER 43

The chairman was as good as his word. The following Sunday evening as I walked from the lounge to the kitchen I noticed an envelope on the mat by the front door. Quite obviously in view of the time, it had been hand delivered. I opened it and found that there was another envelope inside. This one was addressed to Lucy. Again I put it straight into my briefcase. I never gave any thought to the fact that it had been delivered to my home instead of work. Or, more pertinently, that it came to me at all rather than straight to Lucy.

First thing at work the following morning I rang Lucy and told her the envelope had arrived. I wanted to deliver it personally of course. Unfortunately I had scheduled a meeting with the dealership's star salesman Simon Kendal which was likely to take up a good part of the morning. Kendal was a man who clearly felt he should be sitting in my seat. On arriving at Harvington after my transfer it was not my intention to rock the boat, but Kendal appeared hell bent on confrontation. Barely an hour went by without him trying to cause a problem. He had no interest in my sales process and was determined to do everything his way. Trouble was, for him, I didn't work that way. Conversely, having been at the dealership for several years, he had a large client base but was too lazy to use it properly. Much of what he did was repeat business which is great. He wasn't maximising his profit margins however. Customers dealt with him because to a large extent they had no other choice. The group operated a system whereby when a salesperson sold a car to a customer that customer remained their client every time they bought a subsequent car. It allowed him to sell cars even when he was off work. Another sales person could do all the work, including delivery of the car, and Kendal could then claim the commission. Consequently he was the salesman who 'sold' the most cars so I couldn't afford to lose him in the short term as it would cause too much upheaval. I knew if he listened to me and acted on my teachings it would improve his profitability and increase his salary but he was having none of it. He was in his own comfort zone and another example of a salesman who was far too fond of his own voice, often failing to listen to what the customer was saying, resulting in lost sales. Almost everyday I was fielding complaints from customers because Kendal had failed to ring them back. John Hatton told me to tread gently with him, but then Kendal tried to knife me in the back. Metaphorically of course.

A prospecting night had been organised just before my arrival. All the sales team were given lists of former and current clients to ring in the hope of convincing them to call at the showroom to buy a new car. However, no one bothered to structure the content of the call. It was yet another example of the Hatton Groups 'get on with it' policy. Prospecting nights are part and parcel of a sales person's role but if not done correctly they can be seriously counter productive. It's no good just picking customers at random. The exercise needs planning and when the client answers the phone, after introducing themselves the first question a sales person should ask is, 'I hope I'm not calling at an inconvenient time?' If it is then tell them politely you'll call back another time. By all means try to arrange a convenient time but don't push it. I also believe that calling clients out of the blue should only be done before seven in the evening because after that I think it becomes intrusive. I don't like it happening to me, so why should we believe motor trade customers are somehow different? My 'I don't believe in prospecting being done unprofessionally' became 'I don't believe in prospecting' when reported by Kendal to John Hatton. Despite my protests, John gave me a real ear bashing. However, I'm not a man who bears a grudge.

The previous Friday a customer who had picked up his car the month before walked into the showroom, clearly in some distress. Kendal had gone home so I dealt with the guy. Turned out he had bought his car on a finance package and in the absence of a Business Manager at Harvington, the previous incumbent having left and not been replaced, Kendal prepared all the documentation himself. He had also structured the deal. He quoted all the repayments to the client, who decided that he could just push himself to afford the car. Sacrifices would have to be made, but it would be a good reason to give up smoking. For the first few months however money would be tight as he was not on a huge salary. When he collected his car he signed all the paperwork and drove away. Kendal neglected to tell him that the agreement was subject to an administration charge, or arrangement fee, of one hundred and fifty pounds, equivalent to more than his monthly payment and payable with the first instalment. This charge is levied by some finance houses on the client for the privilege of borrowing money irrespective of the interest rate charged. There was a time when this charge was always made at the end of the agreement. Now, the finance houses often place a charge at both ends. The cynical view is that as more and more clients settle early, then the finance houses lose out on what is an extra source of income. It caused our client to go overdrawn, pushing him further into debt, as the bank charged him for his overdraft and all because we had failed in a simple duty of care to explain fully his finance agreement. I think customers deserve better! Simon Kendal was being paid in excess of 40k a year. Why does the motor industry reward such mediocrity with alarming regularity?

I feel quite sorry at times for the manufacturers and the workers who screw the vehicles together. All the billions spent on getting a vehicle from the drawing board to the showroom and then they often have to rely on a lazy sales person with no qualifications to sell the product. The industry is long overdue for reform and perhaps a licensing system with sales people requiring a minimum academic qualification, perhaps even to degree level, and being rewarded with remuneration packages which are not heavily reliant on commission payments to make a living. Of course there are good sales people with little or no academic qualifications, but just because someone has a degree doesn't mean they are lacking in character. And character, or personality, is a vital part of a salesperson's armoury. Obtaining a degree, or diploma, demonstrates a willingness to learn and a level of commitment, something too often lacking in the retail motor trade. The breed needs to improve.

Lucy was desperate to know the content of the envelope so I organised a driver to deliver it on the pretext of taking over some overdue deal files. She rang me just before my meeting.

'I adore you,' she said with some feeling.

'Good news then,' I replied good humouredly.

'It's brilliant. I can't wait to tell everyone.'

'You know the rules,' I answered with some severity. I couldn't be too angry with her though as I well understood how she was feeling.

'I know, but it's exciting. How do I get the copy back to you? The drivers gone.'

'I could come over at lunch.'

'No,' she replied 'if it can wait till Wednesday I have a better idea. Can you arrange some time off?'

Now, I'd only been at Harvington for a week so there was plenty to do and we were short staffed. But!

'Of course,' I said.

'Then come to the house about one.'

Seemed like a cracking arrangement to me!

CHAPTER 44

When Malcolm Prentice told David Thomas, as they completed the eighth hole on the Rednall golf course, that David's wife Lucy was having an affair, the news hardly came as a hammer blow although it did cause him to miss a two foot putt. He had suspected Lucy for some time. Their lovemaking, never the most exciting of occasions, had become more and more sporadic over the preceding months. He caught her on several occasions sending text messages at odd times. Too often, he now realised, he was unable to get through to her mobile as it had been engaged. Was she on the phone to her lover or was it, as she said, just a girl friend? Perhaps he should have questioned her further. He thought that the holiday would help but it proved to be a waste of time. Lucy had been morose and distant often going off on her own or feigning a headache to avoid going out. He was pleased to get home and so, he suspected, was she. After the Hatton annual evening do she came home exceptionally late and he did not hear the usual diesel rattle of a minibus or the slamming of doors and drunken goodbyes. He feigned sleep when she eventually came up the stairs. In any event she went straight into the spare bedroom, something which she seemed to do quite frequently of late.

The following morning she claimed that she hadn't wished to disturb him. Was it the truth? Had she been with someone? Would he have smelt another man on her? There were several occasions when he had been tempted to say something to her but he had not had the courage. It caused him to examine his own position. He had, after all, engaged in a number of affairs over the period of their marriage. His only real hope was that if Lucy was indeed having an affair, then it would not be with a woman. His chauvinistic pride would never accept that.

He also knew that Malcolm Prentice was not enjoying telling him. He was in no doubt that Malcolm had been 'volunteered' by other members of the gang of blokes who drank together one night every week. Motor traders all, there would be those who would revel in the news and those who would be sympathetic. Malcolm was from the latter group.

'How long have you known?' he asked as they shouldered their clubs and headed for the ninth tee.

'The rumours have been circulating for sometime,' Prentice answered.

'So it's just rumours then,' but he knew they were true.

Prentice just looked at him with a pained expression

'Why tell me now?' David asked.

'I couldn't let you win the hole,' Prentice answered with slow smile.

Despite the annoyance that David felt he had to smile. The response was typical. Still, he couldn't let Lucy get away with it. He asked Malcolm the obvious question and when told the name he realised he shouldn't have been surprised. Although he had never met Joe Quinn, Lucy frequently spoke of him and always in glowing terms. He himself had spoken to Quinn on one occasion when he asked him to keep an eye out for a car for Lucy. He had asked all the Hatton Group's sales managers the same question. Looking back he could not recall anything untoward in the conversation.

He let Prentice set his ball on the tee and then as he was about to pull the club back into the backswing he repaid the compliment by coughing and asking what Prentice thought he should do. Prentice stopped the swing but his concentration was broken.

'If it were me I'd punch his lights out, but it's not my decision to make,' he answered.

David rested on his club pondering the answer. He was tempted to speak again but allowed Prentice his shot and was satisfied when he topped the ball and sent it no more than fifty feet. He took his own shot and was immensely gratified when the ball flew a good two hundred and fifty yards down the fairway. He was not going to let the revelation affect his golf. He had decided to ring Lucy as soon as they finished the round. Better to catch her off guard at work. If the allegations were true, what to do about them was a different matter. Certainly he was realistic enough to know that he had been the first to stray in their marriage and indeed in their relationship and that he could hardly blame Lucy too much. Still, it hurt his male pride and he had no intention of being made to look foolish. He would challenge Lucy first and then see how things developed. He would take a perverse satisfaction in telling his parents. Perhaps some of the blame that had been laid at his door in the past would now be deflected somewhat. It would be an interesting few hours but right now he had a golf match to finish. And win, especially as they were playing for a pound a hole.

CHAPTER 45

Lucy replaced the phone. She could not believe how easily she had lied. So now David knew, or thought he did. She should have known that someone within the company would eventually say something to him. After all, the rumours had been circulating for some time and despite her protestations that she and Joe were just good mates, she knew that she had not been believed. Tonight would not be a pleasant evening by the fire in the Thomas household. Lucy had also had enough. For her the charade had to end. She knew she had fallen in love with Joe and the knowledge filled her with both delight and dread. Would she leave David? Would Joe leave Lynn? No matter what, she knew it all had to be resolved and quickly. Her proud boast that she was always in control was beginning to haunt her now. She knew that everything was well and truly spinning out of control. She rang Preece and he answered, abruptly, on the first ring.

'Nigel Preece.'

'It's me,' she said softly.

'Mrs. Thomas!' he exclaimed, seemingly pleased to hear her voice. 'How are you today?'

Lucy ignored the question and continued,

'I can't go on with this Nigel. I'm going to tell Joe everything. I'm beginning to believe my own lies. I actually got excited when Joe sent me the fake letter from the chairman and now someone has said something to David, so I'm putting a stop to it.'

'Not again,' thought Preece. He could feel his anger and impatience rising but he kept his calm as he answered,

'I understand the pressure Lucy,' he said as gently as his frustration would allow. 'I think we need to discuss this face to face before you do anything rash don't you? I have some purchase orders here. Perhaps you'd like to drive across and collect them?'

Lucy could feel herself wavering but she knew what must be done. She told him she would be there in twenty minutes. She signed herself out at reception knowing that her trip to head office would not be questioned and drove round to the main showrooms. She found a parking place with ease and went to the side entrance avoiding the need to go through the main showroom. It was the entrance favoured by the directors and equipped with a coded security door. She had been given the code several years ago and it had never changed. She went up the flight of stairs to the first floor and headed down the corridor to Preece's office, avoiding the Directors secretary in her small office cum reception area. She passed the open door to Fox's office and was pleased to see it was empty. John Hatton's office was also empty but she could hear the voices and the ringing phones from the fleet department alongside Preece's office. She knocked once on his door and walked in. Preece was on the phone and motioned her to a chair whilst he finished the call. Lucy was by now very frightened of him but she was in no doubt that he would never physically assault her. Preece ended the call and swung in his chair to face her.

'Now Lucy, tell me all your troubles,' he said, smiling benignly.

'I can't do this anymore Nigel, it's asking too much and it's all getting out of hand. Joe Quinn is one of the good guys.'

So it was true thought Preece. Lucy had fallen for Quinn. Preece sighed, the smile fading as he lent towards her.

'You're prepared for the consequences?'

Lucy nodded but even as she did so she could feel herself beginning to weaken.

'Do you really want the truth out in the open? Let me spell out for you what it will be like. Your life won't be worth living. Those pictures will go round the company after we have made sure that David and your in-laws see the copies first. Everyone will either be laughing at you or leering at you. Face the facts Lucy, they really are extremely lewd. And who will know when they were taken? We can soon remove the dates. My guess is that David will think they are of you and Quinn. Do you really want him to know that it's Stuart Green in the photos? In any case Stuart wasn't married when you slept with him, but you were. And what of Quinn? Do you think he will want anything to do with you? And if you try to tell him about our little scheme what will it achieve? Everything we have done so far is deniable. Quinn is a proud man with a huge ego. The letter you have only ties you to him. He will see you as a whore. As will your family, friends and your colleagues. I'm genuinely sorry you have fallen for Quinn, and I know you have, but you always knew that the relationship could never amount to anything. The trade off is that you get to keep your marriage, your home, your job, your reputation and most of all, your daughter. No Lucy, you'll keep quiet. This ends when I say it ends and not before,' he finished, his voice never having risen above a soft, sinister whisper.

Lucy sat through the whole tirade without attempting to interrupt. It was a speech from Preece that she would never forget. Or forgive.

'You bastard,' she whispered quietly.

'It's been said before,' he replied and rocked back in his chair. His tone softened. He knew Lucy would stay onside and he was prepared to cut her some slack.

'Look,' he said, 'you know how much is at stake here. I promise you it will soon be over. Keep your side of the bargain and you can destroy the photos yourself. And may I remind you that although Quinn thinks he's destined for the top, I know I am. Play your cards right and I will not forget it.'

She stared at him, hating him with her whole being and said,

'I don't trust you.'

Preece smiled. 'I don't care. You'll have to because as I have said, one word out of line from you and your world collapses.'

Since her disturbed childhood Lucy had always been proud of her ability to contain her emotions in public. This time she could not prevent the tear that rolled down her cheek. Preece showed no concern. She knew that he was right and she hated him all the more. Her private rebellion was over.

'One day Nigel, I will get even with you,' she said with as much venom as her frayed nerves would allow.

'I doubt that Lucy, I doubt that very much.'

Preece stood and opened the door giving clear indication that the conversation was at an end and that she should leave. Lucy left the way she came. When she got back to the car she sat for several minutes to compose herself. She knew there was no option but to continue with the charade. She was tough enough to come through the situation and as she sat she began to plan. David she would deal with tonight. She would deny everything and claim that she and Joe were just good friends. She would bed him tonight. He would believe her. She also knew that she could not just drop Joe. It would cause too many complications at this moment. She had to wait until Nigel was ready. She didn't like it, but so be it.

'Still,' she thought, 'there's no reason why a girl can't have a bit of fun in the meantime.' Despite herself she managed a wry smile. Wednesday afternoons were about to become times to remember. For however long the affair lasted she would make the most of it. Perhaps a solution would present itself but if not, well, no matter how much it hurt, she would get over Joe. She would have to.

CHAPTER 46

A warm, still, overcast September morning in North Yorkshire with just a hint of moisture in the air. Near perfect conditions for what I was about to undertake. As I locked the car in the car park at Brampton Raceway I shuddered involuntarily as the adrenaline began to course through my veins. Today would be a pleasant diversion from my personal and professional problems. I was here at the invitation of the circuit owner, Neil Marriott, to drive a prototype sports racing car.

I first met Neil some six years earlier. I had decided to try my hand at Karting, a form of motor sport which I felt I could just about afford. Neil was present at the meeting with his son Anthony, who was having his first race. Anthony proved to be woefully slow. Neil, on the other hand, was quite quick and it was clear that he had some motor sport experience. I was surprised to find that Neil was a member of the aristocracy and that his family owned a sizeable chunk of North Yorkshire. We raced together in a few Kart endurance meetings and I had been invited to Brampton on several occasions to drive some of Neil's impressive collection of mainly historic cars. Despite being one of the wealthiest men in the country Neil is, like the rest of his family, one of the most down to earth and laid back individuals I have ever met.

Like so many other race circuits in Britain, Brampton Raceway is built on the site of an old World War Two airbase. In 1938, the then Duke of Brampton, Neil's grandfather, was approached by the air ministry with a view to purchasing some two hundred acres of remote farmland for what would be England's most northern bomber base. In an act of extraordinary generosity the Duke refused to sell the land opting instead to lease the land for ten years for a peppercorn rent of just £1. His reasons weren't entirely philanthropic. He reasoned that by leasing the land he would not have the aggravation of having to buy it back, in what might become a competitive market. And if there was a War and it was lost, he doubted that pounds, shillings and pence would be of great value under the new Nazi regime. The airbase was duly built and saw its fair share of action, before being handed back to the Duke in 1948. The land was returned to the plough but the perimeter roads, runways and many of the buildings remained intact. Neil's father became interested in motor sport in the early 50's and with the help of a few like minded individuals formed a club. The members then began to arrange race meetings on the old airfield using oil drums and straw bales to mark out a course. The circuit developed with use, the oil drums and straw bales giving way to steel and tyre barriers, and went through good and bad times before Neil, for want of pursuing a life of his own, persuaded his father to let him run it. Where Neil's father had been reluctant to change, he positively embraced it and set about a period of modernisation. With the help of some Government and EU subsidies he redeveloped the track building proper spectator banking which also helped with noise reduction although in truth owning the land around made sure that there were very few environmental issues. A permanent grandstand was built opposite the pit lane which was in itself widened and provided with a row of purpose built lock up garages. To the south of the circuit an industrial park was developed, utilising many of the old station buildings. Whilst not the biggest circuit in the country, it has become an impressive and popular facility hosting rounds of several British championships, track days and a permanent race school. Little did I know that this day was to give me the biggest fright of my life and in many ways shape my destiny.

Neil rang me the previous week to ask if I would like to try the new car. I was pleased to accept. Then my stomach sank slightly when he told me that the car had been designed and built by Anthony to the regulations of the 750 Motor Club.

The 750 Motor Club was formed in 1939 as a means for owners of the then vastly popular Austin 7 motor car to meet each other socially. It was not long before these gatherings turned to the subject of competition. Thus, the 750 Formula came into being for a two-seater sports racer powered by the 750cc Austin 7 engine. This provided an outlet for the skills of the home constructor and specials builder many of whom went on to become leading figures in the higher echelons of motor sport. Over the years the club has expanded to become one of the largest motor clubs in the world with the 750 Formula cars subsequently being powered by an 850cc Reliant engine and latterly an 1108cc Fiat engine.

Despite my reservations I was intrigued. Anthony was a good lad even if I found him a little shy and a bit of a geek. I had nothing to lose however and I accepted Neil's generous invitation despite getting some grief from both women in my life.

Approaching the pit area I paused for a moment by the guardrail just beyond the pit lane exit. The circuit was in use for what appeared to be a general testing day as there were several different types of car circulating. I leant against the rail for a few minutes, composing myself and enjoying the scent and sounds of the circuit. A heady mixture of hot oil, high octane fuel, overstressed rubber and the ear splitting fever pitched howl of a high revving single seater or the ground vibrating rumble of a big bored V8. Turning, I spotted Neil in his racing overalls halfway down the pit lane in animated conversation with Anthony and a large man, who I recognised as Big Jeff, the full time mechanic who tended Neil's ever increasing collection of interesting cars. A big, usually affable and straight talking 'scouser' with a brilliant sense of humour, he possessed the largest pair of hands I had ever encountered, which were completely at odds with his manual dexterity.

I walked down the back of the pits and approached the trio through the back of the garage. Neil saw me coming and greeted me warmly. Jeff took my hand in his great maw and almost shook my arm off, whilst Anthony muttered a shy 'Hi' before busying himself on his lap top.

The car certainly looked the part and was clearly no home built special. I have tested some cars which proved to be so slow they would have had difficulty getting out of their own way. Pristine in white, there were no sponsorship decals to disfigure the sleek lines unlike some of the more garish machines out on the track. The only badge was a small red oval with the word Marriott etched in silver letters. After a good look round the car I went off to change into my flameproof racing suit. I also visited the toilet as the last thing I wanted was a full bladder, in case I had a shunt. By the time I returned Neil had rejoined the circuit.

I sat by Anthony who had returned to his seat on the pit wall with his computer and clipboard. I was expecting stopwatch timing but they were clearly utilising the latest technology. I was hugely impressed.

I was still a little apprehensive about driving the new car and watching some of the quicker and more powerful cars flash by did nothing to ease the growing tension. There was clearly a great disparity in speed between some of the different classes of car. Neil did a five lap run and then returned to the pits. His best time for the 2.1 mile lap was just under 1 minute 53 seconds. Very impressive. Out of a racing car Neil is a pretty lethargic individual, but put him behind the wheel and he is a very rapid racer. Not as rapid as me though and despite our friendship I knew he would be fighting all day to set a faster time than me. As he came to a halt and popped the seat belts Jeff and Anthony lifted the engine cover. Jeff immediately began to make some adjustment. What he did I knew not, the car sounded perfectly healthy to me. Neil gave me some advice regarding the track conditions and warned me about some of the quicker cars before telling me to climb aboard. I stepped into the cramped cockpit before sliding down into the snug driving seat. The regulations state that the car has to be a two-seater, but even two people of my height and build would find it very cosy. Neil reached in and pulled the belts tight around me and I gave a last tug on my driving gloves and flexed both hands. Our differing heights also meant some padding had to be used on the seat so that I could reach the pedals in comfort. As Neil stepped back I reached across and adjusted the rear view mirror. The visibility was largely obscured by the rear wing but I could see all I needed to see. I hit the starter button and the engine caught first time. Everything around me vibrated uncomfortably. I knew it would cease as the car got up to speed. Or at least I hoped it would! I was so nervous I was holding my breath and had to make a conscious effort to exhale. I let the engine idle for a moment and checked all the gauges. Everything looked normal and Neil gave me a thumbs up as I gently eased out the clutch and trundled down the pit lane. Everything felt right and my apprehension, along with the vibrations, began to dissipate. I was born to do this.

The circuit itself very roughly resembles an upturned Wellington boot when viewed from the air. The pit straight, formed from one of the old perimeter roads, is actually a long gently sweeping curve which tightens slightly more to the left at about three-quarters of its length. This bend is taken flat out before breaking hard and coming down through the gears into a very tight right-hander. From there it's back on the power, a short straight followed by another right hander, another short straight and then the quick 'ess', a right left sequence which leads on to the back straight which had once been the main runway at RAF Brampton. Flat down the straight and then a forty five degree left followed by a tightening curve to the right, then another short straight followed by another right turn and then the hairpin. Hard on the brakes and keep well to the right it provides a good, if opportunistic, overtaking spot. It is the scene of many a coming together and a favourite spot for spectators. As you exit the corner it's hard on the power and let the momentum build as you feed into a right hander. Still accelerating and changing up through the gears and on to a short straight with the pit lane entrance to the left and then it's into a long, tightening, right hander which leads back onto the pit straight. This final corner is the key to a good lap, exit speed being crucial to attaining maximum velocity down the pit straight. The lap record in a 750 Formula car stands at 1 minute 51.264 so Neil being two seconds off the pace in a new car wasn't a bad effort.

As I exited the pits I glanced to the right to make sure the track was clear. I needn't have bothered as the pit lane marshall had given me the green light but it's an old, and good, habit. I accelerated hard up the gears, took the gentle left hand kink, hit the brakes for the right hander and promptly spun! Fortunately, I saved some embarrassment by keeping the engine running and I moved quickly away and did a couple of steady laps, keeping well out of everyone's way, just to get the feel of things.

The car felt superb. It was as good to drive as it looked. It was quick, responsive, well braked, stuck to the road like glue and inspired confidence. It felt like an extension to my body. Man and machine in harmony. The real test, for both me and it, would be when I pushed it to the limits. Having settled in I did two quicker laps and then came in. Anthony and Jeff both came rushing over and pushed some sensors into the tyres for temperature readings. Neil stood impassively by and then waved me out again. I did a ten lap run and then returned to the pits. Neil was deep in thought and to my surprise I found that my quickest lap was faster than Neil's and only three tenths outside the lap record. Despite my being quicker, Neil was as pleased as punch and Anthony was positively glowing with pleasure. As we discussed things Jeff fussed over the car, checking levels and re-fuelling. I took several pulls from a bottle of water to avoid dehydration. I felt I was losing fractions in the final corner thus compromising my speed on the straight. I was lifting just a shade too early and feathering the throttle for just too long. Neil suggested I did another run and I was heading back to the car almost before he finished speaking.

I took the out lap steadily, checking the gauges and warming the tyres and brakes. There were other cars still circulating several of which were Formula 750's like the Marriott. I wondered if I might benefit from a tow. Travelling close behind another car allows it to punch a hole in the air thus lowering the wind resistance for the car behind. At the end of the third lap I was still allowing myself too much of a 'confidence lift' in the final corner. A misnomer if ever there was one. It was a lack of confidence which was causing me to briefly lift my foot from the throttle. I groaned inwardly, determined that this lap I would keep my foot hard down, fighting the fear. Coming down the back straight I was overtaken by a much more powerful single seater. He was quick in a straight line but not quite so agile in the tighter corners relative to his straight line speed. I stayed in his wake through the tighter bends and then tried to stay as close as possible as we accelerated towards the final turn. He began to pull away. And that's the last thing I remember before waking up in hospital the next day!

Neil told me that he had wandered down to the final corner to watch and apparently as I turned in, without lifting off the throttle pedal this time, the inside rear tyre just clipped the kerb. It was enough to throw the car off line but I kept my foot down as the car twitched to the left. The opposite lock would have been instinctive and he reckons I glanced momentarily to my left presumably as I calculated whether I was going to make the turn. It would only have been the merest of glances. Unfortunately the car in front chose that moment to have a drive shaft fail and in a heartbeat my right front clipped its left rear as the stricken car moved right to get out of the way. The Marriott lurched up, air got beneath it and it performed a back flip before slamming down, upside down, on the tarmac. Fortunately the roll hoop protecting my head didn't break but as the car left the track it dug in and flipped back on to its wheels before rolling to destruction along the pit wall.

Needless to say when I awoke the next day I had a monumental headache. Amazingly I hadn't broken any bones but I had dislocated both shoulders. The extra seat padding had meant I wasn't quite strapped in as tight as it seemed and my shoulders had moved against the straps. I had heavy bruising, was deeply concussed and very, very lucky to be alive. I was off work for a month. It turned out to be a very critical month.

CHAPTER 47

Preece could not believe his luck. He had just received the news that Quinn had been injured and would be off work for at least a month. Not normally given to overt shows of emotion he nevertheless punched the air with delight. He picked up the phone to tell Freddie Fox and couldn't quite hide the elation in his voice when he imparted the news. On the other end of the line Fox didn't smile. Yet another complication to sort out.

'We need someone into Harvington quickly. Morale is bad enough at the moment and I don't want any more staff leaving or lost profit opportunities,' he told Preece.

'How about Jim Ashton?' Preece asked, 'he'll do a holding job until we find a replacement.'

'Quinn hasn't been sacked Nigel,' Fox responded having correctly sensed the euphoria from Preece, 'and I'm not about to stick the boot in when he's in hospital. It would not do the company image any good at all. Talk to John. Between the two of you, you can sort it out.' Fox cut the connection abruptly and Preece immediately rang John Hatton.

Hatton was feeling tired and thoroughly fed up. Despite his best efforts Quinn was digging a hole for himself and he knew, despite the accident, that a hard decision would soon have to be made. Now this. He was not surprised when Preece came on the phone. He sounded like a man who had just won the lottery.

'I've spoken to Freddie and we think we should put Jim Ashton into Harvington until Quinn recovers,' Preece told him. Hatton took note of the fact that it appeared to have been sorted already and told Preece, with an air of resignation, to go ahead.

Preece hung up without further discussion. Jim Ashton was just right for his purposes. Preece turned on his computer and logged into the used car stock file for the Harvington branch. He quickly identified four cars and then changed the stock dates so that they showed in stock for far longer than the company's ninety day stocking policy. He had no doubt that Ashton would find the information and report back that Quinn was clearly failing to control the stock. It would be yet another nail in Quinn's coffin. Before ringing Ashton however Preece rang Stuart Green and then Lucy. Green was over the moon with the news. Lucy was not. Preece was not surprised that he detected the note of concern in her voice. He had always thought of her as being a very hard individual but of late he had begun to modify his opinion. Despite her telling everyone who asked that she and Quinn were just good mates he knew different. As, he suspected, did everyone else.

Lucy was in fact devastated. She did not want Joe to go racing but she could find no way to stop him. She sent him a text on the Thursday morning and was surprised when he didn't reply. Now she knew why. How would she get to see him? Lynn would be in close attendance and for the first time in a long time she found herself suffering from an attack of jealousy. She wanted to tell Preece where to put his job and everything else. The news of Joe's accident had already begun to spread throughout the firm and it came as no surprise to Lucy's two colleagues when she slammed the phone down and ran from the room. They were in no doubt that she had rushed to the loo in tears. They were right. Lucy shut herself away from prying eyes but not ears. Several other members of staff heard her sobbing but didn't truly realise why. Some thought it because of Joe. They were only partially right. That morning Lucy had taken a test at home. As if her life wasn't complicated enough to her dismay the test proved positive. She was pregnant. Worse, she did not truly know which of the two men in her life was the father, David or Joe.

CHAPTER 48

I spent a full week in hospital. My shoulders were put back into their sockets whilst I was unconscious so I did not have to endure what I am told is a very unpleasant experience. Not that it could have been any worse than the pain I was in anyway. I was bruised from head to toe and my head ached fit to burst. Every joint felt like it had been twisted inside out. I could barely move. Not that I was going anywhere. I was dizzy and nauseous. In short, deeply concussed. Even when I shut my eyes the room continued to spin. When the paramedics delivered me to the hospital I was immediately given drugs to keep me unconscious. A scan revealed no brain injuries so it did not prove necessary to keep me in a controlled coma. None the less, it was going to be some days before I could walk. I had plenty of visitors but I didn't want to bother with anyone. Some of my former colleagues from Mildenhalls, who owned several dealerships in the area, popped in and one manager visited from the Hatton Group. It was of course a long way to travel and I was deeply touched that Bob Dance made the effort. Lynn came up on the afternoon of the accident. Neil of course made certain that she was OK to travel and insisted that she stayed with him and his family. Lynn and Neil's wife Natalie, known to everyone as Nat, get on very well so it wasn't a problem. Lynn visited every day staying for varying lengths of time. There wasn't a lot she could do to lift my spirits. I thought I could detect a certain coolness in her manner. I was too busy feeling sorry for myself to let it become any sort of issue. I assumed it was because she was unhappy that I was injured and that I had caused her some worry. I was only partly right. I kept trying to remember what had happened. Despite Neil telling me I just could not recall. The one thing we did know was that the accident had been my fault, albeit exacerbated by a set of unforeseen circumstances. No worries about the car having broken even though it was now lying in bits. Anthony and Jeff called in one afternoon and accepted with good grace my apology for having destroyed their creation. I assured them that it was the best car I had ever had an accident in! Anthony looked suitably gratified. The normally affable Jeff seemed to alternate from being pleased I was on the mend one minute to wanting to do me more physical harm the next. Still, he did present me with the Marriott badge from the car.

'It's the only bit that's not broken,' he said mournfully in his melodious scouse accent. It was only after they left that Neil told me that both of them had leapt from the pit wall, without a thought for their own safety, to come to my aid. Jeff physically manhandled some of the bodywork whilst Anthony turned off the fuel pump to negate the risk of fire. Both of them were eager for me to have another go when the machine was rebuilt. Had I been either of them, or Neil for that matter, I don't think I would have contemplated having me near their car or track again.

Then of course there was Lucy. I couldn't ring her and she couldn't visit me. It made a long week even longer. After a few days bed rest my headache began to ease and the leads and drips were gradually taken away. I had been given morphine to help ease the pain. I was very careful not to self administer more than was necessary having heard all sorts of stories about going cold turkey. The only cold turkey I wanted to experience was the one left over at Christmas. After seven days I was released back into the world. I could still barely walk but there would be no lasting damage. I had been so very fortunate which only served to reinforce my belief that I was invincible. The doc told me to take it easy, get plenty of rest and re-acquaint myself with living. I wasn't sure how I felt to having to have another three weeks off work. Perhaps time spent reflecting would turn out to be a blessing in disguise.

It didn't. As soon as we got home Lynn cut loose. She retrieved my mobile phone after the accident and read a text from Lucy. The questions and accusations came thick and fast. She resisted the temptation to ring Lucy but it would only be a matter of time. In the meantime I was going to be put through the wringer. Luckily Lynn had made several plans for the next few weeks involving family and friends so I knew she would not do anything too hasty.

Despite her animosity Lynn settled me in before leaving for work. I turned on the mobile for the first time in a week. Nothing happened. I thought at first it was broken and then realised that it needed charging, having been left switched on. I rang Lucy on the landline. She was clearly pleased to hear my voice and said she would ring back. Why spend my money when she could spend the Hatton Group's cash? Ten minutes later she rang me back and we talked for an hour. She admonished me gently for the accident. I wasn't facing up to anything because I didn't feel I needed to. Work was off the agenda for the next three weeks anyway. It didn't matter to me that the trading results showed that Harvington was slipping rapidly backwards.

When I first transferred to Harvington, three of the sales team left within days and only one of them actually left the company. The other two transferred to Rednall. When I complained I was told that the transfers were agreed long before the management shuffle. Nigel did not allow me to replace them despite the fact that I knew several good people who I could draft in. He cited the new recruitment policy as the reason why. But what did I care? Within a few months I would be his boss and he would have to dance to my tune, and the stupid recruitment policy would be the first thing in the dustbin. Despite his seeming friendship he had pissed me off over the last few months. He hadn't kept me supplied with stock and I had helped him to get rid of the embarrassing cars that he had bought. My profit per unit suffered dreadfully and I didn't think he had done enough to protect me from the wrath of Freddie Fox. Just prior to my accident Fox sent a memo out to all the managers regarding stock preparation before sale. Stuart Green claimed on his arrival at Harpley that I was guilty of allowing a car to be sold without being prepared and that I had arranged for the customer to bring it back at a later date. The implication was that I avoided the car being reconditioned to inflate the profit during that month. It was completely untrue and fortunately I possessed the evidence to prove it. Green and I had yet another heated conversation. Or rather I got heated and he tried vainly to apologise. He is a brave man when your back is turned. When confronted though, he shows his true colours. He is a coward. Fox named me as the guilty party in the memo and despite my sending him a true account of what really occurred I never did receive a retraction or an apology. Nigel knew the truth and although he appeared sympathetic to my cause I was beginning to have doubts about his honesty and integrity.

After charging the mobile I took it back to bed with me. Lucy rang me a little later and we talked for another hour. For some reason the conversation came round to babies. But not for long. After she ended the call the phone rang again within seconds. It was the chairman. I was touched that he should ring and he assured me not to worry, everything was proceeding as planned and he had decided to make a big announcement at the end of October regarding the future of the Hatton Group. It was not long to wait. He then revealed that John Hatton was standing down from the committee for the time being, as he was going to oversee another project. I couldn't see what difference it would make anyway as the committee had never met but I wasn't going to discuss the point. Apparently there was some minor updating needed doing at Rednall and he was moving his office from there to the administration building in Flushing Road. His temporary office was right next to Lucy's. I had no reason to be concerned or so I thought.

After three weeks of sick leave at home I was well rested and ready to return to work. Lynn subsequently backed off, probably as a result of the impending visit of her aunt and uncle. Lucy of course was a great help during my convalescence. Her phone calls and text messages kept me amused and helped to relieve the boredom. I never gave a thought to the phone bill. Despite speaking with her every day, I was missing her. We needed to resolve our relationship for everyone's sake. The Friday before I was due to return to work, Lucy rang me with a concern. She overheard one of the office managers discussing phone bills with John Hatton. A new phone system had been installed a few months previously which recorded all the outgoing calls. Had we been caught out? Too right we had! There is none so blind as those who cannot see and I must have had my eyes removed. Lucy fretted about the conversation over the weekend. She was not wrong to be worried. When I arrived back at work John rang me and after enquiring of my state of health, summoned me to a meeting at Rednall. When I arrived it was clear that something was wrong as Jane Hatton was also in attendance in her role as the Human Resources manager. Without much preamble and a complete disregard for any formal procedures I was facing, along with Lucy, a disciplinary meeting. I could have challenged the meeting but what was the point. Jane knew absolutely nothing about the correct way to run a disciplinary hearing. It was clear that my failure to respond to her advances caused her great offence and no doubt more than a small amount of jealous anger towards Lucy. We were guilty as charged though, no matter what we said or did, and we both knew it. I tried to do the decent thing and take the wrap for both Lucy and myself. John was happy for me to do this; he just seemed to want everything settled with the minimum of fuss. Jane was having none of it however and clearly wanted a show trial. Common sense eventually prevailed and the whole thing resulted in us both receiving a recorded verbal warning for misuse of company time and resources. A lot of fuss for very little in the end. Still, John had made his point. Jane looked suitably smug at my discomfort. At least I had the satisfaction of knowing that all she could do was dream about sleeping with me. She would never have the real thing. Unfortunately I didn't get the opportunity to see Lucy as I was ushered out of the building.

On the way back to Harvington from the meeting the mobile rang. I answered it without pulling over.

'Are you drilling her?' boomed the familiar voice of the chairman. So he'd heard the rumours as well.

'Not sure I get your drift Mr. Chairman.'

'I think you do' he said. But it was a good natured response. At least Reg was broad minded. 'Welcome back, I know what's just happened,' he said laughing. 'It's just John flexing his muscles. He's not a happy man at the moment and he had to be seen to be doing something. Just keep your head down for the next few weeks and keep your nose clean. I have a contract here for Lucy which should please you both. I'll see that it gets to you and then you can deal with it. I'll speak to you soon.' Then he rang off. There were so many things I wanted to ask him but what the hell, my reward was getting closer.

CHAPTER 49

Jack Swift replaced the phone in its cradle and with a huge sigh sat down. He looked across the desk at a smiling Nigel Preece and said, 'I can't believe this, is he really this stupid?'

Preece rocked back in his chair and placed both hands behind his head.

'No, not at all. In fact, the bloke is very intelligent and, if I allowed him to be, a very good manager. Trouble is, for him, he has a monstrous ego and we've pressed all the right buttons. He believes what he wants to believe. I suppose it's a bit like kids and Christmas. They believe and carry on believing even when they suspect Santa doesn't exist. The bigger the lie the more plausible it can seem.'

'You're telling me Father Christmas doesn't exist?' Swift asked with a mocking smile.

Preece smiled back but didn't respond. The charade had probably gone now as far as it needed. Quinn was as good as finished.

'What happens next and what about Lucy Thomas?' Swift asked.

'I'm not worried about her Jack. She's in deep and she won't cause us trouble. As I said before she has far too much to lose. I think though that it's time to wrap this up. We've achieved everything and much more than I thought was possible. Its gone on far longer than I actually intended and its been a good laugh as well. I just have some small details to work out and then I think we can give Mr. Quinn the good news. Want a little wager on how he responds?'

'Not really, but what do you think will happen?' Swift asked.

'He'll resign and drop Mrs. Thomas like a hot brick. He won't admit to anyone that he's been conned. I think he'll probably take a pragmatic view and try to get a job with another group. He's finished with the Hatton Group and I have no doubt that by the time we've spread the word he'll be finished in the industry as well. When he realises that it will be too late for him to be a problem to us. If he starts squealing it will just sound like sour grapes. Jane Hatton hates him with a passion. I have no doubt that when anyone gets in touch regarding a reference she'll make sure it's a bad one. We just have to make sure that she doesn't give anything in writing. The woman is thick enough too. There are probably only two things that I agree with Quinn about. One is the lovely Mrs. Thomas and the other is that Jane Hatton is the ugliest woman I have ever met. If you stuck an apple in her mouth she would look just like one of those stuffed pigs at a banquet,' he said with a wry smile.

'Give over,' said Swift, 'you know you'd love to warm your hands on those huge knockers!'

'I can think of nothing worse. I've got to spend the morning with her doing a disciplinary tomorrow. John insists that someone sits in with her as he's not certain she knows what she's doing. He's right. The sales manager and one of the salesmen at the Cradley branch have been caught doing a little free enterprise. A bit of front end discounting for their own benefit.'

'How does that work then?' Swift asked.

Preece took out a pad, pen and calculator from his drawer and proceeded to explain.

'Let's say a new car has a retail price of £15000 including VAT.' He tapped some numbers on the calculator. 'This gives a basic price for the car of £12765.96 and a VAT content of £2234.04 making £15000, right?'

'If you say so,' Swift nodded, beginning to wish he hadn't asked.

'For ease of working out we'll assume the dealer has a profit margin of 10% based on the basic price giving a profit of £1276.59. A customer visits the showroom with his part exchange which we decide we don't want so the manager gets it underwritten by a trader who tells him it is worth £9600. We haggle a bit with the customer and decide to 'over allow' on the trade in by £400.'

'So the customer has got £10000 for his car,' said Swift, trying to look interested.

'Correct. He then asks what discount is available if he sells his own car privately and the sales manager decides to split the profit and give the customer a 5% discount for a deal with no trade in. With the saving in VAT this amounts to £750 so the customer signs the order with the proviso that he can sell his own car if he so wishes and take advantage of the discount. The sales manager decides that should the part exchange come into stock he will give it a stock, or stand in, value of £9250.'

'But the car's worth £9600,' Swift said becoming slightly confused.

'Also correct. He's shifting profit from one box to another on his accounts. We don't pay profit to the salesman on trade deals so the salesman loses a bit of commission whilst the department retains the same amount of profit. The sales manager sells the car for £9600 and the salesman on his 10% gets just over £50 instead of just over £85. Every little helps.'

'So you cheat your own staff?' said Swift, beginning to see the logic.

'This is the motor trade remember. Some groups do pay trade profit to the salesman but not us. In this case though the sales manager and his salesman are mates so a couple of days before the car comes into stock the salesman rings the customer to see if he has sold his car privately. He hasn't because he's been greedy and asked way too much for the car. The salesman points out to him that anything he gets over £9250 is worth considering because with his £750 discount it will be like getting more than £10000 for his car. So he tells him that he knows someone who is looking for a car just like his but can't afford more than £9350. The customer accepts because he's making an extra £100 overall. They get the trader to give the customer a cheque for £9350 and £75 each in cash for themselves. On the basis of 'what we haven't had we won't miss' we don't lose out because we were prepared to give the discount anyway. Or that's how they are trying to justify it. Of course we have lost out and we can't allow free enterprise can we? The customer is better off by £100 as is the trader and the sales manager and salesmen are £75 tax free to the good. The only loser, apart from the company, is the VAT man, who has his revenue cut by,' and he tapped out more numbers, '£111.70. And who cares about the VAT man? Geddit?'

'I think so but it's a bit complicated and what if the customer says something out of turn.'

'That's exactly what happened,' said Preece smiling. 'The customer happened to drink in the same pub as John so the two young men are in a bit of bother.'

'Will they get the sack?'

'Not if I can help it. They'll get a severe slap on the wrist and then we'll see if the process can be refined and I'll have a cut,' Preece answered throwing back his head and laughing uproariously. Dodgy place the motor trade.

CHAPTER 50

I arrived at Lucy's just after one the following Wednesday. The chairman had again kept his word and on the previous Monday evening a large manila envelope had been pushed through my letterbox. When I opened it, it contained another envelope for Lucy. I guessed what it was and it made me feel a lot better after the meeting with John and Jane Hatton earlier in the day. The following day I arranged for the letter to be delivered to Lucy at work and she rang and asked me to meet her at her house on the Wednesday afternoon. I readily agreed and told the staff that despite only just returning to work I would be absent after twelve on Wednesday. Nobody seemed very surprised. If we thought that no one noticed that we were both absent from work on Wednesday afternoons then we were being naive. Still, after four weeks apart I couldn't wait.

By Wednesday I seemed to be walking around with a permanent semi erection. Lucy greeted me at the door. To my disappointment she had dyed her hair blond. As I didn't want to spoil the moment I didn't make an adverse comment. Once inside she immediately flung her arms around me and held me tight. As we broke our embrace she avoided my lips and turned away. This was not a good sign. She showed me into the lounge and handed me the letter from the chairman which turned out to be a contract. I expected her to be almost gibberish with excitement but something was clearly on her mind and she appeared much 'underwhelmed' by the whole thing. I sat beside her on the sofa and began to read. The letter required her to sign the contract, get it witnessed and returned to the chairman. It was an impressive document. Two pages long and with a copy for her to keep. Even I was surprised by the numbers being offered. As I continued to read, Lucy suddenly slipped her hand into mine and pulling me towards her she whispered softly,

'Let's go to bed.'

The ache in my groin was telling me that this was a very good idea. We both stood and she led me from the lounge. At the foot of the stairs she turned and kissed me with more passion than I could ever remember. She almost dragged me up the stairs and believe me I was more than willing to follow. Such was her haste that as we reached the top she stumbled and fell pulling me down with her. As I landed she rolled and was suddenly on top of me. We never reached the bedroom. She seemed to have three pairs of hands as she removed my trousers and jockeys and her own underclothes. As she lowered herself on to me we both gasped and she gripped me fiercely with her slender thighs. It was fast and furious and over in seconds. Well, it had been some weeks. We lay side by side panting and then she suddenly raised herself on one elbow and looked down at me. I started to speak, to apologise, but she placed a finger on my lips and then I noticed a small tear escape from the corner of her eye and run down her cheek. I reached up and brushed it away and as she kissed the inside of my hand she looked straight into my eyes.

'I'm sorry,' she whispered huskily, 'I love you very, very much' and with that she pulled me to my feet and down the corridor towards the bedroom. For some odd reason I couldn't help but notice that the Monet print on the wall wasn't quite straight. I was almost tempted to reach up and straighten it but then lust got the better of me and we entered her bedroom. Her mood was definitely a lot brighter.

An hour later as I was dressing and feeling very pleased with myself she asked me to go back downstairs and fetch the contract. I did so and when I returned to the bedroom she was up and sitting on the bed running a brush through her hair. I handed her the contract and a pen and she signed both pages with a flourish. I witnessed it, gave her the bottom copy, folded the other and put it in my inside pocket. Job done in more ways than one. I sat beside her and put my arm around her shoulders.

'We can't go on like this,' she said sadly.

'So what are we going to do about it?' I asked.

If I was expecting a revelation I was sadly disappointed.

'I don't know, I just don't know,' was all she could say. I held her close.

'I have to go,' I said.

'I know, and I have to fetch Annie.'

She suddenly snapped out of her melancholic mood and kissed me.

'Go on,' she said, 'we'll sort it out.'

She grinned. I let her go, stood up and walked away. At the bedroom door I turned and paused.

'I love you,' I said.

'I love you too,' she answered. 'Go on,' she said smiling, 'I'll speak to you later,' and then she threw a pillow at me. I ducked and stepped out the door laughing, little knowing that I would only ever hold her one more time.

CHAPTER 51

After Joe left, Lucy sat for some time brushing her hair feeling, despite the circumstances, surprisingly warm and content. A part of her had dreaded Joe arriving. Two days earlier she had visited her doctor who confirmed her pregnancy. In truth she already knew this was the case as she had just missed her period for the second time and normally she was as regular as clockwork. Another problem she definitely didn't need and one that would become extremely difficult to hide if her life didn't soon get sorted out.

She also knew Joe didn't like her new blonde look but he never mentioned it. She had done it in part to spite him. She was so angry when she received the news of his crash. Angry, but relieved that although badly hurt he was not paralysed, or worse, and was expected to make a full recovery. She missed him dreadfully. The week he spent in hospital was awful. She couldn't visit him as he was so far away, and nor could she ring him in case Lynn was present. She was elated when he came home. During his convalescence they talked most days. It helped, but she really wanted him with her and yet a part of her rebelled at her own feelings so she dyed her hair knowing that he hated fake blondes. There was even a part of her that hoped Joe would be angry and walk away from her but he had apparently turned a blind eye. He had looked and then ignored the colour as though she had not done it. She regretted the decision now and would let the dye grow out.

The disciplinary had been a further complication. The situation frightened her more than she cared to admit. Still, at least John Hatton agreed that any correspondence regarding the matter would be given to her at work and she felt sure that John would keep his word. The whole episode would remain confidential provided there were no further transgressions. Jane she wasn't so sure about. She was clearly not happy with John's decision. Joe had warned her that Jane could be trouble, but there was nothing to be gained by worrying. She had enough on her plate.

As she sat on the edge of the bed, she realised that for a couple of hours she had suspended reality. Making love with Joe was just so good. Making love to David or indeed to anyone previously, had never given her the satisfaction and the inner warm glow that she felt with Joe. Despite Green's photographs, the thought of which still sickened her, she never realised that the many different ways to make love could be so pleasurable and she richly enjoyed giving herself completely and wholly to Joe. She found herself so relaxed with him and she had become quite adventurous. She performed acts with, and on him, which she had never contemplated before and which she would once have found disgusting. Their mutual passion made her realise something of what she had been missing over the years. She realised that despite all her bravado and flirting, her life had in many ways been quite sheltered. Joe was attentive, gentle and yet passionate. Today was the first time he had put his own needs before hers and yet she knew there had been a good reason. She loved Joe. She could imagine spending the rest of her life with him. Yet even though the thought gave her a warm glow the icy hand of reality gripped her and she knew it would never be. She had wanted to tell him she was pregnant. She thought seriously about another abortion but decided to wait a little longer. Surely there must be a solution. She didn't cry but resigned herself to let fate decide. Rising from the bed she dressed quickly and left to meet Annie from school. She rang Joe later and they chatted for a few minutes. He was his usual cheeky self and his mood lifted her spirits again.

The rest of the week passed for Lucy without further complications. She was not looking forward to Friday. Joe told her as they lay in each others arms on the Wednesday afternoon that he and Lynn were going away for the weekend. She accepted the news, warm in a way that Joe had been able to tell her to her face, trusting absolutely that she would not be angry. She wasn't angry but Lucy was jealous and it wasn't an emotion she enjoyed. On the Friday evening, as she sat in her car outside the office, she sent him a text telling him to be careful. What she really meant was, 'don't sleep with Lynn,' and she knew she was being unreasonable, yet she couldn't help it.

As she parked her car at home her mobile rang. She hoped it was Joe but as she glanced down she recognised the number as that of Nigel Preece.

'What do you want?' she snapped.

'Don't be like that Lucy,' he said not unkindly. 'I've rung to give you some news. I'm going to reveal all to Quinn on Monday so I want you to take the contract into John Hatton first thing on Monday morning and ask him to verify its authenticity. You can back up the contract with a copy of the chairman's proposal countersigned by Quinn. Tell him who gave it to you and then make yourself scarce. I'll do the rest.'

Lucy snapped the phone shut and sat for some time in the car. Her stomach churned. She felt sick, helpless, and not for the first time that year, tears rolled down her cheeks. This time however she didn't weep silently. She sobbed loudly and beat the steering wheel in frustration. She wanted to be as far away as possible from Rednall and it took her several minutes to regain her composure. David was already home and she was determined that neither he nor Annie would witness her distress. She got out of the car and walked to the door. Annie greeted her with her usual customary excitement but Lucy just wanted to be alone.

The rest of the weekend dragged by but in truth that was what she wanted. She was dreading Monday. David had the weekend off but they didn't do anything. He couldn't even be bothered to visit his parents and the only time he left the house was to stand outside with a cigarette. Their conversations were muted and stilted and not even Annie could lighten the mood. She longed to be able to speak with Joe or at least send him a text. She looked at her phone several times more in hope than expectation but it remained silent, the screen empty and in the end she turned it off. Lucy was deeply worried and very frightened. Then, in the middle of Sunday afternoon, she began to experience stomach cramps. She guessed the cause of her discomfort and in the privacy of her bathroom she mis-carried. At least she had one less problem to worry about.

CHAPTER 52

The weekend following my Wednesday afternoon assignation with Lucy, Lynn and I went away to attend the wedding of a mutual friend. It was his fourth attempt at marriage, a real glutton for punishment. Despite our growing animosity towards each other both of us felt that we should still go. Lynn also informed me that Mavis and Alan were coming down for a few days the following Wednesday. Under the circumstances I thought I accepted that news with good grace. It was certainly not something to look forward to. I had also arranged to have the Monday off work as I needed to have my six month dental check and my annual physical at the docs. I did not appear to be suffering any residual effects from the accident but I wanted to be sure.

The weekend was actually quite pleasant. We caught up with a few old friends and I think both of us forgot all our respective problems over the two days. There was not one cross word or snide remark between us. I heard nothing from Lucy. I sent her a couple of text messages on the Sunday but got no response. I knew David was also having a weekend off and she too was playing happy families. I wasn't worried because everything was slotting nicely into place.

On the Monday I waited until Lynn left for work and then rang Lucy at her office. I reached her voice mail and left a message for her to ring me. Half an hour later she still hadn't returned my call so I rang again. Again the call went to her voice mail. I tried her mobile but it was turned off which explained why she hadn't replied to my texts. Perhaps her battery was down? I then rang her colleague Mandy who sat on the opposite side of the desk from Lucy. She answered almost immediately and I asked if Lucy was there.

'She's out of the office at the moment. I'm sure she'll ring when she gets back.' Did I detect something in her voice? I didn't ask where Lucy was. At least I knew she was at work. I couldn't however shake off the feeling that something wasn't right.

Then my own phone rang. I recognised the chairman's mobile number on the screen and answered quickly.

'Mr.Chairman, how are you?'

'Now then you little wanker. I'm fine, and yourself?' he asked with his customary good humour.

'Yeah, I'm well.'

'Good,' and then the voice changed from the chairman's rich brogue to a voice I vaguely recognised, 'because you are about to get the shock of your life. Let my friend here talk to you.'

I was bewildered. What the hell was going on? I heard the phone being passed across to someone and then a very familiar voice came across the airwaves.

'Listen carefully you little Geordie prick.' It was Nigel Preece. 'You've been had son.'

I was stunned into silence. This could not be happening.

'Even you will be realising by now that you have not been dealing directly with the chairman. The truth is that he thinks you're a useless prick. Why would he ever bother to contact you? There is no promotion and there never was or will be. At least not for you. I set you up. I played you for the arrogant, egotistical fool that you are.'

Every word was like a kick in the groin. I knew he was telling the truth. I wanted to respond but anger and frustration were causing the words to stick in my throat. I realised I was beginning to sweat profusely. I really was, for the first time in my life, rendered totally speechless. How could I explain this to Lucy? Turned out I didn't have to as Preece delivered the final, crunching, body blow.

'Cat got your tongue pal?' he went on nastily. 'You're out Quinn. I reckon by the end of the week you will be history. And don't worry about Lucy; she's been in on this charade all along. She was always loyal to me.'

He couldn't have hurt me more if he had stuck a knife in my gut and disembowelled me. I felt faint.

'I, I don't believe you,' I managed to stammer softly and without conviction. I was utterly crushed.

'No? I bet you haven't managed to speak to her today have you?'

The silence from me said it all. No. NO. NO!

'I thought not,' he continued, 'and nor will you. She took the fake job offer to John Hatton first thing this morning. He was completely stunned. He knew nothing about it of course and she had to tell him it came from you. After all, your signatures on it as well as the pretty good forgery of the chairman's. Quite an actress is Mrs. Thomas. I've just come off the phone from John. Apparently Lucy burst into tears and fled. I have no doubt John will be ringing you shortly. I can just see you trying to blame someone else. Remember I've been with the company for a lot of years. I'm a trusted and loyal servant. Nobody is going to believe you. What have you achieved in your time with the company? One good year followed by a complete cock up and an affair with a married staff member who you lied to in order to get her into bed. You appear to have seriously abused your position,' he sneered.

'You bastard Preece. I'll have you for this.' Yet the words rang hollow. I had never felt, or been, so angry, humiliated and worse, impotent in my entire life.

'Really?' Preece laughed, 'and just what do you think you can do?'

I knew he was right. I slammed down the phone, cutting off his laughter. Had he been there in the room with me I would have killed him with my bare hands. And Lucy too.

Almost instantly the phone rang again. I snatched it up.

'Lucy?'

'It's John. You and I need to speak.'

I met him that evening. He presented me with a copy of the 'chairman's' letter to Lucy and the contract as well as a note from the 'chairman' signed by me months earlier. If only I hadn't returned the copy's I received but then what would it have proved? I had been in turmoil all day but I remained silent. What could I do? I was beaten and I knew it. Well and truly stitched up. Jim Ashton was there taking notes. I refused to say anything other than finally saying 'no comment' which probably just made me look guilty. 'No comment.' The two words that all guilty criminals utter. I could see nothing in Ashton's face other than complete contempt. Clearly I was now the company bad boy who had seriously abused his position in order to take advantage of a member of staff. I guessed that was what my other colleagues would also be thinking when the word spread. If it hadn't already. John was clearly angry and exasperated. He ended the meeting by saying that I was suspended on full pay whilst all the circumstances were investigated and that I was to have no contact with any member of staff. Especially Lucy Thomas. I was past caring. I handed him my letter of resignation. John read the letter and I could see the disappointment in his eyes. He looked at me and asked softly, 'Are you sure this is what you want?'

It wasn't but there was nothing I could do. The thought of going through any sort of disciplinary procedure with Jane Hatton sitting smugly in attendance was enough on its own to make me walk away. I had been well and truly done up like the proverbial kipper. I was crushed and humiliated. Besides, what would be the outcome? I was guilty of letting my balls and ego rule my brain and would now have to suffer the consequences. Preece was right. It would have served no purpose to have accused him or anyone else. I could prove nothing without Lucy's support and she had clearly taken me for a fool. I had believed in her. How could any woman do what she had done? Right there and then I was too numb to be angry. I just wanted to be as far from Lucy Thomas and the Hatton Group as possible.

I thought I had hit rock bottom that night as I worked my way through a bottle of whiskey. I hadn't. One week later Lynn pulled out in front of the truck.

CHAPTER 53

With some of the remains of his meagre cash Jake bought a ticket for a seat on the National Express coach to Harpley. By the time he arrived in the evening he was cold, hungry and beginning to feel the first pangs of desperation. He needed food, a hot drink, warmth and a place to sleep and think. The coach had been held up on the motorway and was running late. He would be unable to contact the accountant tonight. Stepping off the coach he spotted the internationally famous twin yellow arches and whether the food and coffee was junk the place was open and almost empty.

The very last of his cash went on a hamburger, fries and coffee which he consumed with relish. His thoughts were interrupted by a gang of four teenagers dressed in trademark baggy jeans and hooded tops. He guessed that they were planning to have some sport with him when he left. He looked like a tramp, fair game for a bunch of teenage thugs. This put Jake in a dilemma. He knew he could take them all down but he did not need any trouble or, if they got lucky, a trip to hospital. As he left the restaurant sure enough the four got up to follow him. Out in the street they taunted him but Jake, ignoring the foul abuse walked on, not knowing where he was going but determined to get away. Then two of them pushed past and turned to confront him. Jake had nowhere to go and knew that it was fight or take a beating. There was no chance of flight. He stopped in his tracks. He was pushed from behind and then from the front. Just then he became aware of a car pulling into the kerbside. A door slammed and then an accented voice asked,

'Now then lads what's tha doin' like?'

Jake turned and saw a casually well dressed man, older than he and shorter but there was something about him which made Jakes insides churn.

'Fuck off old man or we'll do you as well as worzel here,' said one of the gang.

'I think not boy,' the man answered with a heavy hint of sarcasm and just enough menace to stop the boy in his tracks.

'Let him by now,' he went on quietly but with a calm authority. Jake seized the opportunity and pushed past the two boys and stood beside the man who didn't acknowledge him. He was keeping his eyes firmly fixed on the boy who had spoken and who was obviously the leader. Jake saw the two boys at the front tense and knew what was coming but before they could react the man said,

'Just ask yoursenn this. There's a tramp and a shortarse stood in front of me and me and ma mates are gunna give them a kicking. Question is, why would a bloke dressed in designer gear climb out of his nice warm Range Rover and come to the rescue of a tramp, unless he knows summats I don't?'

Jake saw the uncertainty in the boy's eyes. Were they asking themselves, 'is this scruffy looking man an undercover cop?' It was probably not unknown for the local force to disguise themselves in trying to catch some of the local drug dealers. And one of the thugs kept glancing at the other man as though he recognised him. Three of them began to relax unsure of what to do but the leader was still spoiling for a fight and his ego had been rattled. His hand came out from his pocket holding a short blade. He lunged at the older man who stepped back ever so slightly which put the boy off balance. The knife missed and the man rammed his fist straight into the boy's solar plexus causing him to double up. The knife hand came up as the boy straightened and the man grabbed the wrist, twisting the arm around and forcing the boy to the pavement. The knife clattered free and fell from the kerb into a rain gulley. The boy screamed in agony as the man twisted the arm to the point of breaking. His companions immediately turned and ran.

The man bent over and whispered menacingly in the boys ear,

'I'm going to let you up nice and slow and then your gunna fuck off just like your mates. Understand?'

Jake didn't hear the answer. The boy was allowed to rise very slowly. He was whimpering now and as he stood the man gave him a shove and he ran, holding his injured arm and not daring to look back. With that the man turned to Jake and thrust his arm out.

'Joe Quinn.'

'Jake Smith,' Jake answered and grasped the proffered hand shaking it firmly.

That first handshake formed a bond that would never be broken. Neither of them would ever be able, nor indeed did they try, to define what had passed between them, or why it was.

'Well Jake, you look like you need a friend. Let's get out of here.'

They climbed in the car. Jake was wary and although the cheap food had revived him the stress of the last few months was beginning to take its toll.

'Where can I drop you?' Joe asked. His accent had changed, softened and Jake realised he was from the north east of England, a Geordie, trying and failing to lose his accent, and that it was probably the stress of the moment that had accentuated his tone.

'I have nowhere; I only arrived from London an hour ago.'

'What brings you to Harpley?"

'I'm looking for a business associate. Michael Nelson, he's an accountant.'

Jake saw the look of concern on Joe's face.

'Was he a friend?'

Was? Jake immediately noted the past tense and his stomach began to tighten.

'No, he has something belonging to me.'

'Jake, I'm sorry to have to tell you this. A Michael Nelson died today in a fire at his office. The police are treating it as a gas explosion. The building was gutted. The poor bloke had only moved here ten days ago and wasn't yet open for business. Word has it that he'd had enough of high rents in London and thought this would be a good place to spend the rest of his career before retirement. It seems he was interviewing for a new receptionist and one had only just left the building when she heard a small explosion. She thought at first it was a car back firing. When she turned around the place was in flames. According to her the place was packed with unopened boxes presumably containing all his business records. She was lucky. She can't remember smelling gas. I suppose the leak could have been in the shop below which was empty. The street is still closed off. What with the explosion in London today everyone is understandably a little nervous.'

Jake couldn't help himself. Joe gave him a quizzical look as Jake threw back his head and laughed. So, the accountant had taken the box and tried to open it. Surprising really that he hadn't tried before. In the act of opening it he had triggered a small, but extremely powerful pressurised incendiary device. The resulting fire would have been highly intense and with luck the inevitable investigation would be inconclusive.

Jake would never find out the truth. Sadiq Kahn and Michael Nelson both died as the result of acts of kindness and curiosity. Kahn had received an offer for the flats which was too good to refuse. A supermarket chain needed the site for access to land at the rear. Jake never noticed the planning application notice outside the flats. Nor had he taken note that one of the flats was already boarded up, the tenants having already left. Only two weeks earlier Kahn had heard a disturbance at Jake's flat. Fearing squatters he entered the flat through the broken front door. He was accompanied by one of his rent collectors. Two youths fled the scene but not before they had ransacked the flat. Kahn and his wife tidied the place up and replaced the lock. Neither of them went down to the garage assuming that the youths had gone no further than the kitchen. Not being able to contact Jake, Kahn instead contacted Michael Nelson. They had spoken previously about the sale of the flats and Kahn was becoming increasingly concerned that his tenant would not return before the sale of the flats was completed.

Nelson had dealt with Jake for some years. He knew that Jake was not what he seemed but he paid well and on time and he was happy to look after his affairs. He knew he worked abroad a lot but he knew Jake was no builder. His hands lacked the roughness or callousness of an artisan. Nevertheless he felt a responsibility for his client and he too was becoming concerned, particularly as he had decided to relocate north having grown tired of life in London. A lifelong bachelor and not in any sort of relationship he chose Harpley purely for its proximity to the waterways, having fallen in love with the notion of eventually retiring on to a narrow boat and exploring the nations canals and rivers. Kahn gave him a key to the new lock and asked him to give it to Jake when he eventually returned. Nelson entered the flat, picked up the few days mail and placed it with the rest of the unopened mail which Kahn had previously placed on the hall table. He also left a letter for Jake asking him to contact him. He satisfied himself that everything was in order in the flat and then went down the internal stairs to the garage. He noted the broken lock, passed through the door and then saw the inner door hanging from its hinges. The youths had just prised the door when they heard Kahn upstairs and fled empty handed. Kahn never realised that they had been in the garage and he never looked. Nelson observed the cans on the shelf. It never occurred to him that it was odd that they should be locked away. In any case his attention had been drawn to a metal box of a type which was not unfamiliar to him and the AK47 resting in the corner. He wasn't familiar with guns and surmised that it was some sort of sporting rifle. Fearing another break in he removed the metal box, correctly assuming that if his client had taken the trouble to have it locked away, then it contained something of value. Leaving the gun worried him but he wasn't about to leave the flat with it, much less store it at his home. He thought briefly about calling the police and then decided against it. The box went with him to Harpley and hearing of the explosion at the block of flats in London, curiosity got the better of common sense. He broke the lock on the box and died.

As for Kahn, the night he arrived back at the flats with his family from a trip to his parents in Luton he thought he saw a movement at the curtains on Jake's flat and hoped he had returned. The hour was late, he was tired, and he decided to check in the morning. It was a decision that would cause the death of himself, his family, the remaining six tenants in the flats and Michael Nelson.

Joe took Jake back to his flat believing him to be suffering from the shock of hearing about Nelson. Whilst Jake showered and shaved for the first time in months Joe made some far reaching, if somewhat impetuous decisions. Despite Jake's exhaustion they talked into the small hours. The only disappointment for Jake was that Joe was straight but by morning Jake had a place to stay and the offer of a job. Despite knowing that he possessed a small fortune deposited in a London bank he was aware that he could not risk any attempt for now to access it. Besides, he had nowhere to go. For the time being at least, Jake had stopped running.

CHAPTER 54

If Buxton felt any lingering doubts regarding Stuart Green's guilt they were dispelled by a set of twelve black and white photographs lying before him on his desk. The twelve photographs were just a small selection of graphic images of Green and Lucy Thomas, some dated, some not and some with Green's face obscured, discovered by one of the search teams in a locked briefcase in Green's attic. Both Green and Lucy were naked on a bed and in a variety of different positions. There appeared to be no doubt as to what they were doing. In one picture, Lucy was on her knees facing Green as he smiled towards the camera, his penis apparently in her mouth. Another depicted her on her back with her nakedness exposed to the world. Buxton could not help but admit to himself that she was, or had been, a very attractive young woman. He let his eyes linger on the image but there was no lust in his gaze, just pure anger.

'What a waste,' he thought.

The attic yielded much more evidence. A further locked briefcase contained still more pornographic images. All of them were handed to DI Kirk who vaguely recognised some of the models. He then realised that they were photographs of staff members from the Hatton Group but these images had been crudely doctored. Green, he presumed correctly, had clearly taken photographs of the staff and then transposed their heads on to the bodies of naked models. There was also a batch of photographs of both men and women with young children and several computer hard discs also containing the same type of material. He immediately took the evidence to Buxton.

The images sickened Buxton. Adult pornography he could live with but children were a different matter. At least there were no pictures of Green with young children. Nevertheless he would be having quiet words in ears which would ensure that Green would have a very uncomfortable time in prison.

Buxton knew that Davies was still not convinced that Green was the guilty man. Even now, with the discovery of the pictures, he was still trying to argue that he may be innocent of murder and asked Buxton to accompany him to the incident room to review further the CCTV images. Reluctantly, Buxton agreed.

Davies turned on the monitor and inserted the disc into the machine. They watched the runner come into view from the direction of the town and turn into the lane. Then Davies switched discs. The second disc was the recording taken from the industrial buildings beyond the roundabout. It was still clear enough to pick up the runner crossing the road and passing beneath a road sign. At this point Davies stopped the machine, rewound it, and then replayed the same section. This time he did it frame by frame. Buxton sighed impatiently.

'Well, just tell me.'

'The runner boss, runs under the sign. He doesn't pause or duck. He just goes straight under as though it's not there.'

'So?'

'Stuart Green is six feet tall. For him to run under that sign he would have to duck. The distance between the bottom of that sign and the ground I estimate is around six feet. I'm six feet and when I walked under it I ducked instinctively. Green would have done the same. There is no way Green could have gone under without ducking especially when moving at pace. He would have no choice. The runner doesn't so it can't be Green.'

Buxton stood back. He couldn't fault the logic but he still believed Green was the killer.

'So what you're saying then Andy is that the runner is not the killer. So we eliminate the runner.'

'Or the runner is the killer and we have the wrong man. We should be looking for someone well under six feet tall. Someone like Joe Quinn.'

Buxton dropped his shoulders and smiled but it was a smile without mirth.

'No Andy, Green is our man,' he said forcefully. 'The runner was an avenue that we needed to investigate, but could be it's turned out to be a red herring. We just didn't see it at the time. Perhaps it was just simply someone out for a run who was in the wrong place at the wrong time and it threw us off the scent a little. Whoever it was they probably turned down the lane, ran past the house and carried on towards the mere. No doubt they took one of the many exits from the park. Not all of them are covered by CCTV.'

'So how did Green get to the house then?'

Buxton pursed his lips thoughtfully before answering.

'With Preece perhaps?' And then his mood darkened as he continued. 'Look, what is clear is that Green and Preece are both crooks and are going down. They've been fiddling the company and the revenue for years. Given their apparent relationship, Mrs. Thomas was probably in on it as well. Perhaps she was going to blow the whistle. Murders have been committed for far less than the sums of money involved here. Perhaps she was getting greedy and wanted a payoff as well as ditching Green. Maybe she was shagging them both.'

'But Mrs. Preece would have had to have been involved as well. She would have seen Green.'

'Not necessarily. Green could have been in the boot. It's not a long journey from the Preece home to the mere or maybe she is in on it. She's no doubt benefited from the cash.'

'But the timing doesn't work. We found fingernails and nose droppings remember. The killer had some time to wait and Preece leaves only a couple of minutes before the killer.'

'So he arrived by a different route. There are other ways to get there on foot.'

'But if he went on foot the direct route would have taken him under the CCTV cameras. He would have been very marginal on time if Mrs. Green left the house when she said she did.'

'So she lied. She's done it once. Remember she originally said she had been at home and then changed her story. Maybe it was her?' Buxton exclaimed with enough sarcasm to let Davies know that it would be useless to argue further. But Davies wasn't about to give up.

'There are other things boss.'

'Go on,' said Buxton sighing.

'Fingerprints, phone, position of the car seat and Green is left handed.'

Buxton remained silent and Davies took this as permission to continue.

'Other than the fingerprints we expected to find, there were no prints in the stolen BMW yet we found a fingernail. We know it came from Green but do we seriously believe that he removed his gloves to bite his nail and then was careless enough to just flick it in the car?'

'People with habits do things subconsciously or maybe he bit the nail earlier and it stuck to his clothes before falling off in the car. Or maybe he had only half bitten it and it caught in his glove.'

'Then how do we explain the phone in Lucy's handbag which had blood on it?'

Buxton smiled, still prepared to indulge Davies because he was content in his own mind that he, himself was right.

'She dropped the bag and the phone fell out. Green picked it up, put it in the bag.'

'Then why leave it at the scene?'

'Because he picked up the knife, then maybe someone or something disturbed him. He panicked and fled.'

At this Davies gave Buxton a very dubious look. He knew he was getting nowhere.

'What about the seat position? Green and David Thomas are both six feet tall but the seat had been positioned for a much shorter person.'

'So he slid it forward to make us think exactly that.'

'The pathology report states that the killer used his right hand to stab her.'

'Actually Andy, the killer used a knife. Look I know Green is left handed but it doesn't mean he can't use his right hand.'

Buxton slapped his young protégé on the back and smiled.

'Good try Andy but we have our man. Look at these photographs. What type of man has photographs taken of himself in bed with another mans wife? What type of person was she? Loving mother or tart?'

Davies shuffled the photographs. He to was quite shocked by their explicit nature and was not looking forward to informing David Thomas of their existence. How would he react to seeing his wife pictured, her eyes closed in bestial passion in the arms of a man who was supposedly his friend? He shook his head sadly and handed the images back to Buxton.

'We'll talk to Green again and then I'm going to have a conversation with the CPS. I want Stuart Green charged with the murder of Lucy Thomas and I'm convinced that Preece is involved so I think it's time to bring him in. He'll be facing fraud and embezzlement charges at the very least and with a bit of luck and a bit more co-operation from Mr. Green, conspiracy to murder,' Buxton said as he placed the photographs back in their folder. Davies was still far from convinced.

Later in the day Buxton got his wish. When shown the pornographic images of young children and given a graphic account of what happened to people associated with child pornography in prison Green visibly paled. Then Buxton showed him the pictures of him in bed with Lucy. Green knew it mattered not one bit that she had been heavily drugged and knew nothing of what happened that night. He hadn't even penetrated her. It had been stupid getting his mate Tim to take photographs but it was only meant to have been a joke. He just wanted to take the stroppy cow down a peg or two. He knew he should have destroyed them as Preece had done with the copies they had shown to Lucy. Indeed he had assured Preece that he had done just that, but it was too late now. And worse, Tim couldn't help him as he had died in a car crash on the motorway only a few months after the party. It was the final straw and he knew he was doomed. He couldn't admit to blackmail it would just implicate him further. Green asked for a break to consult with his solicitor and Buxton granted him fifteen minutes.

Buxton needed a coffee and stopped at the machine as they walked towards their office. Davies continued down the corridor without him and as he stepped through the office door the phone rang. He snatched it from its cradle with a curt,

'DS Davies.'

'DI Moore. Is Bob there?'

'Sorry, no. I can get him or take a message,' Davies replied.

'It's alright and it's probably not important. Tell him that I forgot until after his call that Quinn's name came up in a minor investigation about a year ago. We had a spate of beatings over a period of a few months. Dark alley jobs. Apart from one fellow no one was badly injured. Turned out all the victims were involved in the building trade and all had at one time or other worked for Quinn's company. It was such a tenuous link that we didn't follow it up. It would probably have been more of a surprise if they hadn't done some work for Quinn. Thing was though, the guy who did get hurt, one Frank Holmes, actually volunteered Quinn's name as being someone who he might have upset. He tried to convince us that Quinn was running some sort of cartel. I was the interviewing officer and at the time Holmes was getting a hiding, Quinn was with me at a sporting dinner. I was going to speak to Quinn but then Holmes changed his story so it went no further. There were no more beatings either.

Holmes was reported missing this morning and his body has just been fished out of the river. He was known to have money worries and was a drinker. He was separated from his wife and it seems he was due to meet a mate who went to his house when he didn't show up. He couldn't raise him on his phone and his van was in the drive so he reported it to us. It appears Holmes was in The Ferryman on Monday night and drank too much. The barman claims Holmes was quite depressed and was asked to leave. All the indications are that he fell in the river and drowned or possibly decided enough was enough and jumped.'

'Could he have been pushed?' asked Davies.

'He could, but there's no evidence to suggest it. We'll do the routine of course and try to establish if anyone saw anything but he left before closing time and the river bank route to his home will have been quiet at that time of night. There are no railings either as you walk under the bridge near The Ferryman.'

Davies thanked him for the call and went in search of Buxton who was still at the coffee machine trying to get a drink. He related the call from Moore. Buxton dismissed it as being irrelevant.

'We may not like coincidences but they do happen.'

Davies got Buxton a coffee from the machine and they returned to the office. Buxton decided not to ring Moore back and settled back in his chair and closed his eyes. Davies knew it was futile to attempt any further conversation. Buxton would be dead to the world for the next ten minutes.

For Green, under the circumstances, Guy Pepper was the worst solicitor that he could have appointed. Pepper listened to all the evidence that Buxton had produced and knew that a half decent barrister would get Green acquitted of murder, if indeed the case ever came to court. Green was under no illusions now. He was going to jail for theft. No matter how the charges were dressed up, he was a thief but that was infinitely better than going to jail labelled as a 'nonce'. He did not need to hear Buxton's graphic account of what life inside would be like. He had heard enough stories and Pepper was about to prey on those fears.

For Pepper, paedophiles deserved everything they got and more. Pepper's own younger sister had been snatched from a playground when he was supposed to be looking after her. Even though she had been found quickly her rescue came too late to prevent her from being violated. Pepper never truly recovered from the guilt. He also knew, and previously worked with, a male barrister who had suffered similar abuse. They were charged as professionals to do their best to defend their clients but if the client wanted to plead guilty who were they to argue? It did not take much to convince Green that if he was going inside at least if he went down for murder the charge would give him some kudos and Pepper felt sure he could fabricate a good enough story to show that Green had been a victim. Perhaps even a crime of passion. With luck he would be out in a few years. After all, life didn't really mean life anymore did it? Pepper did not just dislike his client, he now detested him with a passion. Pepper also knew that Buxton was aware of the rape of his sister.

When Buxton came back Green informed him that he would confess to the murder of Lucy Thomas on condition that any charges relating to child pornography were not pursued. Buxton smiled and told him that he could make no promises but he would make the correct recommendations. Neither Buxton, Davies nor Green noticed the slight smile on Pepper's lips. Green also said that he would make a statement implicating Nigel Preece. He wasn't going down alone.

Davies was stunned by this turn of events and still remained less than convinced that Green was guilty of murder. Something, he was certain, was seriously wrong with the whole scenario.

CHAPTER 55

Jake closed the folder on his desk and rose to put it away in the filing cabinet. Then he had second thoughts and put the folder and its contents through the office shredder. It was one less problem to bother about. He was a little subdued. For a few days after a kill he often felt this way. In its own way it was probably something akin to post-coital depression he surmised. He sat, closed his eyes and allowed himself the luxury of letting his mind drift back to the previous Monday evening. He didn't often look back but sometimes reliving the moment helped to lift his spirits.

He remembered leaning on the garage door for several minutes, hating the wait. Yet perversely, the waiting was worthwhile. The anticipation heightened the buzz. He heard a door close and remembered straining to hear the footfalls on the pavement. He had exhaled slowly, controlling his breathing and ridding his body of some of the heightened tension. No rush. A quick scan around him. No one in sight. His victim came round the corner. It took only a split second to verify the walker's identity and then he moved quickly and stealthily forward. The deed was done in seconds. Another life ended. He walked away, not hurrying and not looking back. He knew that if he were caught he would probably be classified as a physcopath but what did he care? They, whoever they turned out to be, had to catch him first.

He didn't miss his old life at all now. How could he? There was still a chance that someone somewhere had a file with his name on it but he doubted it. It had been several years now and nothing had happened. No tap on the shoulder or knock at the door. Soon, he would take up the offer of a Directorship which Joe kept offering. Perhaps he could even risk a visit to the bank. Proving the accounts were his might prove difficult but not totally impossible.

He had been seriously worried in the weeks after the death of the accountant but he couldn't have run anymore. There was nowhere left too run. If the papers had been found then so be it but as time passed by he thought it more and more likely that everything connected to him had been destroyed in the fire that raged through the accountant's office block. Despite the near hysteria surrounding the London bomb, the explosion in the office block had been attributed to a gas leak in a faulty water heater. Jake was lucky. Life now was good and occasionally he still got to ply his trade as he had done earlier in the week and as he had done a year and a half earlier when he murdered the step parents of Joe's dead wife Lynn. Now that mission he had really enjoyed.

Murdering them had been a pleasure. When Joe told him all the stories of their behaviour he almost felt he had done society a favour. He dealt with them as a present for Joe. Although he loved Joe it would also send him a message. They would never be lovers but their lives were now inextricably linked. He had taken a taxi from Harpley to Rednall and hired a plain white van for the journey north. No one would take much notice of yet another white van.

Parking two streets away from Joe's former in-laws home he entered their house in the early hours of the morning, the domestic locks taking only seconds to yield to his skills. The air was thick with the aroma of furniture polish. Joe had told him that the house was so immaculate that nothing was ever out of place. He moved quietly up the stairs, confident that nothing would obstruct his progress, his ears attuned for any sound or movement. Entering Alan's bedroom at the front of the house he found the old man fast asleep and snoring gently. Jake closed the door quietly behind him and felt no compassion at all as he placed a pillow over the sleeping man's head. There was barely a twitch as the body defences came awake and fought for life. He heard the muffled but very weak cry as the legs, unable to thrash around in the thick blankets, gave a slight kick and then were still. Jake counted slowly to two hundred, alert for any movement from the bedroom next door, and then removed the pillow. The eyes were still closed and he felt for a pulse but Alan was dead. Jake replaced the pillow over Alan's face. Joe would view his demise as a mercy killing for the old man's life had for many years been a living hell.

Jake opened the door and stepped on to the landing closing the door sharply behind him not worrying now about remaining quiet. He wanted Mavis awake and better that she should wake herself gently rather than with a start when he opened her door. He didn't want her to scream. He heard her beginning to stir in her room.

'Alan, whash are you doing?' she hissed.

He took a deep breath, opened her door, snapping on the light as he entered.

'Don't be alarmed,' he said firmly and with authority. 'I'm a police officer.'

He flourished his wallet at her knowing that she would not comprehend what it really was but would assume it to be a warrant card. She was severely disorientated by the sudden light and the circumstance. All she took in was a well dressed, smiling man in an overcoat by her bed.

'There's been a break-in further down the street and we are checking doors. Yours was open and we thought there might have been an intruder. I shouted. As no one came down I thought the place may be empty.' She was coming awake now, her eyes blinking rapidly, adjusting to the light. She opened her gummy mouth to speak.

'Alan! Why dint shew lock the daw?' She had difficulty forming the words without her teeth. 'Oh I'm shorry the shtupid idiot would forget hiss own head if it wont screwed on.' She began to rise. 'Alan!' she hissed loudly again.

Jake stepped out on to the landing allowing her to regain some dignity. The door partly closed as she took her dressing gown from behind the door and he heard the chink of a glass as she retrieved her teeth.

'I'm afraid he must be dead to the world,' Jake said without any hint of irony. She came shuffling out of her room and made as if to go into the front bedroom. When she realised Jake was blocking her path she moved towards the stairs. Jake smiled and followed. He let her take the first two steps. She was still grumbling at her husband's lack of response. She turned and was about to shout again but Jake moved swiftly and whipped his scarf round her neck and his other hand across her mouth.

He felt the familiar feeling in his groin as he saw the look of abject terror in her eyes. He could almost smell her fear.

'One sound and I push,' he whispered softly. Jake didn't move his hand but pushed her gently back till her heels were hanging over the step and she was balanced on the balls of her feet. All that prevented her from falling was the scarf held taut around her neck. She whimpered behind his gloved hand and tears filled her eyes. He knew her bladder would be on the point of letting go.

'This is for Joe. You will never bother him again.'

He saw the look of disbelief in her eyes and then he released his hold and her pudgy arms wind milled as she fell backwards. A cry rose in her throat but she crashed down the stairs striking her head on the hall table as she came to rest, her neck bent over at a grotesque angle. Jake followed her down the stairs. He reached for her neck knowing that she was already dead but checking anyway. He saw the expanding pool of blood and smelled the familiar stench as he stepped away not wanting to disturb anything further. He left the way he came and was back in Harpley the following morning.

A knock on the door brought him back to reality. The reverie had done him good. Lizzie dropped another folder on his desk. They shared a few pleasantries and then she left. He knew that Lizzie didn't totally approve of him. He opened the folder and pulled out several pieces of paper, invoices and copies of letters. A plumber in Rednall was having difficulty obtaining payment from a client. He smiled when he saw the name and address. 'Small world,' he thought. Well, David Thomas had a reprieve of sorts but after the dust from his wife's murder had settled then his debt would require sorting. Perhaps his wife was insured and the matter would be settled quietly. If not, well, Jake knew the address. The melancholic mood had lifted from his shoulders and tonight he would visit his favourite bar. He needed another form of release.

CHAPTER 56

The following Monday, whilst Buxton basked in the glory of a crime solved Davies took the day off. He was exhausted and far from happy. The nagging doubts would not go away. They had arrested Preece on the Friday evening. As expected he protested his innocence. In fact he hadn't just protested he screamed that he was not guilty and as they put him struggling desperately into the patrol car, he actually wet himself. Davies had never seen a suspect do that before and he was shocked and disturbed. At the station however Preece readily confessed to the huge amounts of money he had taken in bribes. He had cheated the Hatton Group and the Inland Revenue. He was facing several years in jail for fraud and a large fine to say nothing of the assessment that the Revenue would conduct which would inevitably result in a huge financial penalty. Bankruptcy would be a near certainty. To conspiracy to murder however, he denied everything. He cried several times throughout the interview and Davies had been genuinely concerned about his state of mind. Preece claimed repeatedly that he was not aware that Lucy Thomas and Green were lovers. In fact he seemed genuinely shocked by the revelation. Buxton simply didn't believe him. The interview had been suspended in the late hours. Preece was left in no doubt that he was in for a gruelling session the following day and he knew he was facing a long period of incarceration. He was questioned over the weekend which did nothing for Buxton's mood. Preece had continually broken down and his solicitor constantly interrupted the proceedings further irritating Buxton. However, by Sunday evening they had several hours of taped interviews. Buxton admitted to Davies that he thought Preece would be a basket case before he was released. How to prove conspiracy though was troubling him. It was just one man's word against the other. Buxton noted that Davies was looking exhausted and told him not to come in the next day. In truth, both of them needed a break from the other.

Davies didn't manage to sleep late on his day off despite the efforts of the past few days. His mobile would eventually see to that. He slept badly, the runner still bothered him as did the rest of what he still thought was conflicting evidence and he still couldn't get the feeling from his mind that they had missed something about Joe Quinn. He didn't even know why he disliked the man. It was just an instinct that something about him was not right. Davies was however dozing peacefully when at eight o'clock his phone rang. He almost ignored it but didn't, some sixth sense telling him that it was going to be important. It was.

'Hello, Davies speaking.'

'Hello. Sorry to bother you, it's David Thomas. I need your advice and you said to call at anytime.'

Davies, wide awake now, confirmed that it was fine whilst inwardly regretting the common courtesy.

'I've collected some of Lucy's jewellery from the police station and there appears to be a medallion missing, a St. Christopher. Lucy bought it in Spain a few years ago so I doubt it's worth anything, but she wore it all the time. I just wondered if you knew anything about it or if there was any reason for withholding it?'

'I'm sorry, no. Look, give me an hour and I'll call you back. You managed to catch me just as I was getting up.'

Thomas apologised and Davies broke the connection. He then rang DI Kirk who confirmed that no St. Christopher had been found at the crime scene. His next call was to the police lab.

'Was there any sign that Mrs. Thomas had been wearing a necklace?' he asked Lee Park.

'We had no way of telling. There was far too much tissue damage.'

A dead end? He sat at the kitchen table and pulled out a notepad. He thought back to their visit to Quinn's home. What had they missed? Had they been too relaxed? Quinn answered their questions and had been polite and open. Think! It was hot in Quinn's kitchen. Overpoweringly so, even for the time of year. But perhaps that was just because the house had been closed up all day. The smell? A distinct, if faint, odour of, of what? Burning rubber? Would a contaminated log give off such a smell, or was it something else? What were they missing? Quinn hadn't been surprised to see them. Should he have been? They had shown their warrant cards. He hadn't scrutinised them. But then not many people did. Still, was it a clue to something more relevant? The balaclava? Of course Quinn owned one. He was after all a racing driver. White. Why had he mentioned the colour? Did he know the killer wore black? And what about his next door neighbour, Rachael Mason? Was there more to their relationship than just good neighbours? And Green's behaviour bothered him. Apart from his confession, no one they had interviewed had suspected that he was having an affair with Mrs. Thomas. Not even Preece. Only Quinn had shown no surprise. Was it significant? From what he had seen of Green surely he would have boasted about it to someone if he was sleeping with her? He just wasn't the type to be that discreet was he? And the photographs apparently taken several years ago and before Lucy's affair with Quinn? Did she have an affair with Green, ditch him for Quinn and then return to Green when she and Quinn split up? And all during the time she was married. Was all this a motive for Quinn to murder her? Was Lucy Thomas that promiscuous? Certainly it wasn't the impression that her work colleagues were giving. Or did David Thomas actually know? Had he seen the photographs already? And what was it about the photographs that were not right?

He rang Park again who answered on the first ring.

'Lee, I'm sorry to bother you again. Have you seen the photographs of Lucy Thomas and Stuart Green discovered in his house?'

'I've got them here. Why?'

'Does anything strike you as odd about them? Can you describe what you see preferably without exaggerating?'

'Difficult under the circumstances.'

'Try.'

'OK, two people, one male, one female apparently in the throes of having sexual intercourse.'

Davies could hear Park shuffling the photographs.

'Why apparently?' he asked.

'There's no close up depiction of penetration so we can only assume that's what they are doing. The female has her eyes closed in all the shots.'

'Could she have been unconscious?'

'It's possible,' answered Park furrowing his brow as he studied the images more closely, 'and in none of the shots is the female holding the male. The male is supporting her in them all apart from where he's laying on top of her. Her arms are by her side and her legs are not pulled towards her as you would expect. The one where her face is to his groin he could actually be holding her by the hair.'

'Could it just be violent sex?'

'It could, yes.'

'Could the photos have been staged?'

'Again it's possible. What you see may not be what you get. I suppose it's a matter of interpretation. You're not happy about this case are you?'

'No. Everything just seems too easy.'

'Have you read all my report?'

'I started to but got called away so no, not yet. Why?'

'Look, on balance the evidence points to Green being the perpetrator. However, there are a few pieces of evidence which I think need closer consideration.'

'Go on.'

'Firstly, the two bloodstained mobile phones. Although they both revealed clear prints the bloodstains were smudged and on the thinner sides of the phones.'

'Your point being?'

'Whoever handled the phones was obviously wearing gloves, which you would probably expect. They were both picked up though in almost exactly the same positions which indicates that they were handled with some care. A deliberate, rather than a reflex action.'

'And secondly?'

'The knife in the bin. I accept that your man could just be so arrogant that he thought he could get away with it but why not just toss the knife in the river and why weren't the gloves with the knife in the bin? And where are the gloves?'

Davies almost held his breath as Park continued.

'The cigarette butts are clearly the remnants of cigarettes smoked by Green. The finger nails are his and the dried colloidal mucus is from his nose but there is a problem.'

'Which is?'

'There's too much of the stuff. The area around one of the cigarette butts had a high concentration of dried mucus. We bagged a further small quantity at the scene and more in the car but there is no evidence of him excavating his nose and then wiping his finger either near the garage or in the car. It's faintly possible the stuff was on his clothes but unlikely.'

'Was all the evidence planted?'

'Can't say for definite.'

'Your best guess?'

'I'm not ruling the possibility out. Look, Green almost certainly suffers from rhinotillexomania. That's a compulsive nose picker to you. I'd try to find out where he wipes his finger. He may eat some of it of course, many people do. I've read somewhere of a lung specialist in Austria who claims it strengthens the immune system. My first port of call would be to check his workplace. I'd start with the underside of his desk.'

Davies thanked him and slammed the phone down in its cradle. Bloody Buxton! An image of Quinn again came into his mind. Quinn had been in Green's office earlier on the day of the murder, yet they had never questioned Green about his visit. A mistake? And what about the missing St. Christopher? Buxton! He knocked something over when they sat down in Quinn's kitchen. Loose change scattered on the work surface. Was there something else?

Davies pulled out a map of the county and spread it on his kitchen table. Despite being a bachelor, the flat was always tidy, just in case he got lucky. Not that he had much time for relationships but he could hope. He studied the map closely and then found some map pins. Firstly he placed a pin at the crime scene and then one after the other at Green's address, the car park at the picnic area, Preece's home and to the south, Quinn's home. Was there a link? He couldn't see it. Then he took the pin from Preece's home and looked again. Was he manufacturing a link? This time he spotted it. The park and the homes belonging to Green and Quinn were all by a waterway. But what did it prove? Nothing. If Quinn was involved how could he have got from Rednall to his home? A boat would have taken far too long. Days even. Besides, his neighbours had sworn that he was at home. The canal still bothered him. What was he missing? Then he remembered the conversation with Sergeant Bill Russell the day after the murder.

Davies used his mobile and was relieved to find that Russell was still on duty. Russell confirmed that there had been an attempt to steal a boat, the Joey B, from Woodgate basin. He stuck a pin in the map. It was enroute from Rednall to Harpley but did it have anything to do with the case? Having nothing better to do he decided that it would do no harm to check.

Instead of going to the gym as he usually did on his day off, Davies decided to take out his mountain bike. It was then that he had a revelation. The towpath. All the canals and waterways had a towpath. Was it possible to get from Rednall to Harpley via the towpaths? He knew the answer before he had finished asking himself the question. Of course it was and as he looked at the map he realised that not only was it possible, it was also a more direct route. He rang Russell back and got the name of the boat owner, a Mr. Godfrey, who reported the attempted crime. Russell asked him what was going on. Davies didn't elaborate.

He quickly donned his cycling gear and set off. His first port of call though wasn't the canal. He went back to Mere Lane and quickly measured accurately the height of the road sign. It was just less than six feet, confirming again his reservations. The only indication that there had been a major crime in the area was a sign asking for help from the public. He was now totally convinced that Green was not the runner.

Next, he remounted the bike and headed towards the canal and when he reached the towpath he turned in the direction of Harpley. He rode at a steady pace and found the going surprisingly easy. As he rode his unanswered questions kept running through his mind. There was also the apparent suicide in Harpley. Was Quinn connected to that death as well? Despite Buxton's feelings on the subject, Davies distrusted coincidences especially when they began to mount up.

There were very few boats on the canal at this time of year and very few walkers. Within forty minutes he reached Woodgate basin. He quickly established that he had a problem. With so many canals feeding into the basin how did he get from one towpath to the other? He saw the sign taking him to Harpley except it was pointing in the wrong direction. There were several boats moored, one of which was the 'Joey B' and Davies was pleased to see a plume of smoke emanating from the smokestack indicating that the owner was likely aboard. He dropped the bike by the towpath and knocked on the hatch. A dog instantly barked and a few seconds later the hatch opened emitting a cloud of cigarette smoke followed by a scowling, long haired, elderly man who asked sharply and rudely, 'What the fuck do you want?'

Davies, although taken aback, quickly explained who he was, showed his identification, verified that the man was Mr. Godfrey and then asked him about the attempted boat theft. The man's demeanour softened only slightly as he motioned Davies to follow him into the interior of the boat. A half hour chat and a mug of very strong coffee revealed an intelligent and warm hearted individual beneath the gruff exterior. His recollection of the events was clear and concise. He had been walking his dog when he saw someone trying to steal his boat. He shouted and whoever it was fled on a bike much like the one Davies was riding. Then he fell off. The dog, a Jack Russell, gave chase, more in hope than expectation. The rider remounted and rode away in the direction of Harpley. He was reasonably sure though that the dog had sunk his teeth into the thief. He hadn't seen which way the rider had come but he was almost certain it was from the direction of Rednall. He was very certain it was a man because of the tight fitting cycle outfit.

'I know the outline of a woman when I see one!'

He himself had walked up the towpath and gone across the bridge and then down the opposite bank. This explained to Davies the route to Harpley. He confirmed this by asking Godfrey about the different canals. The bridge was roughly three quarters of a mile upstream. Davies wondered whether the rider had been trying to steal the boat or merely using it as a bridge. He didn't explain this to Godfrey but he was convinced that this was what had happened.

Davies thanked Godfrey for his help and decided against riding to Harpley. He had enough to think about. He had not gone far when the tyre blew. It didn't matter. He reached into his rucksack and pulled out a can of Seal & Flate. As he did so he suddenly realised what else had been nagging at him about the visit to Quinn's! The garage! Why did Quinn have a can of Seal & Flate on the shelf when there was no sign of a bike? The shelf was above four empty brackets. What had the brackets supported? Davies thought he knew.

His thoughts were interrupted by the ringing of his mobile phone. The call was from Andrew Mason. By the end of the conversation Davies knew that he had to voice his concerns to a higher authority than Buxton. Buxton was convinced he had the right man and was so stubborn that he would not change his mind. Davies recognised that he could be risking his career but he knew it was the right thing to do. Having one's uncle as the Chief Constable could sometimes be an advantage.

CHAPTER 57

Andrew Mason had been suspicious of Rachael for some time. She had changed in very subtle ways. She now always wore make up even when gardening and putting on her make up at the start of the day, as she always did, seemed to take just that little bit longer. She had always been smart even when casual but there was smart and there was smart. Now all her clothes appeared to have designer labels attached and every week she came home with some new item. Her hair never seemed to be out of place. Worse, it had been months since they last made love and even then, for her the act had clearly been a chore.

When the two police officers visited their home the previous week, Andrew would have done almost anything to have caused a problem for Quinn. He didn't like him and guessed that Quinn was not a fan of his either. He could not contemplate however that Quinn was Rachael's lover. He knew Quinn flirted with her and that she responded but he doubted that Quinn possessed the intellect to satisfy Rachael and she, he felt sure, would not pursue a relationship just for sexual gratification.

On the Friday evening he had caught Rachael chuckling to herself in the kitchen as she put down her mobile phone. She claimed it was just a friend sending her a joke text but she had been reticent about the caller's identity. Lying didn't come easily to Rachael and although it had disturbed him he hadn't pursued the matter. They ate dinner in near silence. Rachael had been distant, her mind clearly elsewhere. Later he tried to make love to her. Not for the first time over the past few months, she refused his advances, feigning tiredness. He waited until she fell asleep before going downstairs. Her mobile was in her handbag. When he checked the message box on the phone it was empty. Even the list of missed and received calls was blank. Did everyone apart from him always delete every text and call record? He doubted it and was now even more convinced that Rachael was hiding something from him. He thought about hiding the phone or taking the SIM card out. In the end he did neither.

The following day he spent working in his study while Rachael busied herself around the house although he wondered just what it was that took her so long as the place was always pristine. In the afternoon she went out claiming that she needed fresh vegetables. The boys were coming home for Sunday lunch. How would they react if their mother was having an affair? He wondered if Rachael was meeting someone somewhere. If she was, he was certain it wasn't Quinn because his Range Rover was still parked outside the garage.

When Rachael returned she had indeed bought vegetables.

Saturday evening passed much like Friday. He realised that they had drifted apart, but for her to have an affair was a different matter. He could, she couldn't!

He was glad when Sunday lunch came around. Rachael cooked her usual superb roast. The boys were their usual cheery selves and it had been an enjoyable family occasion. No matter what happened between them, they had raised two fine boys. As was customary after Sunday lunch Rachael and the boys went for a walk. Normally he went too. On impulse he decided not to go. After they left he went through to the kitchen to make a coffee and saw that Rachael had left her handbag and phone on the kitchen worktop. Andrew couldn't help himself. He checked the call records and they were still blank. There were no messages in the inbox and no record of any texts being sent. Then he looked at the list of telephone contacts. To his surprise there were only four male contacts listed by first name. His own, the two boys and a Joe. He knew she had Quinn's number, as did he, as they kept an eye on his place when he was away. He checked his own phone and confirmed that it was Quinn's number.

He began to think that he was being stupid and worrying needlessly. Rachael wasn't having an affair. They were just going through a bad patch. It happened to the best of marriages. He was just feeling insecure. Perhaps it was an age thing? Still, he had to be sure. He hit the menu button on Rachael's phone and selected messages, create message and tapped in "I LUV U" before, after a seconds pause, hitting the send button. The screen showed a request for a number and he scrolled down the list of contacts to Quinn's entry. He paused again before confirming the number and hitting send once again. Then, when he saw 'message sent' come up on the screen he panicked. How embarrassing could this turn out to be if he was wrong and he surely was? Only a few seconds later the phone beeped with a reply.

'ME 2'

Andrew felt his stomach heave. He knew Quinn was out having seen him drive away earlier. No doubt he was having Sunday lunch at the golf club as he usually did. He replaced the phone on the worktop, returned to the lounge and collapsed into his chair by the fire, fighting hard to control the rage and humiliation threatening to overpower him. This could not be happening! Not to him! Rachael could not do this! Not with Quinn! He slammed his hands down on the chair arms, rose, opened the drinks cabinet and poured himself a large whisky. Shaking slightly he tossed the golden liquid down his throat with one swallow. His anger began to subside to be replaced by pure hatred.

When Rachael and the boys returned they were in good spirits, despite the rain. With a great effort of will he made sure that the rest of the day passed normally. After the boys left, quite late, they sat for some time watching the news. When they went to bed he kissed her on the cheek and said 'Goodnight' but he made no attempt to make love to her. Inside he was seething and thinking long and hard about Quinn. In the early hours, unable to sleep and having replayed various scenarios over in his mind, most of which had Quinn coming to a grisly and painful end, he got out of bed and went downstairs. Staring at the dead embers of the fire he suddenly realised what it was that had been troubling him all week about the events of the previous Monday evening.

It was the lights. When he had been out having a cigarette he had seen the light go out in Quinn's study. But Quinn had still been sitting at the desk. When the light came on in the lounge Quinn was already sitting down in his chair. Andrew had seen no one else. How could Quinn have achieved this? Had he really been at home after all? Andrew didn't have an answer.

Despite his feelings towards Quinn Andrew abhorred violence, but he was an intransigent man, a characteristic which often provoked people to the point of losing their tempers. No amount of reasoning with him could ever alter his stance if he believed he was right. His attitude was that he was always right and that anyone who disagreed with him had to be an idiot. Whenever he felt threatened with harm his defence would be to fall back on his favourite saying that 'violence is the last refuge of the incompetent' as though it conferred on him some moral superiority. Only once in his life had this failed to protect him when a colleague became so exasperated with his refusal to accept common sense that he said,

'You know Andrew; you really can be a pompous, self righteous penis at times. Personally I much prefer the saying that you should never let your sense of morals get in the way of doing what's right' and then he punched Andrew square on the nose! He looked down at the now prostrate Andrew and continued with a very satisfied smile on his face,

'I'm sure you're right but I do feel so much better,' before turning away flexing his painful hand. Andrew, his nose bleeding profusely, made no attempt to rise until his assailant left the room. Despite his colleague tendering his resignation Andrew never forgot the pain, or how humiliated he felt as other colleagues failed to come to his aid and smiled at his perceived loss of dignity. They too had grown tired of his arrogance. The truth was that he was a coward. Rachael had once been mugged and even though Andrew was close enough to intervene he let the attack play out before coming to her aid.

Andrew was frightened now of Quinn. He also knew he needed to find the truth. He was reasonably certain that Quinn would not assault him if Rachael was present but he couldn't be absolutely sure. As he glanced up from the fire he saw the answer to his dilemma.

On the Monday morning he took the card left by Andrew Davies from the mantelpiece and rang the young officer later that morning from work voicing his concerns and making a suggestion. Davies thanked him for the information and promised that he would keep him informed. He also asked Andrew not to do anything precipitous. Andrew still didn't believe that Quinn was guilty of murder. As for Rachael, if she and Quinn were sleeping together, he knew exactly when he could catch them out. As usual, on Tuesday evening, he would be away. He knew he could not cancel and also knew that it would be late when he finished work. But if he were to return home very early on Wednesday morning?

CHAPTER 58

Wednesday November 27th.

It's funny the thoughts that run through the mind as we lay in our beds. Take this morning. Rachael spent the night and when I awoke this morning she was laid beside me with her head nestling in the crook of my arm. I just love the contented purring noise she makes when she's asleep after a good romp. I had been very touched by her 'I LUV U' message on the previous Sunday afternoon. I was at the golf club having lunch but I still found time to send a text back. I've not mentioned it since. She caught me at a moment of weakness when I'd just had a drink. I knew then that the time was not far away when serious decisions would have to be made about our relationship.

As I lay there staring at the ceiling I couldn't help but smile at how things had turned out. Lucy dead, Stuart Green charged with her murder and both he and Nigel Preece being investigated for accepting bribes, defrauding the company and Customs and Excise. How many charges would they eventually face? The rumours coming out of the Hatton Group suggest that the police are paying close attention to Green's collection of pornography and that Preece has suffered a mental breakdown. Did I care? Not one tiny bit. The whole story has been headline news in the local press and on the local radio and it's even made the nationals.

The murder and subsequent arrests completely overshadowed the death of Frank Holmes who had, according to all the reports, either fallen in the river or taken his own life on the same evening that Lucy died. Little did they know. Holmes knew the rules when we gave him work. As did the others who tried to break away from our little cooperative. We gave them all a second chance but Holmes went back to his old ways of giving a price and then going back for more money. By cheating the customer he was also cheating on me and I can't allow that. He will have boasted to others because he's not the type to keep his mouth shut. His death will send out a clear message to all our 'subbies.' Step out of line and they know the consequences. My attitudes changed after I left the Hatton Group. Am I a bully? Perhaps, but I'll never be the statue again, always the pigeon.

Jake dealt with Holmes in his usual efficient way, just as he dealt with Mavis and Alan. Holmes had even moved house but it is easy to find people nowadays. Most of us can run but we can't hide. As the rotund and toad faced Holmes left the pub Jake stepped out and simply pushed him into the fast flowing, swollen river. No fuss or drama, a problem solved. Jake knew that Holmes was a non-swimmer and his cries for help fell on deaf ears as he was rapidly swept away. Some people just never learn. My way or highway. Better yet, Quinn's way or no way.

I knew Mavis was not Alan's murderer. I always thought he would be the one to kill her not the other way round. She couldn't kill him, she would have had no one to abuse. Jake was away that night. I tried to contact him and his phone was off so I went round to the flat. He was out and when I questioned in him the following morning he just said he was out on a job. Then I found out Mavis and Alan were dead. Jake was with me at the time. I saw the look on his face and said, 'Thank you.' He just smiled.

The Hatton Group was in total disarray. Had the Group been a company quoted on the stock exchange then the shares would have plummeted. Pity really, I could have bought a few. I've no doubt the company will survive although the adverse publicity will have a knock on effect on its business for quite some time.

Thinking back it must have been about three years after leaving the company that I bumped into Preece and Green again. My life of course changed dramatically over those three years. The three of us were at a sportsmen's charity dinner. I had no idea they were going to be there and I don't suppose they were expecting to see me either. When I saw the two of them I made a point of seizing the initiative. I crossed the room and greeted them both like long lost friends. I shook both their hands enthusiastically hoping to catch them off guard. Preece, however, responded in a similar manner. Green was a little more reluctant and kept making nervous glances at Preece. Naturally I bought the drinks. My time with the Hatton Group was never mentioned and neither was Lucy Thomas. They were both complimentary about my business career and sporting achievements which were beginning to be widely reported by the local media. What really took them by surprise was when I told them they had been dealing with me indirectly through the used car sites. We parted that night the best of friends. Or so they thought.

After that night I made a point of calling in personally at the Harvington branch every couple of weeks or so and buying the odd used car. I always paid a little over the odds and also made sure that Green got a little something for his trouble. Of course I have kept records of every transaction and my books are exemplary.

The job at Harpley proved too big for Green, as I knew it would, and the company transferred him to Harvington. Preece also found his career stagnating although he was made a director of a new company the Hatton Group formed. This turned out to be some management think tank which did not trade and had but one share wholly owned by the parent company. He was the director of nothing, which was just as well because he couldn't direct traffic on a children's play mat. How ironic that almost the very scenario that he conned me with should actually come to fruition albeit in a truncated form.

Harry Morgan left Rednall only a few months after replacing Stuart Green. He hated the branch and found lots of mistakes that Green left behind including customer complaints, which Green had failed to resolve by simply ignoring them. Morgan's own complaints fell on deaf ears. Another cock up by Freddie Fox trying to fix something that hadn't been broken in the first place.

I have often heard me mam say that revenge is a dish best served cold. With Nigel Preece, Stuart Green and particularly Lucy Thomas, five years is long enough for my revenge to have been the coldest dish. I would gladly have waited twenty five years if that is what it would have taken. As I've always said, I'm not one to bear a grudge; at least not once I've got even! Despite my new found fame and fortune they should all have remembered one of my favourite maxims, I-NEVER-LOSE.

When I plunged the knife into Lucy's neck my only regret was that she didn't suffer longer. Still, at least I had the satisfaction of knowing that the last face she saw in this life was mine. I may not have been her last thought, but I was her last vision. And believe me I know that as I lowered her gently to the ground she knew precisely who it was that ended her life.

There is no such thing as the perfect crime but this one has been a pretty good effort. I knew I would need a bit of luck to carry it all off, even though my planning is always meticulous. Besides, nowadays I'm a lucky guy, right? Show me a stretch of water and I'll walk on it! Nevertheless as I lay in bed and allowed my hand to move towards Rachael's nipple I reflected that I had committed some mistakes and that things had occurred which I hadn't foreseen.

Befriending Green worked out better than I could have hoped. I was no longer a threat to him so he had nothing to lose. Paying over the odds just confirmed to him, and no doubt Preece, that I was a complete numpty who they could both exploit. The lads who run both my used car sites would no doubt agree and I'm sure they will be pleased to know that I will no longer be buying some of their stock. Over the past couple of years Green has given me no end of personal information. I already knew about his predilection for pornography but even I was surprised at the extent of his collection. He even boasted to me about his sexual activities with his wife. I know all about his kids and his wife's hobbies. It was very useful knowing when she would be out. I did seriously consider having an affair with her and then decided against it. He may not have been sufficiently bothered. Hell, he might have wanted to join in!

I've also studied his habits. He bites his nails. Not all the time so that they are down to the quick, just when they need cutting. He also picks his nose. I'm sure he doesn't always know when he's doing it until he's finished having a good broggle and then he examines his finger end before wiping it under the desk almost in embarrassment. I'm sure he thinks no one notices. It's surprising how many men do exactly the same.

On the Monday Lucy died an opportunity presented itself to complete my plan which was too good to miss. I knew the time was ripe as it was a week when the moon would be full. I was in Green's office when a salesman walked in needing him to look at a car. He had just bitten the nails on one hand and flicked each one casually on the floor. He had also been at his nose. We hadn't completed our business so I waited in his office for him to return. Using a sheet of paper it took seconds to sweep up the nails into a plastic used vehicle document wallet. Then I ran his ruler under the desk and caught the dried nose droppings in the same bag. When he came back I offered to buy him a coffee and he accepted. I knew he would take the opportunity for a fag break. We stood outside in his favourite little corner where he always went for a smoke. When he finished he dropped the cigarette end on the floor and put his foot on it. He never screws the butts into the ground. I kept him talking long enough for him to light another and then got a bit of luck. One of the other salesmen came looking for him and he extinguished the half smoked cigarette and dropped it on the floor. Using the end of a pen I flicked it into the plastic bag along with a couple of other dog ends which were of the same brand. I knew that Green always smoked alone and I knew that the yardman would have swept the floor that morning so all the cigarette ends were from that day.

I then went back to his office and we completed our business. When I left I made sure that my mobile was still on his desk. He never noticed that it wasn't my regular phone and nor did he notice that I kept a pair of gloves on the whole time I was with him. He came after me with the phone and handed it back. Until that day the phone had always been kept in a thin plastic case and after I left him I placed it carefully back in the same case. It was this phone that I left in the BMW after killing Lucy.

That same night I left home at a quarter to six leaving the lights on in the kitchen and hallway. I also left the heavy drapes open in both the lounge and my upstairs study. All the windows are covered by light net curtains. I'm old fashioned that way. Two standard lamps, one in each room, were left on and plugged into timers. I was dressed in the appropriate clothes for cycling and avoided putting on the luminous smock until I was clear of the house. I had a rucksack with a change of clothes and I took a can of Seal and Flate just in case of a puncture.

As Rachael moved beside me I suddenly remembered that I had bought two cans of the stuff. The remaining can was still on the shelf above the brackets where I had hung my two bikes. I made a mental note to get rid of the can later when I got up. I doubted that it would be of any significance.

The mountain bike along with a foldaway cycle, Seal and Flate and cycling gear had all been purchased for cash and from different outlets. The mountain bike was light and easy to carry and I never let the wheels touch the ground until I was on tarmac. I cycled over to Rednall using the back roads. It was a route I had travelled many times before over the previous eighteen months.

Traffic was light and I set a reasonable pace arriving at Webbers Wood at around quarter past seven. I chained the bike to a tree in the undergrowth, took off the luminous top, put it in the rucksack along with the helmet and jogged down to Lucy's home. I set an easy pace and it took me around fifteen minutes and I hardly saw another soul. I knew that if Lucy followed her usual routine she would be going to the gym very shortly. I had been watching her ever more closely over the preceding three months. Prior to this I had only kept an intermittent eye on her. I would drive by every couple of weeks or so just to make sure she hadn't moved. Jake helped of course. I knew exactly when she changed her car. As the nights began to lengthen I stepped up my surveillance to almost every other night during the week. Had the opportunity not presented itself, or she not done as she usually did, then I would have postponed her death for another time. As I said, it could have taken twenty five years or more if necessary.

I used to sit astride the bike in the coppice opposite her home, sometimes using the fold-away cycle having driven across to Rednall in the Range Rover. The fold-away spent most of its time in the back of the Range Rover. It was handy for short trips. I just looked like any other two-wheeled commuter. There were several times when I was tempted to call out to Lucy but I never did. What would have been the point? During the summer I photographed her in the garden using my hideously expensive digital camera fitted with a telephoto lens. I was surprised to see that she was still wearing the St. Christopher. I almost sent her a copy of the photo, and then thought better of it. Why put her on her guard? I deleted the images. Every once in awhile I would ring her mobile, usually in an evening or at weekends. I used the code to withhold my number of course. It would have annoyed her and irritated the hell out of her husband. I didn't do it too often in case she changed her number. Even if she had, I would have been able to obtain the new number from someone at Hatton's.

I positioned myself outside the garage giving plenty of time for the security light to extinguish itself. Then I deposited some fingernails, nose detritus and two cigarette ends on the ground. The half smoked butt was a gem. It would look as though the killer had been disturbed in the act of smoking. I heard the back door rattle in its frame as someone closed it and I pressed send on the mobile phone that Green had handled earlier in the day. The text message, written earlier, went to a second mobile in my rucksack. This phone had also always been kept in a thin plastic case. Both phones had been purchased some three years earlier each from separate outlets and service providers in Rednall. They were both cheap pay-as-you-go phones for which I paid cash and although no one insisted, I registered them in the names of Stuart Green and Lucy Thomas respectively explaining to the sales assistants that they were being bought as presents. I reasoned that after three years there would be no chance of anyone remembering me as the purchaser. The chances were that the two assistants would have long since moved on. I knew which service providers Green and Lucy used so any correspondence would not arouse suspicion. It was highly unlikely that either of them would read it anyway the likelihood being that any letters would be treated as junk mail and end up in the bin. If either of them had changed providers then I reckoned they would be more likely to chuck away any mail assuming it was connected to their old phone. The risk was worth it. The top-ups were always paid for in cash and always in Rednall. The cards went through the office shredder.

The phones were never used, or turned on anywhere other than within the towns boundaries and then only for short text messages. Simple things like 'MEET ME' or 'OK' or 'WANT U' or 'AT WW' At Webbers Wood. It was so easy to have the phones at the wood. There were so many places to hide them. I used to leave one or the other in a box in a hollow tree. No one ever discovered either of them in the hours they were there. Why would they? Sometimes I would leave one phone switched on in the car when I was on the fold-away. Then I would ride to one of their respective homes, stop close at hand and then turn on the other phone to either send or receive a message. I was sure I'd read somewhere that a phone company could provide the location of a phone when it had been in use either by satellite coverage or triangulation from a couple of transmission masts so I reasoned that if anyone did check it would be enough to point towards two people arranging clandestine meetings. The final message read,

'PLSE DONT END THIS'

I counted the seconds knowing that I would have very little time, whoever came round the corner of the garage. If Lucy's husband David came round the corner and discovered me, a swift kick to his gonads would have allowed me to escape. He might be big but he's not hard. Fortunately it was Lucy and as she walked between the two cars, I gave her no chance. All the pent up rage, hurt, humiliation and anger went into that one knife thrust. I planned to cut her throat but I couldn't be that clinical. I was oblivious to the spurting blood although I realised later I was covered in it. I held her as she fell and I saw the look of recognition in her eyes. It pained me not at all. Not one tiny spark of compassion. I lowered her gently just so that she would have time to look into my eyes and know. I tore the St. Christopher I had given her from her neck.

'Mine I think,' I whispered. If she heard me I cared not. The medallion was a family heirloom worn by my Grandfather in the Great War and I wanted it for someone far more deserving. I brushed the second phone across her lips and squeezed her lifeless fingers around it. She had of course dropped her bag and keys and I picked them up and put the phone in the bag. Any DNA would be hers. I got in the car, dropped the knife on the seat, reversed out of the drive and pulled away.

I drove steadily back to Webbers Wood, not wanting to draw any attention and parked almost out of sight of the road. The phone registered to Stuart Green I dropped in the rear footwell, hoping whoever found it would think it had fallen out of the drivers pocket. I then emptied the last fingernail and the remaining contents of the plastic bag in the front footwells. Then I got calmly out of the car and locked it. I retrieved the mountain bike and rode down the towpath to Green's home throwing the BMW keys into the canal as I went. I knew as soon as the keys left my hand that I had made a mistake, as I suddenly remembered the drivers seat. Not being very tall whenever I get out of a car that isn't mine, I always slide the seat back on its runners. This time I didn't. Too late though now. At Green's house I left the towpath, went up the bank and into the snicket at the rear of his house. I opened his back gate and the blood stained knife went into the refuse bin just inside his garden. I knew the bin wouldn't be emptied until the following Friday and in any case I expected the police to have found it by then. There was always the chance that someone from the household would use the bin but most people don't look inside a bin as they put rubbish in. Anyway, probably all the better if Green or his wife handled it. If anyone questioned why it had been so easy to find the knife, I was hoping that it would be put down to Green panicking or just being arrogant enough to believe that he could get away with it.

I cycled back to Harpley using the canal towpath, a much shorter route. It was only twenty four miles which took me a little over an hour at the pace I rode and that despite a mishap at Woodgate basin. I tried to be a bit clever. The towpath turns back towards Birmingham and you have to turn that way before crossing at a bridge a little further upstream. As I turned I could see a light swinging on the opposite path and guessed rightly that it was someone out for an early evening stroll. I hoped they didn't have a dog. There was a line of narrow boats moored so I had the bright idea of untying one at the bow end and pushing it across the canal. How was I to know that someone was living on it? It was he who was taking a walk on the towpath and he had a dog, a yapping Jack Russell. I heard him shout,

'Oi! That's my fucking boat!' as the bow hit the far bank. I jumped aboard at the stern and ran along the barge jumping off at the bow. I mounted the bike but as I did so the front washed out and I landed heavily on my shoulder and grazed my face. The adrenaline was really pumping now and I was quickly up and back in the saddle. Sadly, not quick enough to escape the dog. As I remounted the damn thing bit me on the ankle. The bite broke the skin but the dog obviously didn't like the taste as it let go and I pedalled away. It gave chase half heartedly and soon gave up. It didn't hurt at the time as much as I expected but I did favour the ankle for a few days after. I also knew I was going to need a tetanus shot which was why I visited my friend at me mam's local hospital the following day.

Back at home, I stopped in the woods that back on to the old gravel workings near the house. I dismantled the bike and threw the wheels into one of the pits and the frame into another. I doubted that they would ever be found as the pits are very deep and long since filled with water. No one dives in them as they are far too murky. In the wood is an old hunting lodge. Actually it's a shed with a concrete floor but that is what it had been used for before I bought the wood. I don't allow any shooting. I'm not against hunting, I just don't want my peace and quiet disturbed. Earlier that day I placed a plastic ground sheet on the floor and as I unlocked the door I stepped on to it. I stripped off quickly and put all my gear in an old bag. Then I rolled up the sheet and put it in another bag. I then took my change of clothes and trainers out of the rucksack and dressed quickly. I put a brick inside the rucksack and tossed it far out into the pit. I entered my house by the side door being careful to avoid the light sensors. All the cycle gear went into the burner. The following day the ashes and any remaining scraps of clothes went into the canal. Ever since the boiler has been kept working at a high heat.

I had a quick shower and my change of clothes also went into the burner later that evening. Unfortunately the smell of burning rubber persisted throughout the house for a couple of days. I caught the last few minutes of the match, having removed the mannequin from my chair. I left the TV on when I went out and used the video recorder rather than the DVD or Sky plus to record the game. I wanted no possibility of a digitised recording giving me away. I watched the tape later. The match was a total bore with no goals and no controversy. The tape went into the river in the early hours along with the mannequins. I had purchased two mannequins and used one in the study and one in the lounge. They had been backlit by the two timed standard lamps. I knew Andrew would see them as he went out for his half time cigarette. By the time the match finished I was back. Just. The fold-away bike also found itself in a watery grave but a hundred miles away. The bag with the sheet in from the shed, packed now inside a plastic bin liner, went into a skip near me mam's house. I watched it being taken away to the landfill site a couple of miles away. I knew that if asked, Andrew and Rachael would both swear that I had never left the house that night. I couldn't be out in the Range Rover, Andrew's car was blocking me in and no one, apart from Jake, knew about the bikes.

Rachael began to stir. I could feel myself beginning to be aroused but my thoughts were interrupted by the sound of a car engine in the lane. Or was it several engines? I thought perhaps it was my mind playing tricks but as I was about to caress Rachael I heard a loud knocking on the door. I was expecting a building team at eight to begin a new conservatory and wondered if they had decided to start early because I was the boss. I was not impressed, for Gods sake it was still dark. Whoever it was had just ruined my morning shag. Still, there would be other times and with any luck Rachael would agree to leave her prick of a husband and move in with me. It's time I had someone to share my life. Besides, her culinary and cleaning skills will come in handy! As I got up the knocking got louder. I put on my silk robe and headed downstairs. The photograph of me mam on the dresser made me smile and I was reminded of one of her favourite sayings,

'We always get what we deserve.' Well, I reckon she's dead on the money. Big house, big car, big successful business, a working class Geordie boy made good. I'm rich and I enjoy all the trappings that wealth brings. I once read somewhere about a Chinese philosopher who reckoned that 'he who knows that enough is enough will always have enough.' I reckon he was either the richest man in China and just patronising the peasants, or he was a real loser. I could close the business tomorrow and if I live to be a hundred I won't get through my fortune but it will never be enough. I want Moreton Jeffries to be the largest house building company in the country with developments in every major city. I am one of life's winners, a major player and I feel truly invincible. No one gets in my way.

I went down the stairs and as I crossed the kitchen I noticed the St. Christopher on the side. Rachael will love it when I give it to her later and no doubt she'll reward me in kind! The hammering on the door grew louder and as I unlocked it and threw it open intent on administering a bollocking, I immediately experienced a serious sphincter moment and was instantly reminded of another of mam's sayings,

'If God don't come, he sends.'

But two plain clothes police officers, one irate husband and a whole posse of uniforms in body armour is surely taking the piss!

AUTHORS NOTE

While Quinn's Way is a work of fiction I have tried to base it in reality. Nevertheless any characters depicted within the story are the work of my imagination and any similarity between persons either living or dead is entirely coincidental.

Quinn's story also pre-dates the Government scrappage scheme, a laudable initiative designed to protect manufacturing jobs within the motor industry. Did it work? Well certainly I know of many motor dealers who were rubbing their hands with glee at the increased sales and increased profits. I was told of one sales manager who was boasting that during this period he was being paid in excess of ten thousand pounds per month! Was this what the Government intended? I think not. Ten thousand pounds per month and no academic qualifications needed. Mind boggling.

Many stories and anecdotes were related to me during the research for Quinn's Way which I have not used in the narrative. They included the Directors of quite a large dealer group awarding themselves astronomic pay rises in the months leading up to their company entering administration.

Perhaps the strangest tale however was one in which I was personally involved. A former colleague came to see me as he had just been dismissed from his sales position within a family owned medium sized dealer group. He had decided to sue the company for wrongful dismissal and believed that he was owed outstanding commission for cars he had sold. Even to me, with only a rudimentary knowledge of employment law, it was apparent that correct procedures had been ignored. Now I think that most sensible people would be of the opinion that a dispute such as this would be better settled out of court and indeed that was what my former colleague was hoping. The company felt otherwise and the dispute dragged on for over five years! It should be said that there were some quite complex legal issues raised and mistakes were made by the tribunal service but nevertheless five years, some seven industrial tribunal hearings, which included appeals hearings, and an equal number of county court hearings all paid for by you and I, the taxpayer, to settle what should have been a minor dispute. Imagine the cost to the company in legal fees alone as they were represented at the majority of the hearings by a barrister. And that's before factoring in the cost of managers time. I myself wrote to the sales director and managing director of the company concerned but my entreaties were ignored.

The sums involved are worth noting. After a four day hearing my colleague won his case and was awarded £1108.39. The company were allowed to deduct £595.45 from the award which had already been paid to him in Jobseekers allowance leaving a net figure of £ 512.94. The company declined to pay as they were in the process of suing him for depreciation on his company car and for fuel drawn on his company fuel card after his dismissal. My colleague had kept his car in the hope that it would force the company to negotiate. He carried on using his fuel card but always accepted that he would have to pay back the cost of the fuel used. Despite an assumption made by the tribunal panel he did not use his company vehicle and was ultimately instructed by the courts to return the car. You might well ask why the dismissing officer did not obtain the company car keys and fuel card when dismissing my colleague. This alone I feel showed gross incompetence but as far as I am aware the manager was never disciplined.

Ultimately the matter of diminution was settled in the county court the company being awarded £400 and £244.92 for fuel. A good result as far as my colleague was concerned as he had agreed with me that £900 would have been a fair figure! Given that the company had refused to pay his tribunal award he employed the same tactic as he believed that he was still owed outstanding commissions.

Due to procedural errors and appeals and despite two judges urging the company to settle, the case dragged on. Sadly my colleague misunderstood a part of the appeals process and the company were awarded £252.60 in costs at one hearing. He was however allowed to continue his claim for outstanding commissions. At the subsequent hearing the company produced two sets of commission figures both of which they stated were definitive!

The subsequent tribunal awarded my colleague £396.88. He had won just £607.75 net in total for his efforts. When he first came to see me he would have settled for £2000 so it could be argued I suppose that the company had won. But how many tens of thousands of pounds had been expended to save £1400? Consider this also. My former colleague was dismissed by the company because they felt he was incompetent. In truth, he was a very competent salesperson but a very incompetent administrator. But did he actually cost the company money? Certainly he did not make as much profit for the company as he should have done. But what of the manager who dismissed him and the senior personnel who backed not only the decision to dismiss him but also the long campaign to defend the company in court. As far as I am aware not one of these members of staff was disciplined in any way. With a decision process so badly flawed and intransigence and incompetence rife it was small wonder that the company eventually found itself in administration. A sad and ignominious end to a once proud organisation.

Sadly, companies like the one above are not unique. I have recently seen life from the customer's point of view. I have been appalled at the lack of professionalism of some dealers. I actually wanted someone to really sell me a car. Many salesmen were just not interested failing in many instances to obtain basic information from me like my name and address. As for being able to present or demonstrate the product they wanted me to buy? Whatever happened to basic training?

However, not every motor dealer is as incompetent as those above or employs characters as corrupt as some of those depicted in Quinn's Way. I have been privileged to work within some fine institutions. Principal among these has been the Hartwell Group based in Oxford whose training programmes were second to none. The Cambria Group, a relatively young company, is also beginning to make its mark.

There are of course many more. Let no one be afraid to walk into any dealer to buy a car but always remember, do the research and don't be afraid to walk away.

I am also indebted to Mike Godfrey, Managing Director of the Amvale Group, who has been a very highly valued friend and colleague for more years than either of us would probably care to remember. And to my family without whose unstinting support Quinn's Way would never have seen the light of day.

Steve Gray
Malvern 2010